BEGINNING OF TIME

BEGINNING OF TIME
A TALE OF ANGELS AND DEMONS

THE DISASTROUS ALLIANCE
BOOK ONE

ADRIANA RODRIGUEZ

THE PAPER HOUSE
PUBLISHING

Copyright © 2024 by Adriana Rodriguez

All rights reserved.

No part of this book may be reproduced in any form or by any electronic or mechanical means, including information storage and retrieval systems, without written permission from the author, except for the use of brief quotations in a book review.

To my friends and family who made it all possible.

Thank you.

CONTENTS

✦✧✦ Prelude ✦✧✦	1
1. Prince Wonwoo Has to Deal With The Idea Of Marriage	13
2. King Titanosaurus's Proposed Idea For An Alliance	31
3. On A Horrible Windy Day, It Was Love At First Sight	61
4. A Beautiful Date With Royalty...Goes Horribly Wrong	81
5. The Untimely Demise of the Princess of the Demoniacal Kingdom	97
6. The Threat of A War Coming; Nightmares Plague Prince Wonwoo	123
7. Prince Scamander's Early Desires For Revenge; A Dark Path Is Born	137
8. The Promised Dynasty Gets A Surprise	153
9. Preserving the Good Name of Ellowyn	173
10. It Was All A Fake Out! Prince Wonwoo Miraculously Lives	185
11. The Outlaw Prince Deals With...Well, Being An Outlaw	195
12. Seeking Refuge In A Far Distant Clan	223
13. The Life Beyond the Two Kingdoms	245
14. A Fiery Vengeance Unquenched; The Wolf Prince Loses His Mind	279
15. The Prince Is Captured By the Demoniacal Kingdom	289
16. Prince Wonwoo? That Name is Dead. More Like...	307
✦✧✦Postlude ✦✧✦	331
✦✧✦ Bonus Scene ✦✧✦	359
A Mini Guide Into The World of Beginning of Time	377
About the Author	455

✦✧✦ PRELUDE ✦✧✦
THE TRAGIC END OF THE PRINCE OF THE PROMISED DYNASTY

~ Few days ago... ~
~ July in Terra Cycle 1118 B.E. ~

"He went this way! Hurry!"

It was the middle of the night, and the full moon hung over the star-filled sky. There were very few clouds floating around. They were thin, no sign of any kind of rain, and they drifted lazily through the sky. Being the month of July, it was not too cold in the night breeze, but it was not too hot either. It was perfect weather to take a night stroll.

The usually quiet forest of Divine Kingfisher Woods was interrupted by a rushing army chasing after a creature. The brightly colored creature, which the moonlight revealed to be a young male cave lion, ran through the undergrowth with nimble speed.

✦✧✦ PRELUDE ✦✧✦

Leaves brushed against his fur and prickled at him in a way that made him wanna stop and scratch. He did pass by some thorny flowers, which cut into his skin. He grit his teeth to suppress the groans of pain.

"He's getting away! Pick up the pace you lousy good-for-nothings!"

The cave lion flicked his ears. Lifting up his head, he disappeared in the thick bushes, and the army followed after where the cave lion went. He breathed heavily, looking back and parting the leaves to get a good view while also not exposing his location.

When they cut down the bushes, they were greeted with an empty field. His skin jumped at the sight of them, slapping a paw over his mouth to suppress the scared gasp. He wished he could control the pounding of his heart. He continued to look on in curiosity. They all stared in disbelief when they were met with no sight of the cave lion prince.

"Curse the wyvern! He's gone!" one of the soldiers shouted, throwing their sword to the ground in a fit of rage. "Just when we had him!"

The cave lion felt himself catch a huge breath of relief. The relief was more short-lived than he had expected. The commander of the army stared at the army and lifted up his head. The cave lion watched as he flared open his nose to get a good catch of his scent. He lowered his head and began to snarl.

"No, he's not!" the commander growled at the soldier, making his way to the front of the crowd. "I can still pick up his scent. He's nearby. And he's hiding! Like a coward!" He turned to the army.

"Don't give up yet. Remember why we're here. Search the entire cursed forest ground for him. Leave no rock unturned. Dig holes! Cut down trees if you must! We will find that lowly excuse of a prince and capture him! We will make him pay for his crimes!" He put a paw to his chest. "For the King of the Demoniacal Kingdom!"

The soldiers, having gained a new surge of confidence after the speech, pressed a paw to their chest and shouted:

"For the King of the Demoniacal Kingdom!"

As the soldiers searched Divine Kingfisher Woods, the lion prince, hiding far from where they were at and having masked his scent the best he could, watched them as they ruthlessly uprooted nature to look for him. He took a deep breath in, clutching his chest fur, before he slowly backed up.

The lion prince knew the Demoniacal Kingdom; they were ruthless and merciless, a Kingdom of creatures who worshipped and believed in the darkness and the sins. Where the lion prince was from, the Promised Dynasty, they were inhumane compared to him. His Dynasty believed in good and purity and preached it as their founder had over 100 terra cycles ago. A total difference. But their difference wasn't the reason he was being hunted down.

6 months ago, the lion prince had made a horrible mistake that proved to be a breaking point for the fragile peace between the two Kingdoms. That horrible mistake turned out to be murder. He had murdered one of their own. Because of this mistake, the Demoniacal Kingdom decided to declare war on the Promised Dynasty and call for the lion prince's head.

✦✧✦ PRELUDE ✦✧✦

His father, the King of the Promised Dynasty, made sure to hide him well in the castle with his mother before he ran out to fight. But it had failed *(somewhat knowingly but unexpectedly)* when the King of the Demoniacal Kingdom sent a secret army after the lion prince. They raided the Promised Dynasty castle, killing the guards in one swift blow, and charged straight for him. The lion prince had to leave his trusted soldiers and mother, the Queen of the Promised Dynasty, to the savage claws and jaws of the army. He didn't even know if his mother was still alive since she had been attacked brutally, or if she had died moments after, for as soon as he ran into the woods, he could hear the army chase after him.

He managed to throw them off by heading into Divine Kingfisher Woods, a forest just a few feet short of Halcyonwick (the town where the Promised Dynasty made their home), as he knew they would not be familiar with the territory. This was a forest that had been formed ever since the creation of the very land. It was a forest of thick vegetation, lots of trees and vines hanging around. Only those who know the landscape could maneuver through the forest. For a moment, the lion prince had the upper paw. He saw the army struggle while trying to chase him. He breathed a sigh of relief. That is, until he noticed that they brought large swords that were strong enough to cut down the large vegetation of the forest unlike regular battle swords. It was as if they knew he would flee here. He mumbled to himself with what little breath he could catch. Just when he thought he was safe.

Now, he was a prince on the run. An outlaw.

The lion prince didn't think he was going to live a life of crime, but it was happening. It was bound to happen anyway, with the terrible action he had done. He couldn't do anything about it, nor could he do anything to turn back time as much as he wished and prayed. He had to accept the situation he caused and hopefully, hopefully, find a way to make it all go away.

Right now, all he had to focus on was getting out of here alive.

If I stay here any longer, they'll eventually find me, have me arrested and do Gods knows what before they execute me, the lion prince thought. He slowly started to back away, looking behind him and side to side. *I have to keep running. I have to leave the Promised Dynasty and lay low until I can make a return. Maybe, I can find help from–*

SNAP!

His heart sank at the sound of a twig snapping. His ears slowly drooped.

The soldiers had stopped once they heard the snap. They looked around but didn't seem to know where the sound was exactly. There was confusion amongst the soldiers as they tried to pinpoint the source of the sound. He could hear various sentences from the soldiers, ranging from "Did you hear that?" and "What was that?" and "That was probably a squirrel or a bird." Before the lion prince could rejoice on how stupid the soldiers were, a tiger soldier caught the direction of the noise and soon bore his eyes into the lion prince.

"Over there!" the soldier said, pointing to the lion prince. "He's over there! The lion prince!"

✦✧✦ PRELUDE ✦✧✦

The lion prince swallowed as soon as the commander followed the soldier's point, eyes narrowed in a death stare.

Shit.

He had been found out.

"See what I told you all? GET HIM!" shouted the commander.

Without another second thought, the lion prince broke his cover and ran. The soldiers chased after him as soon as he stood up, hot on his tail. He could hear them shouting: "There he goes!", "After him!", "Don't let him get away!" He shoved through the thick vegetation, not minding the scraps and cuts and the soreness his body endured. Behind him, his ears could catch the sound of the soldiers' thumping paws catching up to him. He did not look back, but he could imagine the horde of predators chasing after him like he was a helpless rabbit.

He was so tired, he wanted to give up. He forced himself to keep going. For the sake of his Dynasty and his parents.

The lion prince shut his eyes.

No, no, no! Why do I keep messing things up?

He felt the landscape change underneath his paws, and he caught himself before he tumbled down. *Woah!* Coming to a sudden halt, he found himself standing on the ledge of a cliff. The roaring river of Dragon's Wrath below him deafened him. He did not need to lean forward to see where he was. The lion prince backed away to safety, heart pounding, breath ragged, and looked back. Now he was truly stuck. He whimpered to himself and looked around.

What do I do, what do I do?

He had a few options he could attempt: He could try to leap the cliffs and make it to the other side. He lifted up a paw to measure the difference between him and the other side. *Could I even make it?* But he'd risk not calculating correctly and fall straight into the river below. *Yeah, I don't think so.* That was definitely off the list. He could also run to the side, following alongside the riverbank until reaching the ravine and leaping from there. The distance from the ravine was shorter than where he was now. It was a definite possibility, but there was a problem to that solution; the land is far too unstable due to the rushing waterfall. One would have to walk alongside the cliff with light pawsteps. He couldn't possibly jump down it at top speed without the dirt collapsing underneath his paws and burying him in a landslide, entrapping him until the Demoniacal Kingdom came along to dig him out and arrest him.

There was no escape for him.

He still breathed heavily, looking to the night sky. He prayed to the God of the Moon, the God of the Night Gau, to guide his night path. He prayed to the Goddess of the Heavens and the God of Hell, Okalani and Azrael, for their fair judgement when he would have to meet them. He went beyond to pray to the Creator herself: Ellowyn.

Great Ellowyn, please forgive me for all I have done. I know I have committed a great sin, but I assure you it wasn't intentional! Okalani, Azrael, please judge me well. Wherever you send me, I will accept it.

He narrowed his eyes.

✦✧✦ PRELUDE ✦✧✦

The lion prince had to make a decision, and he knew there was no other choice.

The lion prince looked down and back behind him. The army soon came into sight, their eyes radiating hunger and lust. Time seemed to slow down as they lunged at him, weapons in paws (or mouths), claws and teeth ready.

He closed his eyes.

For the Promised Dynasty. I'm sorry, Mother. Father.

Without hesitation, he intentionally slipped as he purposefully backed up and found himself plunging to the raging waters below. While his body slowed during the fall, his mind raced on everything that had led up to this moment. From his childish antics as a cub to his mistake to the war. It all flashed in front of his eyes. Nothing could be done to stop this. He accepted his fate.

He saw the army staring over the ledge of the cliff, their eyes narrowed in slits. They paced back and forth in frustration as they knew their mission was a bust. There was a brief moment where the lion prince smirked. *Losers.* The prince especially locked eyes with the commander, who stood over the edge with fury sprawled on his face. He had recognized the commander. The voice was familiar, and the figure was distinguished.

He was no commander whatsoever.

It was the very prince of the Demoniacal Kingdom himself.

The prince of the Demoniacal Kingdom watched as the lion prince disappeared underneath the waves. His eyes kept a close attention to see him tumble and struggle, his head briefly emerging to possibly catch a breath, but eventually, he lost sight of the lion prince. He was truly gone.

"What an idiot!"

"We can hurry and catch him at the bottom of the riverbank!"

"Now hold on. We must wait for His Highness's orders."

He stamped a paw on the ground, his tail swaying back and forth in aggressive lashes as he tuned out the voices of his patrol. Curse that lion prince to the wyvern king. He didn't expect to lose the one he wanted dead that easily. He wanted to be the one to punish the lion prince! He wanted it to be him to pass judgement onto the lion prince for his crime! It should have been him! He now knew his father would not be pleased to hear this news.

We should have been faster, he thought to himself, curling his lip and looking up to the night sky. *We could have caught up to him while he was lingering about on the edge. Now he is at the mercy of their Gods, and they won't go hard on him despite what he's done...*

"Prince Scamander?"

The wolf prince, Prince Scamander, snapped his ears back to the one who called him. Reality snapped back in a painful way when he finally focused back on his patrol, and he rubbed his head. It was the tiger soldier who had found the lion prince hidden. He had approached the wolf prince who had all his attention focused on him.

✦◇✦ PRELUDE ✦◇✦

"What are your orders, Your Highness?" the tiger soldier asked.

The wolf prince turned his head back to the river, its deafening roar echoing through his ears. He would normally call that they follow towards the end of the river, but he shook his head. He's heard enough tales about this river, and he was not about to risk losing his loyal subjects over such a powerful force of nature. No one should have to suffer, other than the lion prince. He frowned.

"Retreat back," the wolf prince ordered. "There is no use standing here anymore like ducks in a pond. We cannot risk being caught by anyone in the Promised Dynasty. By morning of the next day, we will search for his body, whether alive or dead."

"Do you not wish for us to head to the riverbank?" someone had spoken out.

Prince Scamander pinned his ears back hard. *Yes, idiot, I want you all to get THAT DAMN LION PRINCE!* He shook his head, ignoring his bubbling anger. "It's too dangerous. Besides, my father is going to need some support to take down the Promised King. Half of you shall return back to the Demoniacal Kingdom, while the rest will follow me back to the Promised Dynasty."

"I will follow you back to the Promised Dynasty, Your Highness," the tiger soldier volunteered.

Three more soldiers also volunteered after the tiger soldier, and the wolf prince nodded to them. "Alright, you four follow me back. The rest of you: Head back to the Demoniacal Kingdom and await for me and my Father. Let's go!"

They all turned tail back towards the forest, Prince Scamander in the lead. As they ran back, the wolf prince narrowed his eyes. Anger surged his body as he thought back to the lion prince. He was so close to reaching him, so close to capturing him. He was so close to having his time to shine as the true heir of the Demoniacal Kingdom and have closure for the crime the lion prince committed on his family. He shut his eyes.

You may have won this time, Prince Wonwoo of the Promised Dynasty, but I will find you eventually. Whether you've died in that river or by whatever miracle you survive. There's only so much running you can do, but it will all catch up to you in the end. Once I do, you'll be sorry to have ever been born!

CHAPTER I
PRINCE WONWOO HAS TO DEAL WITH THE IDEA OF MARRIAGE

✦✧✦ ~ *7 months before the war...* ~
~ *December in Terra Cycle 1117 B.E.* ~

"Prince Wonwoo!"

Within the large land, a huge forest sprawled many miles. One city made this forest its home, and that city was known as Halcyonwick. In the city of Halcyonwick, a huge Dynasty resided and made Halcyonwick their home. This Dynasty was the Promised Dynasty. The Promised Dynasty was a group of animals who worship and believe in all things relating to the goodness of their Gods, their Creator and the Heavens. Halcyonwick was a glamorous and beautiful city, with buildings as tall as an oak tree and lights that burned as bright as the sun itself. Beneath the large beauty, small homes and businesses strewn around the city.

PRINCE WONWOO HAS TO DEAL WITH THE IDEA OF MARRIAGE

It was just around 2 hours after Dagny's Peak. It was a nice Friday with a bit of a chill coming due to winter having kicked in. Dynasty members were leaving their jobs to return back to their families, children and youngsters leaving their tutors after a long day of teaching to have some fun, and many of the residents of Halcyonwick took to the streets to find themselves whatever they needed for the next week. Business was still alive and much more than it had ever been.

The usually quiet street of Grace St.–the main street that led to the city square–was suddenly filled with chaos as two male cave lions ran, being chased by a pack of hyenas. They were fleeing the angry creatures, who were snapping their jaws at their legs. The residents let out a shocked gasp, talking to each other about what was going on as they pointed.

One of the fleeing cave lions, a large pale tan-furred cave lion with a slowly growing brown mane and light brown tuft on his head, let out a guffaw.

"Look at that! Who knew that these tiny guys could run so fast!" he commented.

His friend, also a cave lion dark brown in appearance and only a little bit smaller than he was, looked at him with wide eyes. "P-Prince Wonwoo, please, w-we need to s-stop!" he called out, panting. "T-They will only be more angry if we keep running! L-Let's just–Talk to them! HHAGGHHHH It's hard to breathe!"

"No way!" the cave lion, Prince Wonwoo, retorted. "Why should we? They provoked us first, Cayman! So it's only fair to provoke them back! Plus, they're not much of talkers. So why bother?"

"But–!"

"Just keep running!"

They continued to run deeper into the city until they ran into a particular street full of vendors named Farmer Route. This place was home to the low ranking members of the Promised Dynasty, those who either couldn't afford the high life or willingly chose to become farmers to help the city and their Dynasty. The various creatures looked at the cave lion pair and hyena swarm in fear as they scrambled to get out of the way. Some of them yelped in fear, some shouted, some of them cursed in the vain of the Gods. Some vendors went ahead and slammed their businesses shut with gates.

Prince Wonwoo couldn't help but have a laugh. Hyenas were the natural enemies to lions, but he never knew how much fun it was to poke fun around them. Most of the time anyone could handle his jokes; it was one of the many strong qualities of the lion prince. But the hyena cackle had snapped sooner than he expected.

These hyenas better loosen up from time to time, hehe.

The lead hyena, the matriarch hyena, suddenly managed to get a hold of the lion prince's tail by clamping down hard on it, and he let out a confused roar. "OW!"

Well, there was the end of the fun.

The lion prince stopped abruptly in order to throw the hyena off. It did work, at the cost of him losing his footing since the hyena had not let go of his tail. She pressed her paws firmly on his

PRINCE WONWOO HAS TO DEAL WITH THE IDEA OF MARRIAGE

shoulders and towered over him.

"Got you now, you rotting living corpse," she snarled at him.

"Well, now that isn't very nice, isn't it?" Prince Wonwoo said rather sarcastically. "You hyenas need to learn to chill out, sometimes."

His friend Cayman, who was still running away, looked back when he heard Prince Wonwoo's roar, stopping. "Prince Wonwoo!" he shouted before being tackled by the hyenas. "UMPH!"

"Hey, leave Cayman alone! He had nothing to do with this!"

Two other hyenas pinned the prince down along with the female. They snarled at him, jaws salivating. The lion prince blinked. He was now at the mercy of the Gods.

"That other lion friend of yours is definitely involved if he's with you," the other hyena that had pinned the prince growled.

"Yeah, he's not gonna get away from this. He's got to learn the consequences just like you have to deal with the consequences."

"Ew! Guys! Watch it!" Prince Wonwoo said, raising an arm. "Seriously. Do you not know who you're salivating on??!"

"Yeah," the first hyena that spoke jeered, "the royal pain in the ass!"

The hyenas laughed rather obnoxiously and in an ear-splitting tone.

"Excuse you!" the lion prince growled. "Rude! It's Prince Wonwoo of-"

The matriarch hyena snapped her jaws in front of his face, causing him to flinch. "Shut your annoying trap! We know who you are, and we don't care!" She frowned. "Do *you* know who you're messing with?"

"Yes?" the prince answered. "But also, I don't really care who you guys are, because you're all stinking-"

"*We* are the Night Stalkers!" the matriarch hyena snarled an interruption. "One of the greatest gangs to exist in the Promised Dynasty!"

A gang? This cackle was a *gang*? The lion prince flicked his ears. "Well, shit, did I ask if I cared?" he asked. "You hyenas are not Promised Dynasty. You're just refugee Demoniacal Kingdom bullies who harass others for no reason. You don't learn from your sinful ways. Sooner or later, my dad *will* kick you out for good!"

The matriarch hyena raised her round silver gray ears. The mention of the lion king definitely got her attention as well as the other hyenas. For a moment, they faltered. She pursed her mouth into a tiny "o" shape before her grin took over again. "OH! Ohhhoho, you think that's going to scare us? You think we're nothing to you, huh? Today you will learn, dumb lion. I'll *show you* what we really are." The hyena looked at her friends with a sly grin. "Well. What shall we do with the great Lion Prince of the Promised Dynasty who harassed us for no reason, y'all?"

PRINCE WONWOO HAS TO DEAL WITH THE IDEA OF MARRIAGE

The hyenas cackled amongst each other. Now Prince Wonwoo was getting a bit concerned. If he didn't do something to get him and Cayman out of this situation, no one would come to their aid in time. Especially since the bystanders would not do anything to involve themselves with the situation. He could feel their stares, seeing the fear as they backed as far away as they could. They were afraid, and he was making it worse by not freeing himself and Cayman from the hyenas.

Come on, Prince Wonwoo, think! The lion prince scolded himself, shutting his eyes. *They're depending on you since you are the Prince and the future King of the Promised Dynasty! You got to prove your place on the throne! Now think...*

"D-Don't do anything!" Cayman shouted, squirming to desperately free himself. "I beg of you! If you do something to him, King Jung-hwa and Queen Cora won't be as kind as they are–"

"Who cares what the King and Queen will do?" the matriarch hyena mocked. "What are they *even* going to do? Unleash your oh so omnipotent Gods that hide from the mortals on us? Pah! They're too soft and generous to give out punishments. Unlike us hyenas. *Especially* us from the Night Stalkers!"

The venom in the hyenas' voices didn't help with his thoughts. He fluttered open his eyes, gazing at them with furrowed eyebrows. He wanted to claw their silly smiles off their faces, he so badly wanted to show who really was the one in charge here.

"We're sorry! Really, really sorry! Please, can we talk about this?"

"Talk? Hmmm, lemme think... No."

She and her cackle yet again obnoxiously laughed. Prince Wonwoo's claws unsheathed. He so badly wanted to rip them to shreds.

"We're not one to talk, little lion," one of the hyenas who had Cayman pinned said, further pressing their paws down on his body. "We would've loved to talk things out, if your friend here wasn't being a complete ass for no reason."

"Yeah, and for that, you suffer the consequences your friend caused," another piped up, cackling.

"Leave him alone....!" Prince Wonwoo growled.

"Hey! I got an idea: Let's rip the Prince's face apart!" one of the other female hyenas pinning down Prince Wonwoo shouted out a suggestion.

What?

"Tear his limbs off!" another chimed in. "Slowly! One by *o n e*!"

The more he heard the suggestions, the more anxiety sat in his stomach. Injuries from hyenas were not to be taken lightly; he had seen wounded soldiers and guards who took nasty bites and scratches from hyenas in the Demoniacal Kingdom. No other creature could amount to such terrible wounds.

"Those all sound like great ideas," the matriarch hyena said. "I love myself a good little mauling and disfiguration. Permanent reminders for ALL to see. And by the looks of it, everyone has their full attention on us." She looked down at the lion prince. "Let's start with that pretty little face of yours." She lowered her

PRINCE WONWOO HAS TO DEAL WITH THE IDEA OF MARRIAGE

head and pulled back her lips to reveal her large fangs. They were sharp and also stained dark yellow.

The sight of those ghastly fangs sent a cold shiver. The lion prince began to beg.

"Wait now!—" he pleaded. "Hold on, hold on, let me-I- Can I say something–" When the hyena matriarch didn't listen, he began to wail out. "H-HELP! HELP!! SOMEONE HELP MEEEE!!!"

"PRINCE WONWOO HONEYCUTT!"

An intense, powerful roar pierced the tense air. Everyone had froze in their place, the hyenas widening their eyes with a whimper. The hyena matriarch didn't show fear, but Prince Wonwoo saw her dark spotted pelt jolt a bit from the roar. Craning his head back, the lion prince saw a large pale male cave lion with a tuft of mane on his head and a flowing golden robe approaching. The prince called out to him.

"Father!" he cried out. "Thank the Gods!"

"Thank the Gods indeed!" Cayman prayed. "They've heard our pleas!" He looked at the hyenas with a proud smirk. "How's that for omnipotent?"

They slammed his head to the ground in retaliation.

The King did not look at his son or his friend, instead bearing his eyes on the hyenas. The ones who pinned down him and his friend (which was the whole cackle) yelped at the sight of the lion king and ran back where they came from, passing by the King as fast as they could. The matriarch hyena, however, did not move from her place, and she met the lion king's gaze with fierce determination.

"Help me..." Prince Wonwoo could hear the faint whines from his friend as he curled up to himself, paws on his head and shivering. "Great Ellowyn...please save me...I don't want to die..."

"Don't worry, Cayman, I'm still right here for you," Prince Wonwoo directed to him softly. "My dad will set these hyenas straight. Just stay there and stay still. Don't move a single muscle."

"I-I am..I am..."

"Let my son and his friend go, Atiena," the lion king said in a deep and booming voice. "I'll see to his punishment, for that is my job as his father and his King and not your responsibility."

"What are you going to do to him, King Jung-hwa of the Promised Dynasty?" the hyena, Atiena, challenged, pushing the lion prince's head down on the ground with more force. "Slap him on the wrist? Bring your almighty Gods down to give him a smack? Tell him *'Don't do that again?'* and leave it at that? He'll keep doing his obnoxious behaviors unless he's given a proper *brutal* punishment!"

Dynasty members around them gasped in shock at Atiena's words. She was speaking as if she was still a member of the Demoniacal Kingdom.

Not surprising she's speaking like this, Prince Wonwoo thought. *She and her cackle are refugees of the Demoniacal Kingdom, and will always be Demoniacal Kingdom members. They can't change that about them. They'll never learn the ways of the Gods and become members of the Promised Dynasty. They never change. They never will.*

"You know, you and your Queen are the worst the Promised Dynasty has to offer," she continued, practically spitting in King Jung-hwa's face. She kept pressing down hard on Prince Wonwoo's head, making him groan out in pain. "I thought you would be better than the conditions in the Demoniacal Kingdom. You don't know the suffering that goes on in the Promised Dynasty because you're all so stuck up and thinking you're like the almighty beings of those Gods you worship. Well, you're not! There are better animals to lead the Dynasty than you. For example: me."

The lion prince widened his eyes, listening to the muttering whispers and murmurs from the crowd. Atiena did not just challenge his father.

She'd be dead meat before the first round even began! He thought to himself rather comically. It was the only time right now that a joke could alleviate the fears he was feeling. *I'd like to see her try.*

The lion king, King Jung-hwa, took another step closer, staring at Atiena with a blank face, and grabbed the hyena matriarch by her neck without warning. With force, he threw her off of Prince Wonwoo and onto the streets. The lion prince twisted his head to see where the hyena matriarch was, his shock as equal to her's. There was a loud thud, a crack and a pained yelp as Atiena rolled on the ground. She got up slowly, lifting up her front leg. Judging from the way it looked, the lion prince concurred that she had broken her leg in the fall.

"You monster!" Atiena howled. "You broke my leg! You're no better than King Titanosaurus!"

Prince Wonwoo blinked, his mouth dry. He had no words for what he had witnessed. There was only a twinge of satisfaction for Atiena getting what she rightfully deserved. *Serves you right for hurting me and my friend and challenging my Father.*

"And I'll break more than your measly leg if you don't get out of here in 5 seconds," the lion king threatened, placing a paw in front of him and tossing his head to the side. *"Leave!"*

Atiena finally yelped and ran with a limp to follow after her cackle.

Once she fled, the lion king looked back to his Dynasty members, nodded at them, then looked down at his son. Prince Wonwoo did not get up from the ground. He stared at his father.

"Hey dad..." the lion prince said with a sheepish smile.

"Get up and come with me back to the castle," the lion king ordered. "I have something very important to tell you."

No "Are you okay, son?" or "Glad I found you before the worst happened" or "What did they do to you? Did they hurt you?" or "I'll do something so that they will never be a problem ever again!"

Nothing?

Okay then.

"But first: Take your friend home first."

At that moment, he heard his friend groan.

PRINCE WONWOO HAS TO DEAL WITH THE IDEA OF MARRIAGE

Oh! Prince Wonwoo rolled onto his belly and got up on his paws, looking behind him. He totally forgot about his friend. Cayman still laid on the street, curled up, shaking, paws on his head. He was whimpering to himself, praying and apologizing under his breath. The lion prince felt completely bad for him. He shouldn't have had Cayman involved in this situation. He walked up to him and gently nudged his shoulder.

"I'm so sorry, dude," he said. "Are you okay? Did they hurt you?"

Cayman got up and shook his fur, brushing a paw on his shoulder. "No, I'm okay," he answered. "I'm good. They didn't bite me. Or scratch me or anything, thank the Gods in the Heavens. But they put a lot of their weight on me, and my muscles ache." He looked at Prince Wonwoo. "How about you? Are you okay?"

"Yeah. I'm starting to get a massive headache from the way Atiena pushed my head on the ground."

"Oh no, that's not good. But thank the Heavens they didn't do anything far worse to us. Thanks to your Father as well. Who knows what would have happened had he not came along!"

"Yeah, indeed..." The lion prince offered his shoulder. "I'll take you home."

Cayman leaned against his friend's shoulder, relaxing his tense muscles. "Thanks, Prince Wonwoo. I'm in your debt, along with your father."

"What? No no no. There's no need; there's no debt to pay to me or my Father."

"...I'm sorry."

"No, don't apologize. It wasn't your fault. I shouldn't have dragged you into my mess."

Cayman waved a paw. "Hey. What friends are for. I wasn't going to leave you to those Demoniacal hyenas anyhow. So don't worry about it." He looked back at the vendors and farmers, who stared at the two with narrowed eyes. He cleared his throat and addressed them: "I apologize everyone! There's nothing to see here anymore! Please carry on with...whatever you all were doing."

They still stared at the two cave lions before shrugging off what had happened and returning back to what they were doing. The two lions looked at each other and chuckled.

"I'm not as good as you or your Father with giving commands," Cayman joked.

"Yeah, leave that to us next time," Prince Wonwoo teased, lightly bumping him with his rear. "Alright, let's go home finally."

Cayman nodded. "Yes. I agree. 100%. Let's go home. Where not a single hyena will ever disturb us ever again!"

As Prince Wonwoo and Cayman walked out of Farmer Route and back to the main city, the lion prince felt a sinking feeling in his stomach.

"Come with me back to the castle. I have something very important to tell you."

He couldn't help but wonder *what* exactly did his father have that was so important for him. What was his father needing him for?

PRINCE WONWOO HAS TO DEAL WITH THE IDEA OF MARRIAGE

Hopefully it wouldn't be something *that* important.

∽

"King Titanosaurus of the Demoniacal Kingdom wants me to DO WHAT to his daughter?"

Prince Wonwoo stepped back from the throne in shock. After taking his friend back home, he went back to the castle and was already greeted to the sight of his parents on their respective thrones. The guards protected both ends of the lion king and queen from below and by the thrones. His father had beckoned him with a paw to join him by the stairs. The lion prince had already been nervous because from the way they sat in alertness, something serious was about to happen. Once the prince complied and sat down, he was already hit with the thing his father said would be important. No build up, no prep talk or anything. No. It was immediately straight to the point.

"He wants you to marry his daughter–Princess Okome Snapdragon of the Demoniacal Kingdom–as a means for an alliance between the two Kingdoms," King Jung-hwa repeated himself, explaining.

Yep. There it was. Marriage. An *arranged* marriage. A marriage that he had no say or decision on. That kind of marriage. That was the important matter for King Jung-hwa to tell him.

The lion prince shook his mane aggressively. An alliance of the Promised Dynasty and the Demoniacal Kingdom? That had to be the most absurd thing he ever heard of. But that wasn't his main focus right now. "No-Absolutely NOT! I do *NOT* want to marry someone from the **DEMONIACAL KINGDOM OF ALL PLACES!** Never EVER! Father. You *can't* be serious!"

"King Titanosaurus *is* serious," his father said sternly.

"Doesn't this go against what King Saturhorimau wanted for the Promised Dynasty?" Prince Wonwoo asked. "What King Boipelo made for the Dynasty after his demise!?"

"It is rare for King Titanosaurus of the Demoniacal Kingdom to ask for help," his mother, Queen Cora, said. "But it is for a good reason; Coldwyvern and the Demoniacal Kingdom are slowly falling into ruins because of the war. King Titanosaurus can only stoop so low to finally agree that we should not have let the Great War Between Good and Evil divide us and make us weak. This alliance will help build us together and make us stronger as before. It will help us become one again. Just as the Gods intended all those terra cycles ago."

The lion prince's ears twitched, and he shook his head. "This is a *jinamizi*," Prince Wonwoo groaned, placing a paw on his head. "We're basically just shitting on King Saturhorimau and his ideals."

"No further questions or comments, young man, and watch your profanity in front of me," King Jung-hwa said. "You're not a cub anymore, you're 20 terra cycles old. It's time you grow out of your childish personality and learn what it means to be royalty. You will one day have to succeed me and make these tough decisions."

"But can't I marry someone from the Promised Dynasty?"

"King Titanosaurus of the Demoniacal Kingdom already offered you his daughter. You know he would never in a million terra cycles do something this nice."

"But I don't know her!" Prince Wonwoo wailed. "How am I to marry her when I do not know who she is or what she really is like?"

"That is why we're going to arrange a date for the two of you. So that you can know each other and eventually fall in love." King Jung-hwa narrowed his eyes at his son, who groaned aloud. "You *better not mess it up,* or we will see another war that we do not need heading our way. Do you understand me, Prince Wonwoo Honeycutt of the Promised Dynasty?"

The lion prince, noticing his father's serious tone, whimpered to himself and straightened his posture. He knew his father wasn't playing around when he addressed the lion prince by his full name. He bowed. "I understand, Father," he said. "If you say this is for the good of both Kingdoms...I will believe you and do what you wish. I'll do it. For our Dynasty."

The lion king clapped his paws together. "Excellent! Then we'll get preparations started! King Titanosaurus of the Demoniacal Kingdom will be arriving next terra cycle in January."

"Next terra cycle!?" Prince Wonwoo was caught off guard yet again. Why was he not given days to prepare? More months!? January was basically next month! The look on King Jung-hwa kept him from making an outburst again.

He bowed his head again. "I-I'll be prepared as best I can for when the princess arrives." He gritted his teeth. "Please excuse me."

"You're dismissed," King Jung-hwa said.

The lion prince made his way to his room, passing through the line of guards. He felt bad for ignoring the ones who were genuinely concerned for him, but he didn't want to meet them while he was like this.

What was his Father thinking? Arranging him, the Prince of the Promised Dynasty, to the princess of their rival Kingdom? How was he even meant to present himself to his enemy? Especially the princess!? The. *Princess!* A princess is royalty! Someone far more important than an average farmer! PRINCESS! A million thoughts ran through his head as he opened his bedroom door. He froze, his eyes widening.

Could he even find himself having some feelings for the princess of the Demoniacal Kingdom? Prince Wonwoo let his mind also wander on what the princess would look like. He knew the King and Queen of the Demoniacal Kingdom were dire wolf mixes, along with their son. From what he had been told on what they looked like (being dire wolves with King Titanosaurus's lineage having draconic-like features thanks to King Wyvern deciding to go the extra step and take a wolf bride), he could imagine the princess as a pretty she-wolf. A pretty she-wolf who would look as pretty as her mother, with eyelashes as luscious as she would be–

He swiftly closed the door after that thought then crashed onto his bed.

He proceeded to scream into his pillow.

CHAPTER 2

KING TITANOSAURUS'S PROPOSED IDEA FOR AN ALLIANCE

~ In the eyes of the King of the Demoniacal Kingdom... ~
~ December in Terra Cycle 1117 B.E. ~

Few miles from the city of Halcyonwick was another city that situated itself on the base of a mountain range. That land was the home of the Demoniacal Kingdom. That city was Coldwyvern. It was not much a city, rather it was more of a small town compared to the large city of Halcyonwick.

A town named after its founder, Coldwyvern's infrastructure can only be described as old, with homes built from scratch terra cycles ago and buildings that were wearing out from the cold mountain breeze. A few had collapsed, remaining that way since no one wanted to repair it. Some newer buildings that had been built were out of the ordinary, appearing large and majestic to

KING TITANOSAURUS'S PROPOSED IDEA FOR AN ALLIANCE

make up for some of the old buildings that still stood. Basically, Coldwyvern was trying to copy the style of Halcyonwick's, with a touch of a medieval feel to it.

Within the inner circle of the town, a huge black castle stood tall and proud. This was the only building in Coldwyvern that was always under constant care, for it was the home of the Royal Family of the Demoniacal Kingdom. It had been built from black cobblestones, stuck together over the years by mud. It had taken hundreds of Kingdom members, and a few had died during the project but that hadn't stopped them from canceling. Many rumors have surfaced of the castle being cursed, but that could be a different story for a different time.

Inside this grand castle, it appeared as dark as the starless new moon sky. The only light that showed was from the windows of the sun outside. Various paintings of the Demoniacal Kingdom's history, from its founder to a recent painting depicting the birth of the current King's children, sprawled the main hall that ended towards the throne. Barely visible in the dark lighting, a large, massive wolf made his way down the grand staircase and through the main hallway, his head raised. This was the wolf king of the Demoniacal Kingdom. He was a muscular wolf, snout appearing as if he had slammed his face into a door as a pup and never recovered from it, coated in all black as the night itself that helped him blend into the darkness with only a dash of white fur on his head and blue snake-like patterns wrapped around his legs that could give him away to anyone who looked closely enough. His piercing yellow eyes scoured his surroundings, looking intently for something. Around him, his subjects made up of various carnivorous predators had their paws (or *whatever appendage they had depending on their kind)* on their chest in the presence of the wolf king. He looked to them, and at once, they called to him:

"King Titanosaurus of the Demoniacal Kingdom!"

The wolf king, King Titanosaurus, looked at one particular individual and swiveled to them. "Where is my son and daughter, Tokira?" he asked. "I have been searching for them in their rooms, but they're empty."

Tokira, a Caspian tiger, had kept still when King Titanosaurus approached him and met his eyes. "Prince Scamander and Princess Okome are with Her Majesty Queen Zirconia of the Demoniacal Kingdom, Your Majesty."

From within, the wolf king sighed. At least his family was together and safe.

"Where exactly?"

"By King Oromir Memorial Fountain, Your Majesty. Town square."

King Titanosaurus nodded his head. "Thank you." He left them to their own desires as he turned around towards the castle doors. Two guards noticed him approaching and grabbed onto the ropes that helped open and close the large doors. He passed them a glance and headed out.

The Demoniacal Kingdom was lively around this time of hour. Rows of businesses and small homes lined the streets. Passing individuals headed from building to building, creatures even heading to their homes. When some of them noticed the King,

KING TITANOSAURUS'S PROPOSED IDEA FOR AN ALLIANCE

they stopped in their tracks to put a paw to their chest out of respect. King Titanosaurus acknowledged a few of his subjects, making his way out of castle grounds and towards the main heart of Coldwyvern.

This was his town, one he inherited rightfully. King Oromir, King Titanosaurus's father and the King before him, had made sure to keep the Demoniacal Kingdom as independent as possible, away from the Promised Dynasty. Despite his young age at the time, he had helped build the town with his father, King Titanosaurus's grandfather and founder of the town: King Wyvern. It was rather an impressive feat for a teen such as King Oromir to build such a grandiose town with the land's most feared creature.

The wolf king remembered the stories.

Specifically, the story of the Great War Between Good and Evil.

Long ago, King Wyvern and the Promised Dynasty's founder, King Saturhorimau, lived together when the world was created by Ellowyn the Creator and the Gods. It was a time before the Kingdoms were formed, and everyone lived as one in a huge group. There was peace, unity and harmony in the land created by Lavian–the God of the Land and Sea–and Wuxjun–the God of the Skies–, since both King Saturhorimau and King Wyvern helped guide the creatures. The two were close friends, having met when they were just children. King Wyvern was an orphan, lost without a family. By sheer luck, he had met the cave lion cub, and they struck a conversation that would lead to their friendship. Close in fact, they considered each other brothers. The two soon became the leaders of the group, steering and guiding them to safety.

Things would change, however, when the young cave lion would be chosen by the angels of the Heavens to be the land's preacher. King Wyvern, in his jealousy that all attention now focused on his best friend and sworn brother, one day ran away. During his time gone, he had discovered and began to practice a form of magic never before seen: dark magic. Once King Wyvern returned and introduced the new darkness to everyone, some creatures began to follow him, challenging the ways laid out to them by the Gods and King Saturhorimau's sayings. They worshipped the wyvern dragon as their new leader. Rebellion soon formed in the land not long after as two factions–the early Kingdoms in a sense–fought one another.

This alarmed King Saturhorimau, who was all about preaching the ways of good in the name of the Gods. The sight of everyone who had once lived together and called one another friends or a partner now divided in hatred and distrust was devastating to King Saturhorimau. The cave lion had attempted to talk things out with his best friend. King Wyvern, who was already lost to the forces of the sins, refused to listen and only offered King Saturhorimau an ultimatum: give up the land and his Heaven blessed status to him, or die by his dark magic along with those who oppress him.

King Saturhorimau broke off his loyalty to King Wyvern after being given this ultimatum, further devastating and breaking the wyvern dragon's heart and sending him into madness. In the buildup before the war, King Wyvern taught his dark magic to his allies, building up their strengths. King Saturhorimau also built his allies' strengths. He continued to preach Ellowyn's word and

KING TITANOSAURUS'S PROPOSED IDEA FOR AN ALLIANCE

the Gods' kindness. He prayed and prayed for them all and he asked the Heavens for a blessing.

Eventually the two factions–the ones who supported King Wyvern and the ones who supported King Saturhorimau–went to war. This Great War Between Good and Evil, as it was called, was a major mark in history, lasting for one terra cycle. Many lives were lost, and some generations would be affected. There was no victor in the end, and the two agreed on a treaty to separate themselves from one another for good. King Wyvern made the Demoniacal Kingdom, and King Saturhorimau made the Promised Dynasty.

That's the way things have been for many terra cycles.

Until now.

It did not take long for King Titanosaurus to get to the town square. Right in the center sat King Oromir Memorial Fountain, a grandiose black marble fountain. The large wolf king observed with interest. King Oromir Memorial Fountain was a large fountain in the middle of the town square constructed with a sculpted statue of King Oromir to commemorate his contributions to the city with King Wyvern–the founder, his Father, King Titanosaurus's grandfather–floating on top of him. King Wyvern was the one that was spraying out the water, while King Oromir just stared. King Titanosaurus didn't entirely understand why King Wyvern was here (since after all, King Oromir did contribute to the development and creation of Coldwyvern instead of sitting around all day) but he didn't question it that much.

I apologize, Father, King Titanosaurus said to himself, lowering his head submissively. *I know you built this town for us alongside Grandfather for the Demoniacal Kingdom, for us to be independent and forever cut off from the Promised Dynasty. But we are struggling, and I cannot keep the Kingdom going forever when there are forces way out of my control. I'm losing members. We need help. The only help we can get is from the Promised Dynasty. ...Please, if you're watching and hearing me...forgive me.*

He darted his eyes towards the statue of King Wyvern.

Forgive me, Grandfather, if you happen to be listening as well.

The wolf king lifted up his head in a haste, shaking himself. He could not be weak in front of his people. He had to be strong. He looked down at himself and up ahead. At the edge of the fountain, past the running, screaming children playing freely in the town square, a pretty white she-wolf with silver gray paws and an emerald studded collar sat on a bench with two adult pups curiously leaning on her shoulders. She held an unrolled scroll that she and her pups were looking at. King Titanosaurus had found his family. He padded up to the three of them. He caught a bit of the she-wolf's words.

"*And with a mighty roar that could be heard from every corner of the land, King Wyvern split the land between him and King Saturhorimau, creating our wonderful town that is Coldwyvern today.*" She twitched an ear upon feeling King Titanosaurus's presence and looked up at him. "Ah. Hello, dear," she greeted him.

"Teaching history to our kids, Zirconia?" King Titanosaurus said with a smile.

KING TITANOSAURUS'S PROPOSED IDEA FOR AN ALLIANCE

His Queen nodded at him. This was Queen Zirconia, a dire wolf from humble origins and his beloved wife. With her pretty eyelashes and gentle demeanor, he knew from the moment they met that she was to be his future Queen and the mother of his children. Speaking of said children, his kids–a dark blue wolf with light blue eyes and a blue-gray and white she-wolf with mint green eyes, a tuft of sky blue hair on her head and wearing a black diamond necklace–leapt towards their father excitedly as he approached them.

"Father!" they said in unison, hugging him.

For a brief moment, he smiled. These were his children, the future of the Demoniacal Kingdom. They were his pride and joy, his hope for his Kingdom. But, with things happening, he knew he needed them more than anything. He let his smile drop. "It's King Titanosaurus of the Demoniacal Kingdom to you, children," he said jokingly though serious, rubbing both of their heads.

"We're not kids, Dad!" the blue-gray and white she-wolf said. "We're adults!"

"Yeah, we're way beyond the pup age!" the dark blue wolf agreed with a curt nod. "Way too old and cool to hang out with anyone younger than us!"

King Titanosaurus sighed at them, but it was not an annoyed sigh. "Glad I found you guys. I went to both your rooms but didn't see you two there."

"Is something the matter, dear?" Queen Zirconia asked, perking up instantly.

King Titanosaurus looked at her, looked around him, then back at her. "This is not the place to discuss such personal and urgent matters," he said in a hushed tone. "Come back to the castle with me, all of you."

His children tilted their heads at him. They were confused. Queen Zirconia, however, flattened her ears. She knew when her husband mentioned anything about personal problems, it meant something bad was happening.

She quickly closed the scroll she had and tucked it in her pouch that she was carrying. Hopping off the bench, she ushered her children forward.

"Come along, kids," she urged. "Important business is your concern too that you will have to learn." She nosed her son especially, who crossed his arms. "You especially, young man, don't brood now. For once you take the crown after your father, you'll be the one making the decisions around here."

"Awww! But I wanted to learn about how King Wyvern mastered dark magic!" the wolf prince groaned, begrudgingly heading back to the castle. "*I* wanna learn how to use it too!"

"That will have to be saved for another day, Prince Scamander," Zirconia told him.

"But I thought that *was* going to be today! You promised!"

"I'm sorry, dear, but important matters come first."

The wolf prince, Prince Scamander, although he complied, frowned. He let out a grunt of disapproval, looking away with tail rapidly twitching. Queen Zirconia frowned, getting frustrated

KING TITANOSAURUS'S PROPOSED IDEA FOR AN ALLIANCE

with having to deal with his stubbornness. His sister, noticing how upset he looked, shoved him playfully. Prince Scamander looked at his sister with a raised eyebrow.

"Race ya home!" she teased, crouching down. "Last one there is a rotten Promised Dynasty member!"

His expression changed almost instantaneously like a light bulb. He lowered the front half of his body, hind quivering in the air.

"HA! You think you're faster than me? You're on, Okome!" Without warning, Prince Scamander took off.

The she-wolf, Okome, temporarily froze. She looked back to her parents with an expression that could be identified as "What the hell?" King Titanosaurus stood in his usual monotone stance, while Queen Zirconia let the corners of her mouth crook up in a soft smile. She gestured to her as if saying, "Well? Go catch up with him!"

She finally gave chase.

"Hey! Cheating! You didn't count!"

"Later loserrrrrr!!"

The two royal siblings ran ahead as their parents watched in amusement. Citizens of the Demoniacal Kingdom made way for the two rambunctious royal siblings. The wolf queen bumped her shoulder on King Titanosaurus's shoulder, following after their children.

"Our son truly takes after you, doesn't he?" Queen Zirconia said to King Titanosaurus. "With all his frowning and brooding and eagerness for the darkness. He'll make a great King."

The massive wolf, stoic, managed to crack a faint smile at his wife.

"Just like his great-grandfather," the wolf king said.

King Titanosaurus got his children situated in front of the stairs and Queen Zirconia sat on the throne, observing them. The wolf king checked on the soldier guards that stood by the carpet and made his way to his throne. The prince and princess and the guards placed a paw on their chests.

"My subjects," he started, "it is with a heavy heart I must announce: it is time that we make a formal alliance with the Promised Dynasty."

Both the wolf prince and the wolf princess jolted in their pelts. They didn't hear that right, did they? Queen Zirconia stared at her husband with concern. The guards broke their stance after the royal siblings jolted and stared at the King. There was an instant riot amongst all in attendance as many voiced their opinions and complaints.

"What in the name of the wyvern??!"

"Did I hear that incorrectly or what?"

"You cannot be serious!"

KING TITANOSAURUS'S PROPOSED IDEA FOR AN ALLIANCE

"An *alliance* with the *Promised Dynasty*?! Are you mad, Your Majesty!? Like we'd ever want to be allies with them!"

The two royal siblings looked at each other in concern. While Princess Okome never was one to speak on her feelings regarding personal matters with the Kingdom, Prince Scamander on the other hand felt the same rage as everyone around him. As the future King, he understood the ins and outs of both Kingdoms, and he knew that in order to be a good King, he had to take care of his Kingdom first. An alliance with their rival Kingdom was indeed a stupid idea, and he wondered what made his Father think of wanting such an alliance.

What are you planning, Father?

The wolf king arose from his throne, his fur spiked. "Quiet!" King Titanosaurus shouted. "There will be order!"

The riots quieted down almost instantly, sprinkled grumbles lingering throughout the room. Princess Okome and Prince Scamander shifted their paws, awkwardly looking towards their Father with questioning looks. They weren't sure what to think about their Father's statement, but they decided both to remain silent until they found the perfect opportunity to speak up.

One of the creatures attending, also a massive black wolf identical to King Titanosaurus with a white chest and underbelly, moved his way through the crowd, his piercing ice-blue eyes fixated only on the wolf king. Prince Scamander studied the black wolf; this was his and his sister's uncle, the brother of the King and the other son of King Oromir: Livyatan. His ears flattened. *Oh great.* He knew that he was here to give his opinions on the matter. Knowing his uncle, Prince Scamander knew there was going to be a bit of tension between brothers.

At least he will have some sense unlike Father. I wonder what he will say.

"King Titanosaurus of the Demoniacal Kingdom, I hate to object to anything you say or do, but, are you *certain* of this?" he growled. "An alliance with the Promised Dynasty? Our *sworn rival*, may I remind you? Won't this go against all that King Wyvern and King Oromir made for the Demoniacal Kingdom?! It's risky to make such decisions involving our rival Kingdom with our business."

"Livyatan, my brother," the wolf king said calmly, "I understand your concern, but this is only for the best of our Kingdom." He continued, while looking at his children's shocked, concerned faces: "The Demoniacal Kingdom was doomed from the start. King Wyvern and King Oromir had failed to see that the war damaged our Kingdom. They were young and reckless without thinking of the consequences of their actions."

"What are you talking about, King Titanosaurus?" Livyatan groused with the roll of his eyes. "King Wyvern and King Oromir did what was best for the Demoniacal Kingdom. They broke free from a religious tyranny that would have ruined us all. I don't understand..."

Prince Scamander had to agree with his uncle; King Wyvern knew what he was doing when he declared war on his sworn brother King Saturhorimau. He saw the flaws that he wanted to fix, but the cave lion refused to listen. It was only understandable

KING TITANOSAURUS'S PROPOSED IDEA FOR AN ALLIANCE

that the two went their separate ways and created Kingdoms based on their own beliefs and thoughts. *It's the only reasonable course of action,* he thought. *What was King Wyvern supposed to do? Stay with those who challenged his views? I sure as hell wouldn't.*

Were the two founders teenagers in the buildup to the Great War? Sure, but they had grown past being children to know how the world worked to make conscious decisions. King Wyvern choosing to stray from his sworn brother's cult was his decision that he had obviously thought of before he acted out on it.

It just doesn't make any sense. Uncle Livyatan has a good point to discuss.

The wolf king ignored his brother and continued: "We did not have to live separately, instead, our land could have been one and only divided from within. Because we have ignored the Gods, they have cursed us, and that is why we are falling apart. I cannot appeal to them, so that is why I am turning to the Promised Dynasty for help."

The mention of the Gods drew much hushed conversations. Prince Scamander pinned his ears back. It was a touchy subject to bring up the Gods, since no one in the Demoniacal Kingdom even worshipped or acknowledged them, not even the Creator herself. They believed that the Gods only favored the ones pure of heart, like the Promised Dynasty, and loathed those with evil in their hearts. It's why King Wyvern abandoned them.

The Gods! Seriously?! Dare to mention those cursed beings who have a play in brainwashing mortals into their ways!? Prince Scamander lifted up his ears, twitching. *What is Father planning..?*

Livyatan narrowed his eyes. "How incredibly soft and bold you've gotten, my brother. Mentioning the Gods all willy-nilly like they're your best friends. You KNOW we do not believe them or anything they say! This isn't you, King Titanosaurus. Who manipulated you? King Jung-hwa of the Promised Dynasty? Or Queen Cora of the Promised Dynasty?"

The tension rose again as the vast majority agreed with Livyatan.

"Why would we go groveling back to the Gods?"

"They would reject us the moment we stepped foot on their doorstep."

"I don't want some divine beings interfering with my life! Never!"

The wolf king snorted. "I am not soft! You know me, brother. I would never bow to King Jung-hwa's ways or the ways of the Gods." The wolf king turned his head away. "I only agreed that we can merge our Kingdom with the Promised Dynasty for the good of us. Well, that's what King Jung-hwa said, but I am agreeing on the good of the Demoniacal Kingdom. He doesn't know, of course."

"And why are we relevant to this again?" Prince Scamander asked after minutes of silence from him and his sister. If he didn't speak up sooner, their Father would have continued to drone on off topic without even addressing them.

"Of course!" King Titanosaurus clapped his paws together. He looked towards his daughter. "Princess Okome, I have arranged a marriage between you and the prince of the Promised Dynasty, Prince Wonwoo, as a means to seal the alliance."

KING TITANOSAURUS'S PROPOSED IDEA FOR AN ALLIANCE

The silence had never been stronger. The anger within Prince Scamander was immeasurable as he heard those words. Arranged marriage? A means to seal the alliance!? His blood boiled.

WHAT!?

Princess Okome lifted up her head. "Father, I am...honored, but I am confused," she said hesitantly. "I do not know anything about Prince Wonwoo of the Promised Dynasty. How are we to marry if we do not know each other?"

Yeah. How could she marry someone from THE PROMISED DYNASTY!? Someone she doesn't know! Someone she probably does not WANT! Prince Scamander narrowed his eyes. *Father's got something in his old brain. Uncle Livyatan is right in the fact that he's never like this. Someone manipulated him.*

"King Jung-hwa and I have arranged a date for the two of you to further acquaint yourselves," King Titanosaurus explained.

His body was practically on fire as his hatred exploded.

Oh, no! Hell no!

The wolf prince couldn't be silent anymore. He stood up, drawing attention to himself from those attending.

"Father," Prince Scamander said, his eyes radiating a dark hue, "are you sure this is a good idea? What if this Prince Wonwoo hurts her? What will happen then?" He stepped closer to his sister in a protective manner. "I'm not about to lose my sister to those scums in the Promised Dynasty. Especially from their prince!"

There was tension in the air as the prince visibly shook in anger. Everyone whispered, expressing concern for the wolf prince and wolf princess. None could speak up as they feared the wrath of the young prince. Queen Zirconia rose from her throne to console her son, but King Titanosaurus placed a paw on her shoulder. He reassured her to sit back down as he would handle the delicate situation. She complied with him, nodding. He got up from his throne, raising his paw to his guards.

"I know you're all confused about the situation that is unfolding," he addressed the crowd, "but I want you all to understand: this is all for the good of our Kingdom."

Confused? What in hell do you mean confused!? The wolf prince was beyond anger, he lost all rational thoughts. *We're all* angry, *not* confused!

"But why not find a way to solve our problems amongst ourselves, King Titanosaurus of the Demoniacal Kingdom?" someone asked.

Exactly!

"Because I have tried," he said. "I have tried and tried and all have failed. We're losing members by the day, and we're losing good members. I cannot find ways to recruit members as many fear our darkness and our ways. That's when I began to think: If we alliance ourselves to the Promised Dynasty once more, we will be able to grow our Kingdom again and become as strong as we once were before."

The statement suddenly appealed to everyone except for Prince Scamander. They looked to their king eagerly. Even Livyatan

KING TITANOSAURUS'S PROPOSED IDEA FOR AN ALLIANCE

seemed curious as he stared at his brother with a form of eagerness.

"By strong... Do you mean that we will be able to live independently again?" Livyatan asked.

"Correct, my brother," King Titanosaurus said, pointing at him. "See, once my daughter is married, they will be the new King and Queen of the conjoined Kingdoms."

Prince Scamander's ears jolted up at once. He pulled his lips back in a snarl. The Demoniacal Kingdom and the Promised Dynasty becoming one? He didn't like the sound of that idea whatsoever. Also, his sister marrying a Promised scum? Being booted off the throne by the lion prince!?

This has to be a joke. Father cannot be serious.

"Ahhh, I get it!" Livyatan grinned. "King Jung-hwa would no longer be in power once Princess Okome is married." He stopped. "But...that will mean *his son* will be the one to boss us around."

The guards murmured their disapproval.

"I won't listen to the likes of him!"

"Me neither!"

"He can expect loyalty from my ass."

"HAHAHA! Damn straight! I'll make him kiss it!"

Prince Scamander raised his head up, agreeing with everyone's disapproval. He could agree with their sentiments.

King Titanosaurus quieted the crowd. "True, but my daughter will be there for him. She will give him advice, and he will listen."

The guards mumbled.

"This is ridiculous," Prince Scamander grumbled, lowering his head down again. *Have they forgotten that I will no longer be King if this Prince Wonwhatever becomes the King?* He said to himself, not daring to speak it aloud. *Has Father just practically demoted me for this stupid alliance!? How could he forget about me!!!? HIS SON!!*

"We will be able to gain new members by convincing them to our ways. Who would stop them? Prince Wonwoo? Of course not. My beloved daughter will distract him from ever finding out. Once we gain their full trust and power, we will be even more unstoppable than ever before! We will strike the Promised Dynasty when they least expect it, and we will rule the land!"

Everyone shouted in agreement.

"Down with the Promised Dynasty! Long live the Demoniacal Kingdom!"

"You are absolutely ridiculous, Father!" Prince Scamander bursted out. "How can you do this to us? Do this to Okome!?" He gestured aggressively to his sister. "Have you even thought about her well being? Consider what could possibly happen to her??"

Voices around him sided with his argument.

"The young prince has a point."

"Her Highness would be walking in dangerous territories."

KING TITANOSAURUS'S PROPOSED IDEA FOR AN ALLIANCE

King Titanosaurus slammed his paws on the floor to silence everyone. "Prince Scamander, silence your tongue. Watch who you are spewing your words onto." The wolf king's eyes glared. "Would you really think I'd not think about the safety of my own children?"

The wolf prince narrowed his eyes.

He looked at Princess Okome once more. "What do you say, my daughter? Do you agree on these terms?"

"Say no," Prince Scamander whispered to her as she began to think about the decision. "Please, for the love of the wyvern, say no."

"You're not the one making the decision here," she snapped back at him in a hushed manner.

"I'm trying to protect you from making a huge mistake you will come to regret."

"By the wyvern, brother, you're always protecting me and speaking for me as if I don't have a mind of my own!"

Prince Scamander snapped at her. "Because I am your older brother, and I am doing what is only good for you!" He inhaled sharply, doing his best to keep his composure. "We don't need an alliance with the Promised Dynasty to become stronger. We can find other ways! Father is just spewing nonsense at us."

Princess Okome tossed her hair tuft. "I know what I'm getting myself into."

The wolf prince felt his composure crumble as he shook his head aggressively, getting up on his paws. "By the wyvern! No, you do not! How are you not listening to a word I am saying!? You're absolutely crazy right now to believe Father's decision! Now believe me. Say no to this."

Princess Okome flinched at her brother's sudden movement. The wolf prince saw this and felt a huge wave of guilt crash in his brain. He shouldn't have worded that as if he was angry specifically at her. He hated the idea of getting angry at his sister, but he wanted her to know that he was not angry at her. He was just angry at their Father making her decide on something she had no control over.

"Okome, I'm sorry, I just–"

"Prince Scamander!"

King Titanosaurus's bark startled the two of them. The wolf prince put a paw on his chest.

"Do not bother your sister with your thoughts. This is her decision, and her decision alone."

Prince Scamander growled, but he felt a paw gently rest on his shoulder. He looked over to his sister, who smiled at him. He looked away from her and sat down, scowling. As much as he was getting frustrated with her, he knew he could not be mad at his sister. All he wanted was to make sure she would be okay and live happily. But how could she live happily with someone she's being forced to love, marry and bear their children? That was what frustrated Prince Scamander; the fact that she did not see this point upset him. That made his heart ache.

KING TITANOSAURUS'S PROPOSED IDEA FOR AN ALLIANCE

The wolf princess seemed to falter for a moment. Prince Scamander knew that she was reconsidering her choices, but he could see her eyes leaning on the idea of agreeing with the alliance. No matter how much she thought of her brother's words, he knew that she wouldn't entirely listen to him. She finally stood up and put a paw on her chest.

What are you doing? The wolf prince stared unblinkingly. *You can't seriously think...*

"I will do it, King Titanosaurus of the Demoniacal Kingdom," she answered. "I will agree to this betrothal. For the Demoniacal Kingdom."

Amidst the mixed cheering and chanting, Prince Scamander scowled at his father. This could not be happening! Did their Father not know what that meant for the both of them? He casted a glance at his sister, who met his gaze. He was definitely going to have a talk with her about this.

"I can't *believe* Father did this to you!"

Once the meeting was at a close, and the two siblings were free to go, Prince Scamander roughly grabbed his sister by her arm and dragged her down the hallway, up the staircase, and to his room. She examined his room; from the very few times she had been in his room, she could tell her brother had a thing with all things dark. His walls were covered in a dark blue, similar to his pelt but more identical to that of the night sky, with the ceiling reflecting that. A wallpaper of the night sky was plastered on the ceiling, and chandeliers in the shape of stars hung. Rows of shelves populated one corner of the room that were filled with books, a pot that contained a live Venus fly trap (something Princess Okome found strange that her brother–the Prince of the Demoniacal Kingdom–would enjoy such a plant to keep as a pet), and small little figurines of King Wyvern.

The wolf prince closed his door ever gently so that it wouldn't slam then finally unleashed his anger once they were settled.

"How could he do this!? Manipulate you and sell you away to this Prince Wonwoo like you're some cow in an auction!?" Prince Scamander vented, pacing around his room as his sister sat down on his bed. "Absolutely outrageous! And this whole alliance thing! Trying to unite the Demoniacal Kingdom with the Promised Dynasty? **HA!** Father's getting a little too old, ain't he? The mere idea of our Kingdom becoming one with the Promised Dynasty will never happen in a million terra cycles! No. Not even a million terra cycles. More like it will never happen AT ALL! We're completely different in our ways and our ideologies. There's no way we could ever get along and there is NO WAY we will be able to convince any Promised Dynasty members to join us! That's just ridiculous! This is going completely against what King Wyvern and King Oromir made for us! How could you agree to this?!"

Princess Okome rubbed her arm and gazed at her ranting brother with fear. "Brother," she started once he had finished, "I understand your concern, but you do not have to worry about me."

"NOT WORRY ABOUT YOU!?" The dark blue wolf patted his chest in an attempt to calm himself down. "Okome, my dear

KING TITANOSAURUS'S PROPOSED IDEA FOR AN ALLIANCE

sister, you're younger than me. Of course I'm going to worry about you."

"Younger than you I am, but I'm an adult just as you are. I'm old enough to make my own decisions."

"Not old enough!"

"I'm 21!"

"And *I* am 23, two terra cycles older."

Princess Okome flipped her hair tuft. "Why does it matter anyway? If I agree on something, it should be final."

"I was trying to tell you against it!" Prince Scamander growled. "There is so much wrong about this, this is just a recipe bound to fail!" His light blue eyes began to fog in red as tears welled. "Please, why can't you listen to me?"

"I do listen to you, brother," Princess Okome reassured. "I take your advice. But I believe it's time you let go of your overprotection of me."

His eyes stretched out, appearing as if they were gonna jump out his skull. Princess Okome continued.

"Scamander. Brother. Beloved brother. Listen to me. I love you, and always will. Nothing will ever stop me from loving my big brother. But we will have to live our own lives eventually, and that will mean that we cannot depend on each other as we are now."

"I don't want to think about it *that* early."

"Soon you'll be King, I'll be Queen. We will not have time to be around each other anymore."

"I won't be King," Prince Scamander snorted, tossing his head to the side.

Princess Okome twitched an ear. "Whatever do you mean? You're the rightful heir to the throne. Of course you will be King."

The wolf prince turned his gaze away from her. How did she already forget? "You heard Father. Right? When you marry that Prince Wonwoo-whatever-the-fuck-that-name-is, you will be Queen, and *he* will be King. Then, when you have a hybrid child with that whosit, that child will be the rightful heir. I will lose my rights and be bumped down to the second heir like Uncle Livyatan. Then third-in-line when your child's child is born. So on, so forth."

Princess Okome stared sympathetically at her brother.

"Basically, Father demoted me from the throne without outright saying 'Oh, by the way, Prince Scamander is no longer the rightful heir to the throne. It's Princess Okome now and her lineage,'" the wolf prince said sarcastically.

Princess Okome scoffed at him. "Father did not mean that."

"Oh yes he did! I am the firstborn, the first in line to the throne. But this alliance...I am demoted from the throne."

"I won't allow it."

"You really don't have a choice. You're now our only hope for future heirs–"

KING TITANOSAURUS'S PROPOSED IDEA FOR AN ALLIANCE

"NO, not that! I don't care, I want children. But I won't make them rightful heirs. I will have you retain your birthright."

The wolf prince looked back at her with shock written in his eyes. He tilted his head. "How... Isn't that against the rule? That just sounds a little...unordinary. Like...why deny your children of their given rights? Don't do that for me."

"...You're mad because of that, aren't you?"

Prince Scamander lifted up his ears. "What? No. Of course not! Why would I be mad at you!? I could care less about my status at this time. I have already said: I'm worried for *you*." He huffed. "We don't know what this Prince Wonwoo is actually like and how he will treat you. Yeah sure, he's a Promised Dynasty lion. But we don't know how he really is, you know what I mean? Like, what if he does something to you?" He dug his claws into the carpet beneath him. "What if he rejects you? Harms you? *Physically* hurts you?! All the possibilities are endless."

"Brother, he's a Promised lion through and through. He would never stoop that low and do something so heinous. It's against their moral code."

"You never know!"

The wolf princess chuckled and lowered her head. "You really are more concerned over my well-being than your own status."

"Did you just not hear what I said NOT EVEN A MINUTE AGO!?"

Princess Okome laughed. She swung herself off the bed and went up to her brother. She rested a paw on his head and gently ruffled it. "You're getting worked up over nothing," she said. "The alliance will work out. I know so." When he hadn't responded, she added: "I promise you: I will take care of myself."

"Promises, promises. No promise is a good promise. Why promise when you can't uphold it?"

Princess Okome frowned. Was her brother really that cynical about life? "Should anything happen, I will be sure to let Father know," she told him.

"And me," Prince Scamander added with a grumble.

"Yes. Of course. I will be sure to let you know as well."

"I mean it, sister. With all my being. If Prince Wonfuckery does something to you, and I mean *anything at all*, I want to know. You tell me first before telling Father. That way, I can personally whoop his ass straight to King Wyvern!"

The wolf princess shook her head. "No need for that."

"Oh there will be a need! You just watch!"

Princess Okome stared, lifting an eyebrow. She knew where her brother was going with his statement. "I'm watching."

"Yeah. Yeah, I'm gonna kick his ass. Like this! But more simplified of course." The wolf prince bunched his muscles and lunged at her, wrestling with her in a gentle way on his bed. She laughed, batting at his ears and neck. They continued to roll around, play batting and biting one another.

"Just like this!" Prince Scamander continued to bumble on, softly taking her ear into his jaws. "And this!"

KING TITANOSAURUS'S PROPOSED IDEA FOR AN ALLIANCE

Princess Okome continued letting her brother toss her around until she came up with a funny idea to play on him. "Oh yeah? Then what happens if he...fights back?" she teased.

"Oh, don't you dare!"

In one swift movement, she swept her brother off his paws, making him fumble. She grabbed him by the shoulders and slammed him onto the bed, pinning her paws on him. Prince Scamander looked rather shocked at Princess Okome, almost finding it hard to believe that she actually did something in their play fights that she would never normally do.

"What if Prince Wonwoo did that? Hm? What would Father say if he found out the rival prince from our rival Kingdom beat our beloved prince in combat?"

He tried to call her out on it.

"Cheater!"

"How did I cheat? I did what any creature would do in combat." Princess Okome playfully flicked her brother's nose, feeling him flinch.

The wolf prince stared at his sister. "...Touche, sister. Touche."

As much as he was a pain in the ass, Princess Okome was grateful for her older brother and having him around. He had protected her the moment she was born, and he had never left her side. He made sure that she was well taken care of. Those were the happiest moments in her life, and she never wanted them to ever go away. She wasn't sure how her life would have been had she been an only child.

She wanted to enjoy every moment with Prince Scamander until the day she got married.

Once I'm married... She let out a sigh... *we'll never be close as we are now ever again. The time I spend with my brother will never be frequent when I am Queen. Especially when I become a mother. I'm sure that's what he's more worried about. I'm gonna make sure he knows I'll still be here, even if we are far apart and focused on our duties.*

"Just... Promise me something, will you, sis?"

A paw on her chest brought her out of her daydream, and she promptly got off her brother. Prince Scamander was never one to ask for promises, so she knew it was time for things to get serious. She fixed her fur, making herself appear professional. The two sat side by side. "What is it?" she asked him.

Prince Scamander looked at her with a look that screamed "Please listen to what I have to say." For a minute, her heart stopped. What was he going to ask her? Promise him to still keep his status on the throne?

"Take care of yourself for me," he admitted in a soft breath. "Always remember that I will always be there for you. So will Mother and Father. But I, more specifically. No matter what troubles may happen, don't forget to call for me."

Princess Okome sighed a happy sigh. "Of course, brother, I promise," she said, taking his paw into her's. "Just cause I'll be spreading my wings and living my life doesn't mean I'm going to entirely push you away. You're still my big brother at the end of the day and my biggest pillar of support. I'll always think about you. I'll always want you in my life until the end. No matter where I will be."

Prince Scamander leaned closer to her, resting his head on her shoulder. Princess Okome could tell how tender her brother was, but his face read to that similar to their Father. "Do you *really* promise?" he asked with more sternness. "*Promise* promise? Like this isn't some false promise most make that they don't fulfill. Like a real promise?"

"Yes, I *do* promise," Princess Okome huffed, chuckling to herself and petting his head. "I *really* do promise."

The wolf prince narrowed his eyes. Princess Okome could tell he was still untrusting of her words, and she knew that no matter how much convincing she did, it wouldn't get through to her older brother. All she could do was be there and hug him. Finally he relaxed and let out a fat sigh.

"Thank you, sis. Thank you."

The wolf princess leaned her head on her brother's head. She closed her eyes and sighed contently.

"You're welcome, brother. I love you."

"I love you too."

CHAPTER 3
ON A HORRIBLE WINDY DAY, IT WAS LOVE AT FIRST SIGHT

~ 6 months before the war...~
~ A day after the New Terra Cycle Day ~
~ January in Terra Cycle 1118 B.E. ~

Why did it have to be today? Why are we meeting now?! Great Ellowyn, help me not make a fool out of myself!

Prince Wonwoo stood outside the castle surrounded by his guards. Yesterday was the celebration of the new terra cycle, otherwise known as the New Terra Cycle Day. It was a huge celebration, with howls and cheers and bottles flying once they saw the moon at its highest point. Prince Wonwoo had celebrated with his parents and his friends, doing stupid things and taking a lot of shots.

ON A HORRIBLE WINDY DAY, IT WAS LOVE AT FIRST SIGHT

Now it was over, and it was a new day of the new terra cycle. Today was the day that King Titanosaurus of the Demoniacal Kingdom would be arriving along with his daughter, Princess Okome of the Demoniacal Kingdom. The lion prince couldn't help but shake as he tried to stay still. This was happening too soon. He should be resting, not meeting the princess! Fidgeting his paws, he stared at his parents; they were talking to some guards about something related to the Demoniacal Kingdom.

Why can't this happen later instead of the day after the New Terra Cycle day? Prince Wonwoo thought to himself as he fixed his mane. *This is still too soon for me. I don't feel prepared. Hell, I'm not even IN THE SLIGHTEST prepared!! I'm so sleepy! And also a tad bit hungover..*

"Cold paws, Prince Wonwoo?"

The lion prince turned to the voice who spoke to him; it was a medium sized raccoon with gray fur and a dark mask and stripes. They stood on their hind legs as they observed the fields beyond the gate.

"Don't worry, I was the same too when I married my wife," he said. "I once ran out on her on our first date! She never lets it go, it's funny!"

"Very helpful," Prince Wonwoo said with sarcasm, twitching his tail. He didn't want to sound rude, but the raccoon wasn't helping with his anxiety. He needed time to calm himself, to mentally prepare for his life changing forever. When a gust of wind blew, he hurriedly fixed his mane. Stupid wind. What was going on today with this weather? It hadn't been like this before. Did today just *have* to be windy? It was as if the Gods–specifically Wuxjun–were testing the lion prince.

Yeah, well I don't appreciate it! he cursed.

A nose pressed into his shoulder, followed by a rush of air. His flesh jolted at the sudden touch.

"Don't mind him, Prince Wonwoo," a white horse told the lion prince. "He's just being dumb to try and entertain you."

"Hey!"

"Oh. I'm not at all, Hakuba," he said to the white horse, Hakuba, turning his attention back to the gate. He could trust Hakuba; they had been friends ever since he was a cub. "I know it's how he acts."

"You guys are mean!"

They brushed off the raccoon's remarks.

About 10 minutes went by, and the anxiety within the lion prince's chest grew bigger and bigger. There was still no sight of King Titanosaurus or his Kingdom. Prince Wonwoo tried to take deep breaths, clutching his chest fur. He could feel his intoxicated heart desperately trying to escape right now. The grass swayed in the wind ever so gently. How could the winds be calm on the grass yet act so rough on him?

"King Titanosaurus is taking quite a long time, isn't he?" another guard, a maned wolf, said after moments of silence.

"Well, Coldwyvern is some few miles away from Halcyonwick," another responded. "I don't blame him if it takes half an hour to get here."

"It better not take that long!" Hakuba neighed, stomping her hoof on the ground. "He can take all the leisure time he needs on any other day except for today!"

Please don't come today, please don't come today, please don't come today, the lion prince thought to himself. *I can't calm down. I'm going to pass out if this continues any longer–*

"I see him! I see King Titanosaurus of the Demoniacal Kingdom!"

Every guard stood on high alert. The lion prince jumped once again in his own skin at the loud, shrill voice. The fear made his heart skip so fast that it couldn't get back into rhythm.

I'm so going to die right now. Morana, Goddess of Death, if you're here, please take me now.

Atop Hakuba the white horse, a small sand-colored meerkat bounced with its black-tipped tail erect. It patted the horse's neck as it shouted. "Alert the King and Queen of the Promised Dynasty at once!" the tiny creature said to Hakuba.

"We're aware."

Prince Wonwoo might as well make a tally of how many heart attacks for today from all the surprises that kept happening. This time, his father had miraculously popped up beside the lion prince's side, along with his mother on the other side. The lion prince could feel his mother's warm gaze as she fixed up his mane.

"You're going to do just fine," Queen Cora reassured her son. "Just be yourself, and you'll be fine."

"Just not too much, or else you'll scare her off," King Jung-hwa teased, bumping his head onto his neck. He also took a moment to flash a playful wink at Queen Cora, which made her face turn red.

"Jung-hwa!"

He tried to not look at his parents, instead, he focused on the opening gates.

The first sight the lion prince was greeted with was an enormous black wolf with a streak of white fur on his head and blue snake-like patterns that wrapped around his legs. Prince Wonwoo was shocked at the sheer size of the wolf; his muscles rippled through his skin, and he was as tall as King Jung-hwa, only a few feet taller. He had a small round snout and face which resembled that of a dragon. He also had small sharp blue scales on his cheeks.

The lion prince swallowed nervously.

Wow.

"By the Gods... He's MASSIVE!" the raccoon said in shock, putting his paws on his snout.

"Larger than King Jung-hwa!" the meerkat observed. "I never seen a wolf THAT enormous! Let alone any other creature as big as His Majesty is."

"Look at those claws.." Hakuba breathed, her flanks quivering. "They're ginormous."

The lion prince twitched his ear at them. He agreed on their statements; the wolf king of the Demoniacal Kingdom was indeed a large creature. Probably helped by the fact that he had wyvern dragon blood in him. All thanks to King Wyvern, no doubt.

Surrounding him were a few Demoniacal Kingdom guards. They were of various predators, from the smallest canine to the biggest bear Prince Wonwoo had ever seen, and they looked rather unfriendly. King Titanosaurus looked around him before he gestured to his party to follow him. Prince Wonwoo eventually spotted two individuals that caught his attention; on both sides of the wolf king, a dark blue wolf and a blue-gray and white she-wolf looked around in curiosity. Prince Wonwoo noted their posture and appearance and finally concluded they were the wolf king's children.

So that must be Princess Okome of the Demoniacal Kingdom, Prince Wonwoo thought, looking at the blue-gray and white she-wolf. He studied her further.

Indeed, she was a pretty she-wolf, with a tuft of light blue fur similar to Prince Wonwoo's and mint green eyes that hypnotized his gaze. She also wore a purple necklace that contained a small piece of a black diamond. She was slim and sleek, her pelt shining in the sunlight. Her smile was bright as she poked her brother to speak with him. The lion prince felt something jump up in his chest.

Okay, I won't lie, he admitted to himself, *she is kind of pretty for someone who is from the Demoniacal Kingdom. I wonder how she truly is when we talk.*

He could already feel his heart beating fast the longer he stared at Princess Okome. She had a gentleness to both her expression and her body language, and she appeared to be a friendly she-wolf. Curiously, Prince Wonwoo turned to study her brother as well.

The wolf prince looked more identical to his father, dark and brooding, with a dark blue pelt and a frown that could easily make you go nuts and wanna shout "Hey, come on! Smile, man! Your frown is ruining everyone's mood!" at him. He had a similar build to that of King Titanosaurus, except less muscular. He looked strong though, intimidating enough to scare everyone out of their wits. His eyes were the same color as the sky, light blue, just as hypnotizing as his sister's mint green eyes. Except, he didn't radiate the same bright energy Princess Okome had; instead, the wolf prince glared at every Promised Dynasty member with a stare that was screaming "I really, really wish I wasn't here right now, and I also hate all of you Promised creatures."

He met Prince Wonwoo's stare and narrowed his eyes at him. The lion prince couldn't suppress a gulp when he noticed his paws flexing.

Ooookkaaayyy, don't mess with him, duly noted.

"Welcome King Titanosaurus of the Demoniacal Kingdom," King Jung-hwa greeted, bowing his head. "It is an honor that I welcome you and your Kingdom into our city of Halcyonwick." He nodded at Queen Zirconia and their children. "I also welcome you, Queen Zirconia of the Demoniacal Kingdom, and your lovely son and daughter."

"Thank you, King Jung-hwa of the Promised Dynasty," Queen Zirconia replied, slightly tipping her muzzle down in a small, stiff bow. "It's a pleasure to finally meet up in person and talk once more in a civil manner."

"A pleasure indeed, Queen Zirconia of the Demoniacal Kingdom," Queen Cora replied warmly.

So this must be the Queen of the Demoniacal Kingdom, Prince Wonwoo had concluded. She was much different from her husband, appearing like a...well, a normal wolf. She was petite. A total difference from the hybrid that was King Titanosaurus. She had a light silver pelt with gray tipped paws and yellow crescent-like ear tips. She also sported a collar that was embedded with shiny emeralds. Her pink eyelashes complemented her pretty appearance, and they batted lovingly at her family. The lion prince could see where the wolf princess got her good looks.

"It's very....radiant, King Jung-hwa of the Promised Dynasty," the wolf king said. "But pleasant enough that I can tolerate just for the day."

Holy shit! The lion prince was thrown aback at how deep and menacing his voice was. It was deeper than his father's. That made him shrink in his pelt. He stood tall despite wanting to shake like mad.

"As radiant as the gates of the Heavens!"

"...Right." The black wolf looked at the lion prince. "So, I presume this is your son and future heir, Prince Wonwoo of the Promised Dynasty?" he asked.

King Jung-hwa proudly lifted up his head. "That's him." He nodded at him. "Introduce yourself, son."

No, no, please don't put me in the spotlight right now! Prince Wonwoo drifted his gaze to Princess Okome, who stared at him with interest. Her tail swayed side to side. He sighed softly in a way to not raise suspicion. *Ohhh. Gods, help me.*

The lion prince stepped up.

"Hello, King Titanosaurus of the Demoniacal Kingdom," he greeted, bowing his head. "It's an honor to meet you. Along with Queen Zirconia of the Demoniacal Kingdom. My name's Prince Wonwoo. Of the Promised Dynasty, of course. Prince Wonwoo Honeycutt of the Promised Dynasty. I am the one that you desire for your daughter to marry." *Why are you making yourself sound like a fool!? Just be professional! AHH!*

The black wolf stared stoically at the lion prince, unfazed by his stumbling. Every single unblinking glance from his bright golden eyes made his pelt prickle, and he felt he was being judged.

What are you looking for in me? he said to himself. *Seeing if I am fit? Seeing if I am a good choice for your daughter? Or rather re-thinking this whole arranged marriage and deciding "Yeah, nah, there's no way we're gonna follow this absolute buffoon of a future King; we're gonna continue our separate ways"? I'm right, aren't I?*

He finally blinked and nodded slowly. "It is nice to meet you officially, Prince Wonwoo Honeycutt of the Promised Dynasty," he said. "Indeed. This is my daughter, Princess Okome Snapdragon of the Demoniacal Kingdom."

ON A HORRIBLE WINDY DAY, IT WAS LOVE AT FIRST SIGHT

The blue-gray and white she-wolf stepped up once she was commanded to and placed a paw on her chest. "Prince Wonwoo Honeycutt of the Promised Dynasty," she said. "It is an honor to meet you."

Prince Wonwoo lifted up his ears. *Oh Gods! She sounds beautiful. So much different from her father.*

"'Honor to meet you,' you don't know what you're saying, sister," the wolf prince grumbled.

Those ears flattened once he heard the wolf prince's voice. *Oh Gods, he sounds* awful *and just like his father. Not in a pleasant way.*

"Ah, forgive my grumbling young man; this is Prince Scamander Snapdragon of the Demoniacal Kingdom," King Titanosaurus said, jerking his muzzle to him. "The rightful heir to the Demoniacal Kingdom."

"Not after this marriage I won't be," he continued to grumble.

"Hush, dear," a white she-wolf with silver gray paws reprimanded gently, nipping his scruff. "Mind your manners."

"Ow. Mother. That's humiliating," Prince Scamander grumbled.

Prince Wonwoo couldn't help but snicker to himself when he heard that. It reminded him of the times he'd act out and his own Mother would snap at him the same way Queen Zirconia did. The only thing about that was that she punished him as a cub.

The humiliation to be punished by your Mother in front of everyone as a grown adult! It's what you deserve for acting out like that.

A strong gust of wind rushed through the fields. Prince Wonwoo felt his fur spike up from the cold. The Demoniacal Kingdom members grumbled as they puffed out their fur. He looked at them curiously. He wondered why this little puff of wind bothered them when they lived right by a mountain, which he knew would most definitely be colder than here.

King Jung-hwa lifted up a paw to shield his eyes. "This wind is atrocious," the lion king said. "A way to start the new terra cycle huh? With some of Wuxjun's winds? Come, let's go to the castle. We have a lovely banquet prepared for you all." The lion king waved a paw enthusiastically. "Come. Come along now."

The Promised Dynasty guards looked at each other in a joint suspicious concern.

"I'm not sure about this, letting the Demoniacal Kingdom blindly enter our castle," Hakuba said softly. "Even if they're under watch by all of us. I feel it isn't enough protection." She looked at her meerkat friend. "Hey, Luta. Keep an eye on them for me."

The meerkat bowed its head. "Sure thing, Hakuba."

The Promised Dynasty guards lined up by the entrance to the castle and watched carefully as the Demoniacal Kingdom entered the sacred ground. Prince Wonwoo looked back to watch Princess Okome; she delicately stepped inside the castle and stared in awe. She stared determinedly at the colorful tiles, tracing the patterns with her paws. She whispered something to Prince Scamander, to which he perked up at her and listened. He seemed to have nodded and agreed to whatever she was saying but went back to his usual stoic self, lazily drifting his gaze around.

Yeesh, he's never happy, isn't he? Prince Wonwoo thought, shivering. *Or even a tad bit lively. Except only around his sister. Even then, she's trying to make conversation with him, and he has to act as if I spat in his food. Definitely the true son of his father. And the true blood of King Wyvern.*

The lion prince saw the wolf princess bound up to him after she had failed to talk with her brother. It took him a while to process before his eyes went wide and his ears flattened. His tail twitched.

Crap, she's coming my way. What do I do?? Idiot! Act natural, act natural.

"Your castle is simply magnificent," Princess Okome commented, smiling at him as she brushed close to him. "Such beautiful and tender work done to it and mesmerizing patterns that I could stare at for hours! It's so much different from Coldwyvern's castle."

"R-Really?" Prince Wonwoo stammered. "How's your place back home like?"

"It's not that different. It's like yours, but more...tch, how do I describe it?" She looked around the castle, tapping on her chin before she looked back at him. "More dark."

"Dark?"

"Dark. With no vibrancy or life to it."

"Ah. I see."

"Yeah..."

The two continued to stare as they entered past the throne room, her eyes only breaking away for a second to continue gazing at the architecture. He could already feel the burning gaze of Prince Scamander searing through his pelt. As if the awkwardness of the conversation wasn't bad enough. He refused to look back, but he could imagine that the wolf prince had an aura of darkness emanating off of him while standing and staring at him like he was his prey. His ears flicked.

Dude, chill. I'm just making small talk with your sister.

"What do you mean by no vibrancy?" Prince Wonwoo asked, pushing his thoughts deep down.

"There's not as many paintings as you guys have," Princess Okome explained. "Well, there is, but even they're just as dull as the paint. They're all a display of our Kingdom's history up until our births. A dull timeline for all to see and rather exaggerated. But here. Your wallpapers are also so colorful and bright, in such a beautiful array of orange and yellow. Like a field of paradise. Also your stained glass." She pointed up to a stained glass image of Ellowyn. "Such a beautiful array of colors and life to them. How they depict your history with such radiance... I've only seen dark colors most of my life." She shrugged. "You get used to it after a while, but it gets really, *really* bland."

The lion prince frowned. "Oh. That's really boring."

"Right!?" She pawed his shoulder. "Finally someone gets me."

He blushed at her touch.

King Jung-hwa led the two Kingdoms into the dining hall and immediately the castle servants got to their paws. Most appeared nervous at the sight of the Demoniacal Kingdom, treading lightly around them. The lion king gestured Prince Wonwoo to his spot at the dinner table and even invited Princess Okome next to him. The wolf princess appeared ecstatic, but she stopped herself, an aura of uncertainty emerging from her gaze. She hesitated in her decision, and Prince Wonwoo knew why. She looked over to her father, where he gave a slow nod of approval. She smiled and hurriedly joined the lion prince, bumping his shoulder.

"I get to sit next to the prestigious Prince Wonwoo of the Promised Dynasty," she happily announced as she made her way.

He grinned at her warmly, returning the bump, then looked back to the gathering Kingdoms. Prince Scamander sat wedged between his mother and his father. He stared at where his sister was and glared at Prince Wonwoo. The lion prince kept his eye contact on the wolf prince.

Although the lion prince was afraid of the wolf prince's energy, he couldn't help but find it amusing to tease him. He was laughing on the inside.

Yeah, your sister ain't gonna sit with you today, buddy, Prince Wonwoo said in his mind, lifting up his head. *What are you going to do about it? Nothing. Deal with it. Hehe!*

The wolf prince narrowed his eyes further and scowled, teeth bared.

You're one overprotective sibling, aren't you?

He continued to glare until the wolf queen nudged him and drew his attention away from the two.

Yeahhh. Let Mommy set you straight.

"I wonder what you guys have for large banquets!" she said as the servants brought out glasses and plates. The lion prince was distracted from his game with Prince Scamander, which made him jolt his head to her. He patted his mane.

"Oh! I think you'll love it," Prince Wonwoo answered, helping with arranging her plates and utensils. "At least...I hope you will."

Princess Okome chuckled. "You hope? Trust me, and pardon my language, but our food is undeniably shit."

"Is that so?"

"Yes so. Hopefully one day, after we get married, you get a taste of our banquet food. Then you'll see."

"I *cannot* wait." The lion prince said that sentence with much emphasis to hide his sarcasm.

Finally, the servants brought out the food, from the fattest pigs known to all life to even the vegetarian side of salads and fruit, and Prince Wonwoo saw the lights shine in Princess Okome's eyes.

"Oh that looks elegant!" she said. "Look at how well prepared the food looks! So gorgeous and elegant indeed. Yep. Definitely better than ours!"

"Here, I'll help you."

ON A HORRIBLE WINDY DAY, IT WAS LOVE AT FIRST SIGHT

The wolf princess placed a paw on her chest. "My~! What a gentleman, hehe~"

The lion prince twitched his muscles in embarrassment, feeling his cheeks flush.

Maybe this won't be so bad after all.

It was a bit of a calm dinner between the Kingdoms, but now, while King Jung-hwa and King Titanosaurus discussed business with each other, Prince Wonwoo and Princess Okome were in the lion prince's room. He made sure to tidy it up before she had arrived per his parents' requests to leave a good impression on him. He made sure of that, folding his blankets and alighting a lavender candle to freshen up his room. The scent worked well, for Princess Okome commented on it. He was still awkward around her; they managed to hit it off well, but he felt he was a fool everytime.

Why can't I just be normal around her? He asked himself as he sullenly watched Princess Okome study his room intently. *She's just a creature like any other. It's just cruel to be so...foolish around her like she's the problem. She's really nice.*

"It was delicious, Prince Wonwoo," Princess Okome said. "Everything was just perfect! Put the good word for me to the chef, will you?"

"Oh. Yes. Of course, Princess Okome," Prince Wonwoo answered. He lowered his gaze and sighed. "Sorry, I'm not sure how else to...talk, you know? I mean, I know how to, but-Uhm. You know what I mean. Sorry."

"It's okay. I mean, we are just getting to know each other, so I don't blame you. Honestly, I'm more worried about what I will say to you and your family."

"What do you mean? You're doing an amazing job!" Prince Wonwoo had meant it; in their small talks, he found himself immersed with what she told him. "I'm like, actually interested in your Kingdom that I normally would not have batted an eye at! You're not as repulsive as the hyena cackle refugees that moved here a while back. Even my parents welcome you fondly."

Princess Okome flattened her ears, her fur flushing a bright pink. She fanned herself with her paw. "You're too modest, Prince Wonwoo. You know we're not all that bad." She paused. "Can I tell you a story? Our story?"

Prince Wonwoo perked. "Of course."

The wolf princess laid down on the carpet, tucking her paws underneath her. "This is a story about King Oromir," she began, "and how he left such a profound impact on the Demoniacal Kingdom."

King Oromir? Prince Wonwoo knew that name; he was the son of King Wyvern, the first Prince. He didn't know much about him, due to the fact that he was much more elusive than his own Father. He was curious to know more about him. And what better way to know than from the grandchild of King Oromir herself? He also laid down a couple inches away from Princess Okome, wrapping his tail around his body.

"You see, when King Oromir was only 12 terra cycles, he began to involve himself in his Father's affairs. He helped King Wyvern make decisions, certain ones that would become part of our daily lives. 3 terra cycles later, he became the King. See, his Mother–Queen Skydamire–died after his birth, so there was no one left he could learn the ways of being a King. So, he took the mantle early and plunged the Demoniacal Kingdom into the path of total isolation. Many adored him, many loved that he was their King, however, a small few did not like how self-absorbed he was."

Prince Wonwoo lifted an eyebrow. "Really?" *A King acting like his people still hated by those in his Kingdom? That's ironic.*

Princess Okome nodded. "I've only heard small bits from my uncle, as my Father does not talk much about him, but apparently all the things he did for the Demoniacal Kingdom was out of his own selfish deeds. He hated the Promised Dynasty with a fiery passion, so much so, he wanted to make sure no contact with your Kingdom was in place. But only because he had a vendetta against them. I think that's what got him killed in the end."

"How did he die?" Prince Wonwoo inquired. "In school, the teacher told us that he was assassinated by an unknown assailant. Is that true?"

Princess Okome went silent, deep in thought. He realized that maybe it was a sensitive assumption to make.

"Sorry if that was too much–"

"No one actually knows what happened to him," she finally said without paying attention to his words. "Not even my Father or my uncle. He died after they were born. But, many in the Demoniacal Kingdom believe that theory. King Oromir died during a celebration, a perfect time for someone to strike. Who that vigilante, or traitor, was...well." She puffed at her hair tuft. "That will probably remain a mystery until the end of times."

The lion prince stared, unable to speak at first. He was dumbfounded, he was intrigued. He was...speechless. "Oh wow..." *The son of the founder, and no one knows how exactly you died? A tragic end.*

"After his death, my grandmother–Queen Bernadette–raised my Father until he was old enough to become the King. Now, everyone loves my Father more than they ever loved my grandfather. Although, now...with the whole...alliance plan he mentioned, he might be falling under King Oromir's path. The path of...being forgotten. I don't want that to happen with my Father... All because of our different ideals..."

Prince Wonwoo flicked his ears. The way Princess Okome cared for her Father despite him being in hot waters for such a controversial proposal showed a lot more than he imagined. He can only picture Atiena and her cackle, their toothy smiles and harsh laughter filling his brain. Princess Okome wasn't like the hyena matriarch.

She...cared.

Perhaps I did judge Princess Okome too harshly just because of her birthplace. She is too good for them.

She rubbed her nose, trying to stop herself from sniffling. "I-I'm sorry, I didn't mean to get a little sentimental there," she apologized. "I just worry for everyone."

He cuddled closer to her, laying his tail on her back. "There's no need to apologize for having a heart," he said. "It makes you unique." The wolf princess appreciated the sentiment. She pressed herself onto him, burying her face in his shoulder. He purred. He rested his chin on the top of her head, closing his eyes.

This isn't going to be bad at all.

CHAPTER 4
A BEAUTIFUL DATE WITH ROYALTY...GOES HORRIBLY WRONG

~ One week later... ~
~ January in Terra Cycle 1118 B.E. ~

A week after the banquet, Prince Wonwoo was walking with Princess Okome by Morning Dew Park, accompanied by Hakuba. It was a park with lush green bushes and grass, greener than any other part of Halcyonwick, with a large lake in the center. Various trees scattered the land, ranging from normal trees to fruit trees. He showed her around the park and watched as her curiosity sparkled in her eyes. Prince Wonwoo softly smiled at her.

In those few days after their parents brought them together to meet, Prince Wonwoo and Princess Okome found themselves growing closer to one another from each date they went on.

Their feelings slowly began to blossom as the wolf princess never left the lion prince's side and got affectionate with him. Prince Wonwoo was confused if he was the only one feeling genuine affection towards her, or if they were even genuine because he pitied her, but her behavior showed she liked him back as well, as evident by her clear signs of physical affection. Prince Wonwoo noted how she always loved to bump into him with intent, pressing herself to him.

The lion prince found themselves a spot to rest after walking around the park. Hakuba let the two of them be and headed off in her own direction, but making sure not to be too far in case something happened. Prince Wonwoo took her to the edge of the lake, where a flock of ducks and geese resided. They looked at the two before bowing and returning to feed. He laid out the blanket he took from his room and let Princess Okome sit first. He set the basket in front of them, retrieving bird food he had packed to throw for the ducks, and leaned back.

"This park is so serene," Princess Okome said, leaning close to Prince Wonwoo. "I could stay here all day."

Prince Wonwoo returned the gesture, nuzzling himself closer to her. "Yeah, this is one of my favorite places to be in Halcyonwick," he said, ripping open the bag with his teeth. "When I was a cub, my grandfather, King Boipelo of the Promised Dynasty, would take me here to feed the ducks. It was the best memories I somehow can recall vaguely. They're still a blur, but I can...you know, *remember* them." He smirked at her. "Wanna hear a terrible story?"

"Oh?"

"According to him, I once tried to challenge the ducks and geese, trying to intimidate them with my 'mighty roar,' as he said it, and I ended up getting chased by those pesky Canadian geese." He narrowed his eyes at a pair that floated in the water. "I never liked them ever since."

The lion prince tossed a pawful at the ducks. They immediately gathered at where the pellets were, pecking the ground fiercely. The Canadian geese pair lifted up their heads, but Prince Wonwoo's stare made them not come over.

The wolf princess couldn't help but laugh. "No way! That was terrible for you?"

Prince Wonwoo blushed, crossing his arms. "Yes way! They bit my tail and my ass many times! HARD! They chased me for hours around the park until my Father came in to roar at them."

"That must have been traumatizing for you."

"King Boipelo was more upset, chasing after me to keep an eye but keeping his distance."

The wolf princess reached in the bag to throw some pellets. "He didn't scare them away?"

"He tried. But, he didn't want to harm the geese."

"Oh, wow. I know my family would not let that slide and would have bit the geese back." Princess Okome bit her lip. "And kill them. Without mercy." She blinked. "Wow. Father and others were right: Our families are indeed so different."

A BEAUTIFUL DATE WITH ROYALTY...GOES HORRIBLY WRONG

The lion prince chuckled. He sighed. "After my grandfather passed, things didn't feel the same in this park. My Father and Mother would take me here every few weekends or whenever they were free. I loved it, but it just isn't the same without my grandfather around." He sniffed. "Even now, it still doesn't feel the same. I mean I still have my grandmother, Queen Hawa, but she's too old to do what she once loved. She would try to take me to the park whenever my parents got busy, but overtime her bones wore out and she had to force herself to rest. But...you move on. You make more memories. That's what King Boipelo would want me to do instead of being constantly stuck in the past."

The wolf princess frowned. "I'm sorry for your loss."

He shrugged. "It's okay. It was 8 terra cycles ago."

"I hope he died peacefully."

He nodded. "Despite his strange illness weighing him down, he did. Surrounded by his family. It made him happy, and that was good enough for us."

"I hope your grandmother is also resting well."

"She is. I visit her from time to time."

"Oh she's still alive? That's good." The wolf princess tossed some more food to the ducks. "I heard King Boipelo of the Promised Dynasty was a pleasant King."

Prince Wonwoo looked out to the lake. "He was. Real, real nice. After all, he was the son of King Saturhorimau, my great-grandfather, so all his good nature and gentle heart comes from him. I think you would have liked him. Him and Queen Hawa. Actually! I could take you to her if you wish after the park!"

"That sounds lovely. I think I'd like that." The wolf princess sighed. "I always wonder how I'm so different from everyone else in the Demoniacal Kingdom," Princess Okome said, taking Prince Wonwoo's paw into her own. "With how lively and cheery and happy I am. My whole family is like a walking embodiment of angry sinners."

"No offense, but you are right," the lion prince said, watching the wolf princess study his paw. "King Wyvern was a total mad dragon, I just learned from you that King Oromir was also just as unpleasant as his father, King Titanosaurus doesn't smile, and your brother...Gods, your brother. He's–"

"Annoying? So serious? Brooding that it makes you wanna scream at him to stop frowning and smile already?"

The lion prince nodded.

"Don't worry about offending me, I completely agree with you on all those. My great-grandfather was a power-hungry, selfish dragon who was only jealous of your great-grandfather; my grandfather was a complete narcissist and only cared for himself; my Father *does* smile but only when me, my brother or my Mother are around, and my brother is a whole different being. He's like another King Wyvern."

The lion prince lifted up an ear. "He's more like King Titanosaurus of the Demoniacal Kingdom if I am honest. A complete clone of your Father. Eeesh."

A BEAUTIFUL DATE WITH ROYALTY...GOES HORRIBLY WRONG

The wolf princess did not take her eyes from Prince Wonwoo's paw. "You're not wrong. But, in my personal opinion, he takes more after our great-grandfather." She pulled his paw under her chin to rest. "He's been interested in dark magic all the time ever since he was a pup, and he wants to learn to master it."

The lion prince's heart fluttered. "He doesn't have any?"

"No."

Thank Gods. "Huh. I would have assumed he did already by the aura he emits when he broods."

"They're weak," Princess Okome explained, letting go of Prince Wonwoo's paw. "I mean it's the same for me."

Without a second thought, she summoned a blue flame from her paw. Prince Wonwoo jumped up, his fur spiking. Princess Okome had dark magic!?

"We're born with magic, but it's not until you go through the rigorous and difficult training course that you truly master it," she explained, continuing to let the flame dance in her paw. "This is just baby stuff I'm showing you right now compared to the true magic my father possesses. This flame can't hurt you. It isn't hurting me, so you would be okay. You could touch it if you like."

"Oh wow." *Yeahhh, I'm definitely doing a hard pass on that, thanks.*

With the flick of her wrist, the blue flame extinguished itself right away, leaving behind tiny sparks in the sky.

"It's nothing to be afraid of."

Prince Wonwoo relaxed himself. "Duly noted."

The two sat in silence as they watched the ripples from the lake. They continued to feed the ducks until the bag was empty. When they realized, the ducks waddled away and pecked at the ground. It was only just hours past Dagny's Peak when they had laid back down again.

"Prince Wonwoo?" said the wolf princess.

"Hm?"

"Could you tell me a story about your Gods?"

He promptly stood up, curious. "Well, we have so many stories about them," he replied. "From their births to their grand adventures, it's a whole collection I can tell you! Which one would you like to hear about?"

Princess Okome also stood up, scratching her ear. "Tell me about your– Well, *our* Creator."

"Ellowyn?"

She nodded rapidly.

Prince Wonwoo widened his eyes. He was rather surprised that *someone* from the *Demoniacal Kingdom* would be *interested* in the story of the Gods. He knew all of them rejected the Gods after King Wyvern brought about a new age of darkness. But to see one of them *actually* curious about Ellowyn and the Gods...

He cleared his throat, recalling what he had been taught in school with passion:

"Long long ago in an age that could not be defined, before the land was created, way before even the stars burned in their light, the whole universe hadn't existed. It was only nothingness. An empty void."

"That's terrifying to think about," Princess Okome interrupted, shivering. "Like...the idea of just..nothingness."

"It is," Prince Wonwoo said in agreement.

"I'm sorry, I didn't mean to interrupt. Please continue."

The lion prince wasn't too thrown off by the interruption. So he continued with the tale:

"In this emptiness of the void, there was absolutely nothing. Not even a speck of an atom. The place was in a standstill. All of a sudden, that nothingness just...exploded. WHAM! KABOOM! The explosion soon caused the matter that would be the basics of our universe. From that matter emerged space and time as we know it. This matter scattered in all corners of the nothingness, eventually pushing towards more of the unknown and expanding. One small clump of matter joined together and soon formed what many considered to be the first known being of this strange nothingness. That being of course was Ellowyn.

With Her powers given to Her by the newfound energy, She created the universe in which we stand upon today. She created the galaxy, the stars, the planets, the sun. She created it all."

"All by herself...?" Princess Okome was lost in thought as she looked towards the clear skies. "Wow. That's just...Oh wow. We're standing...on her creation. I see why she's the Creator you all worship." She looked at him. "But all of that must be taxing though."

"Indeed," Prince Wonwoo answered. "Although She was powerful, She could not do all the jobs alone. Carrying the whole weight of the universe grew to wear Her out. That's when She came up with an idea: divide Her job. Using the cosmic matter She gathered, She bundled them up and gave them a form. In total, She created 12 forms who would be born with a purpose."

"Those 12 forms being...the other Gods of yours, correct?" Princess Okome asked.

He nodded. "But these forms were empty husks, a shell with nothing inside. Ellowyn noticed this as they floated about, carrying out their duties in a monotone manner. There obviously had to be more than a shell. A life. So, Ellowyn gave them something important, something important that every creature must have: a heart containing a soul of purity. Using Her own heart, She created and gave these empty forms their own hearts. Soon enough, there rose the Gods we would come to worship."

Princess Okome's eyes shone.

"A great story, ain't it?"

"So very great!"

He purred at her. "Would you like to know more?"

"Yes, please! Tell me more!"

He tapped his chin. "All right, my young pupil," he teased, "I can teach you much more about the Gods. Who are you curious to learn about next?"

A BEAUTIFUL DATE WITH ROYALTY...GOES HORRIBLY WRONG

She appeared a little dumbstruck. "Well, I'm not too aware of your Gods. Uhm..."

"There's the Goddesses of Life and Death: Abella and Morana, Okalani and Azrael the Goddess of the Heavens and the God of Hell respectively, the Gods of the Land and Sea and the Skies: Lavian and Wuxjun, Dagny and Gau the Goddess of Day and the Sun and the God of Night and the Moon, Ayumu and Kishi the Goddess of Dreams and Visions and the God of Nightmares and Omens and lastly, there's Aklene and Ziton the Goddess of Nature and Peace and the God of Destruction and War."

Princess Okome blinked, more lost than ever before. The lightning round Prince Wonwoo had spat as if he was rapping threw her for a loop. She rolled her eyes around as she tried to piece together which God was assigned to what, and it made her sway.

"Oh dear," Prince Wonwoo laughed, holding her steady. "Don't worry about it. They all have their own stories to tell, it would probably take days or a week to tell them all. I'll just stop at Ellowyn."

"Awww but I want you to tell them all," she said in a clearly joking manner. She pouted, her expression radiating irritability. "Ack, I'm getting hungry."

"Oh here!" Prince Wonwoo rummaged through the picnic basket. His paw came across one of the few sandwiches his mom had made for the two of them and handed it to her. Princess Okome's irritability faded, a bright smile crossing her face. Her warmth prompted another purr from Prince Wonwoo.

He couldn't believe that a month ago, he had completely been freaking out over marrying someone from the Demoniacal Kingdom. But after meeting and conversing with Princess Okome, Prince Wonwoo realized it wasn't all bad; the wolf princess was genuinely sweet and kind, and she seemed to share the same feelings he had when they first met.

"Do you really think our Kingdoms will get along well once we become the new King and Queen of the conjoined Kingdoms?" Prince Wonwoo asked, laying on his back.

"I'm unsure if I'm honest," Princess Okome responded, unwrapping and taking a bite from the sandwich. "When my Father announced the alliance proposal, his brother–my uncle–and the guards looked at him as if he just praised your Gods."

The lion prince turned his head to her. "Really?"

"Oh yeah." She paused to take another bite. "I don't know if you were able to see him. The other black wolf with the white chest and underbelly."

"I did."

"That's my uncle, my father's younger twin brother, Livyatan. He's a prince as well but he got bumped to second in line since my brother took his place. Obviously... He was the one to publicly voice his dislike for the alliance."

"Not too surprising." Prince Wonwoo plucked a large stem of grass to chew in his mouth. "Your Kingdom is kind of irredeemable after all they've done in their past. Again no offense."

"No, you're right. No one wants to change. It kind of hurts my soul to see. It makes me feel...out of place in my Kingdom."

"Oh?"

"I want the best for the Demoniacal Kingdom, as much as it sounds bizarre," she continued. "But I...Don't tell anyone I said this yet, but...I also want the best for the Promised Dynasty."

Prince Wonwoo froze, the stem of grass falling from his mouth. *She really means that?* He thought to himself.

"I want the best in the Demoniacal Kingdom in the sense of...wanting to return back to our roots. Return back to how things were before King Wyvern discovered and gave in to dark magic. I heard life was so much more peaceful back then. Why can't it be that way now?"

His mind was ready to explode at any given time. Everything he had thought about the Demoniacal Kingdom had flown out of his brain. Princess Okome had really proved to him that, deep down, maybe there could be some hope for the Demoniacal Kingdom.

But the vast majority are against the old ways, he said to himself. *No one wants to go back to those peaceful days. They're too stuck on the grips of sin that they have rejected the Gods, rejected the virtue of goodness and embraced the ways of the dark. None of them want to be redeemed. None of them* can *be redeemed. But Princess Okome...She's an exception.*

She finally laid back next to him after finishing her sandwich, tucking her paws close to her chest. She huddled closer to Prince Wonwoo. The lion prince still couldn't believe this was happening, but by now he had come to accept it; he genuinely loved Princess Okome, and wanted to enjoy every minute of their interaction. He could almost imagine Prince Scamander's face right about now as he reached out to hold her in a hug.

"When we become the new King and Queen of the new conjoined Kingdoms," she said, resting her head on his chest, "we will make them see your ways."

"Do you think so?" Prince Wonwoo asked her.

She nodded. "I believe so. It wouldn't be too difficult."

The lion prince twitched an ear. "So you're really for this alliance then, hm?"

"I am. I really am. I was a little bit confused at first when my Father proposed the idea so willingly out in the open, but then I realized: This is what our Kingdom needs. We need to come back to our original roots."

"You really are not like a Demoniacal Kingdom member at all... What is this witchcraft?"

After the laughter that ensued between the two, they gazed up at the sky and watched the clouds. They focused on the sounds of the lake and the ducks quacking nearby.

"Prince Wonwoo?" Princess Okome asked after a while.

"Hm?"

"What names do you have in mind for our children?"

A BEAUTIFUL DATE WITH ROYALTY...GOES HORRIBLY WRONG

His ears instantly perked up as he inhaled roughly, choking on the air. He coughed a fit, unable to catch his breath. Did he hear that right?? He couldn't have; his ears had to be playing with him. The look on her face proved he wasn't hearing things.

"I-WELL THAT WAS SUDDEN!" he said between his coughing. He reached into the basket for some water he had packed. How did the topic change from a serious discussion to "what names do you have for our future children we didn't think we'd have together?"

"Whaaat? Too soon?" she teased, poking him gently. "We're going to be married tomorrow, on my birthday of all days."

He finally stopped coughing after getting a sip of water. "I know that, and happy early birthday, but by the Gods, Princess Okome! You gave me a heart attack!"

"Is it bad?"

"No, but you're making it sound as if you're already...well, PREGNANT or something!"

She smiled, tapping his shoulder. "Well. Any ideas?"

The lion prince tapped on his chin, deeply in thought on the possibility that was his future children. "Hmm." Even then, it still felt too soon. He never even thought about when he was going to have children; he was a "go with the flow" kind of guy. To think this early on something that he knew won't happen in another few more terra cycles is just absurd.

Though I guess I do have to now at this point if we are to wed, he thought, looking at the wolf princess. Her smile made his heart skip a beat. *Gods, it's still TOO soon! But... anything for her.*

...Oh! I got one!

His mouth was open but nothing emerged. An idea was on the tip of his tongue. It didn't seem to want to come out. He struggled for a bit before giving up. "How about you start first?" Prince Wonwoo suggested, rubbing the back of his neck. "I got nothing yet."

I guess I don't have an idea.

She smiled and chuckled. "I don't care about what names I have for a son. I feel boys are more easier to name."

"What's that supposed to mean?" Prince Wonwoo jokingly asked, grinning.

Princess Okome gave him a teasing stare. "But: If I ever have a daughter, I want to name her Zora," Princess Okome said.

"Zora?" he asked. "That's an unusual name; I never heard of it before."

"It's such a pretty sounding name I heard one day and I just was like 'Oh I definitely want to name my daughter that when I have one.' And with a pretty meaning behind it too! All the more reason to name my daughter Zora."

"What does Zora mean?"

"It means light or dawn."

Prince Wonwoo flicked his ears. "That's actually a nice name."

"Isn't it?" She poked him again. "Well? Got any ideas yet?"

"Actually I do now-"

"Oh well, now look at this!"

The lion prince's ears shot up at the unknown voice. He jumped to his paws, scanning around the park. The wolf princess rolled to her belly and lifted up her head. The flock of ducks raised their heads as well, scanning the area, and began to honk in one particular direction. He followed their direction and widened his eyes.

Poking their heads out from the bushes were three Demoniacal Kingdom members.

CHAPTER 5
THE UNTIMELY DEMISE OF THE PRINCESS OF THE DEMONIACAL KINGDOM

~ 6 months before the war... ~
~ January in Terra Cycle 1118 B.E. ~

"Look! It's the very prince of the Promised Dynasty with our princess."

Prince Wonwoo held onto a startled Princess Okome as three Demoniacal Kingdom members–a black-furred leopardess, a red fox and a giant panda cladded in dark silver armor–strolled their ways in Morning Dew Park. The ducks and geese trumpeted loudly in fear and flew away, not wanting to be around them. They slinked through like snakes and encircled the two. Prince Wonwoo narrowed his eyes at them and tightened his grip on Princess Okome.

"How did you guys get in?" Prince Wonwoo demanded. "Who gave you permission to enter Halcyonwick?"

"Awww, aren't they just so cute together?" the leopardess said in a sarcastic tone, ignoring the lion prince.

"Yeahhh," replied the red fox, "so cute, it's damn near REVOLTING!" He stuck his tongue out as he shook his head, simulating the action of vomiting. The leopardess and giant panda laughed.

Prince Wonwoo snorted in disdain. *What else do I expect from anyone in the Demoniacal Kingdom?* he grumbled.

"I feel a bit sorry for you, Princess," the giant panda commented. "I can't imagine having to be wed to my rival's son. You deserve better than this."

"Enky! Arvolf! Cyclone! What are you guys doing here!?" Princess Okome growled at them, addressing them by their respective names.

"We were sent by your father to check up on you," the leopardess, Enky, replied.

The lion prince flicked his tail in annoyance. *Oh of course. You only answer to your Princess. I see how it is.*

"Why would Father bother to send his guards for me in the Promised Dynasty? Doesn't he already know to trust King Junghwa's word on making sure I am protected under his guard?" The wolf princess casted a side eye glance at Prince Wonwoo, which prompted him to nod curtly.

"You know your father," the red fox, Arvolf, said. "He...wants to make sure. You know. Like, that you're okay and not in any kind of harm."

Prince Wonwoo took note of the hesitation in his voice. Something wasn't adding up with the red fox's words. The way he paused stood out to him. *He's lying,* he thought. *He's lying about it. Only liars with a guilty conscience can hesitate.* The lion prince wrinkled his nose. *But why even be guilty? You must lie all the time. Why is it different now?*

The wolf princess twitched an ear, also noting the hesitation. "That feels impossible; sure, my father cares about me, but he doesn't really show his affection and protectiveness towards me in front of others. Unless... Oh by the **WYVERN!**" When realization crossed her face, Princess Okome pulled her lips back to reveal her teeth. "MY BROTHER!" she snarled, pressing herself against Prince Wonwoo. "My *brother* sent you guys, not King Titanosaurus! Did he or did he?"

The three looked at each other, sweat beads visibly running down their necks. So that's why the red fox hesitated with his words.

"I told you that lie wasn't going to work," the panda, Cyclone, said.

Arvolf scratched his chin. "Maybe I said it wrong."

Enky twitched her tail, crossing her paws. "I thought foxes are supposed to be cunning and sly."

"Hey! That's racist!"

The wolf princess was visibly shaking as her anger circulated throughout her body. The lion prince could feel it as she pressed against him. "Oh my fucking wyvern, I cannot BELIEVE my brother right now!" Princess Okome growled, rubbing her head with her paws. "He just cannot let go of me. He thinks I'm ALWAYS in constant danger. And he says he's the mature one. 'You're too young,' my ass."

Prince Wonwoo held her paw, gently massaging it. "He really cares about you *that much*, huh?" he asked with a chuckle.

The wolf princess groaned in a way that told him she wasn't angry at him. "I told you. I *hate* it. He seriously has to let go and let me live my life the way I want it." She looked back at the guards. "Well, you three can leave. Now. That's an order from your princess."

"We'd love to, Your Highness," Cyclone said, "but we were given direct orders by your brother, the heir. You already know how Prince Scamander will act when he sees we disobeyed him–"

"I know, I know." The wolf princess crossed her paws. "Throw an absolute tantrum and get my father involved."

"Besides, we never had a chance to meet the future groom of our princess properly."

They encircled Prince Wonwoo and studied him curiously. The lion prince felt his fur prickle. He felt he was being judged, and it made him want to rip their smug smiles off their faces.

"You mean *your* future King?" Prince Wonwoo corrected.

Cyclone squinted. "Whatever."

Arvolf shook his head. "You're no King of mine."

"Nor mine."

"I'm curious," Enky said to Prince Wonwoo, "what names do you have for your future children, lion prince? Our true future King or Queen of the Demoniacal Kingdom?"

"Like I'd tell you," the lion prince said, baring his teeth. "That won't be known until he or she is born. Also, it won't be of the Demoniacal Kingdom. It'll be of the new united Kingdom."

"Awww, come on, give us a little something," Arvolf said, poking his shoulder with a claw. "Any name that crossed your mind. A clue we can use to guess. Whatever. Just say it. Blurt it out loud. I'm dying to know."

"We're all dying to know," the leopardess added.

The lion prince unsheathed his claws. He had completely forgotten how troublesome the Demoniacal Kingdom members were. Though they were guards, they reminded him of Atiena and her cackle. It truly was amazing to him.

"I said I'm not telling you," he snapped. "I'm not telling either of you, or anyone from your awful, irredeemable Kingdom. If there's anyone who will know in advance, it will be my family and Princess Okome."

He looked down at her with a smile. She returned the affection.

"Awww but we're practically your guards at this point," Enky ruined the mood, constantly circling and eyeing Prince Wonwoo. Her tail flicked at every gaze. "Friends at this point. We've known

Princess Okome since she was a pup, as well as Prince Scamander, so we always tell each other secrets and other personal information."

"Yeah, cause you're my bodyguard," Princess Okome mumbled. "And I had no other choice."

Enky did not hear her. "So, come on. Please?"

The lion prince's heart hammered hard. Temptation was high, but he had to force it down. He shoved his face close to the leopardess's, and he growled out each word with clear enunciation.

"I. Said. *No.*"

The three Demoniacal Kingdom guards stared at each other with a smirk before they laughed aloud. Prince Wonwoo flattened his ears. What were they laughing about? What was funny about *any* of this? His fur bristled. Now he was pissed.

"Prince Wonwoo, don't mind them," Princess Okome said, tapping his paw. "Enky, Arvolf and Cyclone like to push everyone's buttons for the fun of it; they're jokesters. Trust me: Don't take it to heart."

"They're harassing me though!" Prince Wonwoo growled. "Harassing *us*! Jokesters would know when to stop joking around!"

"I know, but-"

"Hey! Prince Wonwoo of the Promised Dynasty!"

The two turned their attention to the leopardess. She stood still and let her tail sway in the wind. She smiled at the lion prince.

"I got a proposition for you," she said.

"Oh?" Prince Wonwoo said with a smirk. "Tell me."

The wolf princess tapped the lion prince's paw, trying to get his attention. "Prince Wonwoo—"

"How would you like that I challenged you to a duel?"

Princess Okome shot up from her spot. She bared her teeth. "Enky stop! We're not doing that here!"

"Why not, Princess? I think it's time he's shown the ways of the Demoniacal Kingdom if he is to be the King of our Kingdom."

"This is not the appropriate time right now! He can learn once he and I wed but not now."

"Now hold on, Princess. Let's hear what he has to say."

"A duel?" The lion prince raised an eyebrow. He shouldn't give in to them, but he was curious as a cub.

"Prince Wonwoo, no-"

"Yeah, in our Kingdom, we have duels to prove who's better and at the top. As you can probably tell, I've never lost a single duel in my life, and I've been top guard for all my terra cycles living. So. Here's what I propose to you, *Your Highness*: If I win, you'll have to listen to us and do what we say. If you win, we promise to never harass you again and treat you with the utmost respect."

The lion prince grinned at the challenge the leopardess was offering. He would often roughhouse with his classmates in mini "battles," so the thought of a real duel excited him. If there was anything Prince Wonwoo wanted, it was to show the Demoniacal Kingdom who was superior and who was in charge of them. This was his moment!

The leopardess tipped her head slightly. "So what do you say, Prince Wonwoo of the Promised Dynasty? Do you accept my challenge?"

Princess Okome pinned her ears behind her head. "Enky, don't egg him! I command you to stop! Right now!"

"Oh you're on!" Prince Wonwoo said eagerly, getting into a fighting stance. "I would *love* to prove how much better I am to you Demoniacal scum! Show you who's the rightful King in ALL this Land!"

"Prince Wonwoo!"

The lion prince turned back to the wolf princess. He flashed her a smile. "Don't worry, Princess Okome, it's just going to be a quick fight," he promised. "Done and over with before either of us could blink. It's going to be fine. Now I suggest you step back. I don't want you to get hurt."

Princess Okome obeyed Prince Wonwoo and stepped back an inch, shaking her head. "No, this isn't good, I don't like this," she expressed. "Enky, call it off right now—"

The leopardess beckoned him with a paw. "Come on then. You get the first strike."

The wolf princess snarled. "Enky, you son of a—"

The lion prince bunched his muscles and leapt at the leopardess. Enky immediately crouched and rolled to the side, causing the lion prince to fall hard on his belly. The leopardess jumped onto his back and sank her large fangs on his shoulders. The lion prince's eyes went wide. Well, that was a great first move. He roared in pain, struggling as he tried to kick the leopardess off him. He felt like a bull in a ring.

All while this was happening, Arvolf and Cyclone cheered Enky on. Though Arvolf was more vocal than the panda, who just clapped his paws. He could hear every word from them.

"WOOOOOOO YEAHHHH!!! YOU GO, ENKY!" Arvolf barked, practically hollering. "Kick his royal ass! Show that lion prince what the Demoniacal Kingdom is about! Make him prove his dumb royal status! WOOOOOO!!!"

"That was a good dodge," Cyclone commented.

"Tell me about it!"

Opposite of them, Princess Okome was desperately shouting at Enky to stop.

"ENKY!" she growled. "Stop this RIGHT NOW! I'll see to it that King Titanosaurus punishes you!"

Enky did not seem to hear her, but that threat sent shivers down the lion prince's spine. He thought about the wolf king's massive build and his large, thick claws. He didn't want to even begin imagining the kind of punishment and or abuse King Titanosaurus would inflict on those who have wronged him and failed him.

Pushing away those thoughts and concentrating back on what was going on, Prince Wonwoo reared himself up like a horse and let himself fall onto his back. He'd seen Hakuba do this trick many times as a cub whenever someone unknowingly pounced on her back. While it amused him, he always wondered why Hakuba would put herself in danger. He now understood why she would do it. He heard a muffled yelp coming from the leopardess's mouth, followed by claws digging into his flesh. He winced, ignoring the pain. He got up after a while, inspecting his wounds before looking back at Enky. The leopardess shakily got to her paws and spat out some of Prince Wonwoo's blood she gathered from her bite. She smirked, licking her lips.

"You're pretty good for a lowly Promised prince," she said. "But I'm not done yet. See: We can go on for however long either of us can endure it, there's no limits. The first one to fall and call it quits loses. Loser obviously has to bow to the winner."

The lion prince let out a snort. "Like I'd ever bow before you!"

"Well, I ain't bowing yet."

Prince Wonwoo lunged once more, tackling her and taking the leopardess in his jaws. He finally got a taste for leopard blood, and he relished in it. It made him feel like he was a real soldier in combat. He lifted her up and tossed her towards the edge of the lake. How his muscles itched to run up, push her head underwater, and let her suffer until she tapped on his shoulder, but he didn't act on his impulses. He was even a bit shocked at what his mind conjured. He would be no better than Enky or any of the Demoniacal Kingdom members if he let his actions play out and end in a terrible tragedy.

The leopardess got up and laughed.

"That's all you got?" she taunted, rubbing her arm. "Just a measly bite and a toss? I was expecting more from someone with your status."

The lion prince collected himself for once and finally stood up. It was about time that he handled things maturely. He realized it was becoming more and more ridiculous the more it went on, the thrill no longer enjoyable. He sheathed his claws. "I've had enough," the lion prince said. "Stand down, Enky. I won't fight you anymore. I've already proven my worth."

Enky gaped her jaw. It appeared like she was going to say something to him, but she shrugged her shoulders. "Oh well. No Promised Dynasty member is fun to play with. You're all so stuck up in your good virtues."

The lion prince snarled at her statement. The rushing blood in his ears prevented him from hearing Princess Okome clearly.

"Stop!"

"See: This is why King Wyvern separated from you guys to create the Demoniacal Kingdom," Enky continued. "He was sick that no one would listen to him after your founder, King Saturhorimau, basically converted everyone into your ways. You guys became a *cult*, where King Wyvern was stuck. He was *stuck in a cult!* His discovery of dark magic was the light we needed."

Shut up, you stupid, ignorant spots for brains, Prince Wonwoo thought. *You have no idea what your founder did to this land.*

"Enky–"

"But you guys only saw King Wyvern's powers as an evil darkness. Something against all your precious Gods created. Something that had to be cleansed. There is no darkness in dark magic. There's no darkness in EVIL, really. The only darkness in this place, throughout ALL the land, is your cult! Your religion and believing in this 'almighty' God who struggled to take care of us. What am I saying? You guys will never change your views."

We *will never change!?*

The lion prince unsheathed his claws.

That was it. That was the last straw.

"We will never change?" Prince Wonwoo began. "*We* will never change!? You scumbags will never ever change! Your founder rejected Ellowyn because She knew that he was not fit to lead beside King Saturhorimau. It's not Her fault that She was able to sense the very bitterness growing inside his heart. Every angel in the Heavens and the Gods can read your hearts, and they can see your true intentions. Your founder rejected the very basics of living under good care and love that Ellowyn worked so hard to build. He was jealous of King Saturhorimau because he was chosen. He wanted to be the chosen one! He wanted to spread his hatred to all and make everyone bow to his authority. That's all your founder wanted. That's all your Kingdom knows because he taught you all: hatred and bitterness and darkness. All things evil and against Ellowyn! You should be thanking Her for at least being spared from extinction!"

Enky had dismissed his whole speech. "You're speaking like a brainwashed cult member," she said. "It's really scary how you all wish to force your religion onto us. Yes: forcing us. Your founder forced everyone to accept the word of whatever your Creator God whispers into his ears. This is all your doing, this is all your Dynasty will ever do."

Prince Wonwoo charged at the leopardess.

"YOU WILL LEARN SOME RESPECT, DEMONIACAL SCUM!"

Enky was caught off guard at Prince Wonwoo charging at her. He stopped just a few short feet away from her, towering himself above her. She crouched, her eyes unblinking and her tail between her legs.

"Woah, chill, chill!" she pleaded. "Okay, you win! You win!! I won't speak out against your Gods ever again. Now let me go, please! Don't hurt me!"

"You don't get to beg for mercy," he snarled. "Your kind has deviated away from Ellowyn for far too long to now kneel and kowtow and ask for forgiveness. Take that up to the Creator Herself."

The wolf princess let out a desperate cry.

"Stop!"

The lion prince did not hear Princess Okome's plea as he raised a paw. Bringing it down with all his might, he tore through flesh, but the rage in his eyes cleared his vision when he heard the gargled noises. It didn't sound like Enky at all. Once he saw who he had attacked, his eyes nearly popped out of his sockets.

"...Oh...my Gods..."

Prince Wonwoo had just torn open Princess Okome's throat and chest.

No...

"Princess Okome!!" Enky shouted, her voice straining.

The lion prince shut his eyes when her blood splattered on his face. He was too stunned to wipe it away. When he slowly opened them, he watched in horror as she fell to the ground and bled out, desperate to catch any breath. Every attempt would only exacerbate the blood loss. Her snapped necklace lay in the grass, her black diamond having been shattered by the lion prince's claws. Princess Okome pressed her paw to her wounds, trying to staunch the bleeding. He could see that she was too weak to force her paw against her wound. Even if she could, her wounds were too great for her. She shakily reached out a bloodied paw for Prince Wonwoo for support, her tear-ridden eyes round. Prince Wonwoo froze on the spot, his heart having stopped beating.

How could he approach her after doing this to her? Was she really calling out for his help?

He tucked his tail between his legs, whimpering. What had he done?!

In the chaos, he watched the three Demoniacal Kingdom guards gathering around the injured princess and talking to each other in shock. They all did their best to conceal the wound.

"**OH SHIT!** PRINCESS OKOME! OH FUCK THIS IS NOT GOOD!" Cyclone. "This is too large of a wound for us."

"YEAH NO FUCKING SHIT! Come on, you lazy shits! We must notify the King and Queen of the Demoniacal Kingdom urgently and get the doctors!" Enky.

"We'll never get there in time!" Arvolf.

"THEN HOW DO WE GET THEIR ATTENTIONS?!" Cyclone.

"SHUT UP! JUST! SHUT UP! Here, I-I got this!"

Arvolf lifted up his head and whistled a soft yet clear tune. After he ended the tune, the three ran away to presumably get help as soon as they could.

Prince Wonwoo remained frozen in place, watching the Demoniacal guards leave Princess Okome on the ground. He finally pushed himself to do something and bounded up to the wolf princess. Moving her to her back to keep the blood from pouring out (which didn't help one bit), he immediately pressed his paws to her injuries to try and stop the massive blood loss she was experiencing. Princess Okome winced at his touch for a brief moment, coughing.

"No, no, no, this is not good, not good, the wounds are too deep," he muttered between his hitched breaths. "You're bleeding out too much... Gods...what have I done?? HAKUBA!!! FOR THE LOVE OF ALL THE GODS AND GREAT ELLOWYN, WHERE ARE YOU!?! HAKUBAAAAA!!!!"

The white horse, luckily being nearby, ran up to his side at once. She saw the situation and reared up in panic.

"Oh my Gods!" she exclaimed. "Prince Wonwoo! Are you okay?! What happened!?"

"No time! Please! Go get my Father and Mother!" he shouted, clear desperation in his voice. "Along with the doctors! Bring them fast!"

She nodded. "Got it!"

As soon as she turned around, anxiety spiked in the lion prince's chest. If his parents found out what he had done...

"Wait, no— No, stop, don't get my parents!" the lion prince shouted at her as quickly as he could before she got farther away from him. "Just get our best doctors here! You know who!"

Hakuba looked back. "Don't you want the King and Queen to know about this?" she asked, tilting her head.

"NO!? At least not yet!" Prince Wonwoo shook his head. "No! NO! They can't know I screwed up again! Right now, just— go get the doctors, please! HURRY!"

Without another question, Hakuba galloped back to the castle.

He looked back at the wolf princess and assessed the damage he had caused; his claws tore deep through her throat, exposing muscles and tendons, down to her chest. He could easily see through the torn muscles. He was even able to see a bit of her ribcage. He shut his eyes, shuddering. She heavily bled, staining both her blue-gray and white pelt and the grass around her bright red in her blood. Her sides heaved as she struggled to breathe.

"No no no, this is not good. Please..stay strong," he whispered. "Help is on the way right now. No. No no. Please... Oh, Gods, what have I done, what have I done...?"

The wolf princess slowly turned her head to the lion prince. He saw immense pain in her eyes. She reached out a paw to him, which he took into his. He blinked rapidly to rid himself of the welling tears clouding his vision.

"Princess Okome," he managed to rasp out.

"P..P-Prince..Wonw-woo," she said softly.

"Shh! Don't speak!" Prince Wonwoo urged, pressing down harder on her wounds. "You need to save your energy until we get you back to the castle. You're going to be okay, I promise you." His words were stuck in his own throat. "You will be...You *have* to be..."

Princess Okome winced again, coughing up blood.

"Ah! Sorry, sorry! I didn't mean to press down that hard! Are you okay?"

Her voice finally came through, although it was very choked and gurgling.

"I-I'm...I'm s-sorry...."

Prince Wonwoo looked at her with wide eyes. "Why are *you* sorry!? *I* did this to you! If anyone is to be sorry here, it's ME! It's all my fault!" He shut his eyes, looking away. "Gods, what have I done...What have I DONE!?"

She looked at him, trying to force out words. But none could be said. The lion prince blinked away the tears that were arising.

"Please hang on, Princess Okome," he said softly. "Please. You will make it."

Hakuba, please hurry, he cried in his head. *She's not going to last much longer! She's losing too much blood! Oh Gods..she's going to die. And it's all my fault!*

"Prince Wonwoo!"

The lion prince's skin jolted, and he looked back in fear. In that moment, he had forgotten he called for help, and he was expecting to see the King and Queen of the Demoniacal Kingdom. Relief eased his temporary fear when he saw it was just Hakuba who called out to him, accompanied by three creatures: a capybara, an elephant and a giant otter. They looked at the scene, assessing the situation. He could see in their faces that this was a serious situation they were dealing with.

The capybara immediately leapt into action.

"Jiro, check her vitals," the capybara instructed the elephant. "Reassure the wolf princess as well since she will be delirious and in pain." She then turned to the giant otter. "Get her some fresh water so she doesn't dehydrate, Arkaitz."

The two bowed. "Yes, Carmentis!"

Once the two headed off to their own specific task, Carmentis the capybara approached Princess Okome. She bowed at Prince Wonwoo. "If I may," she gently said, pointing to the wolf princess. The lion prince, though hesitant on wanting to stay with her, removed his paws from Princess Okome's wounds and backed away for Carmentis to handle the rest. Hakuba trotted up to the lion prince to comfort him.

Prince Wonwoo could not move. He watched as the capybara began dressing her wounds, trying to limit the amount of blood flow. His body was in complete shock. He couldn't believe this was happening. Why had he been so STUPID to fight Demoniacal Kingdom members? All while ignoring her pleas and begging. It could have all been avoided, had the lion prince not been such a cub. He looked down at his paws, his eyes widening as he lifted them up; they were coated in her blood, which made his stomach churn.

Princess Okome's blood was literally in his paws.

"I'm gonna be sick," he mumbled to himself, retching.

"Would you like me to escort you back to the castle while they stabilize her before bringing her?" Hakuba asked.

"No," the lion prince answered. "No I..I can't leave her. Not like this."

"You won't be."

Prince Wonwoo lowered his eyes.

"We're losing her!"

The trumpet from Jiro the elephant scared the two. The lion prince raised his head up, ignoring the dizziness.

"What's going on?" Carmentis asked, raising her head up.

"Her pulse is erratic and weakening. She's losing too much blood."

The wolf princess was clearly losing consciousness as she struggled to keep her eyes open. She wanted to say something to the two, but of course she couldn't. Arkaitz the giant otter had appeared a minute later, carefully giving her small drops from the wet moss he gathered, but she couldn't swallow the water. He tried to gently massage her neck to try and get her to swallow, but it failed when she had attempted and started to cough blood. It was rather aggressive this time around, sounding as if she was finally drowning in her own blood.

"No, this isn't good!" Prince Wonwoo softly said, shrinking in his pelt when he saw the giant otter scuttle away in fear. "She's not going to make it!"

He ran up to her again, Hakuba joining behind his trail. Carmentis made room for him.

"I'm sorry, Your Highness," she consoled, "there's nothing we can do to save her. Her wounds are too severe."

I know they are! He wanted to snap at the capybara. *I know, because I did this to her! But, can you please do something else more!? Something to alleviate her pain? Isn't there any alternatives in this situation!?! ANYTHING!!!?* His chest tightened as his claws dug the ground. He wished he could fight back, he wished that he could tell them to keep trying. Keep trying and not give up. He took one deep breath and lowered his head again. Deep down, he knew they were right.

She was beyond saving with these damaging wounds.

He offered his presence to Princess Okome as she began struggling to breathe. That was all he could do now.

"I'm sorry, I'm so sorry," he whispered to her, holding back his tears.

She met his eyes, and her face told him she wanted to say things to him. She tried, but, at this point, she was slowly losing her grip on the life blessed to her by Abella, the Goddess of Life. A frosty breeze passed by them both. Prince Wonwoo shivered. He knew that breeze; a frosty breeze next to a dying or dead creature meant Morana–the Goddess of Death–was right around the corner, waiting to greet their soul into the afterlife. She was waiting for the wolf princess.

He looked at the doctors, who were speaking to Hakuba in a somber tone, then dropped his voice a little bit more to whisper to her.

"I don't care what I would name my son," he said, "but if I had a daughter, I'd have her named after her mother..."

Princess Okome's ears slightly twitched. She smiled softly at him. Her mouth twitched, as if she was trying to speak to him. He pressed his muzzle to the side of her neck, trying not to gag at the scent of blood.

It won't happen now, he said to himself, *to have a little Okome the Second, but it's the best comfort I can give her... But in saying that, I'm sad that our children will never be. She would have been a great mother. An excellent one at that. Morana...please take her into your gentle paws, and don't let her be afraid anymore.*

"Oh, Princess Okome," he said softly. "How am I to tell your brother about...this? How much will he hate me? You won't be able to tell him anything, how I'm not at fault."

"SISTER!!"

Aw shit.

Speak of the Devil.

Hearing the desperate cry from the wolf prince, Prince Wonwoo looked up and saw Prince Scamander frozen in place as he bursted his way into Morning Dew Park. Enky, Arvolf and Cyclone were right behind him, keeping a safe distance for the upcoming storm. The wolf prince's eyes were wide and his jaw gaped. He shook his head, ears flattened against his head. The lion prince was able to make out the word "no" being repeated multiple times from his shivering lips, but he was in too much shock to even hear him parrot it aloud.

Locking eyes with Prince Wonwoo, Prince Scamander broke into a run and lashed out his claws at the lion prince.

"Get the **FUCK** AWAY FROM HER BEFORE I KILL YOU!" he snarled.

Prince Wonwoo felt the wolf prince's claws slice his chest, tearing his flesh open. A stinging pain seared through him. The wolf prince may not have large claws like his father, but their tiny size did a fair amount of damage as it ripped seamlessly like he was made out of paper. For a moment, he feared that he had torn a similar wound like he did to Princess Okome. He, along with the doctors and Hakuba, backed away as Prince Scamander took his sister into his arms, hugging her tightly. Carmentis immediately tended to his wound, which Prince Wonwoo looked to see the damage. It wasn't much, thank the Gods, but it didn't help soothe that spike of adrenaline. The lion prince could see he was devastated, his eyes tinted red with anger and grief.

He caught a bit of his words once the initial wave of shock calmed down.

"Sis...can you hear me? It's me. We're going to take you back. I..." Prince Scamander paused, his face cringing as he forced out the last word. "...promise."

That word definitely meant ill to Prince Scamander, by the way Prince Wonwoo heard him spit it out like it was expired food.

Princess Okome stared blankly at her brother, her focus lacking. Prince Wonwoo sniffed. If only she was able to say her final words had her throat not been wrecked. She reached out to her brother, smiling. She appeared to be trying to comfort him. Prince Scamander widened his tear-ridden eyes, taking her paw and bringing it to his cheek. He could tell both brother and sister had so much they wanted to say. But that chance would never happen. Death was already here, and Morana was waiting for Princess Okome.

After minutes, the wolf princess finally relaxed and let out one last breath, her body going limp. Prince Wonwoo looked in shock. She couldn't be...

No. It definitely could be.

The wolf prince stared at her. Prince Wonwoo could tell he saw that she had grown still, but denial clouded his eyes. He gently patted her shoulder and shook her.

"Okome?" Prince Scamander said with worry. When she hadn't responded, he tried to wake her up. "Okome? Okome! Wake up! It's me, Scamander! Your brother! I'm here, I'm going to take you home! You're going to make it!! Please!!! Please wake up! Please, Okome!! Answer me!!"

No response from her. No life in her eyes.

"Don't **DO** this to me, Okome! **PLEASE! OKOME!!!**"

Princess Okome was dead.

"OKOMEEEEE!!!!"

Prince Wonwoo suppressed sobs as Prince Scamander let out a pained howl, tightly hugging the corpse of his sister. He buried his face in her neck, trembling and crying. Enky, Arvolf and Cyclone consoled the young prince as best they could, though he shoved them away. They respected the wolf prince and stood back, allowing him to grieve. The doctors bowed their heads in respect, Jiro the elephant bringing them close. He also let Hakuba and Prince Wonwoo lean on him as they joined the grieving.

The lion prince could barely grieve himself. His eyes, dry as they were from his emotional suppression, managed to shed a few tears. His heart was completely broken. Princess Okome, the one he cared about and grew to love, someone from a Kingdom that didn't agree with their ideals yet pushed past it to be with him, was dead.

He hugged Jiro tightly, pressing his face to his massive leg. He could feel Jiro's trunk wrap around his body.

It's all my fault. His head was spinning. *I did this, I killed Princess Okome. What have I done? I ruined everything now. It's all my fault. It's all my fault, it's all my fault.*

Prince Scamander lifted up his head. He looked at the Promised Dynasty members with fury. Seeing them in his presence with his dead sister, knowing they did not do anything to help her, boiled his blood. How could they let her die? Did they do that on purpose!? Did they not care about her at all because of who she was?!!

But the moment he saw and locked eyes with Prince Wonwoo, the very creature responsible for this whole mess, the wolf prince's anger exploded.

"You will **PAY** for this, Prince Wonwoo OF THE PROMISED DYNASTY!" he yelled.

CHAPTER 6
THE THREAT OF A WAR COMING; NIGHTMARES PLAGUE PRINCE WONWOO

~ The following night... ~
~ January in Terra Cycle 1118 B.E. ~

War was bound to happen soon. All because Prince Wonwoo had completely messed up big time.

Hours ago, Prince Scamander proclaimed his anger that Prince Wonwoo would pay for the demise of his sister, Princess Okome. After a tense conversation with him, he turned away and headed out of Morning Dew Park and out of Halcyonwick. The lion prince couldn't move due to the grief, and he had to be assisted by Hakuba. The doctors tended to Prince Wonwoo's wounds that he sustained from both Enky and Prince Scamander and led him back to the castle. His mind reeled on the event and the conversation as they headed back home.

"P-Prince Scamander, please," the lion prince had said. *"I-I didn't mean — This wasn't— I—"*

"My Father ENTRUSTED your Dynasty a little too easily," he interrupted with a growl. *"Believing that merging our Kingdom with yours was for the good of our Kingdom. I told her this was a bad idea, but she didn't listen to me. AND NOW! I'M HERE, HOLDING HER DEAD BODY!"*

"Prince Scamander-"

"Stop it. Just SHUT UP!!"

"B-But–!"

The wolf prince glared. "I will see to it that the Promised Dynasty suffers for what they have done. For what YOU have done."

The lion prince tried to approach him, mainly to say a final goodbye to Princess Okome. "Prince Scamander, please." Please listen to me, *he wanted to say.*

He jerked her body away from him, baring his teeth at him. The action startled the lion prince. He growled intensely.

"You better start PRAYING to those Gods of yours, because we WILL be relentless!"

The lion prince shook his head. This was too much to process and handle.

He returned back to the castle where he broke the news to his parents about what had happened, afraid of the wrath his parents would unleash. When he had finished his story, he looked away and trembled. He knew his Father would most definitely be upset, since he had told him that if he messed up, there would be a war incoming. Prince Wonwoo did exactly what his Father warned. He was ready to accept the punishments. He was, however, surprised that they were actually compassionate. King Jung-hwa ran up to Prince Wonwoo and held him in a tight hug. Queen Cora joined as well, putting her paw on her son's shoulder. The lion prince trembled immensely, breaking down in his father's embrace.

"I'm sorry, I'm so so sorry!" he started to cry, nuzzling into his father's neck. "I messed up, Father, I screwed up big time!"

"It's okay…It's okay…" King Jung-hwa soothed.

"It's going to be alright, son," Queen Cora said softly.

"No, NO IT WON'T BE, MOTHER!" Prince Wonwoo wailed. "I CAUSED A FUTURE WAR! ONE WE DON'T NEED! I-I was so stupid, and immature, I-" He hiccuped, lowering his voice. "I'm so sorry, Father. You told me to grow up. I-I did exactly what you told me not to do, and I ruined everything! Why aren't you berating and punishing me?"

"Because it wasn't your fault," the lion king said. "I don't believe what you did was on your own intentions. You and Princess Okome both loved each other, I saw it. Ellowyn knows that those Demoniacal members have no respect for the Promised Dynasty unlike us."

It was my fault. He wanted to say but he kept it to himself. He was too tired to fight back; every part of his body and mind was sore, and he wanted to get over this day.

"We're going to have to take repercussions now since the Demoniacal Kingdom will indeed attack for revenge," King Jung-hwa said, releasing Prince Wonwoo from his arms. He looked at Hakuba. "We'll need to get the soldiers up to shape and the guards on high alert. Can you inform everyone first thing before everyone goes to sleep that there will be an emergency meeting tomorrow morning in the war room?"

The white horse bowed her head.

"Right now, we should all get some rest. We'll need to save our strength for the inevitable day."

As soon as everyone departed, Prince Wonwoo stood still by the stairs. He couldn't move any muscle. The thought of sleeping alone tonight suddenly sounded dreadful and frightening. What if the Demoniacal Kingdom snuck into the castle unsuspectingly and killed him in his sleep? Or what if they kidnap him?

Queen Cora turned and saw her son clearly in distress. She walked back to him, her eyes sparked in fear.

"What's wrong, sweetheart?" she asked him.

The lion prince looked into her eyes. That was one thing he loved about his mother. The way she was so gentle and compassionate when obviously he was in the wrong. The way she could sense his emotions and ask the appropriate questions. It was admirable. Sure, she was like this due to the fact that she had lost cubs before him, long lost siblings of the lion prince, but Prince Wonwoo knew she would have been fiercely loving to all her children had they lived.

He shook his head. "I-I don't feel good... I-I need a guard to watch over me tonight," he admitted. "Probably for the next few couple nights if that's okay..."

The lioness queen nodded and called out, "Hakuba!"

Right away, the white horse trotted up.

"Accompany my son to his room and watch over him," she commanded.

"Yes, Queen Cora of the Promised Dynasty," Hakuba answered, bowing her head. She whisked her tail over Prince Wonwoo's shoulders. "Come along, Prince Wonwoo."

The lion prince felt his fear wash over him when the white horse offered her presence and followed her back to his room.

His room was nothing extravagant, but it was something to help lift up his dampen mood.

Hakuba had opened the door for the lion prince since she could see he was completely exhausted from today's events. Prince Wonwoo was greeted to his room shrouded in complete darkness, which made him promptly turn on the light. As soon as the lights came on with a simple click of the switch, the bright light blinded him. Taking some time to adjust, he looked around. His room was big but not that big. His bed was nestled to his left, pressed against the wall. It laid vertically, like all the beds in the castle. By the foot of the bed, a small desk with a mirror was set.

His walls were painted in light orange and white, with flowers all around.

The lion prince trudged over to his desk, looking at his face. He saw how sunken his eyelids were and how close he was to passing out. He also saw the bandage that covered his chest and shoulders. It was starting to stain, and he knew that he had to remove it.

"I need a new set of bandages," he mumbled, ripping them off. "Or maybe not..Do I really deserve them?"

"I'll go get some, and yes you do," Hakuba said, gently nipping his ears. "I'll be back as soon as I can."

Don't take too long, please, he thought, watching the white horse trot out. He stared at his chest wound. It was dark red and a mess, shining due to the anti-bacterial cream Arkaitz put on it. It wasn't stinging anymore as it did initially. Despite being instructed not to, he so desperately wanted to poke it. The moment he lifted his paw, memories rushed back.

"YOU WILL LEARN SOME RESPECT, DEMONIACAL SCUM!"

"Stop!"

Her blood was still on his paws.

Unable to hold it any longer, Prince Wonwoo rushed out of his room, breathing heavily. He needed the bathroom. He looked around the dark hallways. Where was it!? Why was he suddenly forgetting simple things? Paranoia creeped in as it appeared to him the darkness was slinking up to him. He looked down at his chest. Only his pelt gave him some light but his fear darkened his vision. The shadows creeped up on him, slithering up and enwrapping itself like a snake. His breathing intensified, making his head dizzy. He put his paw on his head, whimpering.

Everything was growing dark.

"Prince Wonwoo? What are you doing out here?"

He collapsed.

"Prince Wonwoo!"

His senses were dulled for a moment. Hakuba had rushed to the lion prince's side when she returned with medical supplies among other necessities and took him back to his room. His head was spinning from the light. He groaned, patting Hakuba's neck. "Nauseous... I'm...nauseous-"

The white horse immediately grabbed the small trash bin and placed it by the lion prince. He finally expelled what he had been holding in for hours. Hakuba tended to it and put the trash bin back where it was after she was finished. She laid next to him in his bed, getting him settled for the night. Opening her pouch, she slowly and carefully redressed Prince Wonwoo's wounds with new bandages. The lion prince struggled to stay awake. Hakuba sensed this and gently encouraged him:

"If you need to sleep, go on ahead. May Ayumu bless you with wonderful dreams."

He couldn't respond to the white horse's statement. He finally gave in to the forces and let his head rest on Hakuba's side.

. . .

THE THREAT OF A WAR COMING; NIGHTMARES PLAGUE PRINCE ...

...

"You did this."

Within the depths of Prince Wonwoo's mind, he was trapped in a dark void. There was nothing in sight, just an empty sea of nothing. Sinking fear was all the lion prince felt.

"Hello?" he called out.

No one answered.

"What do you mean I did this?"

That didn't come from out of his mouth.

Yes, it was his voice, but Prince Wonwoo had not verbally said it aloud. It was as if there was a clone of him. Looking around, he decided to follow where his other voice came from. Though, he was basically lost from the start, since there was no indicator of any kind on where he was going or where he was going.

"You know what I mean. You ruined everything. You ruined MY LIFE! First by killing my sister, then causing the death of my wife and children. Everything I ever cared for is gone, and it was all because of you!"

The lion prince stopped in his tracks.

That voice was now suddenly really strangely familiar.

Prince Scamander?

"I did not kill your sister! Nor did I kill your children or your wife! Nor did I kill your parents!"

"They still died because your Gods' angels came down to slaughter us. If you hadn't lived, if my Father had you executed all those terra cycles ago instead of letting you stay with us, NONE OF THIS would be happening! Okome would still be alive. Clarity...and my beautiful bundles of joy...THEY WOULD BE ALIVE!! MY WHOLE KINGDOM WOULD STILL BE AROUND!"

"Prince Scamander-"

"That's not my name anymore. Prince Scamander died a long time ago. You can refer to me as-"

The revelation was suddenly cut off when a bright flash of light blinded Prince Wonwoo. The lion prince lifted up an arm in protest, and he soon saw the faded spirit of Princess Okome. She appeared as she did when she was alive, minus the wounds on her throat and chest and the apparent faded life in her mint green eyes. His eyes went wide, and he reached out to her.

"P-Princess Okome!" he cried out. "My love, I'm so sorry-"

"H o w c o u l d y o u?"

The lion prince was taken aback at the sudden coldness of the wolf princess. *This isn't like her at all*, he was thinking to himself. She was now acting like her brother, which started to unnerve him. What was going on?

"Huh?"

"How could you?" she repeated her question. "How could you do this?"

"What–?"

"Why did you kill me?"

The lion prince's heart stopped. "I-I didn't mean it— I hadn't meant to–" He shook his head. "You have to believe me! I never meant to kill you! You KNEW it was an accident!"

"No...this wasn't an accident," Princess Okome said, shaking her head. She directed his gaze to her wounds. "Your intent was clear. You wanted to kill me."

"What? NO!" Prince Wonwoo started to hyperventilate again. "I-I love you! I love you, Princess Okome! I truthfully do!"

"You don't love me. You never did."

That tore through him viciously.

"Princess Okome..."

"You only care about your Dynasty. You care about being better than everyone. You care for nothing about the Demoniacal Kingdom or the Promised Dynasty! You NEVER CARED ABOUT ME!"

The lion prince lowered his head, tears welling in his eyes.

I did care about you, *he thought to himself.* I love you. I will always love you, Princess Okome.

The wolf princess advanced closer to Prince Wonwoo and bared her teeth at him.

"You don't deserve the Heavens. No. It's no place for a murderer like you. Go to hell where you belong. Die and go to hell, Prince Wonwoo OF THE PROMISED DYNASTY!!!"

She leapt at him, jaws wide open.

...

"NOOO!!!"

Prince Wonwoo arose in a cold sweat, claws unsheathed, heart racing. His room was pitch black from the darkness, saved from the shimmer of moonlight that creeped through his window. He couldn't calm his hyperventilating panting. He grasped his mane, pulling on his fur to distract his pain.

Calm down, calm down! Prince Wonwoo told himself. *Oh, no, they definitely heard me scream. Mother and Father will rush in.*

Everything was growing light again. He pulled on his mane harder.

Someone, help. Help meee!

"Prince Wonwoo."

The voice startled him, but he remembered that it was only Hakuba and she was there with him. The white horse pressed her nose to his neck, puffing gentle breaths at him. Hakuba's presence began easing Prince Wonwoo's fear, and he focused on his breathing. He allowed his mind to relax and took deep breaths.

"Thank you, Hakuba."

"Are you okay? What happened?" Hakuba asked.

THE THREAT OF A WAR COMING; NIGHTMARES PLAGUE PRINCE ...

"I...I can't sleep," the lion prince said, looking down at his paws.

"Kishi giving you horrible nightmares?"

The lion prince didn't answer her, but he would have said yes. He hid his face underneath his paws. "I see... *Her.* Her ghost, her disfigured spirit...taunting me. Telling me that I deserve to go to Hell for what I did to her."

"It's just the stress and trauma your mind latches onto constantly," the white horse said. "You're in shock. Try not to focus on the negative too much, for that's how Kishi gets to you. You know that."

The lion prince had known the legends of Kishi, the God of Nightmares and Omens. He and his counterpart, his sister Ayumu, always fought over who would get which individual during their sleep. Ayumu, the Goddess of Dreams and Visions, would visit all (except those who could not dream for some reason), giving them pleasant dreams. Kishi, on the other paw, would target those who are troubled by the day, unable to be reached by Ayumu due to their woes, and plague them with horrible nightmares at night. Ayumu would often try to intervene on his victims to heal them, leading to the two of them battling for dreams. However, as with all the other Gods, one could not defeat the other, for it would lead to an imbalance and corruption of power. So, despite their battles, Ayumu and Kishi would end in a stalemate, coming to some agreements.

"Prince Wonwoo?"

"I know that," Prince Wonwoo answered Hakuba, snapping himself out of the daydream of the legends. "But... How can

I...not..? After everything that happened... It's all my fault... Even she said so herself."

"She?"

"...Princess Okome."

The white horse flicked an ear. "*She* spoke to you?"

The lion prince nodded. "She said...I willingly wanted to kill her. That I never loved her."

"But you know that's all lies, right? It's just a hallucination."

"Of course they're lies! I— I did love her! I wanted to marry her...I wanted to have children with her. I...I never once even thought about doing something horrible to her..."

"See now... That's the spirit."

The lion prince buried his head in his paws, sighing. He couldn't help but still feel dejected at the events at hand. "Gods, what have I done...? Really...what have I done..? I ruined everything..."

"You did not ruin anything," Hakuba said, picking between his shoulders. "It was an unfortunate, cruel twist of fate."

"I...could have done something to stop it. But I was blinded. Blinded by hatred."

"Hatred is a strong emotion, but it is not a sin. Don't beat yourself up over it."

He casted a glance at Hakuba. "You being here really helps a lot, you know? I don't know what I'd do without you..."

Hakuba rested her head on his body. "Everything is going to be okay, Prince Wonwoo," she said. "Whatever happens, we will get through this together. As a Dynasty."

Her words made Prince Wonwoo suddenly feel like he was a cub. He rubbed his muzzle into her flank, purring.

"Thank you, Hakuba… Thank you."

The white horse yawned and moved her head towards his bed. "Remember that I am here for you. Try to get some rest. May… May Ayumu bless you.." Her words drifted off as she fell asleep.

May Ayumu bless you with wonderful dreams, Hakuba.

Prince Wonwoo stayed up for a little while, staring at the ceiling and conjuring up the stories of the Gods, until he finally gave sleep another try.

CHAPTER 7

PRINCE SCAMANDER'S EARLY DESIRES FOR REVENGE; A DARK PATH IS BORN

✦✧✦✧~ *That same night in the Demoniacal Kingdom...* ~
~ *January in Terra Cycle 1118 B.E.* ~

Life was never going to be the same without his sister around.

Prince Scamander had returned to Coldwyvern carrying the now cold body of Princess Okome on his back. Enky, Arvolf and Cyclone circled around him to have him in the center, with Enky and Arvolf on both of his sides and Cyclone at the rear. The sun was making its way across the sky. All four of them kept rather silent, not making eye contact with each other. Not like there was anything that could be said anyway after everything that went down today. Prince Scamander carried his sister delicately and made sure that she wouldn't fall off him. He stared at her expression; it appeared she was asleep, only dreaming about good things. She didn't even look like she was in pain as she was a few hours ago.

Instead, she was...at peace.

King Titanosaurus and Queen Zirconia immediately ran out of the castle into town square when they heard the news and approached Prince Scamander. A few other Demoniacal Kingdom members gathered around in shock, whispering to one another. He felt a stab strike his chest as he looked at his parents, laying Princess Okome on the ground. "Let us through," King Titanosaurus ordered, making the crowd part for the King and Queen. Queen Zirconia profusely cried and howled the moment she laid eyes on her bloodied body, pushing herself towards her and nuzzling herself into Princess Okome's fur. She hugged her daughter tightly and did not want to let go. King Titanosaurus had an expressionless face, but he eventually gave in and let tears fall from his face. He placed a paw on her head and bowed.

For once, Prince Scamander saw his father vulnerable.

"No! My daughter, my precious daughter!" Queen Zirconia wailed. "Noo! This can't be real! What has happened to you!? Who did this to you?"

King Titanosaurus looked to Prince Scamander, his face reading that he was demanding an answer. He can only fumble in his words, for he was grieving just the same as his mother was.

"I..."

"Look at what has happened, my brother," Livyatan growled, aggressively shoving his way through the crowd. His five children, Prince Scamander's cousins, also padded up into the center alongside their Father and gathered around Princess Okome to offer their condolences. "You gave your trust in the Promised Dynasty, believing that they will help us, and our princess lies dead in front of our eyes. DEAD!"

King Titanosaurus casted a glare at Livyatan. Prince Scamander watched curiously. He looked like he wanted to snap at his brother, tell him to shut up and sit down, but he didn't. He was in too much pain to even fight back. Even if he did, what could he say? His brother was right, and he hadn't listened.

One of his cousins, Dorudon, sat beside Prince Scamander and rested his head on his shoulder. The wolf prince froze at the touch but eventually returned the sentiment. He never shared moments like these with his cousins, but this time it really proved helpful.

"I'm sorry for your loss," he whispered. "We're all going to miss her."

The wolf prince sighed, letting his eyes shut. "Thank you," he murmured. "Thank you..."

Livyatan flattened his ears against his head as he continued.

"My beloved niece–your own daughter–is dead, and you know why."

The wolf king's eyebrows immediately furrowed into a frown. His muzzle wrinkled.

"I cannot believe I let my guard down in front of King Jung-hwa of the Promised Dynasty," he snarled. "I see now, this was just a scheme to have the Kingdom killed! It was just a test, to see how close we can get to him and his Dynasty, and it worked."

Livyatan bared his teeth. "Precisely true, my brother. Now he will find a way through our weakness and kill us all off for good!"

Prince Scamander twitched his ears at his uncle's words. That theory suddenly stirred ideas in his brain. Was the lion king of the Promised Dynasty actually sinister underneath his kind persona and had planned to bring the Demoniacal Kingdom closer to him so he could massacre them all? Kill them all to finally get rid of dark magic? To finally get rid of the "sinful beasts?" He blinked. That made sense to him in his head. Why else would the lion king want to marry his son to someone from the Demoniacal Kingdom of all Kingdoms? *Especially* the princess of the Demoniacal Kingdom? It seemed a little too suspicious.

Of course! They too want revenge, but it's to either convert us back to their cult or be eliminated!

The wolf prince stood up from his place and sat next to his grieving mother. The wolf queen, having sensed his presence, moved away from Princess Okome and pulled her son into a tight hug. She let out another wail, choking on her tears. He leaned onto his mother, burying his face in her shoulder to ease her pain. He sighed. He was glad he was able to find comfort with his mother at least.

"He...Prince Wonwoo killed her," Prince Scamander finally said, bringing himself to deliver the news. He looked at Enky, Arvolf and Cyclone from the corner of his eyes; he couldn't reveal that he sent them unless he wanted to experience the wrath of his grieving Father. He had to come up with some lie that explained why he was near the Promised Dynasty. "I...had gone out for a walk when I was alerted to the cry of a crow. Sensing something wrong in my gut, I followed, and I ran to the Promised Dynasty."

"Prince Wonwoo?" Queen Zirconia seemed beyond shocked. She sounded as if she did not want to believe what her son had said. "This...That can't be..."

King Titanosaurus consoled his wife, rubbing her back with a gentle paw.

"I saw him with her, Mother," he continued. "Saw him standing over her body as her life bled out. I saw...his claws coated with her blood. He...killed her."

"This cannot go unpunished!" Livyatan said, flashing his large dark blue claws. "They've killed her, our beloved princess! Princess Okome's death must be avenged! The Promised Dynasty must pay for what they have done!"

Everyone around them murmured in agreement.

I agree, Prince Scamander said to himself, moving away from his mother and digging his claws into the ground. *My sister didn't deserve this! She shouldn't have died! They must pay.* His ears pinned back. *Especially Prince Wonwoo. The bastard ruthlessly killed her! When I see him again, I want to be the one to rip his throat out! Along with his heart! Rip it out and let him bleed to D E A T H!*

"I will gather with my best soldiers for a war meeting tomorrow morning, and we will discuss from there," King Titanosaurus said. "It is best now that we get some rest. We'll have my daughter properly buried after the meeting. You're all dismissed."

With the flick of his tail, he and Queen Zirconia headed back to the castle, herding Prince Scamander with them. He looked back at the gathered crowd; while the other Kingdom members left, the guards delicately lifted and carried Princess Okome's body towards the funeral home. He frowned, his muzzle wrinkling. How badly he wanted to run up to them and pull her away from them. How he wanted to bring her back to the castle and lay her in her bed. How he wanted to scream "RELEASE HER AT ONCE! SHE DOES NOT BELONG THERE!"

But he could only watch. Watch and accept the reality that Princess Okome was in fact dead.

She didn't deserve this, she didn't DESERVE THIS!

His room had never felt emptier.

Prince Scamander opened the door to his room, and immediately turned on the light to see better. (He had night vision, but because of the whole ordeal, he only saw darkness.) He looked around, his heart heavy. Nothing felt normal in his room. All he saw were faint images of him and his sister. He saw the two of them chatting and playing to no end until either their mother or their father showed up.

Shaking his head clear from those memories, he walked over to his closet, grabbing a small ladder that rested on the wall and a small box. He then headed over to his shelves where his Venus fly trap sat on the top shelf and set the small ladder down by the wall. He climbed it slowly.

Another memory surfaced.

"Brother, how are you going to take care of that plant when you put it so high up?"

"Firstly, 'it' is a he, and his name is Fern. Secondly, I'll be keeping this small ladder so I can use it to give Fern what he needs."

"Okayyy. Also, how do you know Fern is a guy?"

"...I don't know. He just seems like a Fern kind of guy...guy."

"Heh. You're so strange, brother."

Their interaction for when Prince Scamander first brought home Fern the Venus fly trap stuck with him as he delicately showered him and gave him a small fly. He watched Fern shut his mouth, snapping with lightning speed. He gently patted Fern and climbed back down, shoving his stuff back in the closet. He collapsed onto his bed and laid there, groaning in misery.

Why? He began to lament. *Why did it have to happen? Why did fate have to be so cruel to us? I already miss you, Okome.*

His mind was just as heavy as his heart was. He just couldn't believe his sister was gone. The time spent with her, from the day she was born to their crazy shenanigans. That time was now gone. What was also gone was her future. The wolf prince would never see her living life to the fullest, married to a loving creature and with children.

It was all gone.

He pulled the blankets over him, huddling into his pillow. His bed was warm, and it reminded him of his sister's embrace. He sighed. If only his Father hadn't agreed to King Jung-hwa's idea, hadn't agreed to the proposal. If only his Father had refused! She would have still been alive.

It's not fair.

He closed his eyes.

None of this is fair!

His head ached terribly from the emotions and the grief. He realized something that he wished he hadn't; tomorrow would not only be an exhausting day of preparing for her funeral and burial, it would also be painful knowing it would have been her 22nd birthday. The day she and Prince Wonwoo were to wed.

She should still be alive! You should still be alive!!

His heart began to squeeze in anger. Tears ran down like a tiny river. Why? Why was this happening!? The questions raced through his head and had no way of getting out. His muscles tensed as he struggled to compose himself. Rest was a struggle, and it only brought more pain. Whenever he closed his eyes, he only saw Princess Okome and her dead eyes.

I just want you here with me, sis, he choked. *Please...*

Deep within, a growl sounded in his throat.

You better start praying to your Gods, Prince Wonwoo, he growled. *They won't save you when I come for you.*

BEGINNING OF TIME

"It's him! The one destined. He is here."

Far away, in territory unknown, a small creature with the body and face of a chicken and the wings of a dragon–a cockatrice–resided in a dark cave. It sat in its nest, eyes closed, surrounded by the glowing crystals of various colors. The crystals were slowly pulsating in their light, dim but bright enough. The cockatrice was meditating, channeling the energy of the crystals within. It was the only way for the cockatrice to keep its emotions in perfect harmony.

Its meditation was suddenly interrupted by the sound of hoofsteps beating on the ground. The cockatrice slowly opened its eyes after feeling the disturbance and looked back in annoyance, greeted by the sight of a creature it didn't expect to see. A winged horse with dragon scales and a bright yellow headband over its eyes bursted through the cave, leaving a trail of dust in its wake. The crystals shone on the winged horse's light blue and yellow scales. Long snow-white whiskers and mane flowed in the wind. It kept its distance from the cockatrice. The cockatrice recognized this creature: it was a longma. More importantly, this longma was a particular Council member in the Heavens. Not just any regular old council member.

He was the Head Council in the Heavens.

"After tens of thousands and millions of terra cycles, he has returned. His quest for revenge is soon, I have sensed it," the longma grumbled. "Sooner than we expected. The universe as we know it will end. It will be erased."

"Why does it concern you this badly, Song Feng?" the cockatrice asked with a sigh, getting to its feet. "You know that you and the Council will live through it. You are immortal."

The longma, Song Feng, shook his head, fixing his mane. "It's still a concern to me since this is our universe, Waccruwk," he answered the cockatrice, stomping his hoof on the ground. "My existence is not of importance in this matter. I am saying that everything we know right now will be gone if the one destined seeks out his revenge. Mortals are at risk. Have you not sensed it?"

The cockatrice, Waccruwk, stretched out his wings, flapping them. He preened his wings to get rid of loose feathers. "I have. But how do you know for certain if he will arrive at all?" Waccruwk asked curiously. "What if Providence had prevented his rise to power?"

"We have seen it! The signs were there from the start. We have been predicting this since the very first fabrics of this universe began to thread and intertwine! Do you not remember the prophecy?"

"Of course." He gestured over to his crystals. "It's written within my crystals and repeats in my brain like a parasite I can't get rid of. *'When Gau's Coup Day comes and the sun rises completely void, a dark creature with the blood of the dragon and a heart of vengeance and grief shall seek. He will be the one destined to bring chaos and destruction to the universe, and he will challenge the Heavens.'*"

The longma felt his whiskers twitch. It wasn't the entire prophecy, but it was the beginning part of it. He lowered his eyes.

BEGINNING OF TIME

"...You haven't forgotten."

"The question now is: Have *you* forgotten that I was outcasted because of the prophecy? Surely you shouldn't have, since you were the one to banish me after all."

Song Feng swished his tail in regret. "No."

"Then certainly, you have not forgotten that, in the prophecy, I am the one who will *'supposedly'* be responsible for the one destined's powers when the day raised by Gau comes. *'He who controls the dark creature with the tick of the clock will be guided by a creature with the knowledge of time.'* Surely, you have not forgotten about that part."

"That I also came to talk about." Song Feng took one step closer to Waccruwk. "I'm begging you, friend to friend, do not do this. It's not our fault a prophecy revealed you would turn out cruel."

His feathers ruffled and spiked at the mention of him becoming cruel. "I'm not going to turn out cruel!" Waccruwk hissed. "The dumb prophecy did not reveal I was going to be evil! It just says 'a creature with the knowledge of time.' Anyone with such knowledge that is forbidden could be the one who controls the dark creature!"

"We couldn't take any risks-"

"All this time, I thought the Council was all about being kind to one another. That we do not hate one another nor promote hatred towards an individual. What a fool I was."

Song Feng's ears drooped. "Waccruwk—"

The cockatrice did not want to hear anymore from the longma. He was done with it all. "After much reflection, I see now that the Heavens is filled with lies and deception. Hidden behind a mask and a glowing halo. You angels follow a being who Herself had terrible actions."

The longma appeared offended. He tossed his head to the side. "That's not true!" Song Feng stomped his hoof firmly on the ground. "Waccruwk, stop this! You've let your pain and sorrow consume your heart and drive you mad with grief!"

The cockatrice narrowed his eyes at the longma. He wished that he could see Song Feng's look, but of course with the headband, he couldn't. It was strange to him; after his exile from the Council and the Heavens entirely, Waccruwk grew bitter, and the bitterness awakened one of the most dangerous powers his kind was known for: his death stare. As an angel, he was supposedly "freed" from this "curse," but after he fell, he realized his true potential. Because he never had this power when he was a member of the Heavens, he became feared by the Council members, and they started to wear headbands around their eyes so that they would not look into his eyes. Which, when Waccruwk started to think about it, was extremely stupid; they were all immortal, given immortality the second they were all created, so why would his death stare frighten them?

It doesn't matter now. Song Feng, his friend and potential lover, had abandoned him, and there was no going back. To him or back to the Heavens. There was no way he could forgive him.

"I didn't let the pain consume me," the cockatrice said menacingly. "I only saw the truth and embraced it. Unlike you. You fools let yourself be blinded by the Gods so willingly that you fail to see the flaws the great Ellowyn had. I tried, tried so hard to make you see it, I wanted to make you see where your allegiance is and see that you're in a cult. But of course you were and are blinded by the Heavens just like everyone else has been. Creatures like you, with so much faith and so little rational thought...they will never change."

The longma's eyebrows lifted. "Waccruwk..."

The cockatrice ran his wing over his head. "Whatever. I don't care what you try to do with me now. If the prophecy says I will help the one destined, so be it that I will do as told."

"Waccruwk, I'm warning you," the longma huffed. "Do not give the one destined his powers. Do not make me fight you. This is my only warning."

Song Feng threatening to fight him? The cockatrice shivered. Now that was new. The longma was never one for violence, always finding a peaceful solution to any conflict. Even when they were bullied by mere mortals of the living world, Song Feng would want to leave instead of feeding into their words. Times were indeed changing.

The cockatrice puffed out his chest, spreading his wings. He hissed at Song Feng.

"Get out. Get out, unless you wish to fight me right now."

The longma was frozen. He seemed to be thinking. He put one hoof forward, and the cockatrice hissed louder. Waccruwk wanted him to show he could fight. He wanted to have a meaningful confrontation with his old friend. To show him his power. Show him the truth.

That's right, come closer, I dare you.

"Wacc–"

"You don't wanna leave? You really wanna fight me? Do it then," Waccruwk threatened. "Fight me, Song Feng."

The longma's eyes widened behind his headband. He continued approaching. The cockatrice felt his tiny heart racing.

"Fight me. FIGHT ME, SONG FENG! I want you to show me your power! No...Better yet: Kill me. Stomp on me, break my bones, crush my skull, make me bleed. ANYTHING! I FUCKING DARE YOU!"

Stopping a few feet short, Song Feng bowed at Waccruwk. The cockatrice lowered his wings, blinking in confusion. That was why he was approaching him? Just to bow at him??

"So you're a coward who's willing to let everyone die just to preserve your own goodwill even in the face of destroying all evil," Waccruwk said to Song Feng in a condescending tone. "Puh. What a massive hypocrisy you're displaying right now. Some joke. I cannot believe I ever befriended you."

Song Feng did not say anything else to him. There was only sadness in his eyes as he lifted up his head and turned away to leave. The cockatrice flattened his feathers, puffing at him. A coward he thought to himself about Song Feng. Though the longma turned his back on the cockatrice, he swiveled his head back to him. He gave him a final message.

"Don't say I didn't try to warn you. I care about you, Waccruwk. You mean so much to me."

I'm sure you do, Song Feng. I can tell a lie when I hear one.

As much as he wanted to tell him off, Waccruwk did not say any final words to his old friend. There wouldn't be any final words for him. He didn't want to give the longma the satisfaction of having been heard. He kept quiet, standing still, waiting for his former friend to leave.

Sensing the silent message, the longma disappeared.

CHAPTER 8
THE PROMISED DYNASTY GETS A SURPRISE

~ The war... ~
~ July in Terra Cycle 1118 B.E. ~

"So here's how this is going to happen..."

6 months seemed to have flown by like it was nothing. Inside the castle in Halcyonwick, King Jung-hwa gathered his soldiers and guards in the battle room. Among them was Prince Wonwoo, who sat uncomfortably in his seat. His paws shuffled as he listened in on his father's strategies and plans for probably the 100th time. His heart sank; the Promised Dynasty was soon going to go to war with the Demoniacal Kingdom all because he accidentally, unintentionally killed Princess Okome of the Demoniacal Kingdom.

I didn't mean it, he thought to himself. *I didn't mean for that to happen! How could I have been so stupid!?*

He never forgot that fateful day 6 months ago. He clearly remembered the look on her brother's face as he saw his sister lying on the ground, bleeding out her lifeblood onto his paws, Morana creeping in to claim her. The way the wolf prince threw himself at her, pushing him away and cradling her close to his body and howling his heart out. Large drops of tears welled in the wolf prince's eyes and fell as he lifted up his head and gazed at him with burning hatred and vengeance. He had never seen the wolf prince with so much emotion.

His warning was also still loud in his ears.

"You will PAY for this, Prince Wonwoo of the Promised Dynasty!"

The lion prince bowed his head, refusing to look at anyone. Not even at his own parents. He couldn't face meeting his Dynasty members.

I deserve it. I...

"You got that, Prince Wonwoo?"

Someone was directing their question to him. He didn't mean to ignore them, but he did anyway. He sat there, head hung low and his stare blank as his paranoid mind took over.

The Promised Dynasty was on the brink of another war, one they definitely did not need, and a strong lingering feeling by all hung that this would be as grand as the Great War Between Good and Evil. Anxiety rose again, and the lion prince grasped his mane. His breathing intensified.

Everyone here today is going to die because of my stupid actions, and it's all my fault! It's all my fault! Oh, Gods, I'm really going to die after today.

"Prince Wonwoo?"

"Is His Highness okay? He looks...a little anxious."

"Oh, the poor boy..."

"Son?"

Concerned and sympathetic voices caught his attention as he gasped, his chest tight. He looked around the war room, meeting everyone's concerned look. *Oh no. They're all noticing. This is so embarrassing. I have to stop, okay brain? Got it? You can stop now. Go back to prince mode. Please, stop!*

Hakuba was at his side, pressing her snout on the lion prince's shoulder.

"Breathe, Prince Wonwoo," the white horse said soothingly. "You're letting your anxiety get to you again."

The lion prince took in a deep inhale, pressing a paw to his chest. He was able to ground himself and come back to reality in a more peaceful state of mine. He breathed out, feeling his muscles loosen. He lifted up his head. "I'm okay..I'm okay," he said.

The guards didn't appear convinced, not even King Jung-hwa and Queen Cora.

"Please proceed," Hakuba said.

They all listened to Hakuba.

THE PROMISED DYNASTY GETS A SURPRISE

"What really should be important is the safety of Prince Wonwoo," the maned wolf soldier brought up. "They're most definitely going to go after him and will not rest until he's in their grubby grasps. Only our Gods know what they will do to him."

Execute me, Prince Wonwoo said to himself. *What else would they do? Keep me in whatever jail they have to let me rot for the rest of my life? No. They're going to kill me.*

"We'll have our best defense protecting the Prince," a dog soldier said. He directed everyone's attention to the board on the table. He pushed a group of figurines towards one figurine that was supposed to be of Prince Wonwoo while pushing out another group elsewhere. "While everyone is off and fighting the Demoniacal Kingdom, they will protect Prince Wonwoo and ensure no Demoniacal Kingdom member gets through to them."

"Agreed," said the maned wolf soldier. "Let's do a bit of a summary of what is going to happen in the event of an upcoming attack: Battalion 1 will be sent to attack the Demoniacal Kingdom once they strike. They will divide and get into their blind spots as an advantage. The Demoniacal Kingdom is strong, but only in numbers. Fighting one on its own will be easy since they are clumsy. Once we have divided the Demoniacal Kingdom, Battalion 2 will come in from all corners and take out whoever we will have to kill."

The maned wolf soldier paused before continuing. "While the fighting occurs outside, we'll have a group protecting the King, the Queen and the Prince in our secret basement. In case the Demoniacal Kingdom spots them, they will fight them to the death."

The lion king nodded at all the information. "This all sounds very well organized, Rashima," King Jung-hwa told the maned wolf. "I think we will be prepared once the day comes that the Demoniacal Kingdom attack. Have any of you been able to gather intel on a possible date?"

The guards looked at each other with uncertainty. That didn't look too good to Prince Wonwoo. Was there still no information? Nothing!?

That's not good!

Hakuba rested her head on his shoulder, reminding him to control his anxiety.

Man, am I so thankful for you, Hakuba, he said to himself, leaning on her.

A great horned owl soldier raised its wing. "King Titanosaurus had been working all day and all night, preparing his army," it told King Jung-hwa.

"Ah yes, Cornelius. What were you able to gather?" the lion king asked.

The owl, Cornelius, flew on top of the table, gathering everyone's attention.

"He has been ruthlessly shaping up his Kingdom," Cornelius said. "He pushes them through extremes from the crack of dawn until the stars appear at night. But this time, I was able to hear faintly, quote, 'this month shall soon be the time of revenge.'"

THE PROMISED DYNASTY GETS A SURPRISE

Everyone lifted up their heads at once. They murmured to each other.

"So...He's going to attack soon?" Rashima asked.

"Sooner than we think."

"Has he said when exactly this month—"

"KING JUNG-HWA OF THE PROMISED DYNASTY! I SEE KING TITANOSAURUS OF THE DEMONIACAL KINGDOM APPROACHING!"

Prince Wonwoo's heart dropped at the moment the shrill voice of Luta and his meerkat scouts ran up to the war room. Everyone got up at once and stood alert, watching the little critters scuttle in and shriek. Each scout went to their respective masters, and Luta climbed on top of Hakuba's back.

"THE DEMONIACAL KINGDOM IS HERE!" he shrieked, jumping up and down. **"IT'S WAR!!!"**

Prince Wonwoo looked up at the calendar on the wall. His eyes rounded in shock at what month it was. It was July. That month was the same month that the Great War Between Good and Evil also started. Were they preparing all these months in order to attack in that same month? Or was it just a very, VERY strange coincidence?

Please let it be a coincidence!

Although he was trying to keep calm, knowing that the Demoniacal Kingdom was already here didn't help Prince Wonwoo's anxiety. He shrunk, pressing against Hakuba as he breathed heavily. They were coming for him.

The lion king got up, pointing to his soldiers.

"Battalion 1, attack!" he commanded. "Do not wait any further! For the Promised Dynasty!"

There was no hesitation in his father's voice, and it was incredible to hear.

The first group of soldiers, named Battalion 1, immediately rushed out of the room and out of the castle. Prince Wonwoo watched them disappear and instantly heard the sound of battle. It had begun. He winced at every wail and howl from the Promised Dynasty soldiers as they most likely were swarmed by the Demoniacal Kingdom soldiers. His mind can only wonder what was happening to those poor soldiers.

King Jung-hwa continued giving out directions.

"Hakuba! Assemble the guards and rest of the soldiers! Everyone else, get into position! Follow me!"

When King Jung-hwa joined the second battalion, everyone stared shock-eyed at the lion king. Queen Cora got to her paws, staring at him with a gaped jaw. Prince Wonwoo stared at his father. Was the lion king *going to fight with them?*

No... No he can't! Prince Wonwoo shook his head.

Queen Cora reached out to him, grabbing his arm.

"Honey, no! You can't fight!" she said desperately. "King Titanosaurus of the Demoniacal Kingdom will kill you!"

THE PROMISED DYNASTY GETS A SURPRISE

King Jung-hwa looked at Queen Cora with sadness in his eyes. The lion prince could only imagine what he wanted to say. His mouth quivered, but nothing came out. He pulled her into a hug instead, along with Prince Wonwoo. The lion prince felt his fear spike further. His father wasn't going to do what he was thinking. No. No, he couldn't be–

Another cry brought him back to his attention.

It really *was* happening. He grasped his father's neck, burying his face.

There was so much he wanted to say as well, but no words could escape him.

Only silence reigned.

"I love you both so much," King Jung-hwa finally said. "Stay safe." He pushed them to Hakuba and the others. "Take them to the safe cellar at once."

The white horse bowed at once at the lion king and, along with a few guards she gathered, began herding the lion queen and the lion prince towards the basement. Queen Cora tried not to cry but her tears began to run. Prince Wonwoo, shock eyed, looked back. He watched his father nodding to his soldiers before he ran with the second battalion outside the castle.

No...he can't fight, he said. *He can't! He'll be killed!*

Prince Wonwoo gasped, bringing energy back to his frozen state. Pushing Hakuba and the other guards, he tried to run after his father. "Father! FATHER COME BACK!!" he shouted.

Queen Cora called out to him in a horrified tone, reaching out to him.

"Son!"

To no avail. Hakuba whirled around in a heartbeat and grabbed his mane with her teeth, holding onto him. She began dragging him towards the safe cellar. "I'm sorry, Prince Wonwoo," she said through a mouthful of fur. "I have to do this. For your safety and the Queen's."

Prince Wonwoo struggled.

No! No! Let me go!

He couldn't hold in his thoughts and emotions anymore and let out a desperate wail:

"FATHER!!!"

∼

"We can't stay here! We have to save him!"

Within the safe cellar, which was the castle's basement, the lion prince paced side to side. Outside were some guards keeping watch while inside, Hakuba and a select few stood on high alert. Prince Wonwoo couldn't stand the silence, and he only could imagine that the Demoniacal Kingdom was ripping into the Promised Dynasty without mercy. He especially wondered what they were doing to King Jung-hwa. Hakuba tried to comfort him, but he had pushed her away to the point she had left the lion prince on his own but made it clear if he needed someone to talk to, she would be there.

He wanted to scream. He wanted to cry. He wanted to curse Ellowyn and the Gods and the Heavens. Why did he let this happen? Why had he been so stupid to do what he had done? Fate cannot be this cruel if it was meant to be, because Prince Wonwoo refused it to have been fate.

"I know we can't stay, but we have no choice, Wonwoo," Queen Cora said to her son.

"We do!" he shouted back. "We can leave! A-And save Father! Save him before King Titanosaurus of the Demoniacal Kingdom kills him! He is going to die if we don't do something!"

"But they will go after you."

The lion prince huffed. "I don't care! If the Demoniacal Kingdom wants me, so be it I'll sacrifice myself to them and have you guys spared." *If I die...well. At least...I'll know I saved my family and my Dynasty...*

The thought of death made Prince Wonwoo start to panic. His legs shook.

Gods, why am I so weak?

Queen Cora padded up to her son, pulling him into her embrace. "We can't lose you; you're our only heir to the throne. Besides, King Titanosaurus of the Demoniacal Kingdom won't rest until he has both of us dead as well, not just you."

"But..." *But I thought at least, by giving myself up, King Titanosaurus will be a little bit lenient.* He wanted to say that but the words couldn't quite come out. Though, when he thought about it, his mother was right; King Titanosaurus not only blamed him, but he blamed his parents for Princess Okome's death. It wouldn't matter if he died, he would want King Jung-hwa and Queen Cora dead alongside him. There was no way King Titanosaurus would be lenient if the lion prince sacrificed himself.

No Demoniacal Kingdom member had any shred of goodness in them.

They wanted all the Promised Dynasty dead.

"Oh Gods...we're going to die," Prince Wonwoo said.

Queen Cora patted his back softly. "We're not. We will get through this. By Ellowyn's galaxy, I swear on it."

"I wouldn't be certain of that."

The two of them froze. Hakuba and the soldiers pricked their ears up, looking to find the location of the voice. That voice did not come from anyone Prince Wonwoo recognized. When he had looked up to find where the voice was coming from, a pair of gleaming eyes stared back at him. He stared at it for a while, eyes burning from not blinking. The creature leapt at him after a couple of seconds, and the defined form of a tiger was revealed. Time had frozen for everyone in the cellar as they watched the tiger emerge from the darkness. His dark armor revealed himself to be a Demoniacal Kingdom soldier. The lion prince could not get a single breath out when the Demoniacal tiger soldier pinned him down.

THE PROMISED DYNASTY GETS A SURPRISE

"You can pray to your Gods, all you like," the Demoniacal tiger said with a chuckle, "but they won't come down to save you. Not even their pretty little angels."

The lion prince stared in confusion. Where did this Demoniacal tiger come from?? Was he hiding in the basement the whole time? Had King Titanosaurus sent someone into the castle without anyone knowing!? Too many questions ran through Prince Wonwoo's fear-riddled mind but there was no time to find answers; he had to fight this Demoniacal tiger.

"ATTACK!" Hakuba and the guards prepared to attack when the basement doors swung open and Demoniacal Kingdom soldiers dropped in, attacking them. The lion prince glanced up and saw the bodies of the outside Promised Dynasty guards laying motionless, with death sprawled in their bodies. His heart stopped.

They were ambushed.

Prince Wonwoo looked back up at the Demoniacal tiger and pushed up his back paws against the tiger's belly. Able to get his footing when the tiger was shoved off, he tried to run to his mother to protect her, but the Demoniacal tiger pounced again. He clung onto the lion prince's back, claws as big as his sinking into his flesh. He soon sank his large canines into his shoulders, right in the same spot Enky bit into.

"You bastard!" the lion prince roared, reaching a paw behind him to try and claw his eyes out.

"Wonwoo!" He could hear Queen Cora shout. He looked back to where his mother was; she was cornered by the Demoniacal

Kingdom soldiers, stalking up to her like mindless husks. Though he couldn't see their faces, he could only imagine the awful, maniacal grins that stretched out. They were teasing her as they attacked her in random spurts, taking the lion queen by surprise. She swiped at them, but each swipe missed as they jumped back. She looked again to her son with desperation, locking eyes with him. "Wonwoo!"

"Mother!" The lion prince had no second thought and ran straight for the wall. He crushed the Demoniacal tiger between him and the wall. He made sure that the Demoniacal tiger was suffocating and feeling pain. The Demoniacal tiger released his shoulders after minutes of clinging, roaring out a feeble breath. Despite the searing pain shooting from his shoulders, the lion prince made another desperate run for it again towards his mother and the other Demoniacal Kingdom soldiers. He was grabbed by the tail and promptly drug hard on the cold floor. The lion prince tried his best to free himself, digging his claws hard on the stone floor, to no avail. It only made his paws bleed. The Demoniacal tiger then threw him towards the shelves, causing it to crash down on him. Prince Wonwoo felt the sharp wood cut into his skin as debris rained down on him, bruising him and burying him underneath the rubble. The Demoniacal tiger dragged him out of the rubble and pressed a paw to his throat. Seeing how pathetically helpless the lion prince looked, he smirked.

"I never thought I would get my paws on the lion prince of the Promised Dynasty of all animals," the Demoniacal tiger snarled. "It's such an honor."

THE PROMISED DYNASTY GETS A SURPRISE

"P-Please..!" Prince Wonwoo choked out, grabbing on the Demoniacal tiger's arm.

The Demoniacal tiger let out a chuckle and raised a paw, claws unsheathed menacingly. The lion prince widened his eyes, staring unblinkingly at the size of the Demoniacal tiger's claws, before shutting them tight.

This was it.

This is where he would die.

"Get away from my son you evil brute!"

The pressure from his neck was released, and Prince Wonwoo was able to take in a huge breath. He coughed, gingerly rubbing his sore neck. Slowly opening his eyes, he saw his mother having pinned the Demoniacal tiger to the wall. The Demoniacal tiger struggled in Queen Cora's grasp, cursing at her and trying to claw her arm off. The lion prince got up quickly, ignoring the lightheadedness that enveloped his vision for a brief moment.

"Mother!" he shouted with effort.

Queen Cora snapped her head back at him. "Run!" she growled at him. "Run while you still can, Wonwoo!"

The lion prince stared, frozen in place. He looked back at Hakuba and the remaining guards; they were still fighting the soldiers with all their strength. How long would they be able to hold the Demoniacal soldiers? Would it be enough time for Queen Cora to make it along with him? From the looks of Hakuba and the guards, they were growing exhausted.

BEGINNING OF TIME

Prince Wonwoo looked back at his mother, his throat tightening. He didn't want to leave her with these Demoniacal soldiers. She wasn't much of a fighter. She would surely die if he ran now.

"You have to get out of here!" she continued shouting at him. "Save yourself, please! You're our only hope now to the Promised Dynasty! Please, Wonwoo, I am BEGGING you! Before the Demoniacal Kingdom storms in!"

"But-!"

"GO!"

Her roars were cut off by the Demoniacal tiger having freed himself and leaping at her, clamping down his jaws on her throat. She gasped, digging her claws into his shoulders. He stared maniacally at the queen, turning his gaze towards Prince Wonwoo.

The lion prince's heart dropped to his stomach.

NO!

He was not about to lose his mother right about now!

Before he could spring into action, Hakuba noticed the queen in distress, running up and kicking her back legs at the Demoniacal tiger, landing her hooves square on his face. The Demoniacal tiger barely let out a noise of pain as he was caught up by the sudden attack. He had released Queen Cora when he was sent flying to the wall, who let out an awful sounding gasp. The lion prince stared wide-eyed.

"MOTHER!!!"

The white horse turned to Prince Wonwoo and shoved him.

THE PROMISED DYNASTY GETS A SURPRISE

"Go! We'll take care of this!" Hakuba snorted.

"But..." Looking back at his struggling mother one more time, unsure if this would be their last time together, the lion prince ran. *I'm sorry, Mother. I promise you, I will be back; I will avenge my Kingdom!* He shoved himself past the soldiers and out of the basement. Taking a moment to breathe and steady his shaking muscles, he ran down the hallways, his life depending on it. Everything was a blur. He had to focus. He had to get away, run like he was told. Run and never look back.

A voice shouted in the air that he was able to recognize as he ran.

"**YOU FOOLS!** THE PRINCE OF THE PROMISED DYNASTY IS GETTING AWAY! FORGET THE OTHERS! LEAVE THE QUEEN FOR DEAD! GET HIM!!!"

For the Promised Dynasty. I'm sorry, Mother. Father.

Deliberately taking a misstep while backing up, Prince Wonwoo let himself fall off the cliff. He watched the Demoniacal Kingdom soldiers look over the edge, their forms outlined by the shine of Gau's moon, with anger in their eyes burning brighter than the sun. His anxious mind was racing, mainly running with all his past mistakes, but the lion prince was able to find peace in himself knowing he did the right thing. Hopefully, this would let the Demoniacal Kingdom know that he was long gone, taken by Dragon's Wrath, and they would stop attacking the Promised Dynasty. His death would be the end of the war.

Looking at the commander of the army, he made a final glance at him. Prince Wonwoo had managed to run away from the very animal who hated him from the started and wanted him dead:

The wolf prince, Prince Scamander.

In a matter of a second, the lion prince felt his breath knocked out of him as he made the collision with the river.

The river was white from all the frothing produced from the rushing current. Prince Wonwoo couldn't see anything because of the foam. He looked above and around him. He could only see the rocks that settled on the bottom. All lessons and stories Prince Wonwoo learned about Dragon's Wrath were now making sense to him; he knew the river was dangerous, but he didn't think he was going to be this helpless to fight against it.

He tried to hold what little breath he had and let himself tumble down out of sight of the Demoniacal Kingdom, enduring each and every hit from the stones, before fighting a way to get another breath. However, the effort was fruitless as he struggled to gain his composure. His back ached from the collision, rendering his entire body sore. Any movement against the current, Dragon's Wrath slammed back aggressively. His limbs flailed helplessly. He was unable to get his head above the water, which started to concern him. His body was becoming more and more bruised by the forces.

Eventually, Prince Wonwoo felt his chest tighten. He was growing exhausted from holding his breath and losing consciousness. He had to try to get his head out for another breath. He had to try as much as he could. He had to. *Keep fighting!* He kept repeating to himself as he pumped his limbs with fruitless effort. *Keep fighting! Fight it! For the Promised Dynasty!*

Putting up one last attempt to break through the surface, he realized that it was hopeless entirely. He was too weak to make a break for the surface. The waterfall was rapidly approaching, and the current was getting more aggressive. There was nothing he could do.

Despite anxiety setting in, he felt a sudden, strange wave of calm wash over him. He somehow knew it. It almost felt as if Morana herself was holding him, cradling him and reassuring him that it was all going to be okay.

You're telling me to let go... aren't you, Morana? He thought to himself, watching his surroundings darken.

He wasn't sure if he was seeing things or if it was real, but he soon saw ethereal white eyes materializing in a gentle glow and staring at him with a smile as soft as his mother's. The white outline of a paw extended out to him, beckoning him. He weakly reached out to the tender dim figure. *I understand...I don't have to fight anymore. It's already exhausting to keep fighting a battle I can't win... Death will comfort me until I reach the Heavens.*

He closed his eyes.

Goodbye, Father. Mother. The Promised Dynasty. I love you all.

Giving in to this calm, he allowed himself to relax. He already felt comforting paws embracing his body. Morana had his life now, ready to take his spirit out of his body and to Okalani and Azrael. The river kept pounding into him, tossing his body against the rocks. There was no more pain. It was as if the Goddess of Death was cutting off his senses so he could die in peace. That was kind of the Goddess to do.

Bubbles of remaining air he held in escaped his mouth. He now only had a short time left.

The last thing the lion prince heard was the muffled roars of the river and the waterfall. Along with an unusual noise. One that was certainly not natural to the river. First growing loud before fading away into silence.

Tick. Tock.

Tick. Tock...

...

CHAPTER 9
PRESERVING THE GOOD NAME OF ELLOWYN

~ *In the eyes of the King of the Promised Dynasty...* ~
~ *July in Terra Cycle 1118 B.E.* ~

His final interaction with his family pained his heart as he ran out with the battalion.

"Honey, no! You can't fight! King Titanosaurus of the Demoniacal Kingdom will kill you!"

"I love you both so much."

"FATHER!!!"

Their words were clear as day, reverberating in his skull. All around him, the Demoniacal Kingdom swarmed his beloved members as soon as they ran down the stairs, mercilessly killing them off. There was nothing but death and fighting all around

King Jung-hwa. He felt sick to his stomach at the sight and sounds. The cruelty the Demoniacal Kingdom had to pull off to enact such a massacre was beyond him. He had to force himself to stoop to their level, lashing out and killing anyone who attacked him and his battalion. He snapped necks, he tore open major wounds, he did it all. This was the worst part for him, being the one to end a life by his own paws. *Great Ellowyn, forgive me,* he silently prayed after he struck down a Demoniacal soldier. *They brought this on themselves, so I am absolved from the crimes.*

Continuing to clear away the attackers, he could still hear the pained screams of his son as his guards took him and his wife away to the safe cellar. They mixed with the cries of the soldiers. They were shrill and desperate until they faded away into silence. He knew it was for the best; he could not have them in this fight, especially not Prince Wonwoo.

Oh my beloved son, the lion king lamented to himself.

He still remembered the ill-fated day his son came home covered in blood and tears, holding onto Hakuba for dear life. He and Queen Cora were understandably concerned and ran to him at the first chance. Within his eyes, King Jung-hwa could see the fear and shock as they both asked what was wrong. It took him a while to tell them what had happened, but he could hear his pitiful wails to them on how he screwed everything up once he did explain and how he was going to be the one responsible for another war impending. King Jung-hwa consoled his son the best he could. There was no way he could berate his son on something that he had no control over. Why would he have berated him? Despite the crime he had committed, King Jung-hwa believed in fair judgement, and he knew the Demoniacal Kingdom had done something for his son to do something such as that. Yelling at him for something he had been pushed to do would have only worsened the situation.

It was hard to close his eyes, for he could only see his wife and son, their faces littered with fear and misery. He could only reach out to them in his mind's eye, imagining their warm embraces.

I love you both so much. Take care of each other until I return.

Another death shriek brought him back to his senses. He whipped around, staring at his soldier who had tackled a Demoniacal soldier that was sneaking up on the King and instantly killed it. Thanking his soldier, he focused on the situation unfolding, looking for the wolf king to confront directly. That was his goal right now, not slaughtering these soldiers. It was difficult locating him in the sea of Demoniacal soldiers, but once he took care of them, he finally met eye to eye with King Titanosaurus. He dared not take his eyes off King Titanosaurus.

The black wolf king took notice of the lion king after taunting his enemy underneath his paws–a coyote–and smiled, exposing his bloodied teeth.

"King Jung-hwa of the Promised Dynasty," King Titanosaurus proclaimed, moving himself away from the Promised coyote that fled at the first chance it got. "Great of *you* to show up. Where is that lowly excuse of your son? We've got business to handle."

King Jung-hwa flicked his tail. "You would think I'd give up my son to the likes of your Kingdom?" he asked defensively. "You'd have to think twice if you think I'd give in that easily. I did it once, I'll never let that happen again. I know your Kingdom, King Titanosaurus of the Demoniacal Kingdom. You did something that made my son snap."

"Defending a murderer?" The wolf king raised an eyebrow. "That's unlike you, King Jung-hwa of the Promised Dynasty."

The lion king bristled at the word. "He is not a murderer."

The wolf king appeared offended. "Not a murderer? Do you hear yourself right now!? He killed my daughter in cold blood. You cannot deny that he willingly struck her down!"

King Jung-hwa stood there in silence for a moment. Prince Wonwoo had told him how he had been provoked by the Demoniacal guards of the princess, and how she had tried to stop them but was caught in the crossfire. There was no way that could have been his fault. Sure, he had done the blow, but that did not mean he attacked and willingly murdered Princess Okome. He put himself in that situation after his son had told him the events. He never pictured himself killing the love of his life intentionally, and he never could picture his son, the Prince of the Promised Dynasty, intentionally killing his betrothed.

The lion king flattened his ears against his head.

"I believe in second chances."

The wolf king frowned, his fur spiking and puffing out while he snarled at King Jung-hwa. His paws were visibly twitching, his large claws flexing. King Jung-hwa, sensing the wolf king's increasing anger, prepared himself for the moment King

Titanosaurus would lunge at him. He was ready. He could take him on.

King Titanosaurus looked to the side before grinning.

"How ironic of your Dynasty, King Jung-hwa of the Promised Dynasty," he scoffed. "All this preaching and goodwill for hundreds of terra cycles and condemning evil doers and all things vile to the good of your Gods, yet you allow a *murderer* roam free in the Promised Dynasty without locking him up and punishing him. A sin far worse than any petty crime if you think about it. Boy, I bet your *Almighty Creator* is pleased right about now as they roll in their grave." His smirk grew wider. "What was their name again? Ellie?"

King Jung-hwa widened his eyes. How dare the wolf king insult their Creator! Everyone in the Promised Dynasty knew not to speak ill will of the Gods and the Heavens, especially Ellowyn. They owed their lives to Ellowyn, *every creature* gave their thanks for her saving the Universe and allowing life to strive. That was something the Demoniacal Kingdom was lacking after willingly abandoning them. In an instant, he charged at King Titanosaurus, large paws crashing down on his chest. He was done playing along, he was *done* dealing with such a nuisance. The wolf king collapsed to the ground with a hard thump.

"Oh? Did I hit a sore nerve?" the wolf king sneered.

"No one dares to slander the good name of the Great *Ellowyn!*" the lion king roared. "And no one shall dare paint my son in a bad light for something he didn't commit intentionally! This has gone on for far too long, King Titanosaurus of the Demoniacal Kingdom! I'm done dealing with it in a peaceful manner. It's time I take action and end such cruel opposition as I should have done a long time ago."

He went for his exposed throat, intent on finally putting an end to King Titanosaurus's reign, only to miss when the wolf king squirmed himself out the way. He made a run for the castle, which prompted a fight between the two kings that hadn't been seen in terra cycles. King Jung-hwa latched onto King Titanosaurus's back to try and knock him down. The wolf king threw him off and snapped his jaws near the lion king. He was able to get away from the wolf king as he lunged back. He was intimidated that his teeth were just as large as his claws. The wolf king bared his teeth in a mocking smile.

"I knew you'd eventually snap! Just like how your son did!"

The lion king attacked again, but he missed. King Titanosaurus rolled to the side, and he lashed out his large claws against the lion king's shoulder, a sharp stinging pain putting a temporary halt on his attack. King Jung-hwa roared in pain, staggering back. Right at that moment, King Titanosaurus took the opportunity to trip the lion king and knock him down.

The impact of his head colliding with the ground left King Jung-hwa dazed. He looked up weakly at the wolf king, who was stalking up to him in a determined stride; he knew his age would get to him one way or another. He was older than King Titanosaurus, 3 terra cycles older, so he hadn't expected to be in prime condition when he had rushed out to the battlefield.

King Titanosaurus leaned his head closer to King Jung-hwa's, baring his canines. "Nice try, but no."

"At least," King Jung-hwa coughed, "it was an attempt."

"A very pitiful attempt if you ask me."

The lion king spat. "It was all for the preservation of the Great *Ellowyn!*"

The wolf king shook his head, reaching out his paw to slam the lion king's head further on the ground. "How sad. After all these terra cycles, you guys never change with your Mighty and All Powerful Creator who did nothing but cause suffering for us all. How pathetic is it to be this blissfully ignorant?"

"Says the ones who willingly defied Her instead of listening and following in Her ways."

"You'll never see the ways of your cult ruining everyone."

The lion king snarled, only to be interrupted by another force shoving his face down.

"Since you're in my way and won't budge a single muscle, how about I just end your miserable, brainwashed life?" he asked. "Tell me: Any last words for me? Or rather yet, any final *prayers* you got for yourself?"

The lion king had no last words. Even if he did, he wasn't going to tell them to his enemy of all creatures. He closed his eyes, accepting his fate as the wolf king neared.

Queen Cora. Prince Wonwoo. Please, forgive me. Know that I loved you both so much with all my heart. I will see you both soon–

"THEY'VE INTERCEPTED THE CASTLE!!"

He instantly snapped open his eyes upon hearing that cry from the meerkats. King Titanosaurus was frozen just a few inches away from his throat, his jaws salivating. The lion king moved his head to see chaos just outside the doors of the castle.

No.

"THEY'RE HEADED FOR THE SAFE CELLAR!"

"QUICK! PROTECT THE QUEEN AND THE PRINCE FROM THOSE SAVAGES!!"

No.

His mind once again immediately went to two important creatures that were there.

Queen Cora. Prince Wonwoo.

He looked back at King Titanosaurus, growling. The wolf king must have gotten some intel on where the safe cellar was and how to enter without getting caught. How else would any Demoniacal member know about the safe cellar? Was this the plan all along? Distract him, possibly kill him and his wife, and get to their son? Had King Titanosaurus anticipated his confrontation? A million questions ran through his head. His brain boiled and practically exploded in fury.

He sliced his claws across the wolf king's face, causing blood to spray around him. He ignored the drops that tapped his muzzle as he roared and pushed the wolf king off him. It was impressive to anyone if they managed to get the burly wolf king off of them.

Impressive in the fact that no one *(except for Prince Livyatan, but no one knows this of course)* could push King Titanosaurus and knock him down. King Jung-hwa had been the first and only one to do so for the first time in a long while and actually survive. But that was because adrenaline had forced throughout his veins and body and helped him gain the strength he needed to get up.

While King Titanosaurus was recovering from his wounds, the lion king turned tail and made his way to the castle. He realized he should have taken that opportunity to pin the wolf king down and end his reign, but he was better than that. Besides, there was a more important matter he had to tend to. He was stopped a few times by ambushes from the Demoniacal soldiers, but he cut down all of them who stood in his way.

As he fought the soldiers, he heard something heartbreaking.

"SOMEONE GET THE DOCTORS! QUEEN CORA IS WOUNDED AND BLEEDING HEAVILY!"

No. He felt his face draining at such news. *No no no no. No!* "Queen Cora!" he shouted. "Prince Wonwoo!"

"You're just too late, King Jung-hwa of the Promised Dynasty."

Massive paws pressed against his back and claws dug into his neck before he had the chance to lunge towards the safe cellar. Twisting his head, the wolf king once again filled his sight. His eyes were wide with manic that sprawled across his pupils and grinned like a madman.

"I wasn't expecting this turn of events, but life is just full of surprises. So, I deliver one to you right now before you die: surprise! My son's after your son as we speak," he said.

The evidence was all too apparent now for the lion king. This attack, this first intrusion on the Promised Dynasty, was all a ruse just so King Titanosaurus's secret battalion could sneak into the castle and kill Queen Cora and kidnap Prince Wonwoo. He knew that the prince was of their highest priority, so they had to find a distraction for the King and Queen to temporarily forget about their son.

"I knew that you were going to distract me from getting your son, so I got spies to scope out your castle and got my son to sneak in without detection."

King Jung-hwa clenched his paws on the ground below him.

"What have you done to my wife!?" King Jung-hwa growled. "WHO DID YOU SEND AFTER THEM!?"

"You ask about your wife, but not about your son? Bit ironic and a shame. Now, where was I? Oh yes: Killing you!"

Before King Jung-hwa could retaliate, a strong force of impact struck his head once again. King Titanosaurus had taken a big swing to render the lion king unconscious, and he struck him hard in his temple. The pain was quick before it dulled into sheer agony that enveloped his entire head. His sight began to swim as stars clouded his surroundings. He could hear the wolf king's laughter filling his fuzzing hearing. The lion king groaned, trying to fight off the stabbing headache that was attacking him. He fell back down, his body aching.

No. No! I won't allow this! He forced himself to stand up against the pressure, staggering. *I have to...save them. I have to save them! Just another step.*

The wolf king lightly tapped his shoulder to knock the lion king off his feet. Trying all he could to stay up, he collapsed, feeling his brain spin in place. He was pinned by the back of his neck, large claws making him bleed.

"Goodbye, King Jung-hwa of the Promised Dynasty!" King Titanosaurus gleefully cheered. "I'll take good care of your son and your Dynasty."

NO!

This couldn't be it. He had to fight back!

In his blurring vision, he managed to catch a glimpse of a particular creature. Someone that was easily recognizable by his poofed out mane that came in rounds. He was being chased by a group of Demoniacal soldiers, along with a particular dark blue-furred wolf layered in armory.

So that's how they snuck you in, you little rat? He growled in his head. *You pretended... Why are you doing this?*

He watched them disappear out the door.

Prince Wonwoo... Son. Please... Run, run far as you can. Don't let them catch you. I believe in you.

He looked back to the safe cellar one last time. Hakuba had emerged looking for reinforcements to help with the Queen and locked eyes with King Titanosaurus when she saw King Jung-hwa sprawled on the ground barely conscious. She charged straight for him and flailed her hooves at him, neighing out harshly. The wolf king was quick to dodge her attacks, albeit barely, and fled outside, where she gave chase.

"His Majesty is also down! Someone help him!" he had heard Hakuba shrill before she faded away.

Although the lion king was in massive agony, he managed to smile warmly. A sense of peace flooded his brain as he accepted the reality of the situation. He knew his time had been coming to an end, but he didn't expect to go out like this. He was at least happy he could go out protecting his son, his only surviving child.

He's going to be alright, he thought. *My boy is strong. No one can take him down. I'm so proud of you, Prince Wonwoo.*

His eyelids began to sink as soon as one of the doctors approached him in a hurry.

...Queen Cora, my beloved..I will await you in Purgatory. We will see each other again... Our son will be safe...and he will return one day to claim what is rightfully his. My beloved...Cora...

All went dark for the lion king of the Promised Dynasty.

CHAPTER 10
IT WAS ALL A FAKE OUT! PRINCE WONWOO MIRACULOUSLY LIVES

~ A few hours later... ~
~ July in Terra Cycle 1118 B.E. ~

The air was ice-cold.

There was only silence before the lion prince found himself slowly waking up from unconsciousness. "Ughhh..." Prince Wonwoo could only hear the blood rushing in his ears from his pounding heart. It throbbed painfully against him, like an annoying migraine, and he was able to hear every single pulse that his heart generated. He wasn't sure whether to feel intrigued or terrified at this. The chill from the cold air whisked by, making his bones shiver and startling him awake. He looked around curiously, but his blurry vision revealed nothing to him. He squinted.

IT WAS ALL A FAKE OUT! PRINCE WONWOO MIRACULOUSLY LIVES

Is he alive? Is this Heaven? Had he already been judged by Okalani and Azrael? Was he still in Purgatory?

His brain began to hurt from the millions of racing thoughts that came to him. He groaned, rubbing his head. *Shut up, brain, you're not helping.* When he flared his nose wide to take a breath in, he was met with a coughing spell that he thought would last forever. Water spilled out of the lion prince's mouth.

If he was dead, he wouldn't have been hacking this much.

All senses finally came back to him after he coughed out all the water. The first thing he felt was the tightness of his throat, followed by a full body ache that kept him on the ground for a couple more minutes. Every breath he took stung him and made his throat tighten more. The lion prince slowly got to his paws and shook his fur dry as best as he could, despite feeling weak and dizzy. Droplets flew off his soaken fur onto the grass.

Ugh..Gods, how long was I out for? Prince Wonwoo questioned, placing a paw on his pounding head. *My entire body hurts like crazy.* He looked at his surroundings, his vision now having improved. His confusion furthered.

Am I...still in Divine Kingfisher Woods?

It still looked like Divine Kingfisher Woods, though he didn't know this area of the forest. This was beyond where he would have known. He looked around his body then he sighed. Yep. He was still alive. Morana had not taken him. He glanced behind him at the river; this end of the ravine was surprisingly calm amidst the waterfall. He could still hear the rushing of Dragon's Wrath from afar. Somehow, the lion prince had survived his fall and struggle with Dragon's Wrath. He smirked with pride.

I better be in the history scrolls and books in the future for being the first individual to survive Dragon's Wrath!

He brushed his disheveled mane, picking out debris that stuck on him, before he noticed his paw was bloodied. Upon examination, he discovered there was a deep cut starting from his paw pad down to his wrist that exposed muscles and tendons.

Huh. I wonder how I got that, he wondered, tilting his head. *Probably cut myself on a sharp rock while I was being tossed by the currents without knowing it.*

He watched the blood flow at a steady pace.

...Why am I not feeling any pain?

His senses have come back, so why was his wound not stinging right about now? The lion prince curiously stretched out his toes to see if he could get a reaction but still felt nothing. He saw the muscles and tendons move, which both unnerved and fascinated him. He then decided to poke around the wound. Nothing. He blinked.

Oh my Gods... I must be invincible!

After staring and continuously poking at the open wound for a few more minutes, an agonizing pain finally seared through him. Prince Wonwoo's jaw snapped open, wanting to scream but no sound emerged. It was unlike any pain he experienced before. It easily ruled out a stabbing migraine by a loooooong shot. He clenched his teeth, eyes bulging. *Oh Gods! Oh **G O D S**! Ow, ow ow ow ow!! Oh great Ellowyn, this is absolutely horrendous! Ahhhh!!* Crippled from the debilitating pain, he grasped his wrist tightly and raised his head to the sky.

"MOTHERFUCKER!!!"

Okay. I'm not invincible. I'm just an idiot.

After 2 hours of rest, Prince Wonwoo decided to move from the riverbank and journey out of Divine Kingfisher Woods.

He knew for certain he could not return to his Dynasty for the Demoniacal Kingdom would be searching for him. He knew they would not rest until they captured him. It made him wonder how long the Demoniacal Kingdom would truly go on until they found some evidence of him or even find him physically. Would this war, a war over him, continue forever?

The lion prince shook his head. Only Ziton, the God of Destruction and War, would know. He looked back before looking ahead, continuing to leave his Dynasty behind. It was probably for the best.

He now knew the full extent of his injury; he could barely walk well, each step excruciating enough to make even the softest of pressure feel like torture. He rested by a tree to give it a break. He winced from the flare up of his nerves. It was too much pain to even limp. He could only go so far before his wound screamed at him to just stop. He was lucky enough to have basic knowledge for bleeding wounds when he found some cobwebs hanging by trees. He gathered a bunch in his good paw, puffing away any spiders that lingered on with a sharp breath, and wrapped them around his paw. He knew this wouldn't be enough. He needed medical attention, especially since the fact he could feel an infection seeping in from how warm and tender the area around the wound was.

I wish you were here, Carmentis, he thought to himself, thinking about the experienced capybara doctor.

As soon as he finished wrapping, a loud growl was heard. The lion prince felt a shiver run down his spine. He stood up again and looked around before it sounded again. What creature was making that sound? Did someone from he Demoniacal Kingdom find him?

Another growl emerged. Something was off about it. *Wait a minute.*

Blinking, he looked down.

Ahhh!

He was just getting hungry.

He lifted up his head, letting his tongue bathe in the scents of the forest. He tried to whiff out any indication of prey. Preferably something large to fill his stomach. Divine Kingfisher Woods did have some fair share of prey of all sizes.

As his luck had it, he managed to pick up the scent of a deer herd nearby. Immediately going into stealth mode, Prince Wonwoo limped carefully to the deer herd. It had been so long since he hunted, since he had been used to being fed. But he knew now, out in the wild, no one was going to feed him. He remembered the basics of hunting. He made sure to keep himself light on his paws. He slinked into the bushes, peeked through and watched intently; the herd was grazing on the ground, their ears and tail flicking. The deer in this herd were all does, not a stag in sight, and of course, there were fawns nearby. Some nursed by their mothers and others laid on the ground floor. Prince Wonwoo frowned sadly but he shook his head. No time to question. He had to do what he needed to survive. Any wild animal would know that. But the thought of killing a fawn or the mother of a fawn made him sick. Maybe he could sniff out a doe that doesn't have a fawn.

He found that doe, and he thanked the Gods. That doe, with a reddish-brown pelt and pure white belly, was feasting on a patch of grass. She seemed far apart from the herd, minding her own business. She was at peace, her eyes closed as she lazily munched on every stalk of grass. The lion prince bunched his muscles. His eyes narrowed.

Please, Gods, help me succeed in catching this doe.

After waiting for the doe to come within a few feet of him, he leapt. The other deer lifted up their heads in shock at the sight of Prince Wonwoo and began to run, their tails erect as they cried out a warning call. The fawns caught wind and chased after their mothers, wailing in fear. The doe Prince Wonwoo targeted had no chance of running, for the lion prince clamped down on her

BEGINNING OF TIME

back and tackled her to the ground. She let out one cry for help. He swiftly made his way to her exposed throat once he had secured her and sank his fangs deep, pressing a paw over her nostrils.

Warm, fresh blood gushed into his mouth, immediately kicking off his gag reflexes. He did his best to suppress the feeling of nausea and kept his jaws firmly clamped. The doe kicked and bucked, trying to get Prince Wonwoo off him. He winced everytime the doe managed to land her hooves square on his sore body, but he held on. He couldn't give up now. He bit down harder on her throat, and he waited for her to suffocate.

Come on, he begged. *Please. I'm so sorry, but I can't hold on much longer. Please. Just die already so I can eat. Please.*

What seemed like hours to the lion prince was only a few minutes, and the doe was finally dead, her fear-ridden eyes glazing over. Her body gave one last jerk before she went still, a cold breeze chilling them both. The lion prince let go of her throat at last, breathing heavily. Getting to his paws, he bowed at her. *Thank you for your sacrifice, may Morana take you in her loving embrace and hopefully be blessed by Okalani,* he prayed before he laid down and tore into her belly. It had been a long time since he had raw meat, so long, he had initially gagged when he took his first bite into the still warm flesh. He got over those reflexes slowly and ate what he could.

After consuming his fill, he got up, bowed again at her half-eaten corpse, and walked away. He could hear the crows and ravens descending, having scented the lion prince's kill. He picked up his

IT WAS ALL A FAKE OUT! PRINCE WONWOO MIRACULOUSLY LIVES

pace once he heard them cawing away; not only did corvids have a reputation for excellent memory, but they were normally associated with the Demoniacal Kingdom. He couldn't risk having one of them spotting him and possibly report his location.

He ran as far as he could, deeper until there was nothing left around him. Once the caws of the crows and ravens had faded out, he continued at a slow pace. Nervously, he glanced back just to breathe out a sigh of relief at the fact none of them were chasing him. The lion prince had found himself in an abandoned, dilapidated cave after hours searching for another resting place. He hadn't known how massive Divine Kingfisher Woods was. He looked to the sky, observing what time it was. The sun was slowly setting, painting the skies with a dark orange. It was now Dagny's Rest. Prince Wonwoo cleared out any lingering leaves and twigs that were littered everywhere, slapping on the walls to stabilize itself. He dragged in some fresh moss he scouted to use as bedding and circled on it. He laid down and placed his paws in front of his chin.

He had to leave. But where could he go? Where could he start? The land had only been discovered as much as they were able to discover the ocean. Just a tiny percent. It was hopeless.

"Are there really other Kingdoms other than the Promised Dynasty and the Demoniacal Kingdom?"

The voice of his younger self echoed in his mind.

"Not Kingdoms, son," his father's voice answered. "Clans. Some animals who did not want to choose either Kingdoms after the Great War moved on and made their own groups called clans. We keep records on those we

manage to get into contact with just so we can see where they've gone with their progress."

"WOW! How many clans are there!?"

"We don't know. I've only met a few, and your grandfather has met a few as well. But we rarely have proper contact due to how far they live."

"Woahhhhh! I hope I can see these other clans someday!"

The lion king laughed, resting his paw on his son's head. "I'm sure you will someday, son. It will be one of your duties as King of the Promised Dynasty to make sure these other clans can be trusted allies."

He perked up.

That's it!

Prince Wonwoo could seek out the other clans in the land. They would be of help for sure!

Oh, wait.

How much help would they be? He didn't know anything about them, and they most likely don't know about him. He would be a stranger to them, an intruder perhaps, and they would attack him without letting him have the chance to speak. Moreover, if they found out about his crimes, that would be even worse for him. That would definitely become headlines all throughout the land.

Prince of the Promised Dynasty responsible for the death of the most sweetest and innocent Princess from an evil Kingdom. Even if she came from the most horrific of places, murder was a crime far worse than sin itself.

He laid back down in defeat.

No. I can't make myself known to anyone. I have to take matters into my own paws.

Letting out a massive yawn, he let his muscles relax and allowed sleep to overtake him.

CHAPTER 11

THE OUTLAW PRINCE DEALS WITH...WELL, BEING AN OUTLAW

~ 4 weeks later... ~
~ July in Terra Cycle 1118 B.E. ~

He wasn't going to run away.

Prince Wonwoo managed to get himself out of Divine Kingfisher Woods and trek more up north to lands unknown. The unfamiliar territories meant he had to take a break longer just so he could figure out where he was going. It had been weeks, 4 weeks to be exact, and Prince Wonwoo started to get more exhausted by each day. Dagny's sun was pounding on his back, leaving him weak. He remembered of the other smaller clans besides the Promised Dynasty and the Demoniacal Kingdom he learned of from his Father. He knew they wouldn't be of much help, but he

THE OUTLAW PRINCE DEALS WITH...WELL, BEING AN OUTLAW

came up with a plan: in one of these smaller clans he came across, he would talk to them about only staying a few days to recover at least until he regained his strength–physically and mentally–to head back to the Promised Dynasty.

In fact, he knew of one clan he could camp out in. It was a clan his Father had mentioned were great allies with the Promised Dynasty. A clan that existed by the ocean. It was perfect for Prince Wonwoo. He would be far away where no one would find him. The conditions would wash away his scent. It was just perfect.

As he continued more north, the sounds of the ocean caught his drifting attention. It crashed in an unsteady rhythm. Was he already nearing the edge of the land? Curiosity piqued, he ran after the sound. He never experienced the ocean before. He only heard about it via stories and history lessons. It was one of those stories that really intrigued the young lion prince. Above him, the shrill cries of seagulls pierced his ears. He had rarely seen or met any seagulls. They were the ones that would be an omen of an incoming storm. No matter how much anyone would try and talk to one, it would vanish in the horizon, never to be seen again. They were too feisty and wary to trust anyone. He looked up at the flock as he ran, watching their gray and white forms floating in the sky. A few peeked down at him, but they ignored him since he had no food with him that they could snatch from him with their grubby sharp beaks.

The sound of the ocean intensified as he got closer. His heart raced in excitement as he bounded faster. Close. He was so close, he could practically touch it. After everything that had happened, he needed this rush of excitement. Prince Wonwoo finally neared the edge of the cliff and stopped just in the nick of time. He looked down cautiously. The ocean was like a massive lake, a huge body of water deep blue as Prince Scamander's fur seemingly stretching for miles and miles on end. Prince Wonwoo blinked.

Legend has it that Wuxjun created the ocean; according to the tale, Lavian had been extremely mad one day, and he tore the earth that he had gracefully created as a result of his rage. These would eventually be the first documented recordings of Lavian's Rage. Though it wasn't clear why Lavian was so angry, it was speculated that Ziton had some play in it, as evidence from archeologists found old earth with so much damage to them that only Ziton could lay siege. They proposed a theory that Ziton played cruel tricks on Lavian, destroying Lavian's land just for a reaction. That was a whole different story.

Wuxjun attempted to calm his brother down, but the enraged bull God would not listen to reason. He knew he could not physically stop his massive, muscular brother, but he knew he could not allow him to destroy the land in such a manner. So the Asian dragon God looked to their mother, the Creator Ellowyn, for help and was gifted clouds once he finished airing his grievances. When asked why clouds, Ellowyn simply said: "Have your brother cry into them. They will soothe his ailing heart and heal the land." Wuxjun did as Ellowyn told him and used these clouds to collect his brother's tears; soon enough, Lavian's anger subsided overtime as his crying helped him vent without being destructive. There, Ellowyn was able to make Lavian and Ziton see eye to eye and finally make peace. Wuxjun then was able to release Lavian's tears back onto the Earth to heal the damages he had caused, where it rained for many terra cycles, giving rise to what would be the ocean today.

In the distance, a massive humpback whale had breached, impressing the lion prince. He watched the massive sea animal rise out the water, fins outstretched, then crash back into the water. His attention diverted from the whale and towards the waves. It roared louder than Dragon's Wrath. The waves crashed into the side of the cliffside so aggressively, Prince Wonwoo started to fear that it would soon send the whole land collapsing into the massive blue void. He backed up. He lifted up his head and took a deep breath. This was nice, just the right place to camp in-

"Egh!" The salty taste of the ocean stung his tongue, and he instantly gagged. He spat as if he ate expired food. "Ewwwwww, ew ew ew ewww! E W! OH, that's so gross!"

"Never been near the ocean I presume?"

The random voice startled him. He turned around and saw a small polar bear approaching him. His heart raced; polar bears were fearsome creatures, beasts who had no hesitation to kill. However, this polar bear didn't seem at all threatening in her approach. It was small, a female based on her size.

But she was also an unusual looking polar bear. Yes, she was white and appeared like, well, a regular polar bear, but she appeared to have light brown front legs and tinges of dark brown scattered on her body. Prince Wonwoo wrinkled his eyebrows. What kind of polar bear would have brown on their pure white fur? Was she a hybrid like Prince Scamander and his family?

"No, I haven't," Prince Wonwoo answered her question, watching her sit down. He eased up on her after he sensed that she would not be a threat. "This is my first time coming here."

"First time?" the polar bear asked.

"Mhm. I live...more inland." It was hard for him not to reveal where he lived. He had to bite his tongue.

"Yeah, you definitely look like an inlander," the polar bear said snarkily. "And the smell of one."

"Oh how rude, that's not how you introduce yourself to someone," Prince Wonwoo said sarcastically, prompting a laugh out of her.

"Sorryyy. Korikuma. Now tell me: Which clan are you from?"

The lion prince initially opened his mouth. Reality suddenly hit him, and the words were stuck in his throat. He began to stutter.

"I'm uh- From the...uh-"

Does she not know who I am? Prince Wonwoo asked internally, his ears flattening. *Am I not common around these parts? Should I tell her? What if she finds out what I've done? Oh Gods I'm looking like a complete idiot right now, stop it!*

The polar bear looked at him expectantly, her eyes radiating only confusion and curiosity.

THE OUTLAW PRINCE DEALS WITH...WELL, BEING AN OUTLAW

...Well, she isn't hostile. Nor does she look like she would reveal me. I could tell her. Right?

The confidence in Prince Wonwoo returned to him. "I'm from the—"

"Korikuma!"

The lion prince yelped at the booming voice and shrinked. There goes his confidence. Approaching the two was a large, and Prince Wonwoo meant LARGE, polar bear with prominent scars across her muzzle and face. There were also more scars littering all over her body, which indicated some kind of war she had gone through. Her tiny black eyes only radiated displeasure and murderous intent. Now the rhyme about bears made sense. Especially the one on the polar bear.

If it's white, say goodnight.

He crouched, lowering his head and trying to make himself small. He hoped this would at least show her that he meant no harm. He whimpered.

Please don't kill me, please don't kill me, he repeated to himself.

Korikuma sighed with indignation. "Yes, Mother?" she asked.

The lion prince blinked rapidly. That large, battle-scarred polar bear was her mother? That was even worse!

"What are you doing with an inlander?" she growled, staring at Prince Wonwoo. "You know they can't be trusted. We've been over this."

The lion prince shrunk further in fear, unable to escape her hot breath beating him down. His body told him to run, but he couldn't. His legs were solid like boulders, and a lump welled in his throat that he couldn't swallow. He really hated having anxiety.

I don't mean any harm, he said to himself. *I wasn't going to harm your daughter nor did I plan on hurting her in any way, that's a promise.*

"I was just making conversation with him," Korikuma said. "It's not like he was doing anything."

"Well he could have done something! What would have happened to you if I had not found you? What if he kidnapped you? By the Gods! You have to be better than this, Korikuma! One day I won't be around to protect you anymore."

Prince Wonwoo saw within Korikuma's face the same irritation Princess Okome had when she found out the guards had been sent by her brother. It softened his fear.

"Mother," the small polar bear said, "not all inlanders are as bad as–"

"We don't mention his name!" the polar bear roared, roughly grabbing her daughter by her ears. "We do not mention him at all! Ever! We're leaving!" She bared her teeth at Prince Wonwoo. "I suggest you get out of here, inlander, if you know what's good for you."

The lion prince stared, unblinking. He quickly bowed at her, trying his best to still be friendly. He could still feel her presence

THE OUTLAW PRINCE DEALS WITH...WELL, BEING AN OUTLAW

looming over him for a while longer before she finally decided to leave with her daughter.

"Wait, Mother!" Korikuma protested.

"We're done here!"

"But–!"

The young polar bear's words were cut off as her mother dragged her off in a rush. Prince Wonwoo lifted himself up from the ground and looked after the two bears. So much for making a new friend who could have helped him. He followed quickly where they went and soon saw a town appear in his eyesight. He lifted up his head.

A town obviously meant civilization! But this particular one stuck out by the fact it was by the ocean. That had to be the clan he was thinking about!

Waiting for the massive polar bear to disappear, Prince Wonwoo headed to where the town was. He climbed down the cliffside, careful not to tumble and hurt himself more.

When he approached the gates, he was shocked by how welcoming the guards were. They waved at him like he was a regular.

"Welcome to the Shell Clan, traveler!"

The Shell Clan.

Prince Wonwoo tipped his head. This was the clan.

"Excuse me, I don't mean to be a bother," he spoke to the guards, "but I'm just in desperate need to rest for probably a few couple days. May I be so kind as to seek sanctuary in your clan?"

"Oh! You can speak to our leader about that!" one of the guards, a seal, said, raising a flipper.

"Oh- Uh- Who would your King be?" Prince Wonwoo asked. "Or Queen?"

The seal tipped their head in confusion. "What? We don't call our leaders by either of those titles! It's just Shell Broken Savaria!"

"Oh. I see." *Uhm, who?* He definitely never heard of her before. Had his Father not met her when he visited?

"She will gladly show you around the Shell Clan! You can just go on ahead and meet her; she loves meeting travelers like you!"

"Ah. Okay. Thank you kindly." *That still didn't really answer my question. I guess I'll just...figure it out when I get in.*

Prince Wonwoo bowed at the guards then entered the Shell Clan. Passing by the gates felt strange to him. It was as if he was coming back to the Promised Dynasty. He looked around the clan with wide eyes.

It was a nice little beach town. Small homes made of mud and twigs and businesses strewn the streets along with tall palm trees that swayed in the wind. Prince Wonwoo studied his surroundings as he walked the streets. This town appeared more olden, as if it were an old cowboy kind of village. Sand covered the streets, as expected, but Prince Wonwoo didn't mind. It felt interesting, far different from grass or mud.

THE OUTLAW PRINCE DEALS WITH...WELL, BEING AN OUTLAW

Looking around him, the lion prince noticed a familiar pattern with the clan members; majority of them were animals adapted for the sea, or animals that were purely sea animals. He saw seals, sea lions, otters, and so on and so forth. There were some canines and a few cats that walked about, most of them not residents. They were probably here on business deals for their respective clans.

Prince Wonwoo was taken by the scent of the seafood. He pressed his muzzle to his mane, trying to filter out the air for a bit. It didn't help that he could see the dead sea creatures, hypnotized by the dazed, lifeless stare of the fish. He felt his stomach jolt. *I don't see how anyone could live in this.* This was definitely a whole different lifestyle.

A strange, wet flipper patted for his attention.

"Here."

A sea lion had approached him, in his flipper a bandana. It offered the bandana to him. The lion prince took it carefully, wrapping it around his muzzle. Immediate relief rushed him. Even if the smell still lingered, it wasn't that bad.

"Thank you," he sighed.

The sea lion waved a dismissal. "Don't worry about it. We get that not all can stand the stench of the ocean or seafood, so we give it to all our strangers who visit. Hope you enjoy your time here, traveler." It turned to head away.

That's kind of the Shell Clan. "Ah! I apologize that this is random, but, if I could ask something?"

It looked back. "Hm?"

"Do you know where Queen– I mean, Shell Broken Savaria is?"

The sea lion hadn't hesitated in answering his question. It raised its flipper and pointed ahead to where a large wooden house resided. "That large house is the town hall and Shell Broken Savaria's residence. Head in there and ring the tiny silver bell on the front desk that reads 'call for assistance.' One of her servants will approach, then they'll take you to her. She's not a land animal."

No wonder then if I never heard about her. Prince Wonwoo studied the large house. He repeated back the information he was given. "Town hall, ring the bell, wait for the servant. Okay. Got it." He bowed at the sea lion. "Thank you so much."

"Not a problem. Enjoy your time here in the Shell Clan, traveler." The sea lion waddled towards the beach and slid into the water, swimming away into the deep blue.

The lion prince followed where the sea lion pointed, continuously repeating the directions. "Town hall, ring the bell, wait for the servant. Town hall, ring the bell, wait for the servant. It's very simple, Prince Wonwoo, you can't mess this up. Don't screw it up." As he followed the sand-ridden path, he was soon greeted by the smell of cooked food. The taste reached the back of his throat, making his mouth water. He was going to have a good lunch today. His head lifted, desperate to locate the source. He came across a pier that made him hesitate. Taking one careful step, he mentally braced himself to be on the structure, not minding the ocean washing around him. He could hear those on the pier

THE OUTLAW PRINCE DEALS WITH...WELL, BEING AN OUTLAW

whispering about him as he walked on forward. He could care less about their gossip right now. He found himself standing in front of a saloon. It wasn't as big as a building in Halcyonwick, a tiny two story. A roof made of intertwined twigs hung over the upper deck and the entrance. From within, Prince Wonwoo could hear faint chattering and laughter of its occupants.

A black and white penguin exited from the swinging doors, escorting a brown and white dog out, and caught sight of Prince Wonwoo. He waved at him, approaching him. "Hey there fellow traveler!" the penguin greeted. "You look like you need a rest. Come on, come on in!"

The lion prince, although hesitant, entered the saloon.

He was immediately met with the eyes of those in the saloon, and he felt like a fish out of water *(no pun intended, he told himself)*. The conversations had been reduced into hushed murmurs as everyone turned their heads towards him. While the majority were curious at seeing a lion for probably the first time in their lives, there were a few clan members who narrowed their eyes at him in suspicion. The penguin who brought him in raised a flipper at him. "Wait here."

Prince Wonwoo, taken aback, nodded. He watched the penguin disappear behind two large swinging doors that appeared similar to the ones used for the entrance. His mind raced; he never thought a bunch of strange eyes would make him feel sick. He tried to ignore it. He shook his mane and stood tall.

...What am I waiting for again?

The doors swung open again but no one emerged. He looked around, seeing if anyone had noticed it or it was just him being tired...

"Down here, traveler!"

He looked down and made eye contact with who he assumed to be the saloon owner.

"Hi there!" the tiny animal greeted him. "You look exhausted. Come, come! Have a seat!" The tiny animal, also a penguin except much tinier and blue in color, guided Prince Wonwoo and sat him down. "What can I get for you?"

"Oh, I- Uh-" Prince Wonwoo shook his paws. "No, I can't— I don't—"

"Have money? Nonsense!" The penguin waved a flipper. "Our economy is just fine as we are, so this one is on me. Whatever I'm given is only tips, haha!"

The lion prince blinked. "That is...really interesting."

"Ain't it?" The penguin offered his flipper. "The name's Tihkoosue."

"Nice to meet you, Tihkoosue." The lion prince gently took the penguin's flipper and shook it. "So. You run this place all by yourself?" Prince Wonwoo asked.

"Yep!" Tihkoosue answered gleefully. "There's really no place to have any help when everyone here is chill." He handed him a rolled newspaper before leaning on the counter. "So, tell me about yourself, traveler. Where are you from?"

THE OUTLAW PRINCE DEALS WITH...WELL, BEING AN OUTLAW

"...I'm..I'm uh–"

Why was it so difficult to come up with a lie? He always was prideful with his Dynasty. But now, it felt as if it was something to be ashamed of.

He shook his head. "Sorry, I've been through a rough few weeks-"

"No worries! If you're not comfortable, you don't have to say so."

"No, it's- If you promise not to tell, I'm from the Promised Dynasty."

He could sense some clan members snapping their heads at him at the mention of the Promised Dynasty. That unnerved him but he forced it down. His confidence somewhat returned when the penguin's confused face lit up. He pointed at him.

"P-Prince Wonwoo?!" Tihkoosue asked. "Prince Wonwoo Honeycutt! Of the Promised Dynasty? *The* Promised Dynasty?"

He didn't want to question how the tiny penguin knew immediately who he was. His pride was restored, and that's all he needed right now. He jerked up his head, winking at the penguin. "You got that right!"

"Oh, my Gods. It's such an honor to meet someone of the Honeycutt Royal Family from the Promised Dynasty! It's been rather a long time; I vaguely remember your Father and his brother coming by here many terra cycles ago!"

"You know my Father?" Prince Wonoo asked curiously. "And his...brother, my uncle?"

"Yes, then Princes Hyun-sik and Jung-hwa of the Promised Dynasty. I am 10 terra cycles older than them both, but he came by when I first took over this saloon after he became King."

"Oh wow!"

"Yeah! So, this is definitely on the house! Eep! I totally forgot about it! I'll get to it right away!"

The lion prince waved a paw at him. "No worries. Take all the time you need."

Tihkoosue nodded then disappeared behind the kitchen.

The lion prince flicked his ears and unrolled the newspaper. This felt oddly like a scroll, except it wasn't. He was met with words "The History of the Shell Clan," and he lifted an eyebrow. An informative newspaper? He had then realized there were multiple pages like a book. Prince Wonwoo let out a small gasp. What was this!

A... scroll book? Book scroll?... Broll?

The little penguin had returned with a mug. "For your thirst." Prince Wonwoo looked at it. It was fizzy at the top, light brown in color. He pulled it closer to him and took one lap. He lifted up his head. *Woah!* The strong taste instantly hit him, but not in a bad way. He licked his lips, processing what it was.

"Beer?"

"It's one of our finest in all of the clans," Tihkoosue replied. "Do you recognize it?"

THE OUTLAW PRINCE DEALS WITH...WELL, BEING AN OUTLAW

"Sort of, I'm not much of a beer fan, but I've had a few during the New Terra Cycle Day," Prince Wonwoo said. "It's good though! Honest. It's just such a rarity in the Promised Dynasty; my father did mention that they were exported from a far away clan, but he never said from the Shell Clan. He probably forgot."

"Perhaps he did; it has been a long time. We don't make much of a name to the Kingdoms from far away, unfortunately."

"Well, you should. At least to the Promised Dynasty. This is fantastic!"

Tihkoosue smiled. "I'll be back! I'm preparing our signature dish!"

"Take all the time."

Tihkoosue nodded. When he disappeared behind again, Prince Wonwoo started to read the newspaper, drinking at a slow pace. He felt relaxed, as if he were at home. It was definitely kicking in, and he was glad for it. He needed alcohol to destress. He twitched his ears; he could feel stares burning into him. But there was one sensation he couldn't shake off. Someone was approaching him. Rather, more than one creature.

"An inlander!"

"One we haven't seen before."

On both sides of the lion prince, there were two creatures that sat close to him: a silver tabby cat with blue eyes and a crocodile with an eyepatch over his right eye. Both wore feathered hats with an emblem of a shark on it. They stared at him with the determination of a fierce predator. The crocodile hissed, his teeth bared. He ignored them, doing his best to flatten his bristling fur.

What do you guys want? He asked himself.

The crocodile swiveled his snout towards him, eyes scanning him intently. "A lion. He's one fine looking inlander if I say so," he said.

And what exactly does that mean? Prince Wonwoo asked himself. *Fine looking as in I'm attractive, or fine looking like a snack? The message here is very much mixed, reptilian.*

The silver tabby cat ignored the crocodile and pulled out a coin. She balanced it between the table and her paw toe. "Tell me, lion inlander," the cat said, "what's a thing like you doing all the way out here in the Shell Clan?"

The lion prince narrowed his eyes. "That is none of your concern or business," he said calmly. "If you don't mind, I'm trying to enjoy my solitude and drink."

"Oh, it actually *is* our concern and business, lion inlander," the crocodile hissed, grinning. "I know you haven't heard of us–"

"I don't know anyone here," Prince Wonwoo interrupted with a glare, "and I don't care who you guys exactly are. Not trying to be rude, I'm just here to stay and rest before I leave. If you're lucky, we might not have to cross each other's paths after today."

The two looked at each other.

"How rude. Are all inlanders like this?" The crocodile.

"Don't look at me; I left them a long time ago. You know that." The cat. "Anyway. That's not the topic of discussion. How about

THE OUTLAW PRINCE DEALS WITH...WELL, BEING AN OUTLAW

we introduce ourselves first?" She pointed at the crocodile. "His name is Seabury, and I'm Mabel."

The lion prince took another shot, raising his eyebrows. "Interesting." *I didn't ask but whatever.*

The cat, Mabel, poked a paw on Prince Wonwoo's shoulder. "Tell us, lion inlander. *Who* are you? Where *have* you come from?"

How the lion prince just wanted to say, *"I am Prince Wonwoo of the Promised Dynasty, I am a prince! Leave me be!"* But he controlled himself. Where they not here when he told Tihkoosue that he was from the Promised Dynasty? Maybe they didn't hear the first time? Perhaps they had just walked in. Who knew?

He watched Tihkoosue emerge from the kitchen with a large plate consisting of fried fish and a salad in his flipper. He paused upon seeing the cat and crocodile.

"Th-Th-The Sharktooths!" Tihkoosue said in a stutter. "Wh-What are you guys doing here!?"

Prince Wonwoo raised an eyebrow. *How fun,* he thought to himself. *They know each other.*

"We're not here to cause harm, Tihkoosue," the crocodile, Seabury, said, his left yellowish golden eye gleaming. "We're just saying hello to the newcomer and probably have a couple of drinks together. We're not going to steal or start anything, that's a pirate's promise."

The lion prince placed his mug down gently.

Pirates? Like, pirates from fictional stories? What in the name of the Heavens am I listening to? I thought they were just fairy tales for children. They actually exist? Or am I just getting drunk already and hearing stupid things?

The penguin still remained in his spot, suspicious.

"On second thought, since we're all here, make us your special dish as well, Tihkoosue," Mabel said. "It would be great to share with the newcomer." She tossed the coin up in the air before catching it, showing it to the little penguin. "We'll pay you handsomely." She gestured to Seabury, who then lifted up a pouch.

"...You know I don't need any money. Especially stolen money."

"Stolen!?" The crocodile put a hand on his chest dramatically. "The audacity of accusing us! You think we're *that* ruthless to steal from the innocent?"

Tihkoosue was silent. Prince Wonwoo kept drinking.

I feel like I'm in the middle of some family drama.

"We at Sharktooths of the Hidden Cove don't steal, Tihkoosue," Mabel said. "That's against our code. If anything, we steal from robbers and thieves. That's the opposite of stealing."

"Yeah! We're taking back from those lowlives who *do* steal from the poor and the innocent!"

Woah. I am...so drunk right now.

"That's not how it's been lately," the penguin said. "But whatever. I'll be nice and treat you guys just as I was about to treat the Prince of the Promised Dynasty. I'll be back. Again."

THE OUTLAW PRINCE DEALS WITH...WELL, BEING AN OUTLAW

...Well I couldn't expect him to not tell anyone who I am. Now they know.

When he had disappeared again, the duo returned back to Prince Wonwoo. They were circling him at this point like vultures scouting a dead body. They appeared piqued, curious to talk more.

"Ohhh, Prince of the Promised Dynasty!?" Mabel mewed.

"How nice of the Promised Dynasty's heir to show up finally," Seabury said. "Finally traveling to the other clans? Meeting us again to keep the peace after terra cycles of silence? It almost feels too good to be true. Doesn't it, Mabel?"

"It does, Seabury. It's as if all of a sudden they care now."

Prince Wonwoo just nodded, staring off into space as he continued reading.

That's when things took a sudden turn; Mabel snatched up the newspaper with her claws and tossed it aside. She slammed the coin down and brandished a knife at the lion prince before he could question why she did that for. He widened his eyes and stared at Mabel, unblinking, leaving her form in his sight as he felt the intimidating presence of the knife looming over his throat.

What the hell!? He wanted to say aloud.

Seabury wrapped his tail around Prince Wonwoo as if he were a snake. He made sure to get a firm grip on the lion prince so that he wouldn't escape. He stared down at the lion prince, his only eye narrowed. He let out a deep hiss, his tongue threatening his ears.

Mabel hissed. "So. Prince of the Promised Dynasty."

"Yeah?"

"Here's the deal. You may know this clan as the friendliest clan in all of the land, but that's a lie to keep the public eye away from us. These creatures are more deceiving than you think. Do you wanna know the true history of this clan? The true horrors and pain and suffering *your Kingdom* left for us?"

What pain and suffering we caused? This should be interesting to hear because...that's very accusatory. He wrinkled his muzzle at her.

"A long time ago, when the Great War ended and the founders of the Promised Dynasty and the Demoniacal Kingdom split, there were a group of various creatures who found themselves stuck. Some had friends and family in both Kingdoms. Brothers and sisters separated, lovers separated from the one they loved, mothers and and fathers and children torn apart from each other. Who could they go with? Who would they alliance themselves with? Go with their loved ones on the good side, or go with their loved ones to the dark side? They were lost, so they left. They moved outland, away from the inland and away from the two great Kingdoms. They all separated eventually following disputes and formed the minor clans that exist today, the Shell Clan being one of them.

The Shell Clan's founder, Aquiris, oh she was absolutely cruel but not how you would think. She lost her mother and father to the

THE OUTLAW PRINCE DEALS WITH...WELL, BEING AN OUTLAW

Promised Dynasty. Her brother went to join the Promised Dynasty, and her sister joined the Demoniacal Kingdom, but she refused to join either of them, as she felt no alliance for either Kingdom. She intended to make her clan, along with our other allies, rise to enact revenge on the Promised Dynasty and make them pay for tearing her family apart. For terra cycles, Aquiris shaped her loyal members into ruthless and valiant warriors, pirates! Pirates we were back then! Oh what a thrill it was! We raided islands, pillaged, swashbuckled! That was the life! That *is* the life! Then, everything would soon change.

Aquiris had a daughter. She did not agree to her mother's supposed cruel ways and demanded for a change. She had joined a rebellion consisting of traitors and was brainwashed into their ways. She believed the Gods would never want us to enact revenge. Aquiris would not listen to her daughter and practically disowned her for being weak. Her daughter ran away, abandoning the ways of being a pirate, abandoning the Shell Clan, and vowing retribution. 18 terra cycles later, she returned to wage a coup against her mother. It lasted a few weeks, but she succeeded in the end and killed her own mother. The Shell Clan was a mess afterwards, and she became their leader. She reformed the clan into how it looks like today, starting by dissolving the alliances of the other clans to make our clan independent. A clan full of soft-bellied creatures who don't know how to fend for themselves. Many disgustingly revered their new leader, but her reign was short-lived; just some 3 months after taking her place, she disappeared, never to be seen again. Before she disappeared, she had named a successor in the event something happened to her. That successor? It's Shell Broken Savaria. A creature not even related to her by blood. That's when it finally dawned on the clan that their leader too was a coward who did not want to lead at all and wanted us to fall apart."

"And this is all relevant to me...how?" the lion prince asked, grabbing his mug to take another drink of his beer.

The cat's face was scrunched up, as if she couldn't believe at how nonchalant he was acting. "I'll get to that soon," she hissed. "What you do need to know is this: Aquiris was my great-grandmother. My grandmother was the one who killed my great-grandmother, her mother, and reformed the Shell Clan as much as she could before she ran away back to the inlands like a coward. She never intended to take on the responsibility of leading a clan. She was paranoid and feared no one would respect her after she had killed Aquiris. She ran away and soon had a son, my father, with an inlander *Promised* cat, and then I was born. I didn't stay in the Promised Dynasty for long; I fled as soon as I was able to fend for myself and found Seabury, who took me back to the Sharktooths. They showed me that they haven't given up on the old ways, and they had refused Shell Broken Savaria. It gave me hope. A new drive."

The she-cat lowered the knife down to his throat, where his pulse would be. She pressed the cold steel against his pulse. "We will get our revenge. *I* will have my revenge. I will carry out the legacy laid out to me in my great-grandmother's name. The Shell Clan will be mine to rightfully take back and steer back to our original roots. When that happens, we will attack. Your Kingdom and your Gods will fall, Prince Wonwoo of the Promised Dynasty."

THE OUTLAW PRINCE DEALS WITH...WELL, BEING AN OUTLAW

The lion prince widened his eyes. Before he could run, the crocodile lashed out and clamped on his body with his large jaws. The lion prince roared in pain and tried freeing himself to no avail. He knew crocodiles had a grip that couldn't easily be fought off. Mabel backed up, letting Seabury toss him around like a ragdoll.

"Get him, Seabury!" Mabel yowled. "Kill him! Show him no mercy! Sharktooth style! You know the code!"

Seabury heeded Mabel's words. He threw him onto a table full of bystanders once he was done tossing him. Prince Wonwoo crashed into the group, which caused them to scatter away. The lion prince got up hastily. He breathed heavily, his breaths coming in short, ragged pants.

"So what? You want to kill me for something your family did to themselves?" Prince Wonwoo asked angrily.

"No! We want to kill you for ruining our lives!" Mabel defended. "We intend to use you in our example of why the Kingdoms are evil! To show that your founders have made life for those who didn't choose a Kingdom a living hell! And to show that your Gods don't help people like us!"

Prince Wonwoo lashed his tail. It wasn't the founders' fault. If anyone was at fault, it was King Wyvern; he had been the one power hungry, determined to rule all the land. The Gods and the Promised Dynasty played no part in feeding King Wyvern's ideals. He had done that to himself and bent those eager to hear from him to his ways. The way Mabel was speaking made her sound like she was a Demoniacal member.

"Oh, goddammit, no no NO! I have been bar fight free for 8 TERRA CYCLES! I knew not to trust you pirates! Shoo! Get off the table, you stupid cat!"

That irritated voice was Tihkoosue.

HISSSSS!

That irritated voice was Mabel.

Prince Wonwoo growled at Seabury, who was encircling him. He may be drunk, but he could still fight. Seabury smiled and locked eyes at the lion prince, hissing threateningly. A chill ran down his spine; he forgot how deep a reptilian's growl was. It sank deep within his bones. He leapt at the crocodile, digging his claws into his flesh as best as he could. Even though he had thick claws, the crocodile had tougher skin that made it difficult to get a good grip on him. Seabury flailed and bucked like a bull in the ring, crashing into tables and walls. Prince Wonwoo held on as long as he could, slowly reaching one paw slowly to his only eye. When Seabury realized what the lion prince was doing, he whirled his head back, snapped his jaws on Prince Wonwoo's hind leg, and launched him right onto the top table.

He felt his shoulder being stabbed right on the corner, which made him hiss in pain. That was going to leave a bruise for sure. Mabel, seeing the opportunity of the lion prince being disorientated, jumped on top of him, pinning him down and holding the knife above his throat.

"How interesting. This all reminds me of how I killed your Father's brother 36 terra cycles ago," she sneered.

THE OUTLAW PRINCE DEALS WITH...WELL, BEING AN OUTLAW

What?

The lion prince was confused. His Father's brother was Hyun-sik, and he was destined to be King. King Jung-hwa had not been the firstborn, rather he was second-in-line to take the throne. He remembered vaguely of one time his Father mentioning his late brother. He had mentioned that he died in a "freak accident" when they just turned 18, though he did not mention what kind of accident it was.

Is this why Father never mentioned this clan much? Prince Wonwoo thought to himself. *They did something to Hyun-sik?*

"The Promised Dynasty is going to pay for what you have done to my family and my clan," she hissed her threat again. "Your Kingdom will suffer the consequences of your unknown actions!"

Prince Wonwoo narrowed his eyes, snarling. This tiny feline thinking she could bring down a whole Kingdom? "Think again, cat." The lion prince grabbed Mabel by the neck and threw her off of him before she could stab him. She collided with a table and collapsed over it, her pained yowls ringing out. He winced when he put pressure on the leg where his shoulder was stabbed, lifting it gingerly as he quickly and carefully licked the wound. Assessing the damage done, Prince Wonwoo lowered his ears. He brought this to the clan. If he hadn't come along, this bar wouldn't have suffered the damages. The pirates would have never found him and outed him. He finally made a run for the door.

I'll be back for this clan one day, he growled. *When I become King, I will rid Mabel and her stupid pirates.*

As he left the gates, leaving the guards in a state of confusion, he could hear Mabel shouting at him in a victorious caterwaul.

"That's right! Run, Prince Wonwoo of the Promised Dynasty! Never come back! We'll kill you if we ever see you again!"

I wasn't planning on it! I can find another better clan to be with! That or I'll live by myself! Fuck it!

CHAPTER 12
SEEKING REFUGE IN A FAR DISTANT CLAN

~ *1 week and 3 days later...* ~
~ *July in Terra Cycle 1118 B.E.* ~

No clan wanted to accept him.

Just a while ago, Prince Wonwoo was chased out of the Onyx Clan after they had found out he was the prince of the Promised Dynasty who had committed a horrible crime. Word somehow must have spread fast, because every clan the lion prince tried to join wanted him gone and wanted no association with him. First it was the Shell Clan (specifically a group of pirates drove him out called the Sharktooths, yes, *goddamn pirates*), then it was another clan he came across called the Emerald Clan, then another one only for a brief moment called the Fire Clan. Now it was the Onyx Clan, and they made sure that he was far from their established territory, and they meant *far*. That was 4 clans in a row! And they all rejected him!

Kicked me out, Prince Wonwoo reflected. *Treated me like I was a plague!*

They all feared that the Demoniacal Kingdom would locate them if he stayed with their clan. The lion prince couldn't blame them though; if he was King, he wouldn't want any outsider who had committed such a terrible crime joining the Promised Dynasty. (He coughed to himself, thinking about Atiena and her cackle.)

They could have been a little nicer about it instead of running me out without explanation.

But he was starting to get a little concerned; a week had passed with little to no success at all. He adjusted to his life as a nomad, wandering where he pleased, hunting the wildlife, settling in multiple areas. To a few creatures, they would call this a paradise. The freedom of not being restricted to a clan and having only yourself to fend for. The endless amounts of food and water you can encounter and new places you discover on your own. Any creature would immediately dump everything and go on a huge globetrot forever until the day they die.

This wasn't Prince Wonwoo's style of living however.

As much as he thought about it, he can't live as a hermit forever. Hunting wasn't entirely easy, and eating live and raw meat was making him feel sick. He needed to belong somewhere, recover in a safe place, have some actual food, and have more strength in numbers. That was his way of life. But all he could see in every clans' eyes was fear and distrust. No one wanted him.

They treated him like—

A curse.

To be fair, he couldn't blame them for thinking that way, but he wished that they would hear out his side of the story instead of assuming the worst because of what they've overheard. But he also thought of himself, how he would automatically think the same. There was no other way of thinking about it.

He ventured out of the north and went southeast, back towards the inland. It was a beautiful July day, the grass greener than ever before and the wind breezing cold air to combat with the summer heat. Maybe he could find another clan to stay with that isn't from the far edges of the land. Or, if not a clan, maybe a group he could live with. If not a group... He wasn't sure at this point. He really didn't have many options. He could only rely on his chances and his luck—

Grrrrrr.

His stomach began to growl in a familiar tone. It's been a while since he last ate.

He looked towards the sky; Dagny had moved the sun to its highest point. Dagny's Peak. *Oh great, perfect time to get hungry,* he sarcastically told himself. That would be a bit of a problem. Most prey wouldn't want to be out and about at this time as the sun's heat was unbearable in the summer weather. He would have to wait until Gau's First Rise to get some luck.

After some more walking, the lion prince came across a field where a herd of pigs resided. The lion prince froze, crouching down. *What do we have here?* Looks like luck was beginning to be on his side. He never hunted a live pig before, but he definitely had them during banquets. With how small and chubby they looked, he figured this was going to be a piece of cake.

He slowly crept towards the grazing pigs, doing his best to blend into the ground. They ate away without a care in the world. He also made sure that the wind was blowing his scent away from the pigs. Hunting without any cover was a pain, so he decided to wing it. He advanced closer, got within a good distance, broke into a slow trot, then ran and leapt at one of the pigs.

They all squealed and broke up once they saw the lion prince in the air, running in opposite directions to avoid him. The pig Prince Wonwoo targeted fell in his grasp, and the two rolled on the ground. The pig struggled, grunting and squealing in terror, but the lion prince slammed his paw firmly down on the pig's snout. *This is too easy*, Prince Wonwoo thought to himself, making his way to the pig's throat. *You're mine, pig!*

However, this time would be different, and the lion prince would soon regret his life choices.

A different pig ran up to him and headbutted straight into his side, knocking him away from his pig. Prince Wonwoo let out a grunt; he was surprised by the strength of this fat pig. But what also surprised him was the pig had a tough snout, as if it were made out of steel. His breath was instantly knocked from him, and he tumbled on the floor. When he got up, he was again rammed by the pig, joined by the one who he tried to kill. The lion prince didn't understand it; no matter how many times he tried to flee, the pigs would not let him. They pinned him down, forcefully, and even got their teeth onto his flesh. He roared, kicking them away. He swiped his paw at them and missed both of them. He stared with wide eyes.

What bullshit was this!?

The pigs charged again, and the lion prince rolled away. They swerved flawlessly, changing directions to where he was.

"ALRIGHT, ALRIGHT **CHILL!** I'M LEAVING!" he roared at them, running into the jungle ahead of him. He looked back once and saw the pigs had stopped their pursuit at the edge of the jungle. They snorted at him and walked away. He finally stopped and he panted, still watching them until they disappeared in the horizon. He flicked his tail. "By the Gods...what a bunch of rude creatures, unlike deer," he said to himself, huffing. "And those fat pigs would have lasted me a long while. Curse it all."

The lion prince shook himself and looked around. This was a thick jungle, it almost looked like Divine Kingfisher Woods. There were also dense trees that covered the sky, with vines that tangled around the branches and trunks. Some even hung eerily as if they were waiting for a creature to fall into its trap. The ground was lush with large ferns, covering the bases of the trees. Maybe he could rest here, find a clan, and find something easier to eat than those pigs. Now not only was his stomach grumbling, his entire body hurt from bruising. He brushed his mane, sighing. Better to start searching for something.

He headed deeper into the jungle, sniffing at every tree and bush he encountered. The lion prince made sure to keep aware of his surroundings for the vines smacked onto him constantly, threatening to constrict him like a snake. He had to crouch his head to be within ground level, which he can only imagine made himself look stupid. *This is so humiliating that vines scare me. At least no one is around to see me.*

At least...not that I'm aware of. I hope.

He carefully moved them away without cutting them so that he wouldn't damage anything. The ferns brushed the sides of his cheeks, which bugged him after a while. It didn't help that they also tickled his nose. It was stupid humid and gross. There were so many bugs that buzzed around his face, which irritated him. He waved his paw at the bugs, grumbling. He soon found a river and he stared. His mouth began to water, and he smacked his lips. He was thirsty as well.

He padded up to the river. His mind was reeling. What was he going to do if he couldn't find help? Was he going to continue living life as an outlaw, or would he eventually go back and turn himself into the Demoniacal Kingdom?

Whatever happens, I'll just have to adapt to it. What else can I do? The lion prince crouched down at the riverbank and began to lap the water, quenching his throat. *Oh Gods, this water tastes just amazing.* The bugs continued to buzz around him, making him flick his tail at them.

"Hey, hey, hey! Watch out!"

A random voice drew his attention. The jungle went completely silent, not a single disturbance crossed him. Even the bugs that were previously annoying him all flew away in unison. He stopped lapping the water, lifting his head up.

Huh?

...Wait a minute. Prince Wonwoo narrowed his eyes, flicking his ears. *When the forest goes silent, a predator is nearby. That's the number one rule of the wild I remember being told. It can't be me, because the jungle was still alive when I arrived. Something is here. Something–*

Out of thin air, a crocodile sprung from the water, right in front of Prince Wonwoo. His life flashed before his eyes at the sight of the huge beast. The lion prince yelped and reared back. The crocodile snapped down hard on his front leg, keeping a good grip on him. It began to drag Prince Wonwoo into the water. The lion prince tried to dig his claws into the ground so that he could pull himself out, but it failed. The sheer strength of this crocodile was too strong for him to fight it. The lion prince took a huge breath before he submerged.

The water underneath was murky but Prince Wonwoo was able to make out several more gleaming eyes staring down at him. That's when realization sunk in.

He was in crocodile territory.

And he had made himself known by coming onto their territory, springing them to life.

The crocodile that snagged him began the infamous death roll, spinning the lion prince fast. *Woah!* Water rushed into his nose, effectively going down his throat, and the sensation of losing breath kicked in fast. There was nothing he could grab onto, but he tried his hardest, finding something he could to fend off the crocodile. He grew dizzy from the blinding foam. Giving up on trying to grab something, he decided to fight back with his own paws, kicking the water and hoping to hit the crocodile. Something must have worked because the crocodile had stopped rolling and released him.

Thank Gods. Blood clouded his vision as his wound bled all around him. He swam up, breaking his head through the surface. He took a huge breath in, coughing. His leg stung and hurt badly.

Looking up, he noticed a bright reddish-orange monkey alongside what Prince Wonwoo believed to be a leopard with multiple scars in the trees. Studying it further, he realized it wasn't a leopard, but a jaguar. The scarred jaguar lifted up its head once it made eye contact with the lion prince.

"There he is!" the feline shouted to the monkey. "You better hurry up, Vermilion! The crocodiles are getting angry."

The jaguar was right; Prince Wonwoo could hear them hissing and growling from behind.

"I'm working on it!" the monkey shouted, working on something with its hands. "Get out of there, lion! Hurry! Those crocodiles don't stop after one hit!"

The lion prince didn't need to be told twice. He took one stroke and immediately winced. He lifted up his front leg, assessing the damage; it was seriously wounded, close to having been almost ripped off from his body, and it prohibited him from moving fast. The worst part: It was his good leg of all limbs. That didn't stop him from trying to escape. It was extremely painful, but he was determined to get to the shore and make a run for it. He didn't make it far though; another crocodile encircled him and bit on his back leg, right by his flank. Pain seized his brain, causing his muscles to lock up in response. *Shit!* He didn't catch his breath fast enough when the crocodile pulled him underwater. There was another crocodile that swam up and took him by the other leg. The two crocodiles worked together to roll.

This was it for sure. His blood stained the white foams of the water. Prince Wonwoo was too exhausted to fight back. Besides, even if he wanted to, the crocodiles had gotten his legs, so he couldn't kick. He obviously couldn't twist his body around and swipe at them. Water was difficult to fight in, and the crocodiles knew it.

This is it for sure. If it wasn't the waterfall, certainly, it's gonna be by an attack while I am weak and easy pickings.

Multiple crocodiles swarmed in on him, grabbing a hold of him.

Please, Morana, make this pain go away.

He closed his eyes, accepting death.

…

"Is he okay?"

The monkey, Vermilion, looked back at her companion. The jaguar released his grip on the crocodile, letting the large reptile's corpse drop with a thud. The other crocodiles hissed at him and swam away. The feline padded up to the lion, looking down at him.

"He's badly injured, those crocodiles got him good," Vermilion said, crouching down. "Look at those wounds! They nearly tore off all of his limbs! Pretty idiot is definitely new here; everyone knows never to drink here or cross this strip of territory without being accompanied by someone native."

"Pretty idiot?"

"I didn't say anything."

"Yes, you did."

She ignored her friend and began aggressively pounding his back to get him to cough out water, which worked. "How's the crocodile?"

"Good as dead." The jaguar flashed his canines. "And it was the leader of all crocodiles!"

The monkey lifted up her head. "Are you serious!?"

"Yeah, look!"

Vermilion stared at the dead crocodile. She recognized its distinctive scars across his snout and face. It definitely was the leader of the pod. She stopped hitting the lion and raised up her arms. "At long last! We can at least rest with him gone and his reign of terror over."

"For a while. The pod will be back with a more fierce and stronger leader who will want revenge for their fallen leader," the jaguar said with eyes narrowed at the dead reptile. "We will have to be extremely careful until then."

"Oh yeah. Definitely. We better warn Aleena on that then once we get back."

The jaguar nodded. "Indeed. But enough about the crocodile. Your aim was fantastic. I have never seen someone hit two crocodiles in one!"

The monkey brushed her fingers behind her ears. "Thanks, Kitwana. I've been practicing day in and day out on my archery skills for terra cycles. And it paid off! Look! I now have a new way to fend off those stinking crocodiles."

Kitwana nodded at his friend. He looked back at the lion; he appeared as stiff as a log, and none of his muscles twitched. Vermilion continued to pound his back with her hands. He didn't see his sides rising and falling. He pressed his paw down on his neck to try and locate the lion's pulse. Vermilion watched with curiosity. He couldn't feel anything and started to fear for the worst. He moved his paw away from the neck and to the lion's nose, feeling for any breath. He was able to feel short puffs of air. Somewhat alive. It wasn't enough though; anyone could still breathe without a heartbeat for a short while. The jaguar pressed down on his neck harder. *Come on, you beast, work with me. Tell me you're still alive!*

Finally, his paw picked up small rhythmic thumps underneath. The lion awoke for a moment to cough out any remaining water before falling unconscious again. His eyes lit up. "I got a pulse! He's alive! It's weak, but at least it means he will survive."

Vermilion sighed in relief. "Thank the Gods. I guess he should be named after you!"

Kitwana twitched his ears in amusement. "Come on, let's get him back to the Tropic Clan before he bleeds to death here."

"Yeah."

Vermilion lifted the lion carefully onto the jaguar's back, stabilizing him, and the two carried him deeper into the jungle.

"You're truly one lucky lion, let me tell you."

Everything around him was still dull, but Prince Wonwoo could vaguely make out the muffled voice calling to him. He wasn't sure what was happening. He weakly angled his ears, pinpointing to the source.

Me? Lucky? What is that supposed to mean?

Prince Wonwoo wasn't sure if the voice he was hearing was a live creature or an angel calling to him. His senses began to come back to him, and it all ran down to his injuries. Injuries definitely meant that he was not dead. His nerves were flared up, stinging and tingling. "FUUUUUUCKING HELLLLL!" the lion prince cursed, opening his eyes. His vision was blurry, but he didn't see any halo or bright, heavenly light. The only bright light he was seeing was the sun shining down on him. He lifted up a paw to shield his eyes, only for more pain to flare up to strike his brain. "OW!"

Okay, where am I?

"Woah, settle down!"

There was that voice again. Who was that?

His vision cleared and revealed himself in a jungle, within a den. Surrounding him was a brownish black monkey, the bright reddish-orange monkey and the jaguar from on the trees, a bush dog and a llama. The llama had him huddled by his side, pressed in his puffy white fur. The bush dog approached the lion prince wearily with cobwebs and tended to his wounds. He looked down and saw large green leaves and branches wrapped around three of his legs. Cobwebs covered his wounds and held the leaves and branches in place. His memory came back, and he remembered the crocodiles that attacked him, grabbing onto his legs and nearly tearing them off his body. He tried to move, but not even an inch could he move without pain striking him down.

Oh. Prince Wonwoo lowered his head in gloom. *That's why they consider me lucky. I'm still alive.*

"Owwww..." he weakly groaned out.

"Keep still, young lion," the llama said in a soothing tone that reminded him of Hakuba. "Your injuries are severe. It's only luck that you've been found."

Luck. That's all I am. I don't feel like it, though. I am a misfortune to this world. I should be dead. The lion prince placed his head on his paws, staring at the llama. Confusion only spread when he looked around. "Huh? What's happening? Where am I?" he asked everyone present in a trembling voice. "How and why am I always spared from Morana?"

The two monkeys, the jaguar, the bush dog and the llama blinked at Prince Wonwoo with wide eyes. They whispered to one another at the mention of Morana.

"Morana? That's the Goddess of Death."

"Is he from a clan influenced by the Promised Dynasty like us?"

"Maybe?"

The brownish black monkey stepped up to meet him. "My name is Aleena. I am the leader of the Tropic Clan," she introduced herself, bowing to him. "My adopted sister Vermilion and her friend Kitwana–" She pointed at the bright reddish-orange monkey and the jaguar respectively. "–saved you from the crocodiles."

"I can't thank them enough," Prince Wonwoo told Aleena. "It just...happened within a flash, I wasn't able to react in time when they called out to me. You have brave soldiers."

"Yeah, well any animal here in the jungle knows never to go to that strip of territory without at least a partner or weapons with them," Vermilion said sarcastically. "It's common knowledge around here. Even newborns have more common sense than you."

Kitwana promptly smacked her upside the head with his paw, prompting a yelp from the reddish-orange monkey.

"Ow!"

"You really have to watch that mouth of yours," Kitwana growled in a warning. "Not everyone has a sense of humor like you. It can get you killed one day."

"Well, they're no fun then!" Vermilion stuck out her tongue at her growling friend, rubbing the back of her head.

Aleena looked like she wanted to face palm. "Sorry about that," she apologized, "Vermilion can have a bit of a...crude humor."

The lion prince waved a paw. "I've heard worse."

"So...what are you doing so far away from wherever you come from, young lion?" Aleena asked, tilting her head. "Are you lost or something?"

The lion prince blinked. *Am I lost?* He looked away, unable to stand eye contact with her any longer. "I...I had done something horrible for my Dynasty, something I can't come back to..."

"Dynasty? You don't mean..."

He didn't lift up his head. "The Promised Dynasty." He also didn't hesitate to reveal where he was from.

Why bother keeping that secret anymore?

There was a collective gasp from everyone. Aleena counted with her fingers then she looked up at him. "You must be the lion prince!" she said excitedly, pointing at him. "Prince Wonwoo of the Promised Dynasty."

Prince Wonwoo of the Promised Dynasty. A part of him wanted to be cocky at the mention of his full title. *Yeah, I am, Prince Wonwoo of the greatest Kingdom there is!* is what he would say. He would toss his head, puff out his chest, show off how royal he was, the whole shebang. But with all that had happened with the other clans and his near-death experience, he felt that he wasn't worthy of any title of royalty. Especially with what he had done.

There's nothing for me anymore. Even as Prince. So why would I flaunt what is a lie?

"I am," he answered in defeat.

"I've heard of you! Your Father once visited us."

Prince Wonwoo's energy was too low to react to Aleena's comment.

"Well, what are you doing all the way here, Prince Wonwoo?" Vermilion asked with genuine concern after minutes of rubbing her pain away. "What did you do back home that you can't return to?"

The lion prince tensed, his claws unsheathing somehow. *What did you do?* Should he tell them? How would they respond?

He felt the llama press his face on his neck. "You don't have to answer if it makes you uncomfortable," it said. "Vermilion is just a curious one who doesn't understand personal space." It looked back at Vermilion with a stern look.

The bright reddish-orange monkey stuck out her tongue at the llama.

"No. I have to own up to my mistakes at some point." The lion prince looked up at everyone, their gaze full of anticipation. He took a deep breath in and exhaled.

"My Father, King Jung-hwa of the Promised Dynasty, intended to have me married off to the princess of the Demoniacal Kingdom, Princess Okome," he explained. "She was a pretty she-wolf, and I had instantly fallen in love with her when we first met, even though I had massive doubts about the whole marriage and alliance of the two Kingdoms. As the days passed, our love grew stronger than ever. It made me realize: I genuinely fell in love with her. I couldn't care less about the alliance or what anyone said; Princess Okome was the one for me. A week went by, and it was the day before the marriage; we were to wed on her birthday. It was one date, her guards were sent by her brother to check up on her, one of them pushed me to a breaking point so I fought them and..."

The lion prince closed his eyes, unable to look at them. *And.* The rest was too dreadful to recall. He began to tremble as the bad memories came rushing back to his brain. He had to tell them.

They have to know who they're dealing with.

"A-And I...I..I accidentally killed her."

The silence was enough for him to know they were just as shocked as he had been. He opened up his eyes again.

"I understand you all may have mixed feelings, and... and you guys definitely don't have to keep me in your clan," he said. "I will only be a danger. The Demoniacal Kingdom will find you if you keep me. You can drive me out once I heal. Or drive me out now...either or is okay..."

Everyone had looked at each other, confused. Aleena stepped up, taking his chin in her hand.

SEEKING REFUGE IN A FAR DISTANT CLAN

"Who said we were going to drive you out of the clan?" she asked.

"Well... the Shell Clan, the Emerald Clan, the Fire Clan, and Onyx Clan did. All of them. They were afraid that the Demoniacal Kingdom would find them if I had stayed with them. Which...I don't blame them for, and I wouldn't blame you guys either if you feel that way."

"Oh no way did you just visit the Shell Clan," Vermilion said. "They're being corrupted from the inside by those pirates."

The Peruvian spider monkey fixed his tuft of fur. "Who said we were scared of the Demoniacal Kingdom?"

The lion prince lifted up his ears. A clan that doesn't fear the Demoniacal Kingdom? That was new. Practically *every* clan Prince Wonwoo went to would hide their tails between their legs whenever they were mentioned. No one wanted anything to do with them or get themselves involved with them, and for obvious reasons. He couldn't blame them. But the Tropic Clan not fearing the Demoniacal Kingdom?

"Y...You really don't fear them?" he asked.

Vermilion was the one to answer with her outburst. "Yeah! You don't know us well but, we literally fight CROCODILES FOR GODS' SAKES and eat them for breakfast!"

"Well, we don't *eat* them, per se," Kitwana said. "Unless we desire."

"Yeah. Which is...Everyday!"

"Not everyday."

Vermilion stuck her tongue out at the jaguar. That seemed to be a trait of the reddish-orange monkey. "You're killing the mood here, Kitwana!"

Aleena brushed off her adopted sister and looked at Prince Wonwoo with a soft smile. "Ignoring Vermilion. Yeah, we live in a harsh environment, so we're used to danger," she said. "The Demoniacal Kingdom would just be another regular day for us. You don't have to worry about them here, Prince Wonwoo. Here, we look out for each other. We live in peace, in harmony, one with nature and the Gods."

Life surged back into the lion prince when he heard those words. He looked at Aleena with a hopeful shine in his eyes. "Are you...?"

"Prince Wonwoo of the Promised Dynasty, you are more than welcome to stay with the Tropic Clan for however long you wish."

Prince Wonwoo stared at the Peruvian spider monkey. He couldn't believe it. He wished he could jump in excitement and hug Aleena, but his brain reminded him about the state of his body right now. He held back and instead bowed at her. "Thank you so much, Queen Aleena!" he said. "I owe you so much!"

Aleena laughed and patted his head. "Oh, I'm not a Queen," she corrected. "I'm just a leader. Specifically a Tropic Bloom. That's what we call leaders in our clan."

"Ah crap, I'm sorry, I'm just— used to saying King or Queen."

"I know. The Promised Dynasty and the Demoniacal Kingdom are the only ones that establish their leaders as Kings and Queens."

The lion prince shrugged. "Yeah." He felt rude for answering like that, but he was so out of breath and drained in all aspects, he couldn't bring himself to have a normal conversation.

"I can see you're exhausted. I think we can end our pleasantries for today. You go get some rest. Everyone is dismissed."

With a snap of her finger, those who were with her except the bush dog and the llama left (basically only Vermilion and Kitwana). Prince Wonwoo watched the two of them disappear, Vermilion lingering behind to look back at him before Kitwana nipped his teeth at her ear. She shook her head, peeking one last time before leaving. Prince Wonwoo tilted his head.

What was all that about?

"Would you like something to eat before you go to sleep?" Aleena asked, turning her head back to him. "We've got a wide variety of food."

"Uhmm..." Prince Wonwoo hummed, tapping his chin with his only good paw. "Anything will do."

"Okay! I'll get you some crocodile to taste!" She winked and then left. He could hear hooting from the Peruvian spider monkey, followed by a loud response from Vermilion:

"AWWWWW NO WAY!!! YOU'RE GONNA MAKE HIM EAT CROCODILE!? SICK! I CALL DIBS ON CHOOSING THE BEST PART FOR HIM TO TRY!!"

"Vermilion."

The lion prince laughed, pressing himself to the llama. "That's hilarious! But, she's just joking, right?" he asked the llama. When he saw his serious expression, he slowly stopped laughing. "She's...joking..right?"

The llama's face did not change. Prince Wonwoo raised an eyebrow at him.

"...Right?! Ha ha funny??"

Nothing.

He looked away from the llama and turned his attention to the bush dog for answers, who avoided his gaze.

Nothing. Nothing all across the board.

Prince Wonwoo looked back at the entrance of the den. He swallowed nervously.

This was totally going to be a life changer for sure.

CHAPTER 13
THE LIFE BEYOND THE TWO KINGDOMS

~ One month later... ~
~ August in Terra Cycle 1118 B.E. ~

"Hey hey heeeeeeyyyy! Wakey waaaaakeyyyyyy, little pretty royal alllllmightyy liiionnnn!"

The lion prince had been sleeping peacefully in a deep sleep when he felt hands shaking his flank and the singsongy voice. He scrunched his face and grumbled, waving his paw to get whoever was nearby to go away. "Just a few more minutes, please, angel," he bargained, rolling his back towards the entrance of his room, "I feel as if I ate a huge fat pig."

It didn't seem to work when he still felt the hands.

"You forced me to do this."

There followed a crisp **SLAP** across his face, prompting him to awake in a startle.

"AH! AH, OWW! WHAT? WHY, WHO??"

"Wake up! Aleena wants to see you! You better not be dead! Wake up right now!"

He rubbed his eyes as sunlight poured into the den. His eyes finally opened, and he saw Vermilion the howler monkey in his blurry vision. "Oh. Vermilion. It's you." Now the energetic tone of the voice made sense as to who it was. The jungle also came through, specifically his den. He looked around his den; all his essentials, like tables, chairs and bed, were woven by the Tropic Clan members out of vines and leaves and held by stones and sticks, glued together with cobwebs. Although it was a culture shock to him, he had to admire the Tropic Clan for finding use of the old ways instead of advancing entirely.

"Good. You're not dead." The howler monkey chuckled, placing her hand on her shoulder. "I was kind of worried there for a moment...I mean, what?? Nothing!! Haha..."

"Vermilion? What time is it?" he grumbled, letting out a yawn that sounded like a growl.

"Gau is letting the moon rest, and Dagny is barely just lifting the sun," the howler monkey answered, hopping back.

The lion prince shot himself up at Vermilion's answer, ignoring the screaming of his still healing muscles. What she was telling him was that it was basically Dagny's First Rise. "That early!?" he shouted.

"Yeah?"

"...WHY!? Why does Aleena need me *this* early?"

"She wants to take you for a tour of the jungle!"

A tour? He grumbled, resting his head in his paws. He really wanted to sleep in some more, but he guessed he shouldn't continue being a useless member in the clan. He would eventually have to learn of their ways if he was to stay here, know their way of life. Even if it meant waking up this early in the day to begin. He shut his mouth instantly.

"That is, of course, if you're up for it," Vermilion added. "We know you're still recovering from your injuries. Aleena just wanted to make the offer."

The lion prince yawned again, rubbing his jaw. "No, no no. Okay, okay, I'm up then. Tell her I'll meet her in...10 minutes tops."

The howler monkey nodded. "Alright! Do you want me to get you anything to eat before we go? The patrol may take a few hours or so."

"No, I'm okay. I had my fill last night, and I feel so full. I'll probably get a little snack once I get myself out of the den."

"Alright then, if you say soooo." The howler monkey narrowed her eyes in a smug. "It was good, wasn't it?"

"By the Gods, yessssss." Prince Wonwoo had to admit, the crocodile he was given really opened his eyes to a brand new world. He could not stop consuming when he had taken the first bite. He would say that it was now one of his favorite foreign delicacies. If only he had wine with him, then he would truly feel like a God.

"See, I told you it was going to be good. Now look at you, a lover of crocodile meat. It's so good to have someone I can relate to. See you soon!" Vermilion disappeared through the vines.

"See ya, Vermilion." Prince Wonwoo stretched gingerly, making sure not to injure himself further. His waking mind began to reel. Even though a month had passed, he still knew his wounds were not entirely healed. But he had healed enough to the point that he could walk, trot (not run), and crouch to a certain degree. He still could not hunt for himself or bear to drink from the river (not only cause he can't crouch all the way, but the trauma he had with the crocodiles made him afraid to go anywhere near any body of water) and had to rely on the clan to provide for him. He felt extremely terrible, being so weak for all to see and bear with, but no one seemed to mind it at all. They treated him like he was one of them. The lion prince was grateful for this clan and their hospitality.

After much breathing to steady himself, he walked towards the entrance and shoved through the leaves that covered the entrance. He lifted up a paw to shield himself from the sunlight. In the one month he had lived here, he never went beyond the entrance of his den. This time was now going to be different. His eyes squinted. The Tropic Clan had made this jungle their home, and it shows.

Their camp was a large, cut down underground, surrounded by numerous trees around them. They were large trees, with thick vines hanging from their branches. One particular tree stuck out in the middle, standing tall as if it was a statue of a God. That was Aleena's home, the only tree that was never cut down. It had been a sacred home for the leader of the Tropic Clan for many terra cycles. Sunlight poured through the canopy, rays beaming down on the camp below. A warm but comforting wind breezed through and brought fresh air to Prince Wonwoo. He inhaled deeply, taking in the fresh scent of the incoming autumn. The lion prince padded through the camp, basking in the life of the clan. Clan members were roaming and lazing about as children played. He could hear their happy and ear-splitting squeals, reminding him of the Promised Dynasty.

A particular group of children caught his attention when they mentioned something intriguing.

"Fear me! For I am King Wyvern, the most evil creature in all the land!"

The name King Wyvern sent a chill down his spine. Locating the source, his eyes rested on four children: a baby orangutan, an okapi calf, a dhole pup and a gaur calf. He had never seen such animals before anywhere in the Promised Dynasty and was therefore intrigued. The gaur calf was the one who was pretending to be King Wyvern, waving his head around with pride. The lion prince assumed they were pretending to replicate the historical event. So Prince Wonwoo sat down, curious about the group of children and having briefly forgotten about meeting up with Aleena. He leaned his head closer, raising an ear.

"I found myself this great power in the form of dark magic!" the gaur calf said, lifting up a hoof and waving it around as if he had

THE LIFE BEYOND THE TWO KINGDOMS

magic. "With it, I will create a brand new world! Everyone will bow to me! You cannot stop me, muahahaha!"

Huh...It's..kind of almost right, Prince Wonwoo thought. *It's similar, but it isn't word for word what he really told King Saturhorimau. Eh. I shouldn't be harsh; the calf's young. And definitely acting. So.*

The okapi calf and dhole pup pressed against each other at the gaur calf's words, shivering. Prince Wonwoo knew they were pretending, but he could still see some real fear in their eyes. It caught his curiosity; King Wyvern was only known as a threat to the Promised Dynasty, so seeing a clan shiver at his name was an interesting first to the lion prince. His influence had definitely spread far throughout the land.

The baby orangutan stood up, raising its tiny arms.

"Don't be afraid, my followers!" the baby monkey proclaimed. "I, King Saturhorimau, will defend you all and the land from this terrible evil!"

The okapi and dhole rejoiced.

"Praise King Saturhorimau!"

"Long live the Heavens!"

King Saturhorimau!? Prince Wonwoo looked at the little orangutan. *He* was pretending to be the First Lion King?? The tiny baby orangutan pretending to be his great-grandfather was adorable, the lion prince couldn't contain his small laughter. He had to cover his mouth with his paw.

The gaur calf huffed, stomping his hoof.

"Traitors! I'll make you see!"

That calf is really into the role of the wyvern dragon king, Prince Wonwoo thought to himself. *It's just...so adorable!*

"The only thing you'll be seeing is the power of our Creator Ellowyn and Her warmth!"

So is the baby orangutan! Adorable all around!

The four of them then charged at each other, play-wrestling. Prince Wonwoo watched the tiny creatures playfully swatting and batting at each other with trust. He could tell they were definitely best friends. The orangutan, okapi and dhole gently butted with the gaur, letting out happy squeals of victory. Eventually the calf fell in a dramatic way, pinned down by the dhole pup, and the other three cheered.

"This battle is over! We've won!" the dhole pup yapped, bouncing around the gaur calf.

Won? Prince Wonwoo blinked. *We didn't win...*

"No no no! That isn't how it goes!" the okapi calf said. "There was no winner, Shikazu. Remember?"

Well, someone's a smart little ungulate.

"What? I like to think there was," the dhole pup, named Shikazu, said, puffing out his cheeks.

"No, Dusk is right. There was no winner," the gaur calf said, rising to his hooves. "King Wyvern actually killed King Saturhorimau, but he was brought back to life by the Heavens and, along with the angels, declared an end to the war. This terrified King Wyvern. The two agreed to a treaty, but neither claimed victory."

"Yeah."

The lion prince flicked his ears.

Woah. Really smart...That calf knows his history.

"Which, technically speaking, means the war is still ongoing. If you really think about it..."

Prince Wonwoo couldn't shut up his mind. The gaur calf's statement struck him in a certain way. He was right; although the two founders have agreed to end the war, they had never officially said it was *over* over. King Wyvern and the Demoniacal Kingdom continued to be nuisances to King Saturhorimau and the Promised Dynasty in the following terra cycles, even getting into petty territorial disputes that normally would be solved with a simple conversation.

"The war is still ongoing."

Prince Wonwoo lowered his eyes.

I...I guess it is...

Shikazu kept pouting. "Aw, that's not fun!"

"Well, it's history! Didn't you ever pay attention in history class?"

"Yes, but. Come on, Graund! It's fun to pretend that we did in fact win."

"Yeah, but–"

"Alright, alright, enough lingering on this part, let's continue!" the orangutan interrupted the two, getting between them just in case. "Let's get to the best part!"

"Yeah, yeah! The treaty and the formation of the Promised Dynasty!" Dusk said.

The lion prince felt his heart swell back up; he was glad that the Promised Dynasty left at least a great impact to those who could not join them.

"Ohhh yeah this will be fun!"

"Let's sneak the others out of class for this. Come on!"

"Hold it right there, little ones."

Prince Wonwoo looked at the animal approaching them. He was surprised to see it was an elephant with slightly darker gray skin. Unlike Jiro, this elephant was rather small for its size. He also noticed that she had no tusks, which was unusual for an elephant. Questions ran through his head, mainly what happened to them? Had she been born without them or did she lose them in some kind of accident?

Perhaps one day I can talk to her, he thought. *See what wisdom she's collected throughout her years like Jiro.*

The four children squeaked at the sight of the elephant.

"Oh no!" Shikazu said. "We've been caught."

"Rats!"

She smiled at them with warmness.

"If you think you guys can skip class again for another play, think twice," she gently berated them.

"Awww, but Ms. Flayke–" Shikazu started.

The jungle elephant, named Ms. Flayke, wrapped her trunk around the four and nudged them ahead of her. "No questions. Get back to class you rascals."

"Awwwww!"

Prince Wonwoo smiled at the antics of the children. They reminded him of his classmates when he was little and in school. He shook his head, still laughing to himself. They were so adorable in their reenactment. He stood up after they bounded away with Ms. Flayke trailing behind them to make sure they didn't stray away again and looked around, trying to find Aleena. He didn't see her amongst the clan members, who were all busy either sleeping, talking to one another or eating. His stomach slightly rumbled. He figured now was the time to get himself acquainted with the clan as he found a small something to quickly eat.

He approached a small group, consisting of a harpy eagle, a crested serpent eagle and a gorilla. The gorilla had a silver lining on its back, indicating to the lion prince he was male. He hesitated with each paw step. They were all huddled and enjoying breakfast while discussing amongst themselves. Prince Wonwoo looked curiously at this group; it wasn't unusual of species to mingle with others, but the three of them were indeed an interesting trio. A large ape so calmly chatting up with birds as if they were his brothers and sisters when he could easily snap their necks with a squeeze of his hand. That was a sight to surely startle anyone not used to it.

He doesn't appear to be a threat, Prince Wonwoo thought, watching the gorilla rumble in laughter. *He looks friendly enough. I shouldn't be afraid or else he can detect it.*

"Excuse me," he called out warmly, "do any of you know where Aleena is? She was going to take me on tour."

The gorilla looked up, picking the remains from his large teeth. "You barely missed her, lion. She was out just a while ago with us discussing the upcoming patrol, but she retreated back to her den in the tree with her sister," he answered, pointing to the tree.

Prince Wonwoo flicked his tail. "Damn. Thank you kindly."

"She'll be back, but it might be a bit before she comes out. In the meantime. Come. Eat with us." The gorilla padded a spot in front of them.

The lion prince froze, flabbergasted at the proposal, but the kind looks on their faces made him feel safe. They didn't mean him harm, they were looking out for him like any other. He joined them eagerly. He stared down at their breakfast. Their pile was a mix of snakes, eggs and berries. It was an interesting mix, considering the species the trio were, but the eggs were making his mouth water. He sat down, curling his tail behind him. He gingerly poked at the pile. The snakes were giving him the creeps, their dead eyes seemingly staring at him from beyond the Heavens. The crested serpent eagle took notice of the frightened lion prince.

"Snakes aren't that bad," the dark brown eagle said. "They're really tasty. Plus, they're not venomous."

Ahahaha. You're funny, he joked as he picked out a couple eggs and raspberries. He didn't want to imagine the thought of it suddenly coming to life and slithering and biting. "No thanks, I'll pass on the snakes."

The crested serpent eagle shrugged its wings, grabbing one with its talons. "Your loss!"

"So, you're the lion prince, aren't you?" the harpy eagle asked.

Unfortunately. "Yes, I am."

"I couldn't believe it when Aleena mentioned that you would be here with us for however long you're staying. It's like a blessing from the Gods."

I'm a blessing? The lion prince raised an eyebrow, cracking the top of one of the eggs and pouring the yolk out. He considered himself a curse after evading death many more times than normally allowed. Morana must really want his head right about now. When he thought of her, a cold breeze whisked by, warning him.

"It's definitely a good sign for us," the gorilla stated. "With the lion prince here, we are much safer than ever before."

"Ellowyn is truly watching us and keeping us safe," the crested serpent eagle softly chirped, looking to the morning sky. The harpy eagle and the gorilla returned the sentence by looking up and closing their eyes. The lion prince watched them, his heart growing lighter at the fact there were clans out here who believed in the goodness of the Gods. Better yet, he was glad there were creatures out there who treated him no different, despite the crime hanging over his head and his status.

I've committed a grave sin, yet they don't treat me like garbage, he thought to himself. *Just like how my Kingdom protected me after... that day...*

"So tell me, lion prince: what's it like, being royalty and everything?" the harpy eagle inquired.

Prince Wonwoo twitched his tail tip. "It's nothing interesting, honestly," he answered. "Of course people will treat you different, but I like to think I'm just a normal creature."

"But you experience life in a better way."

"Not really? It's just...a normal life."

"Well, it's better than what most of us go through." The harpy eagle snatched up a snake and consumed it without a single bite.

I don't know about that. Prince Wonwoo lamented on the many siblings he had lost before he was born. His mother and father were deeply pained by these traumatic experiences, yet they managed to pull through. He would never get to experience his siblings. He thought about them every single night when he dreamed. He met them in his sleep, he was only able to hug them in the dream. But he would never get to hug them in the physical world. *It's probably different from other traumas, I guess, but I mean... it can happen to any of us, regardless of status.*

"I do hope you will enjoy life here in Tropic Clan," the crested serpent eagle piped up, rousing him from his sorrowful memories.

"Agreed! You'll definitely love it here."

Prince Wonwoo wiggled his whiskers. "Thank you."

"She should be awakening around this time now," the gorilla mentioned, picking up a snake after the harpy eagle and ripping into it.

"Oh. Okay. I gotta go talk to her." He consumed the last of his eggs and berries before standing up. "Thank you again, all three of you," Prince Wonwoo thanked, bowing. "May Ellowyn bless you all."

They waved at him.

"See you on the patrol, Prince Wonwoo!"

Just call me Wonwoo please, he wanted to tell them but bit back the urge. He knew it wouldn't be rude to voice his discomforts, but he wanted to be respectful. He bounded away and looked up at the large tree in the middle. Vermilion emerged from the large hole instead of Aleena, catching Prince Wonwoo's eyes with interest. She swiveled her head back and hollered.

"He's here, Tropic Bloom Aleena!"

The Peruvian spider monkey emerged soon after she had been called, looking down and smiling. She elegantly climbed down the large tree and landed softly on her hands and feet. Prince Wonwoo was impressed at the monkey's grace. He had seen monkeys before, he was even friends with some back home, but seeing one so elegant as Aleena was a new sight. Her movements were adapted for the wild, not for the sophisticated, domesticated life, and it showed. It was rather a beautiful show of adaptation to one's surroundings.

She walked up to him, prompting him to bow.

"Tropic Bloom Aleena," he greeted.

"Good morning. How are your injuries, young lion?" Aleena asked.

He winced when she gingerly touched his injured leg. "I'm okay," he responded. "I'm able to stand for long hours now unlike before. As you can see."

"Yes, I can see. That's good. At least the herbs are working." She patted his shoulder. "Are you going to be okay for our tour? You don't have to if you're still not feeling well. I just want you to get acquainted with our territory."

Prince Wonwoo nodded. "I'll be okay."

She raised an eyebrow.

"I promise. Plus, I don't want to be any more of a useless burden in your clan."

The Peruvian spider monkey didn't appear convinced. "I'm bringing one of our best guards to watch you just in case. She should be here soon." She gently smacked his head. "Also you're not useless nor are you a burden. Stop saying that."

The lion prince pouted. "But it's true!"

"I'm here, Tropic Bloom Aleena."

Prince Wonwoo lifted up his ears and looked to where the soft voice came from. From atop the trees, a small rosetted feline climbed down with the same elegance and grace Aleena had. She approached the lion prince and the Peruvian spider monkey with said elegance. The lion prince's eyes stared intently.

Oh wow.

"Prince Wonwoo, this is Moth," Aleena introduced. "A margay. She's one of the best guards I could ever have. I hope you get along well with her." She turned her attention to the margay. "Moth, this is Prince Wonwoo of the Promised Dynasty."

Moth. Prince Wonwoo parroted the name in the back of his head. *What a pretty name for a feline such as herself.*

"It's a pleasure to meet you for the first time, Prince Wonwoo," the margay, Moth, said with a bow. "Though, not entirely the first time. I've been taking care of you alongside Vermilion when you were recovering." She looked up, tipped her head and smiled.

The lion prince blinked. He was unaware of the clan members also approaching to join the patrol, which included the gorilla and the two eagles. He wasn't sure how to respond, but something about her reminded him of Princess Okome. He stared at her, probably looking like an idiot in the process.

She's really pretty. And she sounds.. .lovely... Like the voice of an angel...

He smiled back at her.

Say something back, idiot. Stop standing there like a dolt!

"I-It's nice to meet you too, Moth," he finally said. Then he finally realized: "...Oh! Oh, I remember you now... You were that sweet angelic voice I would hear when I would be drifting in and out of consciousness. No wonder Ayumu would bless me with sweet dreams after hearing your voice. It's great to finally see you officially."

She just giggled at his response.

His heart jumped at her laughter, realizing what he had just said. *I can't believe you said that aloud!* He smacked his tail on his shoulder, reprimanding himself. *How could you have more confidence casually saying that to Moth than with Princess Okome?* He stopped his thoughts.

"Alright, Tropic Patrol, we're heading out!" Aleena hollered, rising. She went ahead while the clan members she had chosen followed after her. Prince Wonwoo watched the group curiously. It was so strange; normally, the guards in the Promised Dynasty would just stand watch at the gates. They never exactly patrolled. They just guarded.

Moth offered her shoulder to the astonished Prince Wonwoo. "Need some leverage?" she asked.

The lion prince whisked his tail to the side. "No, no. I'm okay! I can...stand..on, uh..stand on my own... Thank you anyway."

The margay smirked. "What? A royal prince afraid of showing weakness in front of commoners?"

He couldn't see it, but his cheeks began to pinken. "Huh?? What, no- I-I appreciate the offer. I— I just–"

"Why do you stutter so much?" The margay squinted her eyes at him. "You're blushing? A little strange. I wonder why?" She raised her head, realization coming across her face. "Ohh! Are you smitten by me already? I didn't even have to try."

Prince Wonwoo's ears stood tall. "What!? I– Uhm—!"

She chuckled at him. "How adorable!" She trailed her bushy tail under his chin, tickling it. "Come on, pretty boy. We shouldn't linger behind any longer."

The lion prince looked away, his face burning hot. Was he already becoming obvious? His heart began to pound hard in his chest. He was glad Aleena hadn't heard, apart from a few clan members who turned their heads curiously. His ears pinned against the back of his head.

Ignore the feelings, ignore the feelings. Just focus on the tour, and it will all be good.

Prince Wonwoo collapsed in his den. He was completely exhausted.

The tour had taken over more than an hour, and he was shown all around the Tropic Clan. He was amazed at how large the jungle was. It was definitely huge and spanned larger territory than Divine Kingfisher Woods. It was all their home, with no rivals (apart from the crocodiles) and friendly allies.

Although he enjoyed the tour, he found himself more immersed with Moth than he intended. His mind reeled on their interaction; the two had bonded well, the lion prince enjoying her snarky and playful personality as she showed him other various parts of the jungle that Aleena hadn't shared to him. Prince Wonwoo enjoyed having her around, though he could definitely see that Vermilion was jealous of her stealing him from her. Vermilion did join on a few conversations, even showing him things as well (such as her favorite scouting areas, the best part of the river, etc.), but she left the two of them alone. Prince Wonwoo saw so much of Princess Okome in the margay, he started to feel a little bad.

Did he like her just because she reminded him of Princess Okome? Would he ever find genuine feelings for her?

Or would the spark die?

He curled up in his leaf bed, tucking his nose in his paws. No. He didn't want to think about it. He couldn't have caught feelings for her that fast. There was just no way. *It's too soon!* he sighed. *I'm not ready for this, I can't be. I should better control myself. For me and for Moth.* He was so exhausted, he wanted to sleep for terra cycles. He closed his eyes, an image of Princess Okome projecting in his mind's eye–

"Hey sleepyhead. I got ya something to eat."

A nose pressed on his head, and Prince Wonwoo raised himself up to see who was there. Speak of the devil. It was Moth the margay again, replacing Princess Okome and with a guinea pig in her mouth. His heart jumped in surprise. What was she doing here? Didn't she have any other important duties to tend to that wasn't checking up on him? She laid the guinea pig down and nosed it to him.

"For you." She smiled.

The lion prince stared at it.

"A...guinea pig," he said dubiously.

"Yes, a guinea pig. Bet you never had a guinea pig before in your life, huh?" she stated in a snarky tone, tucking her paws underneath her chest and belly. "You have the same look every outsider has. 'Am I...eating a pet!? I can't do that! Get that away from me!!' Trust me, you'll like it. Plus: It's the wild guinea pig, not the domesticated one. So don't worry if you think you're eating someone's pet we stole; we're not that cruel."

"I'm sure I will like it," he answered sarcastically.

"Aw, already picking up on my tone! That's cute."

The lion prince took the guinea pig carefully, not minding his heart rate increasing. *You're not helping with controlling my feelings,* he grumbled to himself. *Are you interested in me as well already?* He didn't think to consider a guinea pig as food. It was a bit of a culture shock to him. He sank his teeth into the small rodent and instantly cringed at the taste. It wasn't bad or anything, it was just strange for him to eat an animal that was considered a pet. He swallowed hesitantly, shivering away his gag reflexes. He took another bite since he couldn't get a good hold of the taste, this time chewing it slow.

"Interesting... taste," Prince Wonwoo said with a mouth full.

"Let me guess, chicken?" Moth asked, scooting next to him with intent.

The lion prince, face flushed from Moth's touch, shook his head. "No actually. More like..." He paused. "...Not chicken."

The margay laughed. "You're a funny little lion."

His heart soared. She sounded just like Princess Okome. *Okome, did you reincarnate into this feline?* He asked himself, continuing to eat. His ears drooped.

What's wrong with me? Why was he still thinking about her when he was with Moth? Had he not truly moved on from the wolf princess's death? He sighed, feeling his eyelids sinking.

Maybe it was his heart trying to find new happiness.

My brain's telling me I'm not ready, and I should listen to it, but my heart is being pulled towards her, he rambled, looking at her. *Maybe moving on means getting with her. Would Okome want this?* His tail slowly wormed its way towards her. *What am I doing?*

Moth nudged his shoulder, making him instinctively pull away his tail. "Hey. When you're done, I'd like you to come with me. I want to show you something more in detail."

The lion prince forced open his eyes. "Oh. Okay." *Wonder what she wants to show me?* He asked himself curiously. *Probably something interesting. I can't wait!*

...

He indeed had not awaited. He had immediately forgotten.

Night fell, and Moth awoke a very sleepy Prince Wonwoo. He was confused on why she was waking him up, but then remembered that she was wanting to show him something earlier. He looked away in embarrassment. "Oops, sorry," he had told her. What this something was she wanted him to know, he wasn't sure.

Moth was being a bit snarky with him when he tried asking her what she wanted to show him and where they were going exactly, telling him, "You'll see when we get there~"

"Ha ha," he had responded.

She took him for a stroll outside the jungle. He observed the sleeping clan members before they had left. Some hung on vines, sleeping without any care in the world while some slept in their dens or in a tree. He was amazed at how sound asleep they were out in the open. He couldn't imagine exposing himself to the outside dangers without any form of protection.

Once outside the camp, Moth led the lion prince towards the heart of the jungle. The moonlight shone rather strongly tonight, as if Gau had sensed the two and was jumping in joy at seeing activity. It was here she finally told him where she was taking him. Apparently, there exists a tree that is supposedly as old as the universe. Prince Wonwoo remembered this tree; Aleena had shown him on their tour, and heard the interesting tale and legends from her, but he didn't entirely believe that to be true. He wanted further proof. He wanted to go up to the tree, but the Peruvian spider monkey prohibited him from getting closer to the tree, as it was, of course, old. He respected that, but his curiosity couldn't be contained.

Now, Moth was leading him to this tree, and, while he was nervous about it, he couldn't wait to actually get closer to it.

"Is it really true?" he asked her as they strolled along. "That the tree is, like, super ancient?"

"Oh yeah," Moth replied. "It's SUPER old indeed."

"How come Aleena didn't want me close to it?"

"She doesn't allow anyone near the tree. She fears if we interfere with it, it will shrivel." She pouted. "Also the curse. That's more the huge factor why she didn't want you close to the tree. She's pretty superstitious if you can't tell."

"Oh I know. I am as well. But not like... super super superstitious, you know what I mean?"

Aleena had said it was old, but apparently there was a curse that hung around the tree.

Legends say that many terra cycles ago, before King Saturhorimau and King Wyvern were even born, a horrible war ravaged the land. Information on this war was very scattered and missing. So scattered, only the Heavens would have records of it. A terrible tragedy occurred right in front of the tree. Two lovers–ancient ancestors of the founder of the Tropic Clan–lost their lives: one hanged from the tree for crimes, the other pierced with an arrow to the heart and pinned to the tree. They had been from opposing sides but had found love. They had one child together, and they ran away from their respective homes to live in peace. While it did work, they were still hunted down for their treason and killed. Their child was kidnapped but later survived and returned to the tree, making the camp that would be the Tropic Clan's territory. Because of this, the tree had been called Esme, after the one who was pinned and left to die on the tree.

To be loved.

Now, the curse went something like this: should anyone dare disturb the tree or climb on it recklessly without paying respects, one would be plagued with bad luck and misfortune the lovers had faced while they were alive until the day they die. The clan would also be cursed because of the individual. It sounded like an old superstition to him, and it made his brain run rampant with excitement on wanting to see if it was true. Which was unusual of him since he believed heavily on certain things, but something made him want to find out the truth.

Moth looked back at him. "I mean, how are you not? You're a Promised Dynasty member." She bumped her hind against him. "Now, come on, we're nearby."

The margay broke off into a run, which made Prince Wonwoo chase after her. "Wait!" His body screamed at the sudden change in movement, and he knew he could not run to his fullest. His muscles ached at being stretched. He chased as fast as he could before he gave up and let his body rest. "Wait, Moth! Slow down a bit, won't ya? I can't...run that fast..." He looked up and gasped.

Ahead of him laid the large, ancient tree. From his knowledge of nature, Prince Wonwoo was able to conclude it was an acacia tree. There were many wrinkles on the bark that showed its age. Its many branches stuck out in a unique zigzag pattern and looked like bolts of lightning. The top appeared like a tiny hill, the moonlight showing its lush green color.

"Wow..." he breathed, walking up to the tree. His paw reached out to touch the wrinkled bark, but he pulled it back. He didn't want to do anything to curse his life and the Tropic Clan (or the Promised Dynasty for that matter). He put his paw down, looking at the bark. He could see in the wrinkles that indeed this tree was old. If only he could see the rings and count how many there were to accurately determine its age...

He patted the ground under him, bowing.

I know you don't know me, but I offer my blessings to you both out of respect.

The margay appeared from out of the leaves, startling him. "Magnificent, isn't it?"

"W-What are you doing on the tree?" he asked in shock. "I thought Aleena said it was prohibited to..."

"Remember how I said she was superstitious?"

"Y-Yeah?"

"Well, it's true. She's very easily spooked. But that's because of traumatic things that happened to her when she was little. Not my place to speak about. Anyway. I've been here numerous times in secret, and nothing bad has happened with me or the clan. There's nothing stopping me from being on this tree, I love climbing trees. Kind of my thing, you know? So there's nothing to fear from Aleena's superstitious tales." She reached out her paws at him. "Come on."

The lion prince tipped his head in confusion. Was she entirely right? He thought back on the clan's comments about the crocodile pod that attacked him. They apparently have been their main trouble for terra cycles. Had they moved in because Moth cursed the clan? When he thought about it again, he realized it had to be bogus; crocodiles resided in jungles, so it wasn't too uncommon for a wild pod to live in one. How would a silly little curse bring a natural predator into a habitat it was already accustomed to?

That's stupid.

Prince Wonwoo stared at Moth. She hung from her tail on a branch, arms extended and paws beckoning him. Her body language showed that she was not meaning any harm. He shook his head. "...Can you even lift me up? I mean— No offense to you or your capabilities, I'm a giant lion, and you're...you're a tiny little cat.. I— Uhm."

Moth's eyes softened, her smirk also relaxing into a comforting, warm smile. "Trust me."

The lion prince, hesitant but soothed by her words, reached up and held onto her tiny paws. His heart ascended up to his throat from the sheer force of the small feline pulling him up the tree and launching him towards a branch. "AH!" He ignored the pain in his body as he was being pulled up. He landed and clung onto a thick branch. *A warning would have been nice!* his mind shouted. *That was terrifying.*

He tried finding Moth but she had already disappeared further up the tree. He looked down and saw how high he was. "Ahhh..." He pressed himself further into the branch, whimpering to himself.

Normally he wasn't afraid of heights, but he was still recovering from his injuries. He couldn't risk falling without hurting himself further. He could only rely on not letting go of the branch and Moth.

Gods, please please please don't let me fall. He looked around. *Where are you, Moth!?*

Moth peeked her head through the leaves again, startling him.

Gods! You love scaring me, don't you?

"There you are!" When she noticed his fear, she rolled her eyes in a teasing way. "Oh, come on. You can't be that scared already? We're barely at the top."

"I-I'm not afraid," he stuttered, blushing. "I'm just...I never really climbed a tree in my life ever before. As crazy as it probably sounds to you. Also, my wounds are still healing. My body is still very much sore."

"Meh. You're fineeee, stop being so dramatic."

"I'm not being dramatic!"

Moth rolled her eyes and grabbed his scruff. "Yoink!"

"Woah!" He wasn't sure how to feel at the strength of this margay, but he was sort of glad she could be there to help him up. Even if it meant helping up a tree. Breaking through the foliage, he was greeted with the night sky and Moth's smile. She cleaned away any leaves that stuck in his fur.

"Hey, I would appreciate a little warning next time," he told her, shaking his head.

"I thought princes would be more attending to their appearances," she said jokingly.

The lion prince looked away. "Oh, shush. I mean- Well I wasn't intending on ever climbing a tree this late at night, but here we are," he said in a gentle huff. He looked to the side and let his jaw gape. "Oh, wow."

The jungle was pretty at night. Crickets and cicadas sang their songs and filled the air for all to hear. The moonlight shone on the trees, bathing them in a light silver glow. He was able to see the camp of the Tropic Clan from where he was at from the smoke of the campfire. It was a large hole in the middle of a sea of trees.

"Beautiful, isn't it?" Moth asked.

"Yeah...really beautiful," he replied.

"I just wanted you to see this amazing view. Especially to introduce you to it since I haven't had anyone to just hang out with while sightseeing." She licked her paw hesitantly. "I figured now that we're...friends and all, well. You know. Heh."

"Well, it's very enjoyable, Moth, and I would love to do these nightly sightseeings with you."

"You do?" she asked, batting her eyes at him in a bashful way.

"Yes. I do," he replied. "It's really pretty..." He turned to look back at Moth.

"Now that we're...friends."

The way she paused when saying that sentence was more than enough of an indicator that she too had her own secrets. She was probably feeling the same as he was. Prince Wonwoo flicked his ears, lowering his gaze.

Should he take this opportunity to finally ask her about their feelings?

He lifted up his head.

"Hey. Since we're here, alone... Uhm...Can I ask you a question? Or rather...talk to you about...something?"

The margay, having now delicately balanced and rested on the treetop, looked over to the lion prince. Her paws rested on her chest, within the fluff of her fur. She twitched her ears. "What's up?"

Here goes nothing. "About what you said, about me..liking you..?"

"Yeah?" Before he could continue, she smirked at him. "You *do* like me. Don't you?"

Prince Wonwoo's fur bristled in embarrassment. He looked down. "I- Uhm!" *Idiot, idiot, idiot! She knows! She knows you like her because you're so obvious!* Could he really admit it? They had just met after all, but after the patrol, he found himself growing close to her. He wanted to know more about her, hang out with her more and develop their friendship to see where his feelings for her would go. But he wasn't sure if it was genuine with his feelings or not. He was still, in a way, mourning Princess Okome's death. Could he have recovered that quickly and found love with someone else?

All those thoughts ran in his head, and it made him dizzy.

"Uhh!" *It isn't helping when you're answering like a bumbling idiot as well!*

"It's really obvious," Moth said.

Prince Wonwoo rolled his eyes at her. Her sarcasm didn't help with his thoughts, but he enjoyed it. "Oh really? You think?" he snided, leaning closer to her.

Moth retaliated the sarcasm with her own sarcasm. "Oh yes, I do think indeed. When I tended to you, you would mutter how I was a pretty angel and how kind I was to you. 'I want to see you so badly,' you would say before falling back into unconsciousness. It was so adorable and cute of you, despite not having known me at the time. I was flattered myself hearing those words."

The lion prince flattened his ears, his heart pounding extremely fast against his ribcage. There was no hiding his feelings anymore.

"You can be honest with me."

"I mean...I don't know," he answered in a soft voice. "It's true what I said. I...Well, there was someone I liked once— Loved, I mean. Loved once. It was a long time ago, though." His eyes widened the moment he realized what he had said. He slammed his paw to his head.

I probably shouldn't have mentioned that! Ugh, I'm so stupid! Now she'll think I just love her because of my former love!

Moth didn't seem to mind that, rather she appeared that she didn't pay attention to what he really meant. "What happened? It didn't work out?"

"No, it did. It was all going so well, too well for me. But...something happened, something really horrific, and...it's why I'm here..."

Moth flicked her whiskers in confusion. She seemed curious but obviously didn't want to push further, having sensed that the "something horrific" was said with a tone of pain. "I see. So, then what is it you're really afraid of?" she inquired.

The lion prince was silent. The crickets continued to chirp around them.

"You're afraid of...rejection?" Moth broke the ice.

Prince Wonwoo shook his head.

"Afraid I won't return the same attraction?"

"No."

"Afraid you might hurt someone else who likes you but you don't know or never felt the same about them?"

"No. No."

"Well, what is it?"

"I'm afraid I'll lose you," he bursted aloud. He looked at her with round eyes. "I'm afraid...that I will lose you the same way I lost...the one I loved months ago…"

The margay widened her eyes. "Oh, Prince Wonwoo...I'm so sorry," she sympathized, reaching out her paw to him. "I didn't mean..."

He accepted it, leaning his cheek onto it. "It's okay, you didn't know," he sniffed. "But...I do really like you. Ever since the tour, I've felt a true connection with you. Even before we formally met, like you said. I can't stop thinking about you. I would love to...to be with you."

She chuckled softly. "I knew it."

"Don't ruin the moment," he whined in a playful way, pulling his head away and pouting. "I really *really do* like you! More than like! I love you!"

The two went silent after his confession. He wasn't sure if it was just the moonlight, but Moth's face brightened up a bit as she smiled sheepishly. The lion prince felt his ears burning, embarrassment flooding him. *I can't believe you said that out loud, you idiot!* He couldn't help himself from his self-hatred. What good was he when he's a wanted criminal by the most evil Kingdom in existence? He was only putting everyone at risk by being here. He couldn't be with Moth, unless he was going to risk her life, which he would never do in a million terra cycles.

I'm the worst Prince in the universe, he berated himself. *I'm too much of a mess for her to be with. I'm just self-projecting to her that she doesn't need right now. I'm dumb to think we could even work out while*

I have my own shit to figure out. I'm sorry, Moth. You deserve someone better. I–

She batted him gently, laughing. "I know, I know you do, and I also couldn't stop thinking about you after we met. You're a pretty cute lion if I say so myself. I'd love to be your girlfriend."

He was caught off guard. He flicked his ears. "Y-You do?"

"Duh. You're cute and funny. I also couldn't stop thinking about you after the tour. The way you mooned over me was adorable, I just wanted to hold that dumb cute face that I cared for ever since you joined us forever."

Prince Wonwoo scratched his ears. He could feel his heart pounding out of control at her confession. It made him feel better at his own confession. "Heh. I'm just a dumbass by heart."

"I know. Now, shut up and enjoy the night watch with me, handsome."

The lion prince let out a tiny squeak of happiness. He hobbled closer to Moth, steadying himself on the branch. She pulled him into her arms once he was within her reach, pressing his head to her chest. His face was entirely burning. She was...really *soft!* He looked back to where the Tropic Clan was. It was only just a small reminder of how life was so short and only full of chance and fate.

Especially fate.

He would have died out there in that river, had they not found him in perfect time and saved him. It was only sheer luck that he was found by Tropic Clan members. Had he not entered the forest at all, he wouldn't have been attacked by the crocodiles, and he wouldn't have been found by Vermilion and Kitwana. He wouldn't have been taken into the Tropic Clan. Most importantly, he wouldn't have met Moth, and he would have never had an opportunity to meet her.

It was truly a butterfly effect.

He looked back to Moth; she smiled softly as she stared at the sky, the breeze moving her fur gently. He buried himself in her chest fur, listening to her calm breathing and heartbeat. He looked up without moving his head and took a deep breath in.

There wasn't any urgency to go back home. With Moth at his side as his new girlfriend and a helpful clan leader who treated him like he was one of her own, Prince Wonwoo could truly live here without fear of being hunted down. He could stay with them forever.

"Hey, Moth?"

"Hm?"

"I...I love you."

"I love you too, Prince Wonwoo."

The two rested like this the whole night on Esme, bathing in Gau's moonlight until Gau's Rest.

CHAPTER 14
A FIERY VENGEANCE UNQUENCHED; THE WOLF PRINCE LOSES HIS MIND

~ 4 terra cycles later... ~
~ June in Terra Cycle 1122 B.E. ~

"I am not stopping until we find him. He will reappear."

Within a remote area of Divine Kingfisher Woods, on the northerly tip, Demoniacal Kingdom members tore away as they searched the woods. Prince Scamander planted his nose on the ground, intently sniffing for the lion prince's scent. All he could pick up was a hint of last night's humid rain shower and wet mud. He lifted up his head, rubbing away the mud off his nose. His eyes narrowed as he snarled to himself.

4 terra cycles had passed, and the war was now over. King Titanosaurus and King Jung-hwa of the Promised Dynasty agreed to a peace treaty, and Prince Scamander could not be

more unsatisfied at the outcome. He was forced to watch as his Father agreed with the lion king, his body practically twitching from the boiling anger. The look of the lion king made him want to lunge and tear him to shreds. He was supposed to be dead. His wife was supposed to be dead! How could Father let them still live!? Let alone agree to their terms that their Gods imposed onto everyone?! He hated his Father even further. The wolf prince then learned afterwards that his Father was bluffing King Jung-hwa, as after the meeting, he had pulled him to the side and told him in hushed whispers:

"I want you to keep searching for the lion prince. He's who we need right now. King Jung-hwa we can deal with another day. I just wanted him to be off our asses."

"Do you really mean this, Father?" Prince Scamander had asked him, his curved ears lifting up in excitement.

"You think I'm going to follow the Promised Dynasty and trust them again when I can lose another family member of mine? You're free to keep searching under my secret orders. Just don't get caught is all I ask. If you do, I'll whoop your ass straight to King Wyvern."

"Trust me, Father. Prince Wonwoo is the only one who I'm going to whoop to King Wyvern."

While the conversation was fond, it still did not make Prince Scamander very happy. He had struggled day in and day out to find any remaining traces of the lion prince. The summer heat wasn't helping with the time. He searched for paw prints, spots of blood, clumps of fur, *any* part of him that would give him a lead.

There was nothing, and the only lead he was getting was a cold one.

"Keep searching you lazy sacks of bones!" Prince Scamander barked. "No one will be allowed to rest until I get a piece of information!"

While watching his search party, Prince Scamander felt his mind go heavy. 4 terra cycles, 4 gruelling terra cycles, and the hole in his heart had only grown more. He never thought that his sister would be this much of the light of his life, but now that she was gone, there was no one except for his parents to give that love. It wasn't the same though; he and Princess Okome had shared a deep bond, one that was prevalent since the day of her birth. He knew what she wanted, what she needed, what was on her mind. It was like they spoke to each other in their minds via telepathy.

The last thing he could picture is the sight of her, slowly revealing her children to him and their parents as she smiles brighter than the sun.

I will find Prince Wonwoo for you, Okome, he thought. *I will punish him for you, for taking you away from me. You will not have died in vain. I will give you the peace you deserve. You will finally rest at long last–*

"We've searched all day," someone had complained, snapping Prince Scamander out of his daydream. "We should go home. It's a lost cause anyway, considering how many terra cycles it's been. He'll never be caught, and he'll definitely never be prosecuted for his crime."

Everyone seemed to have gone silent. The air was easily identified as fear. The wolf prince turned his head around slowly.

"Who said that?" he asked. "Who said that this was a lost cause? Which one of you little God fuckers said that!? Make yourself known right now, and bow down to my paws as you apologize."

No one moved.

"MAKE YOURSELF KNOWN RIGHT NOW, OR NO ONE LEAVES!"

They all grew stiff as a log, not daring to breathe. Prince Scamander surveyed his team, narrowing his eyes at every one of them. Someone had to squeal. Someone had to be stupid enough to really speak their mind on such a matter. At this point, the wolf prince had become increasingly tired of a few of his members not respecting him enough. He wanted to make his authority known, he wanted *everyone* in the Demoniacal Kingdom to know that he was indeed the next King to the Demoniacal Kingdom.

How could the Demoniacal Kingdom grow so soft over the past terra cycles just like Father? Prince Scamander snarled to himself. *Has everyone started to believe in Father's beliefs that we should be one with the Promised Dynasty? What happened to the fear we bring to all throughout the land? What happened to our respect? My respect!?*

"May I remind everyone here the very reason we are searching day in and day out is for a wanted criminal of the Demoniacal Kingdom?" he snarled aloud. "May I remind you all that we do not tolerate criminals *or traitors* in the Demoniacal Kingdom! Or do I have to prove an example?"

He pinned his eyes on the very one who spoke out. It was a short pale creamy yellow-furred golden jackal, and they kept themselves low to the ground in an attempt to hide themselves. Prince Scamander quickly snatched them up by their scruff and dragged them out into the open. The golden jackal screeched and flailed. Everyone stepped away from the golden jackal as they scrabbled to their paws, desperately reaching out to anyone to help hide them. No one wanted to. No one wanted to suffer from Prince Scamander's wrath. He knew they knew if they helped this jackal, they would also be punished.

His tail reached out and hooked the golden jackal, pinning him down. Everyone went silent as they watched this happen. He towered over the golden jackal. The golden jackal slowly looked up at the wolf prince, swallowing nervously.

"I-I apologize, Prince Scamander!" the golden jackal finally cried. "Please forgive my yapping mouth! I have no excuse! I pledge my undying loyalty to His Highness and His Majesty of the Demoniacal Kingdom until the day I die. I will never speak out again!"

The wolf prince stared down at them, not amused. It was typical of traitors to speak out, but it was more uncommon that they would beg for mercy. He wanted to instantly get rid of the traitorous creature, but he held back on his thoughts. He wanted to see what the golden jackal had to say for itself.

"Tell me, jackal, you have a family?" he asked the jackal.

"A-A brother, Y-Your Highness," they answered. "He's just a little one though. Almost 6 terra cycles."

"No parents?"

"N-No, Your Highness. They died after he was born."

The wolf prince twitched his tail. "No aunts? Uncles? Grandparents, maybe."

"No, Your Highness. I'm his only family. He has no one else but me."

"Really now?"

The golden jackal kept their head down. "Yes, yes!"

Now it was getting more personal for the wolf prince. The subject of family cut him deep, his heart stung. This random stranger, someone he had no idea who they even are, still at least had their sibling, their brother, alive. That was more than enough of an insult to Prince Scamander. His sister gets to die in such a terrible way by the rival prince, and this golden jackal gets to have his brother still with him?

It's not fair! Prince Scamander growled. He scowled.

It's time I finally assert myself as the rightful heir of this Kingdom.

The wolf prince took one step closer to the golden jackal.

"Then how would it feel if I took away the one thing your brother loves most? How would he like that?" He stretched out his claws, digging them into the earth with intent. "Better yet: How would *you* like it if I just end your pathetic life right now? How would your brother like to know that the prince was responsible for his big sibling's death?"

He lifted a paw.

"How much do you think it would hurt knowing there's nothing he can do? Because trying to go after me, the Prince of the Demoniacal Kingdom? It's a *lost cause.*" He drew the last sentence out with poison dripping.

The golden jackal was visibly trembling. Everyone around them shrunk in their pelts to hide themselves while others stared to see what the outcome was going to be. They cried out.

"No! NO, please! I promise I will never speak out against you! Please forgive me, Your Highness!"

The wolf prince kept his paw lifted and continued to stare at the golden jackal. The sight of such groveling drew a lot of satisfaction. Within the back of his mind, he wanted to show everyone the one thing that traitors deserve: death. The golden jackal had to pay for such disrespect towards him and his family. They had to be made an example of.

All traitors who speak out must learn the hard way!

But Prince Scamander took a step back on the thought.

Sure, the golden jackal had expressed such terrible behavior, but they were a loyal Demoniacal member through and through. What would it do if he killed them? Would it make him look like a good Prince if he decided to kill one of his subjects?

I would be no better than Prince Wonwoo. That was a thought Prince Scamander never thought he would say. *Father would kill, but he thinks first before acting. Plus, Okome wouldn't want this. She'd want Prince Wonwoo punished, not this stranger.*

A cold breeze brushed past him as he thought about his sister. Prince Scamander froze, staring up and around him. The leaves were still and no rustle emerged from either ground or air. He could also see no one had felt the breeze, seeing them all stare intensely at the wolf prince. Prince Scamander blinked. Was that a sign?

Are you there, sis? He asked himself. *Is that you?*

The cold breeze swept by his fur again. He shivered.

The wolf prince rocketed his paw towards the ground, letting it slam within a few inches of the golden jackal's face. They cried out, slamming their paws on their face and reducing their cries to a soft whimper once they realized that the wolf prince had spared them. They looked pitifully to Prince Scamander, waiting for their demise. The wolf prince scoffed at him, lifting up his tail.

"Fine. Get out of my sight before I decide otherwise."

Prince Scamander let the golden jackal scurry away back into the group and looked back to the rest of his search party. He took an intimidating step towards them, prompting everyone to sit up in place. "Anyone else have anything to say about this?" he asked. "Does anyone agree that this search is a lost cause?" When no one had responded with aggressive head shakes, he growled, "That's what I thought. Now get back to searching for any trace of evidence. Find that murderer's path! He will be found."

Everyone returned right away to their duties without another word.

The wolf prince dug his claws in the dirt. The urge to have such control when he wanted to draw blood was hard. But he knew this was the right thing to do, as much as he felt disgusted at such a soft thought of his. Deep within his heart, he felt extremely satisfied at what he had done; he felt great to display his power over his Kingdom. He now would know that no one would dare speak back to him again unless they had something of importance to him. He could imagine the smile on his great-grandfather's face.

He looked up to the sky.

I will avenge your death, Princess Okome. He will pay for what he did to you.

CHAPTER 15
THE PRINCE IS CAPTURED BY THE DEMONIACAL KINGDOM

✦✧✦✧~ *1 terra cycle later...* ~
~ *November in Terra Cycle 1123 B.E.* ~

"Are you certain you don't want to stay here?"

It had been 5 terra cycles that Prince Wonwoo had stayed with the Tropic Clan. In those terra cycles, the lion prince had aged gracefully. He was now 26 terra cycles old, with his mane having grown. It came in rounds, covering his neck and chest. He was now a true male lion. He wondered how his parents would react seeing him all grown up like this.

In those 5 terra cycles, he realized quickly that he couldn't stay hidden forever. It was only when he was on patrol with Aleena that his life came back to him. He couldn't run away from his issues any longer. Was he really the Prince if he didn't come back

THE PRINCE IS CAPTURED BY THE DEMONIACAL KINGDOM

to avenge his honor? His Kingdom was probably in shambles, without a King or a Queen to steer them on the right paths. That was not a pretty thought he wanted to think about when going to sleep every day. He had to return home; he had to let the world know Prince Wonwoo was back, and he was back with a mission for redemption.

The lion prince was preparing his satchel that was given to him by the leader. He looked up at the clan leader. She was a brownish black Peruvian spider monkey named Aleena. He reflected on the first time they had met; she was the clan leader who had taken him into her clan after he was injured by crocodiles, and she has treated him like a clan member and a friend ever since that day. He couldn't be more grateful for her help. He would always remember her. He'd never forget her kindness nor the kindness of the Tropic Clan.

"I would love to, Tropic Bloom Aleena," the lion prince said with hesitation, "but I do believe it's time I have to move on and search out my Dynasty again, whatever is left of the Kingdom. I have to, in order to restore the honor of the Promised Dynasty and the honor of my family."

Aleena twitched her long, prehensile tail. "But you're just as welcome in the Tropic Clan as everyone else. You can stay here with us, in peace. Without any other care in the world. Besides, aren't you afraid that the Demoniacal Kingdom will still be searching for you if you return back to the Promised Dynasty?"

The lion prince lowered his eyes. The Demoniacal Kingdom. It's been a few terra cycles he hadn't heard about them. Aleena's question struck him curiously. Would the Demoniacal Kingdom *still* be fighting over something long in the past? Wouldn't they have found out by now that he was "dead" and moved on? There was only one way to find out, and that's by returning back home.

"I've spent the last 5 terra cycles sitting on my fear of the Demoniacal Kingdom," Prince Wonwoo told Aleena. "Sitting and meditating on my thoughts. And while I still feel anxious when thinking about the Demoniacal Kingdom, I always manage to get my thoughts under control, just like how my guard Hakuba would calm me down. I learned to not care what would happen. If they find me, they find me. If they still have grudges because of what I had done, so be it they unleash it to get peace."

Aleena twitched her ears.

"I also have to go back to bring hope to my people," he told her, turning around. "Who knows what the Demoniacal Kingdom has done to the Promised Dynasty after I ran away all those terra cycles ago. For all I know, my parents might be dead, and they've taken over the Kingdom. I can't allow that to happen. They need their Prince back. They need me back. I have to go home."

"Have you forgotten what they will do to you?" another Tropic Clan member, Vermilion the howler monkey, asked, swinging her way inside Aleena's den.

"No of course not, Vermilion," Prince Wonwoo answered her, gazing at her softly. "I still have nightmares about them. Thanks a lot Kishi. But this is something I have to do."

"I don't know if this is a good time," Aleena voiced her concern. "These are dangerous times."

"Well when is a good time, Tropic Bloom Aleena?" Prince Wonwoo inquired, his voice teetering as he struggled to not snap at her. "Everyday is dangerous for us all. How many more terra cycles do I have to wait until my actions finally catch up to me when I least expect it? I have to act now. Even if there is danger, I have to face it."

The two monkeys looked at each other. He could tell they were both still unconvinced on him leaving, but he knew this was the right thing to do. It was going to hurt that he would have to leave those he made friends and loved on the way, but he needed to do this for himself and for his Kingdom.

It's the best, he thought. *The best for me. The best for the Kingdom. I'll have to remind myself constantly. Who knows. Maybe in the end, when the threat is over, I can invite Tropic Clan back to the Promised Dynasty.* He smiled. *I'll put a pin on that for future me to deal with.*

"I have to confront the Demoniacal Kingdom head on before they get to you guys," he stressed to them. "Especially Prince Scamander." His tail rested on the ground, sweeping it. "Oh, the poor lad...I wonder how fine he's aged."

"Probably aged a lot faster with the hatred and vengeance for you that he's practically an old wolf with a white beard," Aleena said.

The lion prince and Vermilion laughed.

"Have you gotten everything that you may need?" she asked him, inspecting his satchel. "Food, water, medicinal supplies?"

"Yes, I did," Prince Wonwoo confirmed, brushing his tail over her shoulders.

"Weapons to fight back from anyone who attacks you? The pocket knife I gave you?"

He reached into his satchel to pull it out, inspecting it. He was impressed by such a craft; it had been crafted from hand by Aleena herself, with the aid of Vermilion. He admired such dedicated work.

"Yes, yes. I do have it." Prince Wonwoo rolled his eyes. "You're acting just like my mother right now."

She gently punched his shoulder. "I care for my clan members! That includes you!"

The lion prince tightened the satchel to his waist. He looked back at Aleena and Vermilion. "I can't thank you enough," he began. "Both of you and the whole clan. Had you not come along and given me your hospitality, I might have been dead all those terra cycles ago. You took me in when no clan wanted to. You didn't have to take me in, you did not have to treat me, but you did. For that...I thank you."

Aleena smiled and patted him. He could see in her eyes that there was sadness and concern. Those same feelings struck his heart; the two had bonded during his stay, and he considered Aleena to be like a second mother to him. The lion prince had learned a lot from Aleena, and he adapted the ways of the Tropic Clan. So much in fact, he slowly lost himself and the Promised Dynasty. They may have still been in his consciousness, and in his pride, but he found himself more at home in this clan than his Dynasty. But he knew he had to go back to his home. Back to his roots, and confront whatever old grudges may await. He couldn't hide anymore.

He had to be the Prince he was born to be.

"Everyone is a friend to me," Aleena said. "And family. You are family to me, Prince Wonwoo of the Promised Dynasty."

His ears twitched at his formal name. He lowered his head. "I...I still don't know if I am deserving of that title."

The Peruvian spider monkey smacked his chin lightly, lifting up his head. "Hey, what did we say about self-deprecation?" she asked him.

"It's bad for you," the lion prince answered with a sigh.

"And?"

"Bad for your mental health as well."

"So what should you do instead?"

The lion prince's nose twitched. "Be kinder to myself. Say positive things about myself."

She rubbed his tuft of fur. "Good boy." She pulled him into a hug. "Ugh, I'm gonna miss you, you giant furball."

The lion prince froze at the hug. It's not that he didn't like hugs, he just felt confused since this was a random animal that was hugging him. An animal from a clan far away. He put his arm around her, patting her back. "I'm gonna miss you too, Aleena," he said.

"I'm going to miss you as well."

"Me too!" Vermilion howled, throwing herself in the pile. "I'll miss you so much! So very very very much! I'm gonna miss being around you and having you around to bully you."

Prince Wonwoo rolled his eyes playfully, patting Vermilion's hands gently. "Me too, Vermilion. Me too…"

"You take care of yourself, you hear me?"

"I will. I will."

They stayed in their embrace for a few minutes. Prince Wonwoo's heart was slowly breaking, and he did not want to let go. He enjoyed the two of them, and he considered them his best friends. After all, they were the first ones he met in the clan. Vermilion, along with a jaguar named Kitwana (who had sadly passed one terra cycle ago, claimed by the very same crocodile pod that attacked Prince Wonwoo in an act of revenge for the loss of their old leader), had saved him from the crocodiles and brought him to Aleena. The Peruvian spider monkey and her clan treated his wounds, and she allowed him to stay in the Tropic Clan instead of kicking him out.

The lion prince buried his muzzle into Aleena's shoulder, taking in her scent. He wanted to make sure he would never forget her, forget everything her clan had done for him. He did the same for Vermilion.

Once their hug was done, the lion prince began to say goodbye to every Tropic Clan member. The clan gave their prayers and blessings, even the children. He was touched by this; none of them knew him, he had not grown up with them, yet they treated him as if he had been with them since birth. That made the idea of leaving saddening. Knowing he was never going to see them again hurt him.

One day, after he became King and got rid of the threat of the Demoniacal Kingdom, he could seek them out again and bring them to the Promised Dynasty. Where they rightfully belonged.

But there was one goodbye that was going to be painful. One he dreaded to even say those words to.

"I'm...really going to miss you, Prince Wonwoo."

Moth, the margay.

Prince Wonwoo looked up. The small feline had climbed down the trees and looked up at the lion prince with sadness in her eyes. He felt his tail twitching. This was the clan member he slowly started to have feelings for during his stay in the Tropic Clan. She soon became his girlfriend after one night under the starry skies. The feline had reminded him so much of Princess Okome, so much in fact that it began to hurt him and wonder if he was only hurting Moth because of who she reminded him of. After having that talk with her, Moth did not feel any indifferent towards him. She held no ill will about it, nor did she harbor any hatred that she was being compared to Princess Okome, and she continued to love him.

"I'm going to miss you as well, Moth," Prince Wonwoo said, rubbing his ears.

"Are you really never coming back?" she asked.

His breath hitched. How could he answer it honestly without hurting her feelings? Was there even a way? In his mind, he tried to find ways to possibly coat this in the most gentle way he could think of. But nothing came out right in his head that definitely won't sound good if verbally said.

He sighed to himself, lowering his head. The breeze made his mane and tuft flow with it.

The margay gently cuffed his mane. "You can be honest with me," she said.

"I don't want to hurt you for real this time, my love," Prince Wonwoo answered with sadness.

"How have you hurt me? I love you, you love me, we work out any problems we have. There's nothing I see where you have hurt me."

"Well... I'm going to hurt you when I say..I'm not coming back."

Moth sighed. "That's okay. You have to do what you must do."

"But... I really would like it if... if you came along with me."

The margay shook her head. "That offer again?"

The lion prince lifted up his head. "Of course? I love you, Moth. I love you so much. I don't want to leave you. Come with me to the Promised Dynasty; my Father and Mother–if they're both still alive that is–they will welcome you in a warm embrace, and- and you can live with me and be my wife, the new Queen, and-"

"Prince Wonwoo," she gently interrupted, putting a paw on his mouth. "No amount of words can describe the same love I have for you. But my home is here. With the Tropic Clan. Trust me: I'd love to come with you, every fiber of my being is screaming to be with you forever, but I would feel so out of touch. Especially if I became their new Queen. It's just..." The margay had stopped with her snarky and serious replies and she sighed in defeat, letting her shoulders sag. "I just can't leave the place I was born in. I can't lead a Kingdom I do not know about. But I also don't want to leave you. Nor do I want you to leave. It's all...It's all so complicated and painful..."

The lion prince's heart finally broke. That was the last straw for him. He dreaded that answer, but he respected it. He knew himself how it felt to leave home behind him for a new life. He didn't want to push Moth into anything she was uncomfortable with.

He put his paw on hers and looked at her.

"I don't want to leave you either," he said. "But I am unsure about staying here for the rest of my life. If I do, I will never make up for what I have done. I have to go back and face the reality of the situation like a true King. Running away won't make it all go away. I have to own up to my mistake. I have to confront them. Take back my rightful place to the throne. I have to avenge my parents and my Dynasty."

There was silence between the two of them. The wind blew, ruffling their fur. He tried to read her face. What was the margay truly thinking? Hurt? Anger? Sadness? He couldn't tell, for he saw every single emotion. Moth twitched her tail.

"Do you...understand?" he asked.

"Of course I do," she answered rather passive aggressively. "You have to go home and save your Kingdom from the evil Demoniacal Kingdom. Only you can do that. Me? I'll only drag you down."

"I'm not saying that," he quickly jumped on the defensive. "You could never drag me down!"

"No, I know. It's just what I feel. But it is true in a sense if you think about it."

No, not really. Prince Wonwoo sniffed. "I want you to know, I respect your decision. I would never force you out of your comfort zone for my sake. I've made my decision and you've made yours. It hurts, but I know it's the best for the both of us."

The margay frowned. It seemed her heart broke as well. She looked away. "I— Uhm. So...this is goodbye then. Forever."

The lion prince moved his paw away from hers. He was surprised that she didn't mention anything about breaking up with him if they can't be together. Could that mean something deep down? "...I guess it is," he answered somberly, "but I don't want this to be forever."

Moth pressed her head to his mane, rubbing her face against it. "I don't want it to be forever either."

He embraced her, holding her tightly. He didn't want to let her go. He wished it could have been simple to either stay here in the Tropic Clan with her, or find a way to make her come to the Promised Dynasty and live with him. It all sucked, and Prince Wonwoo wanted to cry.

"Do this for me, will you?" Moth asked.

"Of course. I will save my Kingdom and take back my honor. For you. For Aleena. For the whole clan. I will make you all proud."

"I love you," she said softly but audible enough for him to hear. "I love you so much... I'll always love you."

"I love you too, Moth," he replied. "Forever and always. You will be in my heart. No matter where I am. And I know you'll also have me in your heart."

He put a paw to her chest to where her heart was. There was a faint noise he heard from her, like she wanted to say something, but the words didn't come out. Instead, she sadly purred.

Once he freed her from his grasp and stared at her one last time, Prince Wonwoo got to his paws and headed out. Looking back, he saw the Tropic Clan members waving goodbye at him, some shouting blessings and prayers. Though he looked at them all, he couldn't take his eyes off of Moth, who waved sadly before climbing up the trees and disappearing into the canopy above.

Oh Gods, it's been so many terra cycles.

The moment Prince Wonwoo stepped into Divine Kingfisher Woods after days of traveling across the land back south, all his old memories had swarmed his brain. He felt like he shouldn't be here, yet he knew this was his home, where he belonged. The familiarity struck him in both a surreal and calm way.

I'm home. Great Ellowyn, I really am back home. Thank the Gods for this blessing.

He looked over his side, sighing. He already missed Moth and wished that he could feel her against him, hear her soft voice reassuring him. *I did it, Moth. I made it home.* It hurt they had to part ways, but Prince Wonwoo couldn't convince her anymore. He respected her decision and left. Before he had left, she had surprised him and made a passing remark that stuck with him.

"*Maybe one day, Prince Wonwoo, we will meet again. Underneath Dagny's bright sun or Gau's dim moon, Ellowyn will bless us, and we will be together again.*"

He smiled.

Here's to hoping for that day. Now. To take back what's rightfully mine.

Crossing the land, his ears had caught the roaring sound of Dragon's Wrath. Even more memories came back as he climbed the steep ravine up in the opposite direction of the waterfall. He watched the waterfall in awe; he remembered deliberately falling into the raging waters below, fighting desperately to free himself. He remembered how close he was to death back then, and how, despite being afraid, he was comforted by Morana herself. It somehow made the experience less anxious than it was.

He climbed up the ravine after a struggle and landed on the ground. Dirt sprayed in the air like the foams of the waterfall. He dusted off the dirt, coughing. Even though he had healed, his body was sore and ached. He sighed, getting to his paws. The river raged beneath him, awful memories surging. He ignored it and looked ahead of him, blinking.

THE PRINCE IS CAPTURED BY THE DEMONIACAL KINGDOM

Up ahead was Halcyonwick. Although it was not in sight, Prince Wonwoo could tell that he was nearby. He couldn't believe after all this trekking, he would be home.

How would the Promised Dynasty react when they saw their long lost prince alive?

Prince Wonwoo could already hear the voices.

"Prince Wonwoo? Is it really you!?"

"You're home!"

"Our prince is home!"

"Everyone bring out the booze! It's time for a celebration!"

Two voices stuck out to him the most.

"My boy! He's returned! Welcome home, son."

"Wonwoo, my precious cub. You're alive!"

He sighed.

Mother. Father. How I've missed you so. Prince Wonwoo twitched his tail. *Especially you, Mother.* He lifted up his head to the clear skies. *I hope you're watching me. I hope you're seeing me, seeing that I am alive. I lived, Mother. I ran away! Just like you told me. I ran, and I ran good. The Demoniacal Kingdom never got to me, haha!! But it's been too long. Too long I've been away. ...I'm home now. I'm home.*

He looked back down and ahead of him. Was Halcyonwick crawling with Demoniacal creatures? Had the Promised Dynasty fallen. He couldn't tell, but he had to be cautious. He'd have to be on the down low before making his comeback known to all.

Once he found that opportunity, he'd strike. But he needed to have patience. His Kingdom would be his soon enough, and his honor would be restored.

He took one step further.

Prince Wonwoo flicked one ear back.

Someone was approaching him. And fast.

He whirled around at the racing pawsteps and immediately was tackled by a black bear. He was too caught off guard to react to the intruder. The two tumbled on the ground, stirring up dirt, until Prince Wonwoo was pinned furiously down by this bear. Fear hit him directly in the face from the roaring bear. Prince Wonwoo tried desperately to escape, but it was no use. The black bear was too strong for him, and it held him down well. He had to remember the bear rhyme that he had been taught as the black bear raised a paw.

If it's black, fight back.

His eyes widened, heart pounding.

Fight back. Of course!

The lion prince jerked a paw free and swiped at the bear's face, trying to aim for its eyes. The black bear was thrown back, but it bit on his chest and tossed him onto a tree. Stars swirled his vision as the lion prince felt his head collide with the hard trunk before collapsing to the ground. He coughed, groaning.

So much for trying to fight back.

He tried to get to his paws, but black and white spots in his vision forced him down. His head pounded aggressively, swiftly grabbing ahold of each corner of his skull. It made him want to cry out. The bear grabbed him by the throat and kept him pinned against the tree. It raised his head and whistled sharply, hurting the lion prince's ears.

"Hey! Over here!" it shouted. "I got him! I got the lion prince of the Promised Dynasty! He lives!"

Ah...you're a Demoniacal Kingdom member, Prince Wonwoo thought. *Figures...*

His vision began to blur from his pounding headache. He let his head hang, his eyes still looking up. The sound of metal clashing against each other caught his attention, and he knew exactly what it was. Guards approached him in dark silver armor and large smiles on their faces. The armor design gave it away that they were in fact Demoniacal Kingdom. Along with the guards, a dark blue wolf strode in with pride. He was recognizable, though the lion prince was too dazed to really react. He grinned at him, hooking a claw under the lion prince's jaw. Prince Wonwoo's eyes widened at the sight of the wolf.

The very creature who wanted him dead. The only one with a fiery vengeance for him.

"At long last. I knew you weren't dead. You will get what you deserve, Prince Wonwoo of the Promised Dynasty."

Prince Scamander....

Prince Wonwoo groaned, the pain overwhelming his senses, and fell unconscious. The guards were speaking to Prince Scamander, but he wasn't able to understand what was being said. He soon felt chains grasping his paws. He knew what that meant.

He was definitely under arrest.

CHAPTER 16
PRINCE WONWOO? THAT NAME IS DEAD. MORE LIKE...

~ One week later... ~
~ November in Terra Cycle 1123 B.E. ~

Surely, today, he would be executed. He was certain.

Prince Wonwoo clawed another tally mark on the wall of his jail cell as soon as the morning sun shone its rays. Days had passed, multiple risings of Dagny's days and multiple risings of Gau's nights, and now it had been a whole week since the Demoniacal Kingdom had captured him. He was just trying to get back home after he had left the Tropic Clan. But no. The Demoniacal Kingdom just had to be so conveniently nearby to spot him and tackle him. It was as if they were anticipating his return, patrolling, lying in wait until he appeared. *Aleena would be freaking*

PRINCE WONWOO? THAT NAME IS DEAD. MORE LIKE...

out if she found out the Demoniacal Kingdom caught me, he thought to himself.

He moved away from the wall and looked up at the small window in his cell. He stared listlessly at the scenery, lifting his head up to the sky where the morning sun was slowly being pushed by Dagny. A few clouds were rolling in, though none showed any promise of rain. At most he could tell possibly a small drizzle might occur within the hours. He puffed to himself, his face drooping while monotonously fixing his whiskers. Prince Wonwoo wondered why it was taking so long for King Titanosaurus to take him out of this hellhole, put him on some kind of public display for all the Demoniacal Kingdom to watch, and chop off his head while lifting it up for everyone to cheer. It was as simple as that if everyone in the Kingdom hated him–

He shook his head. Prince Wonwoo wasn't sure why he was thinking that way when he already changed his life around.

I lied: I'm still very much scared of the Demoniacal Kingdom, haha, he thought to himself. *I just didn't want Aleena to hear my true thoughts then get all overprotective mom on me and make me stay in the Tropic Clan. Being a "wise philosopher" was the only way to barely convince her to let me go.*

The lion prince laid back down on the cold floor, sighing. He rested his chin on his paws, looking towards the bars. Prince Scamander had indeed grown over the terra cycles. When the two had met again, he appeared to look just like his father. His face was permanently stoned into seriousness, and there was no crack at any happiness. There was only hatred, shaped and hardened from the grief of the loss of his sister. Aleena had been right on the fact that he aged faster from the hatred. The only time he smiled was when he saw Prince Wonwoo. He was happy in an angry, pleased kind of way. The kind of smile that evil creatures had when they had a plot of world domination. He was more than happy to finally chain up Prince Wonwoo and have him thrown in jail.

Seeing King Titanosaurus and Queen Zirconia of the Demoniacal Kingdom again was indeed surreal. It was difficult to look them in the eye, knowing that deep down, despite being from the worst Kingdom, they were parents who were grieving the loss of one of their children. It hurt his heart. The wolf king was understandably angry and happy, though he opted on wanting the lion prince to suffer before he would kill him. Prince Scamander was beyond pissed, speaking up to his father on why not killing him now. Something along the lines of, and the lion prince quoted, "I've waited 5 terra cycles for this moment!" and "Father! How could you ruin this moment for me!?" The wolf king quickly reasoned with his son in a strict manner, and that was that. It was strange, but Prince Wonwoo didn't dare question it himself. Whatever. It would just be a couple days, he had thought to himself. His pain, as well as the Demoniacal Royal Family's pain, would be over soon.

A week later, here he was.

...*What the HELL IS TAKING SO LONG!?*

He couldn't believe that he was *still* alive after a *whole week!*

It really seemed that he was trying to avoid the Goddess of Death, and it chilled him to his bones. It wasn't intentional, he swore on it. Maybe her counterpart, her sister Abella, was fighting with Morana for him to continue living in order to make up for his mistakes. The lion prince felt his shoulders sag. Who knew, honestly? Only the Goddesses of Life and Death, but they weren't speaking to him. So, again he thought, *who knew?*

The lion prince felt his eyelids sink and tapped in a rhythm to try and keep himself awake, watching his claw hit the concrete.

Why even bother keeping me alive when the Demoniacal Kingdom wants me dead? That is the only way I can atone.

Winter was setting in, and Prince Wonwoo curled up to try and keep some warmth. Coldwyvern was truly living up to its name, despite it not being the reason it was named as such. (Well, it was one of the few reasons, but like it mattered to Prince Wonwoo at this current moment.) He shivered, puffing small warm breaths into his paws. If this was King Titanosaurus's definition of suffering, he would have to try to critique the wolf king on how to be better at punishing someone. Probably do something like put him in a torture chamber. One that would send multiple needles throughout his body as he was restrained and crying out for help–

What the fuck is wrong with me?! He berated himself, shaking his head. *Why am I thinking on ways I want to die!? I don't wanna die, at least not yet! Ughhh, I hate myself.*

He had heard pawsteps coming his way, and he perked up at once. They were loud, claws clicking on the hard floor, and recognizable. He flattened his ears, whipping his head around to see the creature. A Demoniacal tiger came into view, teeth bared in a grin. The lion prince narrowed his eyes, tail twitching. After all these terra cycles, he recognized the Demoniacal tiger; this Demoniacal tiger was the one who had ambushed him and his mother when they were hiding, the one who *(may have most likely)* killed his mother.

"Well, well!" the Demoniacal tiger said eagerly. "You're alive after all! What a surprise! We thought that you had died all those terra cycles ago. At least I can look at you in a jail cell, as you rightfully deserve. For now."

The lion prince snarled. "What happened to my mother?" he asked him. "What did you do to her?"

"Oh? No 'it's nice to see you again!' or 'we meet again!' or anything like that?" the Demoniacal tiger teased. "Look who's the rude one now."

"What. Happened. To my mother!?" he repeated his question, emphasizing his sentences while standing up slowly. He dug his unsheathed claws into the cold floor.

"Well, what do you mean?" he answered, leaning on the bars and studying his claws. "I got her good after you ran away! There's no way in Hell your mother, the frail Queen of the Promised Dynasty, would have survived such an attack from me. Before I was chased away, I heard your pathetic guards crying how they were losing her. So. You know."

The lion prince felt an invisible arrow strike his chest, piercing his heart. "No..."

PRINCE WONWOO? THAT NAME IS DEAD. MORE LIKE...

The Demoniacal tiger grinned. "Oh yeah. She's definitely dead. Long gone."

Prince Wonwoo shut his eyes, composing himself before he lunged at the bars. The Demoniacal tiger stepped back in time, staring at the lion prince with a look of glee. He gnawed on the bars and clawed at them, ignoring the pain. The grief was too heavy in his heart, he couldn't bear it anymore. She was dead, and it was all his fault, both the Demoniacal tiger and himself. He tried reaching out to the Demoniacal tiger.

"YOU BASTARD!" he roared. "I'LL KILL YOU FOR WHAT YOU'VE DONE! I'LL KILL YOU!"

"Heh, like to see you try."

The Demoniacal tiger turned to walk off.

"Did you just come here...to TAUNT ME!?"

The Demoniacal tiger didn't respond.

5 more days had passed, and King Titanosaurus finally came down to the jail with the Demoniacal tiger and another Demoniacal Kingdom guard–a Demoniacal black bear, the one who had found him and captured him in Divine Kingfisher Woods–with him. The lion prince was huddled by the corner, trembling. They studied his condition.

Prince Wonwoo was skin and bones. Skinny to the point each individual rib and spinal vertebrae could be counted. He'd gone weak from starvation since they had deprived him of food per King Titanosaurus's request. He was only allowed water, but even then, he was given not enough. He had completely given up on wanting to lash out at them by this point. He accepted the small portions he had been given, though there was a small pile where he had shoved aside the portions. He lifted his head to see them before letting it fall to the ground.

From this sight alone, one could easily tell Prince Wonwoo was a miserable mess.

The Demoniacal tiger and black bear scrunched up their faces in disgust. They had no pity for the lion prince. They instead were practically laughing at him on the inside, damning him that he deserves this punishment. The wolf king, much as he felt the same, kept his neutral face.

"Bring him out to the throne room at once," the wolf king snapped a command to his guards.

The Demoniacal tiger and black bear replied in unison.

"Yes, sir."

The lion prince heard the keys unlocking his cell and the pawsteps of the Demoniacal tiger and the Demoniacal black bear. He closed his eyes, not wanting to look at either of them. He especially didn't want to look at the Demoniacal tiger, who he later found out was named Tokira. Tokira had been the tiger that ambushed him and his mother in the basement. Tokira had killed his mother in cold blood, and there was no way he could ever forgive him for that. The lion prince still remembered that day of the ambush vividly, seeing his mother pinning Tokira before he had freed himself and went for her throat. The fear in his mother's eyes and the cold, satisfied stare of Tokira as he clamped down on her windpipe terrified Prince Wonwoo, and he definitely got nightmares from it.

"What's the matter? Afraid to look me in the eyes of the one who murdered your mother?" Tokira taunted, prodding his ribs.

Prince Wonwoo's pelt twitched uncomfortably; because of how starved he was, he was extremely hypersensitive to the slightest touch. Especially since he had lost so much weight, the Demoniacal tiger was practically touching his bones. He inhaled through his nose.

Ignore him, his mind told him. *He's looking for a reaction that can be used against you. Ignore him, and just breathe. Think about something else–*

Tokira had continued prodding him rather roughly. "Not gonna do anything? Not gonna try to attack me in revenge? Have you gotten that weak? Ha. Some prince."

If he could, Prince Wonwoo would lunge at him and crush his throat like he had done to Queen Cora.

"Tokira, that's enough," the Demoniacal black bear said after a minute of abuse. "Let's get him to King Titanosaurus before his son throws a fit and complains to him about us slacking and gets us killed."

"Pfff" was all the Demomiacal tiger could respond.

The lion prince was finally dragged out of jail (rather aggressively) and into the throne room. Tokira and the black bear dropped him on the floor. He let out a simple groan from the impact, shuddering as he got to one paw. He craned his head to where King Titanosaurus and Queen Zirconia would be at, looking at the two wolves. The two of them sat on their respective golden thrones that shone brighter than the castle. Queen Zirconia looked on with sadness, her head turned to her son. He had accompanied them for this meeting, and he had the same look his father had: anger. Except King Titanosaurus's anger was more neutral since the wolf king never ever showed emotion (from what Princess Okome had told him all those terra cycles ago.)

Prince Wonwoo couldn't look at Queen Zirconia; her face told of the countless terra cycles that she grieved for Princess Okome. It reminded him of the sadness on Queen Cora's face when she mentioned the loss of his siblings. Unlike his siblings, they died of natural causes, not by being killed by another living being. His breath hitched. He wanted to tell her how sorry he was, sorry for all the grief and for all the pain. She deserved to have closure.

They all deserve closure, he added, turning his gaze to Prince Scamander who noticed him.

The wolf prince got to his paws, presumably to confront Prince Wonwoo and go off on him (the lion prince can already hear what he wanted to say to him, how he would pay for the death of his sister, how he was a good-for-nothing worthless piece of shit, the usual Demoniacal curses), but was stopped by the wolf queen, who went up to him and shook her head slowly at him. She was rubbing his shoulder and comforting him with what Prince Wonwoo could only guess was soothing words. He opened his mouth to argue, and the wolf king snapped his head to his son.

"Not. Now," Prince Wonwoo heard King Titanosaurus say.

That had made the wolf prince even more mad.

"Father, I mean this from the bottom of my heart–" Prince Scamander said.

The wolf king interrupted him by raising a paw. He also let out an intimidating growl that could only be translated as "Run your mouth against your King, and you can say goodbye to your speaking privileges." The wolf prince stopped talking, placed a paw to his chest in compliance then sat back down beside his Father, looking bitterly at Prince Wonwoo. He was definitely pissed.

The lion prince could barely move nor could he even stand, but he forced himself up regardless. He could hear the whispering from those who attended and also feel their burning gaze on his pelt. An array of sentences flew by him:

"He's really alive."

"I told you he wasn't dead. You owe me 25 gold pieces after this trial."

"Dammit."

"Look at him. Pitiful."

"Don't feel pity for that worthless excuse of a prince; he killed our beloved princess. He deserves all the wrath our King delivers upon him."

He ignored them and stared at the wolf king and queen and bowed his head.

"Prince Wonwoo of the Promised Dynasty," King Titanosaurus began, his voice silencing the crowd, "I assume you know why you are here in front of the Demoniacal Kingdom today."

"Of course, King Titanosaurus of the Demoniacal Kingdom," Prince Wonwoo answered, not meeting his eyes. "You, along with Queen Zirconia and Prince Scamander, wish that I avenge for...your daughter's untimely demise."

"Not just them."

Another deep voice startled him, and he turned to the source. It was another black wolf similar to King Titanosaurus, with a white chest and underbelly and a sky blue tail. His piercing light blue eyes bore into the lion prince's skin. He sat by the foot of the stairs, on the same side as Prince Scamander, and snorted at him.

"Me as well. You killed my niece."

He suddenly remembered who this wolf was.

"I don't know if you were able to see him. The other black wolf with the white chest and underbelly."

"I did."

"That's my uncle, my father's younger twin brother, Livyatan. He's a prince but he got bumped to second in line since my brother took his place."

Ahhh, so this is King Titanosaurus's twin brother, second in line prince of the Demoniacal Kingdom and Prince Scamander's uncle. The lion prince studied him. *Yep. The family resemblance is uncanny. Grimness definitely runs in this family.*

"You killed my beloved niece, and that is something I will never forgive you for. You will pay for what you have done, lion prince of the Promised Dynasty," Livyatan growled.

Everyone muttered and nodded in agreement.

"Can I just defend myself for like, a split second?" Prince Wonwoo asked, looking back at King Titanosaurus. "Like, my Gods. I have a lot to say on the events as well."

"Why would we want to hear from you? You're a murderer; murderers aren't redeemable."

You are like a clone of the King, it is so crazy, he said to himself. "Because I have my own say? It's not all what you think it is. It would be best if everyone hears my side of the story before the King can come to a conclusion."

The wolf King and Queen looked at each other. Prince Wonwoo couldn't tell if they were offended or they were actually seriously thinking about what he said. He kept his mouth shut, swallowing nervously. He shouldn't say anything else that could further incriminate him.

Livyatan took a threatening step forward. "That's a lie! We know it! You're lying to hide the fact that you are a CALLOUS MURDERER!"

"Brother, silence at once!" the wolf king barked at his brother. "This trial will be fair for once."

For once!?

What is a usual trial in the Demoniacal Kingdom like? Even Livyatan stared at King Titanosaurus with a look of "I'm sorry, what the hell did you say?"

Wait, why am I asking that? The fuck? This is the Demoniacal Kingdom we're talking about!

Livyatan growled at King Titanosaurus but finally complied. He sat down, put a paw to his chest and grumbled, licking his paws. His tail twitched in his annoyance. Prince Wonwoo flinched at the size of his claws. Though they were not as massive as King Titanosaurus's, it was still an intimidating feature.

And he thought he had massive claws.

The wolf king waved at Prince Wonwoo. "Proceed."

"Thank you, Your Majesty." He coughed and composed himself. He finally got himself on all four paws and met the wolf king, wolf queen and wolf prince. "I know you were told that I had killed Princess Okome. While it is true, no one else but I laid the final blow, I really did not intend to kill her. I had no second thought on wanting her dead. It was all an accident. Truly it was. There were outside forces that led to this unfortunate accident."

"Explain?" King Titanosaurus requested curiously, an eyebrow raised.

He looked around the guards, seeing if he could spot a certain leopardess. "Your guard, Enky, was the one to keep pushing me past my limits despite me and Princess Okome many times telling her to stop. She wouldn't listen, and I had to teach her an example. That's when your daughter intervened, a-and...I think you know what happened from then."

The entire room was silent. The wolf king and queen stared in judgement. The wolf queen was more sympathetic in her expression than the wolf king, who appeared to be heavily in thought. Prince Scamander tossed his head to the side, scoffing. He could hear muttered whispers from the Demoniacal Kingdom.

"Do you believe this guy?"

"Uh-huh. Suuuure."

"So he intended on killing Enky AND Princess Okome?"

"I told you not all of them are pure angels! He admitted it himself. He's just trying to save his sorry ass."

"Exactly. Once a murderer, always a murderer."

Prince Wonwoo interrupted the grumbling few. "I did not intend on killing Enky," he said. "Nor did I intend on killing Princess Okome. I only wanted to teach Enky a lesson."

"By killing her!?" Livyatan snarled.

"No!" Prince Wonwoo lowered his gaze. "I mean...maybe I wanted to..."

Everyone gasped.

...*Fuck.*

The black wolf flared open his eyes. He jumped on the gun and pointed a claw at him. "So you admit it!"

The lion prince realized what he said and shook his head. "No! No no! I just...wanted to teach her a lesson! Nothing more! I did not give in to those desires of killing a life so callously!"

"Yet you did with Princess Okome!"

"I never had the desire to harm Princess Okome nor did I want to harm her at all! I loved her! I couldn't wait for our marriage day!" *Gods, you're an idiot, Prince Wonwoo. Why did you blatantly admit you wanted to kill Enky? You should have kept your mouth shut!*

"Lies! All lies! You can't keep pretending that you have a pure soul! You admit to wanting to kill Enky, you admit to having those thoughts of murder! *YOU ADMIT* to the crime! Murderer! Disgrace to your own beliefs and your worthless Gods! You're a worthless excuse of a prince who considers himself holy. What a fucking hypocrite!" Livyatan turned to his brother after slamming the lion prince with a flurry of hatred. "This is enough evidence from the lion prince himself, my brother. He already admitted he wanted to kill *and* he admitted to be the one who *did kill* Princess Okome. He admitted it all!" He flicked his tail. "I'm telling you now, my brother. Execute him, and it will all be over."

"Thank you!" Prince Scamander shouted.

Everyone began chanting for execution.

"Kill the lion prince of the Promised Dynasty. Kill the lion prince of the Promised Dynasty. Kill the lion prince of the Promised Dynasty."

Prince Wonwoo flicked his ears. Deep down, his anxiety stirred in his stomach. Nothing and no one could calm him down, not

PRINCE WONWOO? THAT NAME IS DEAD. MORE LIKE...

while he was surrounded by cold-blooded, power-hungry creatures. He really, REALLY should have kept silent about impulsively wanting to kill Enky.

The wolf king silenced everyone. Prince Wonwoo was expecting to see hatred in his eyes, expecting to hear the final judgement from the wolf king, however, he noticed there was something different in the wolf king. He appeared more...attentive? He had been thinking about Prince Wonwoo's testimony for sure, for he asked the lion prince, "Did you say that Enky was there?"

The lion prince nodded. "Yes, Your Majesty. Along with a red fox and a panda. I wish I could remember their names, Your Majesty, but my memory is quite bad. I apologize."

King Titanosaurus looked even more confused. "Arvolf and Cyclone?"

"Ah. Yes. Them."

He heard some commotion and saw the red fox and giant panda shuffle in the crowd. He finally saw Enky in the crowd too, and he narrowed his eyes at her. He could see the embarrassment rising from her pelt as she tried to hide within the guards. *There you are,* he growled internally. *Hiding. Like a coward.*

Confusion finally settled in on King Titanosaurus. He looked at the lion prince, twitching his ears in confusion. "What? Enky, Arvolf and Cyclone were there? This does not make sense, I don't recall ever assigning them on that fateful day. Why were they even there in the first place?"

Prince Scamander shuffled his paws, looking away and pretending nothing was happening.

"They said that you sent them to check on Princess Okome," Prince Wonwoo answered. "But Princess Okome questioned why you would have sent them when you knew she was safe. Then Arvolf said something that she knew you would never do. That's when she knew who exactly sent them."

"Who did?"

The lion prince blinked.

How much more would Prince Scamander hate me if I ratted him out?... Ah, fuck it.

He weakly lifted a paw and pointed to Prince Scamander, which generated a gasp from those attending. The wolf king turned to his son slowly, ears pinning behind. Prince Wonwoo jumped in his skin; he could practically see the dark aura emerging from the wolf king. The wolf queen also turned to Prince Scamander, who couldn't ignore King Titanosaurus's stare. The wolf prince pretended not to notice his father. It was only a minute that he finally caved in with occasional glances and cleared his throat.

"...I just wanted to make sure my sister was doing okay!" he defended, crossing his arms. "Okay?! I sent them for our own safety because I don't trust the lion King and Queen to be watching and guarding her! Is that bad?"

Prince Wonwoo caught a glance at Livyatan, who had shook his head in agreement for his nephew.

"You sent guards. To the Promised Dynasty. *Without my permission?*" the wolf king growled. Prince Wonwoo was intimidated by how angry the wolf king got. He knew it was in his genes, but hearing his voice drop even deeper than it already was was terrifying. "You told me *you* went yourself to the Promised Dynasty, which I did not allow in the first place. So not only did you go against me, you *lied* to me, your King!"

Prince Scamander also pinned his slightly curved ears. "I did what I did for a reason. Both going against you and lying to you. You weren't going to send any security to accompany Princess Okome, despite the many times I've warned and asked of you! I had to take matters into my own paws."

"He has a point, brother," Prince Wonwoo heard Livyatan mutter almost out loud. The lion prince never thought he would hear King Titanosaurus's brother be as equally insufferable. But what was he expecting anyway from someone in the Demoniacal Royal Family?

"We had a truce," King Titanosaurus growled. "They promised to watch over Princess Okome. They kept their end of the bargain, we kept our end of the bargain! I didn't need to send any security. All would have been fine!"

"But wouldn't you have felt safer knowing your daughter was under the watchful eyes of her own kind as opposed to strangers?" Prince Scamander retorted back, his voice full of venom.

The tension was palpable amongst family, but the wolf king kept to himself, sighing. The crowd whispered, they themselves unsure of how to react. He looked at Prince Wonwoo with eyes narrowed, rubbing his muzzle. If only the lion prince had the ability to read minds. Was he still angry at Prince Scamander? Or was this anger directed at him? The wolf queen whispered something to her husband, and he looked at her fondly. Prince Wonwoo found it interesting how quickly his emotion changed; he remembered what Princess Okome had told him, about how King Titanosaurus's happiness would only show when he was with his wife and children. He stared at her for a moment before finally turning back to Prince Wonwoo and resuming his emotionless stare. He cleared his throat and addressed him in front of everyone.

"I would have you executed for your crimes," he said, "but that would only just solve your problem and not ours. I think it's better we make you suffer with this guilt that afflicts you, wouldn't you agree?"

The lion prince stared dumbfounded. "I'm sorry, what now?"

Prince Scamander snapped his head at his father. So did Livyatan.

"That's right. You, a Promised Dynasty member and a prince, should learn about our ways and why we are hated. You must learn our pain and the consequences of your actions while alive. This will be your punishment. As of now, you're part of the Demoniacal Kingdom."

Everyone murmured. The lion prince was only frozen. This couldn't be happening.

"You're allowing Prince Wonwoo into our Kingdom!?" Livyatan asked. "Are you SERIOUS right now!?"

PRINCE WONWOO? THAT NAME IS DEAD. MORE LIKE...

"Prince Wonwoo," the wolf king repeated, letting it roll off his tongue. "That name is dead to him and to us." He hummed to himself then finally lifted a paw. "From now on, you are Scolamander of the Demoniacal Kingdom."

Prince Wonwoo lifted up his ears.

Scolamander!? SCOLAMANDER?!? That's way too close to Scamander! What is he thinking!? This can't be happening. This can't be happening!

The look from King Titanosaurus proved this was really happening. "If anyone has any complaints on my decision, come forth and address them now."

The crowd shifted, but no one stepped up. Not even Livyatan, the outspoken one with a lot to disagree on, who obviously looked just as pissed as Prince Scamander was. He was tempted at first, having stood up. The lion prince jerked his attention to the wolf king's twin brother.

Was he truly going to say something about the result of this trial? Was he really going to go against his own King? His own brother?

King Titanosaurus noticed him.

"Yes, brother?" King Titanosaurus asked. "Would you *like* to share?"

Livyatan twitched his tail. Prince Wonwoo could hear in the wolf king's voice that he was asking for a challenge. Asking his twin brother "test me and find out, trust me." Prince Wonwoo knew this was the wolf king's way to tell Livyatan he was the one in charge around here. The lion prince shrunk to not make himself known.

Livyatan had heard it too. He flattened his ears and sat down.

"No," he begrudgingly growled out the word.

"Then it is decided on the former prince's fate. Welcome, Scolamander, to the Demoniacal Kingdom. This trial is concluded."

King Titanosaurus got up from his throne and left. Everyone else dispersed out of the castle while some lingered and talked amongst each other, occasionally eyeing the lion prince. He stood awkwardly, unsure where to go. He looked towards the thrones and laid eyes on Queen Zirconia, who caught his attention. The wolf queen smiled at him as she approached Prince Wonwoo, now Scolamander. She fixed his mane eerily in the same way his mother would have. The way she lovingly tended to him made Scolamander think that she must have said something to King Titanosaurus to convince him not to be killed.

"Is there anything I can get you before I get you situated?" Queen Zirconia asked.

The lion prince stared, unable to answer.

Why else would she act so loving towards a stranger? Someone she doesn't even know? Especially someone from an enemy Kingdom??

His eyes drifted up to the ceiling of the castle.

Once again, WHY OH WHY AM I ALWAYS SPARED FROM MORANA!?

PRINCE WONWOO? THAT NAME IS DEAD. MORE LIKE...

Was his life being spared by Abella? Wasn't that against their rule? The one rule that neither Goddesses are to interfere with the lives of the mortals? The one rule that was never meant to be broken after the one incident in the legends from all those undefined terra cycles ago?!

Gods, just please...PLEASE! Let me die! Stop letting me live!

The lion prince looked over Queen Zirconia's shoulder to observe Prince Scamander, still in his place. The wolf prince was visibly fuming, his tail twitching like mad. He watched his father leave, his eyes narrowed. His fur bristled as if he was struck by lightning. There was so much he wanted to say to his Father, but him having left only left him in a bitter state. He looked back at his mother, then the lion prince and spat. The lion prince could see that the wolf prince had tried to at least get his mother's attention but it wasn't working. Seeing his mother attend to him made his anger only fester more.

He got up, flipped his head away, and stormed out of the throne room. The lion prince assumed that he was going to chase after his Father to give him a piece of his mind, but instead, he was heading towards the staircase. He disappeared out of sight towards what he assumed was his room upstairs. Prince Wonwoo– No, *Scolamander now* could hear the wolf prince grumbling aloud before there was a slam of a door.

Both he and Queen Zirconia flinched at the sudden noise. The wolf queen sighed.

"Don't mind Prince Scamander, dear," the wolf queen said to the lion prince, looking to the second floor. "He will get over it eventually. He's just...hurt, that's all."

Hurt wasn't even the right word the lion prince could think of. He only felt what any grieving creature would experience: Outrage. Denial. Desolation. Nothing could ever make these feelings go away, not even in the long run. It was made even worse with the fact that he would be taken in by the Demoniacal Kingdom Royal Family. Meaning that Prince Scamander would have to live with him. The one who had killed his sister.

Now that is super awkward.

Scolamander swallowed nervously.

He wasn't ready for what would be ahead of him in his future with the Demoniacal Kingdom, and especially his future with Prince Scamander.

✦✧✦POSTLUDE ✦✧✦
"MANY TERRA CYCLES FROM NOW, OUR UNIVERSE WILL FALL..."

~ 105 terra cycles ago... ~
~ December in Terra Cycle 1018 B.E. ~

"IT IS A SIGN OF GREAT CATASTROPHE!"

It had been months after the Great War had ended in its stalemate. Saturhorimau, now establishing himself as King of this new Kingdom of his that he had called the Promised Dynasty, was gathered with close friends in the field of their new city when all of a sudden, a large brown fuzzy bear-like creature with an unusually carved mask that bore a frown ran by them. All turned in shock to see what the creature was. It was a Diprotodon, fleeing two other creatures: a Daphoenus and a cave bear. The Diprotodon was yelling in pain and fear, shouting nonsense as he fled from the two creatures. The Daphoenus finally caught up and tackled the raving Diprotodon, tying their paws.

The masked Diprotodon continued to rave and beg.

✦✧✦ POSTLUDE ✦✧✦

"Stop! STOP! PLEASE! LISTEN TO ME! I AM TELLING THE TRUTH!" he shouted. "I'M NOT MAD, I'M NOT MAD, **I'M NOT MAD!**"

"Says the one ranting about how we're all going to die and the world will cease to exist," the Daphoenus said. "By the Gods in the Heavens. When will you see that you're just a crazy old coot, Farlan? That these so-called 'visions' are just a result of your troubled mind not having recovered from your grief? I would almost be sorry for you, had you not continued to go around and rave like a Demoniacal Kingdom member." She tugged the rope tightly in a knot, which prompted a whimper from the Diprotodon. "Now stay down and shut up already. You've caused enough trouble as is."

"Way too much trouble," the Daphoenus's companion–a cave bear–muttered, rubbing his temples with his paws. "The farm's a complete mess after your hollering and ranting."

What is going on here? King Saturhorimau sighed to himself, rising to his paws. *Can I get a single day of just peace? Please?*

"I'm TRYING NOT to cause ANY trouble!" the masked Diprotodon, Farlan, wailed. "Nor am I trying to hurt any of you all! I swear! I'm trying to WARN YOU ALL about the latest vision I had! Please! I SAW IT CLEARLY! A dark creature…marked only by the sound of the clock and free as the flow of time…AND THEN GONE! Everything! This world…GONE, GONE, ERASED! It's **GOING** TO **HAPPEN!!** Many Terra Cycles from now, our Universe will fall!! I'm serious!! SERIOUS! I'M NOT MAD, I'M NOT MAD!!!"

The Daphoenus and the cave bear looked at each other. They shook their heads in frustration and continued restraining the Diprotodon. He continued to wail and scream:

"I AM NOT MAD!! THE UNIVERSE WILL COLLAPSE!!! WE WILL BE NOTHING BUT AT THE MERCY OF NIHILITY UNLESS WE DO SOMETHING!!"

King Saturhorimau tilted his head. What was the masked Diprotodon implying?

"There goes old Farlan," one of King Saturhorimau's friends–a Smilodon–said, shaking her head. "The poor crazed old farmer. Getting himself caught. *Again.* All because he can't shut his yapping mouth."

"It's a bit of a shame," an Eremotherium stated, slowly sitting back down after having stood up in a haste due to the commotion and lifting up his massive claws.

"It is, and he isn't even old. He's roughly the same age as the King, only older by a few terra cycles."

"I guess your brain can just start rotting away at any age."

An Andrewsarchus lifted up its head, shaking its tiny mane on the back of its head. "A shame indeed! Haven't you guys heard of the rumors?"

The lion king's friends began to whisper to each other.

"Rumors?" asked a Thylacoleo.

"What rumors?" a Xenocyon wondered.

✦✧✦ POSTLUDE ✦✧✦

"Come on, Alexandrei, spill!" a Thylacosmilus yapped.

The Andrewsarchus, Alexandrei, narrowed its eyes. "That he obtained dark magic just so he can create chaos?"

Everyone around him gasped.

"What do you mean?"

"Tell us tell us!"

The Andrewsarchus stretched. "Well it's no surprise that, because of the death of his mother at the paws of the Demoniacal Kingdom during the Great War, the bastard lost himself and went mad with grief. But the rumors are that some say he started digging into spells and things no innocent mind should be exposed to as a way to get his revenge on the Demoniacal Kingdom and possibly bring his mother back from the dead."

King Saturhorimau also listened in on the story being woven by his friend. His curiosity peaked.

"How tragic! Poor Farlan." The Xenocyon.

"Poor boy." The Thylacosmilus.

Alexandrei scratched his neck. "It's said he was able to find a way to see through time, into the future, and now because he has so much knowledge, he is just...well. Plain mad. He now speaks in those weird rhymes and only about warnings for the near future that no one pays mind to. They all fear that if they listen to his crazed ranting, they too will be infected like he was and turn just like him. Don't you all remember Xiao?"

King Saturhorimau's heart stopped. *Xiao...*

"Oh yeah. The poor Diacodexis," the Eremotherium said after long silence from him. "Some say she willingly listened to what Farlan had for everyone one time when no one wanted to, and it started to make her mind go nuts. She fled in an attempt to purify herself and found herself in the jaws of a Demoniacal Kingdom member that she couldn't flee from in time. 'We're all going to die!' Those were her last words before she had disappeared."

The Smilodon lifted up her eyebrows. "I remember her! Everyone blamed Farlan for her death because, had he shut his mouth and not worry her of what he had 'seen,' she would have not listened and kept her mind pure."

The lion king also thought about the Diacodexis; Xiao was a petite but beloved little ungulate, with fur as brown as a chestnut and spots as white as snow littered all over. She acted as a messenger and a spy for the Promised Dynasty when the war first broke out. With her speed, she was able to travel from one place to another in a matter of a minute. She was able to escape death from King Wyvern's allies on many occasions. Without her efforts, the Promised Dynasty would have never been able to beat King Wyvern in the final moments. She was hailed a hero after the war, praised and respected by all.

Two months ago was when her accident had occurred. She ran away out of the blue and was never seen again for days. Many tried to stop her from leaving, but she pushed them away, constantly repeating a disturbing phrase: "We're all going to die, we're all going to die!" Everyone searched all day and all night for her with nothing to bring. Many assumed that she was taken by Dragon's Wrath, as her scent had ended around by the river. King

✦✧✦ POSTLUDE ✦✧✦

Saturhorimau did not give up initially but after a while, he too lost hope. It was unusual of him to feel such hopelessness, but it gripped him and did not let go. Kishi had haunted him in his sleep ever since.

About 3 weeks ago, Alexandrei and the Eremotherium went out on a patrol one day, and they finally brought back the mangled, bloody corpse of the tiny Diacodexis that they discovered by the riverbank of Dragon's Wrath. The Promised Dynasty gathered around her, mourning and paying their respects. King Saturhorimau noted the wounds on Xiao's body and concluded it was the work of a Demoniacal Kingdom member. He also noted the fear in her wide, lifeless eyes.

"We're all going to die!"

Her final words rang in his head as he stared into her empty eyes.

"Yeah. So that's why no one listens to him anymore."

An Embolotherium snorted after the tale. "Well obviously. How can we believe what he's saying when it hasn't even happened yet?"

"Did he truly obtain this ability through dark magic like King Wyvern did?" a Hemicyon asked.

Everyone flinched at the mention of the wyvern dragon king.

"You can't just say his name like that, Tuur!" the Smilodon scolded the Hemicyon. "Especially in front of the King!" She pointed at King Saturhorimau.

Tuur, the Hemicyon, lowered their head to their chest. "Sorry. I'm just curious." They looked at the lion king. "Please forgive me, King Saturhorimau."

"You're forgiven," King Saturhorimau answered in a soft voice.

An Epicyon answered the Hemicyon's question. "I like to think so. Think about it. How do you get the ability to see through time with pious magic?"

"..."

"..."

"..."

Everyone was silent.

King Saturhorimau finally got to his paws after listening to the tale, leaving them to their own discussions, and went up to the masked Diprotodon. Farlan noticed the lion king approaching and whimpered.

"K-King Saturhorimau! Please, forgive me!" Farlan cried, lifting up his tied paws. "Oh, Gods so mighty above me! Great Ellowyn! Please, forgive me! Forgive me!"

"King Saturhorimau," the Daphoenus and the cave bear announced in unison, bowing their heads at the lion king.

"What seems to be the trouble this time, Jinsalih?" the lion king inquired the Daphoenus, twitching an ear.

"Your Majesty, this crazed coot–" The Daphoenus, Jinsalih, pointed to Farlan. "–caused so much trouble on the farm today

♦✧♦ POSTLUDE ♦✧♦

that it was starting to make every farmer uncomfortable. They all politely asked him to keep his thoughts to himself, but he snapped at them, calling them, I quote, *'oblivious brainless demons.'*" She narrowed her eyes at him. "He said that we were all blind to the truth, that we were demons as equally as the Demoniacal Kingdom themselves. That's when he destroyed the crops in his crazed rants and then ran off when we tried to apprehend him."

"I-I-I didn't mean my statement!" Farlan shouted. "Honest! I was– I was– Under a lot of pressure, with the vision."

"We already told you to shut up, you stupid, illegitimate bastard!" the cave bear snarled, shoving his face in front of Farlan. "It seems you just can't stop running that useless tongue of yours. Why don't we fix that by removing this dumb mask and tying your muzzle shut once and for all?"

As soon as the cave bear reached out his paw to Farlan's mask, the Diprotodon freaked out. He kicked his back legs at the cave bear. King Saturhorimau noticed his strength; Farlan may be weak, but he had a lot of power to him. He rolled on the grass as he squirmed to repeatedly kick the cave bear, all while crying out incoherently. The cave bear growled and swiped a paw towards his face, trying to break his mask. Farlan managed to dodge it by rolling to his side and onto his belly. He crawled and squirmed, drawing everyone's attention in the process.

"**NO!**" he cried once he got his words together. "NO! NOT MY MASK! DON'T TAKE IT! DON'T TOUCH IT! You cannot see my face...NOBODY'S SUPPOSED TO SEE MY FACE! NO ONE!"

"Stop this nonsense at once, bastard!" Jinsalih snapped, kicking him in the ribs.

Farlan threw his head up in shock.

"*OW!* OW OW OW! ASSAULT! ASSAULT! GET AWAY FROM ME, YOU MINDLESS DEVIL DOG! Y-YOU TOO, DUMB LUMBERING DEMON BEAR! CHAOS WILL NOT GET ME LIKE IT GOT YOU!"

"How dare you talk to Cadwallader like that? Don't you know what he did during the Great War?"

"Don't CARE! THAT WAR KILLED MY MOTHER! *YOU GUYS* KILLED MY MOTHER! HELP! HELP!!"

The lion king felt a growing migraine coming from this argument. He rubbed his head. His Dynasty members were slowly becoming just like Demoniacal Kingdom members. If this continued further, they would tear into each other like those beasts. No. He can't allow this to happen.

Jinsalih jabbed him again. "You're just weak. A pathetic waste of life Abella brought to the land. A bastard that should have never been born. I hope to the Gods that Okalani and Azrael judge you and send you to Hell where you belong."

King Saturhorimau widened his eyes at the Daphoenus. How could anyone say that to someone?! *No one can choose where they're born into*, he thought to himself.

"Woah now, calm down there, Jinsalih. Isn't that going a bit too far?" the Xenocyon asked Jinsalih, who snapped her head at them.

✦✧✦ POSTLUDE ✦✧✦

"Give Farlan a break; the poor lad lost his mother and went mad. Can't we just leave him alone?"

Agreed, let's just leave him alone, King Saturhorimau said in his head. *Especially not tell someone they deserve to go to hell. Even if they are evil beyond forgiving.* His ears drooped, his mind crossing his former best friend at the mention of evil. *It isn't in our place to judge an individual; that is for Okalani and Azrael.*

"We could, Fingal, if he won't shut up!" Jinsalih snarled.

Farlan protested, "W-Well, I am trying to be nice! But you're all pushing me around for no reason! I'm trying to warn you all about danger! I'm trying to be a helpful farmer caring for the Promised Dynasty! I'm TRYING to be useful!"

"Well, you're not *useful*, or *helpful*, or anything! You've never been useful to us when the war first broke out, and you're certainly not useful now at the farm with your lazing about and stargazing and daydreaming that distracts you from work. You contribute nothing to the Dynasty and never will! You're USELESS! You hear me, bastard!? U S E L E S S!"

Farlan began to wail even louder.

"Jinsalih!" Fingal snapped.

"The truth hurts but needs to be said!"

The lion king growled. He could feel everyone giving in to the temptations of sin. The thoughts that rotted the brain and the heart. The same feelings that King Wyvern had submitted to before he turned evil with dark power. That made the lion king clench his chest in pain. He couldn't let that happen to his Dynasty.

He had to do something before a civil war broke out.

"ENOUGH!!!" King Saturhorimau roared.

Everyone went silent after his roar, for everyone knew once the lion king snapped, he was serious.

"All of you! Stop this at once!" He nodded at Jinsalih and Cadwallader. "Back away from Farlan. I will handle this."

Although they scowled at him, they bowed and backed away as told.

"Zakath," the lion king called to his Smilodon companion, "see to it that Jinsalih and Cadwallader are escorted back to their homes at once. While you're at it, check on the farm and its workers to see if there is any damage you can relieve."

Zakath rose to her paws, bowed at the lion king, and bounded up to Jinsalih and Cadwallader. She nudged them forward and back to the city. "You heard the King. Come now, you two. His Majesty will handle this."

King Saturhorimau nodded at her. Zakath began escorting Jinsalih and Cadwallader back to the city, pushing them in front so she could keep their eyes on them. The two briefly looked back. Zakath noticed their scowls and met them with her own.

"Are you questioning Our King?" the Smilodon growled.

"No," they answered in unison.

✦✧✦ POSTLUDE ✦✧✦

"Then get a move on!"

They looked forward, not glancing back.

The King approached Farlan once more as soon as the tension died down, and the masked Diprotodon whimpered. He couldn't see his face, but he could tell that Farlan was scared out of his mind. He trembled and whispered to himself and wept softly. The lion king felt his heart sink at the pitiful sight. He lifted up a claw and reached over to the rope, sawing at it as he delicately cut. Farlan froze but soon knew that King Saturhorimau wasn't hurting him. Once all the rope was cut, the masked Diprotodon got to his paws and bowed profusely at the lion king.

"Thank you, thank you, King Saturhorimau of the Promised Dynasty!" Farlan whimpered. "You're truly too kind! May the Honeycutt bloodline be blessed with happiness and good luck. You truly will reign for all time!"

"Aw, thank you. I do hope I will," King Saturhorimau said with a chuckle. "Now tell me. What's going on? What's all this about the world being erased?"

His friends gasped.

"King Saturhorimau, don't," Alexandrei snorted. "Just. Let him go back to the farm."

"Yeah, we don't need to hear what he supposedly has for us now," the Embolotherium grunted.

"Agreed." The Eremotherium. "We'll all lose our minds if he starts to explain to us about...whatever it is."

Farlan whined, lowering his head to his chest.

The lion king looked back at his friends in disappointment. "Leave me with Farlan to settle things," he commanded. "Return to the city square and wait for me there."

They looked at each other, frozen in place. Fingal the Xenocyon was the only one who went on ahead. The lion king flicked his tail in anger at the rest. Were they not obeying him already just because they don't like this Diprotodon? He couldn't believe it; after all he preached and taught, there was still this much hatred that King Wyvern had in his own heart no less.

He growled deeply.

"That is an order."

They perked up at once and bowed their heads. They passed by the two, casting side glances at Farlan, and crossed the fields. The lion king watched them all go before calling out to one of them.

"Clawtrax!" King Saturhorimau shouted to the Eremotherium.

The large ground sloth turned around.

"You're with me."

Clawtrax bowed his head and joined them.

"A dark creature?"

The trio leisurely strolled through Divine Kingfisher Woods, admiring the beauty of nature. King Saturhorimau lifted up his head, a bird dangling from his jaws; he decided that a serene and bright environment is what Farlan needed to calm down. That, and someone understanding and willing to listen to him would also help. Clawtrax mainly ignored the two, only keeping a sharp eye on the lion king. He lifted his large claws to the branches above and stripped them bare of their leaves, shoving them in his mouth.

"Yes. A really, REALLY dark, DARK creature!" Farlan said, stopping and raising his paws to the sky as the lion king ate. "Dark in pelt, he blended in with Gau's darkest night. There was also a great evil within his heart that had been festering since a life-changing event that turned him more colder than a brutal winter night. He was unlike any I've seen. What's worse: He is related to King Wyvern."

King Saturhorimau's heart jumped. Clawtrax froze after stripping another branch clean, narrowing his eyes at the masked Diprotodon. Mention of the dark dragon always sent everyone in the Promised Dynasty in alert and weariness. It wasn't some name you could throw around in normal conversation willy-nilly. Although it sent shivers, the lion king couldn't help but feel a wave of regret flood him.

"H..How do you know?" King Saturhorimau asked him.

Farlan dropped his paws back down, fidgeting them. "Your...great-grandson."

Great-grandson?

Farlan saw his *great-grandson* in his latest vision? The lion king gently leaned closer. Now he was really curious about what Farlan had seen.

"Tell me more."

The masked Diprotodon lifted up his head. King Saturhorimau couldn't see it but he could tell that his eyes were wide. "Are you sure?" he asked warily. "Are you sure you really want to know what's going to happen?"

"Yes."

"Or are you wanting to know more about your great-grandson?"

"Both. Please."

"..." Farlan sighed. "Follow me."

The masked Diprotodon got up and bounded up ahead. He stopped to look back and nod at King Saturhorimau and Clawtrax. The lion king flicked an ear. Where was he going? He followed after Farlan, Clawtrax hot on his tail.

Divine Kingfisher Woods was a forest known for its thick vegetation. King Saturhorimau and his Dynasty, his allies, had used this forest to evade many attacks from King Wyvern's Kingdom during the Great War. The large oak trees provided great shielding, as it would take hours for the Demoniacal Kingdom members to cut through. The trio ran through the undergrowth. King Saturhorimau soon picked up the faint but clear sound of the river. He shuddered internally; he remembered the terrified look on his friends' faces as they–along with some of King Wyvern's

✦✧✦ POSTLUDE ✦✧✦

allies–fell into the raging force of nature. He never saw a head stick out from the river, nor did he see a paw or leg break through the surface. They were never seen again, presumed dead. The river was so dangerous, it was eventually called Dragon's Wrath, named after King Wyvern, and it was heavily avoided at all times.

They came up by the cliff and followed on the side of Dragon's Wrath. After a few minutes of running, King Saturhorimau found Farlan making his way down a steep ravine. Clawtrax stopped at the ledge and stared below. He sat down.

"You go on ahead, Sire," he said. "I would just be extra weight. I'll be here to keep a lookout and pull you up afterwards. Be careful."

King Saturhorimau nodded and followed after Farlan.

It was surprisingly steep. The waterfall roared loudly against the lion king's ears, a white mist emitting. Tiny rocks dislodged from each step they took and tumbled down to the ravine below. King Saturhorimau breathed in deeply. This ledge was dangerous; because of the rushing waterfall, the sediment here was more loose. They had learned that the hard way during the war. They'd have to tread lightly if they were to make it down safely.

The lion king took one step then found himself dislodging the whole piece of land. The masked Diprotodon had heard the crumble and looked back at the lion king. King Saturhorimau yelped as he tried to recover from his fumble. He nearly lost his footing and was almost sent tumbling before Farlan reached up to grab him and hold him up. The two watched as the large chunk of dirt tumbled and shattered on the ground below. They both sighed in relief. Once the lion king situated himself on steadier land, the masked Diprotodon pulled back his paw.

"I'm sorry, King Saturhorimau!" he apologized quickly. "I didn't- I was just-"

"Don't worry about it," King Saturhorimau said with the wave of a paw. "You saved me. You have a good heart."

He wished he could see Farlan's smile beam.

The two climbed down without any further problems and the lion king looked ahead; the ravine was simply gorgeous. The end of Dragon's Wrath was peaceful, with the water trickling ever so gently. It was hard to believe this was still Dragon's Wrath. It was also as clear as day and not foaming.

"It's so peaceful here..." King Saturhorimau commented.

"Isn't it?" Farlan said. "It's where I go to get away from all the chaos." He trekked alongside the riverbank. "We're almost there. We just have to follow the path."

"Where will it take us?" the lion king asked.

"To a small little pool."

"A pool? What pool?"

"It doesn't have a name I believe. So I call it...Heaven's Eye."

Heaven's Eye. An interesting and intriguing name to him. The lion king definitely never heard about it before.

King Saturhorimau followed Farlan across the ravine until they finally reached a dense, cool area that was shielded by leaves from

✦✧✦ POSTLUDE ✦✧✦

the trees above. The outline of a den became visible. An entrance guarded by vines hung ominously. A cave? The lion king squinted his eyes. He had never seen this before. Was it perhaps made by a Demoniacal Kingdom member during the war?

Farlan pushed through the vines, disappearing. The lion king, startled, raised a paw. Some sort of white mist emerged after the masked Diprotodon entered, slithering up his paw like a snake and surrounding itself around the lion king's whole body. King Saturhorimau closed his eyes, letting himself be immersed in the mist. He could feel the energy of the Heavens, hear them whispering in a sacred language. They were calling out to him, beckoning him to come along. King Saturhorimau opened his eyes. It was safe. He followed after Farlan, slinking his way inside.

The interior was crushed, having been abandoned a long time ago. The roof had collapsed, leaving only a small portion of the original ceiling intact. Old remnants of a table and a chair existed, broken and claimed by the land. Shredded evidence of scrolls lay strewn all around the floor, beyond recognizable. From the looks of it, this cave existed well before the Great War. Someone ancient made this their home. Who that someone was? Well. That was the question. The lion king sniffed for any sign of remnants that would lead to who had lived here, but there was none. No trace of the original owner or anything. The owner must have made sure that nothing could be detected so they wouldn't be found out. This cave was truly abandoned.

Once the two had entered the cave, Farlan beckoned King Saturhorimau to the edge of Heaven's Eye. He stepped up, careful not to step on anything on the ground and stopped in front of the pool. He stared down; it was a rather big pool, about as big as a boulder and as blue as the sky. In the sunlight that pierced through the vegetation and collapsed roof, it shone bright, nearly blinding the lion king.

"What I'm about to show you will be too much for your mind to wrap around," Farlan warned. "I beg of you, Your Majesty, you do not have to do this. I do not wish to harm you. But if you wish to proceed, let me know. You can tell me to stop anytime."

The lion king flicked an ear, heeding Farlan's warning. "No, it's okay. I've been through worse. Show me."

The masked Diprotodon bowed his head. "As you wish. Lay down, relax, and close your eyes."

King Saturhorimau did as he was told. The ground was cold. He shivered a little bit. He could feel the mist again wrapping around him, whispering and calling to him. After a while and some mysterious chanting from Farlan, a strong force of energy surged through his head. He felt himself detaching from his body, and he went limp.

...

"Don't do this."

The lion king finally opened his eyes, and he found himself in the dark. There was no light in sight, no trees, no grass, nothing. Not even a presence of the sun or the moon or the flickering of the stars. It was cold and empty and desolate. There also was a faint sound that kept repeating. He strained his ears to catch the noise.

✦✧✦ POSTLUDE ✦✧✦

Tick. Tock. Tick. Tock.

A ticking noise?

"Prince Scamander, I am begging you! Don't do this!" *The same voice that he heard the moment he was sucked into this emptiness began pleading in a way a child would beg.*

"I have no choice." *Another voice interjected with venom in its voice.*

The lion king jolted at the new voice. Who was that?

"You do have a choice! It's called not doing it!"

"Ahhhahahaha!! Why would I not do this? Are you crazy? I can't simply stop doing something that is very much ingrained into my blood. I always hoped for such power, like my great-grandfather."

"King Wyvern was nothing but a cruel tyrant who wanted to take the land for himself!"

King Saturhorimau turned to that particular voice. So that was his great-grandson. He sounded...just like him. How old is he? How come he couldn't see him?

"He was doing everyone a favor. You don't know that because your Dynasty had been brainwashed for so long into this religion some being in the sky made. It's made you all hypocritical zombies!"

His great-grandson continued.

"He was going to destroy the land! Even the Heavens!"

There was a growl from the second voice that was only malicious. "You don't know anything about him, so you have no right telling me about my bloodline!"

That voice must be King Wyvern's great-grandson, the dark creature Farlan told of. King Saturhorimau observed his tone carefully. He definitely sounded like the cruel wyvern dragon. The lion king couldn't see him as well. Perhaps he wasn't meant to see what was happening in order to not mess with the timeline. King Saturhorimau was only left to hear the conversation between the two.

"I do know when it involves lives on the line!"

"You're even weaker than my Father. I'm going to change all that. I'm going to shape a new world under my command, with everyone bowing at my paws! Better yet, I will have a new universe. Just how King Wyvern would have wanted it."

"Prince Scamander..."

"I already told you that's not my name!"

"I won't call you by your new name. I refuse to. I'm going to put an end to you!"

"Heh. I like to see you try."

"...What happened to you, Prince Scamander? Everything could have changed; my parents believed in you, they trusted you even after everything that happened."

"No they didn't. No one trusted me. Not even your parents."

"That's not true. You could have had a second chance with the Promised Dynasty."

"A second chance without the love of my life and my children? Without the ones who were so callously murdered by your so-called righteous Gods in the Heavens."

✦✧✦ POSTLUDE ✦✧✦

That statement stung King Saturhorimau as if he was stabbed. What possibly happened that King Wyvern's great-grandson would make such a bold statement about the Heavens? If only he could see what was happening, know the whole context and truth on what led up to this moment!

Silence reigned for a while, as though his great-grandson was processing what had been said. He was stunned, too shocked to say anything right away. Finally, he spoke.

"Prince–"

"Prince Scamander is dead."

But he was cut off, King Wyvern's great-grandson tired of it all.

The ticking continued. It grew louder and louder before the lion king had to stop focusing on the sound. He shook his head, his ears aching. What was that sound? Why was it mesmerizing him even though it was hurting him?

"W-What is that?"

"It's the universe. Right in the grasp of my paws."

The lion king raised his ears. The universe? He wished he could see the dark creature holding the universe. So many questions ran through his mind. Was there a power that someone could have the whole universe in their paws? Was such a feat even possible?! It sounded more intense than King Wyvern's dark magic.

What dark magic would his great-grandson obtain...?

"The universe? How did you– What– What are you planning?"

"Something that was destined a long time ago. ...Feel it, Prince Wonwoo."

There was silence. The ticking seemed to have stopped, or at least, quieted down.

This ticking has to be associated with King Wyvern's great-grandson, *King Saturhorimau concluded.* Probably it's something that is meant to convey his inner emotions.

"...What in the..? It...It feels like a heartbeat..."

"Doesn't it? It feels so alive."

"I..."

"Every single creature, every living soul, you can feel them all in one collective heartbeat."

"..."

There was suddenly a squeezing sensation throughout the lion king's body. He gasped, dropping his head down. *What in Ellowyn's name? It was as if a large Titanoboa had caught him and was constricting him to kill him.* The air surrounding him was getting thinner, which was making it harder and harder to breathe. He looked around. *What was going on?*

"What are you doing!?" cried out the lion king's great-grandson.

"Say goodbye to everyone you love, Prince Wonwoo. Everything you once knew, living and in your precious Heavens. It will all be gone. Say hello to a new universe. My universe."

The squeezing sensation tightened. The lion king couldn't get a single breath in. He let out the last breath he was able to inhale. Since there

✦✧✦ POSTLUDE ✦✧✦

was nothing at all in the darkness, his vision didn't change a bit. He did feel his body grow light.

"Wait! STOP!-"

The desperate plea of his great-grandson pierced his heart. King Saturhorimau swayed, unable to accept what was happening. This was his family's fate. Everyone's fate to be exact.

The fate of the universe.

King Saturhorimau suddenly lost consciousness then, in a violent jerk, all he felt was...

Nothing...

...

The lion king jolted to his paws.

A cold breeze rushed through his fur, shaking him awake. He looked around, expecting to see Morana. She was nowhere in sight. He was back here, in the living world. The current living world, that was. The mist that surrounded him slithered back to the pool, leaving not a single ripple behind. King Saturhorimau, breathing heavily, patted his body but found he was unscathed. He sighed, sitting down.

Thank the Heavens.

Relieved to know that he had not died, the lion king looked to the side. Farlan stood as still as a rock, not moving a single muscle. He wondered if he was experiencing what he had gone through. The masked Diprotodon sensed the lion king's fear and got up at once. "K-King Saturhorimau!" he called out. "Are you okay, Your Majesty?"

King Saturhorimau brushed his mane, nodding. "I'm okay...I'm okay.."

Farlan sat down. "Thank the Heavens."

"Did...Is that really going to happen?" he asked Farlan.

The masked Diprotodon lowered his head. "It is," he said. "No one believes me, but...that was real. *This* is real. All too real. I've seen no other path for this dark creature. Nor do I see any good path for your great-grandson. The great-grandson of King Wyvern and your great-grandson will be the beginning of the end for this universe. It's been fated."

"So there's...nothing that can be done?"

Farlan shook his head.

"Nothing at all."

"...I'm so sorry, Your Majesty."

That dejected the lion king. The masked Diprotodon, having sensed King Saturhorimau's dejection, brought something up. "Though we– I mean, you, can find ways to sort of...not make it worse. If that makes sense."

King Saturhorimau looked at him hopefully. "How do I do that?"

Farlan blinked, still looking down. He scratched the back of his head, digging his claws deep. "That I unfortunately cannot answer. I cannot change the course of fate with my intervention.

✦✧✦ POSTLUDE ✦✧✦

...It-It's difficult to explain, I apologize, King Saturhorimau. I truly am. It is for you to decide. After all, you were blessed by the Heavens to lead us."

King Saturhorimau felt his ears droop. Well that wasn't the answer he had anticipated. He was once again dejected.

"I understand..."

He looked back down at the small pool. If the universe gave Farlan this message, it most definitely had to be taken seriously. It could be taken as a sign from the Heavens, even as far as it being a sign from the Gods. As much as he was dejected with Farlan's responses, he still felt determined to know more about this. But he could see where many would not want to listen; it truly was a lot to take in. Especially given the fact that it has not happened yet and will definitely not happen until well after their lifetime. None of them would ever experience the future. But the lion king knew that ignoring the universe and its signs was never a good idea. To be given word from a Council member of the Heavens means that one was worthy to take the information and responsibility. To spit in their face and reject their voices meant you were rejecting the Heavens and the Gods. King Saturhorimau knew better than to reject the wise words of the Gods and angels in the Heavens.

Even though I'm still nothing but a teenager...

"I'm sorry if it sounds like I'm adding more pressure to your shoulders," Farlan said. "I know how difficult you have it already, and this probably made it worse." He put his paws to his head, shaking it. "Oh Gods. This was all a mistake, this was a mistake.

I'm so sorry, I'm so sorry. Please, Great Ellowyn, forgive me. Forgive me, forgive me."

He got to his paws. "Hey. No, no, it's all okay. Thank you for allowing me to trust you," he comforted, reassuring the masked Diprotodon with gentle pats on his back. "I will find a way to warn everyone of this upcoming danger. Let's go home now."

Farlan calmed down at his touch and bowed his head. "Thank you for being willing to listen," he whispered. "It's been a long time since I had anyone to talk to. Truly you are a wise and gentle King. May it never be taken away from us."

The lion king was touched by those words. He allowed the masked Diprotodon to head out first. He stood back for a bit, still trying to catch anything that could indicate even a small bit of history of this cave, before he walked out in defeat. He paused at the entrance.

What Farlan had shown him made his heart sink to his stomach. Everything was going to change for the worst, and he knew there was nothing he could do to entirely prevent it. At least he now knew so that what he did now wouldn't make anything worse. He definitely was going to find ways to perhaps alter the course of history, but how could he do that? How does one change the course of time without unintentionally creating a potentially awful butterfly effect? Impossible, he was thinking to himself!

How can I save my people if I don't even know what to do with this information? King Saturhorimau thought worriedly, frowning. *Would it be even worth telling the Promised Dynasty about this prophetic doomsday? Or would it just lead to panic?*

✦✧✦ POSTLUDE ✦✧✦

He decided it was best to maybe only tell his trusted advisors about what he was told and seen. In no time, he will let the Promised Dynasty know.

Before King Saturhorimau entirely left, he looked back at Heaven's Eye, ears twitching. Something about this pool grabbed his attention, but not in a good way. There was something ominous about it, something that grabbed him and wouldn't let go. Something...

Within the pool, the faint sound of the ticking noise could be heard.

Tick, tock. Tick, tock.

Along with a voice. A voice that began speaking in a warning tone.

Foolish mortals. Your time will run out before you know it... You all will know your ultimate and true God. Your time is fleeting, and you cannot escape. It will be over before you can say your final prayers to your fake God. Your true God is in front of you, and you have ignored Him for the last time.

I will arise at last, and I will be your savior. I will be the beginning...of your end.

✦✧✦ BONUS SCENE ✦✧✦

~ After Chapter 7... ~
~ Song Feng's POV... ~

Song Feng never felt his heart more broken. He knew it would never be repaired back to normal ever again.

After his confrontation with his old friend, Waccruwk the cockatrice, he realized there was nothing to change his friend's mind. He was already set on his own awful ideals, set on his wrong destiny laid out to him by a prophecy. He was even desperate enough that he wanted him to fight him. It pierced and shattered his heart when he heard the cockatrice's shriek. How he cursed and shouted for him to fight, for him to kill him by stomping until his skull was crushed.

◆✦◆ BONUS SCENE ◆✦◆

"Fight me. FIGHT ME, SONG FENG! I want you to show me your power! No...Better yet: Kill me. Stomp on me, break my bones, crush my skull, make me bleed. ANYTHING! I FUCKING DARE YOU!"

The longma walked out of the cave, shaking his head and looking back remorsefully. *How did it come to this?* Even if he could make an attempt to redeem Waccruwk, the votes would definitely be against him coming back to the Heavens. He completely abandoned them, and in turn, he abandoned Ellowyn. Song Feng's ears drooped. The happy memories they had made together were now dead.

Song Feng removed the headband from his eyes, taking in a huge inhale of fresh air to clear his mind. Looking ahead of him, he blessed himself with the beauty of the land. The skies were bright blue and the trees strewn in a beautiful array. He once again closed his eyes and let out a sigh that conjured a cloud. One of the many essentials for an angel was to be able to summon a cloud. This cloud was specially given to them by the God of the Skies, and it would be their transportation to descend to the mortal world and ascend back to the Heavens. It was not like the normal clouds you would see in the sky. Each angel had their own respective cloud that they would spend years mastering and taming.

Opening his eyes, he stepped onto his cloud and, with the aid of his wings, flew up towards the skies. He narrowed his eyes to combat with the rushing wind beating him down. Higher and higher he rode up the skies until he pierced through the clouds. Feeling a surge of cosmic energy, he halted and looked around.

He was back home in the Heavens.

There were no clouds in the Heavens apart from being their ground to them, so all around him was the clear blue sky. Angels of all species were going about, floating around, hanging out with friends or business partners (or regular partners), and minding their business. He frowned at how lively and outgoing all the angels were. Normally, it would lift him with such happiness, seeing the angels and being reminded of how golden and pure it was. But after his meeting with his best friend, he knew that they would all be gone in a heartbeat. And they would never even see it coming. All by some dark creature who will seek revenge.

Some angels noticed Song Feng and bowed at him.

"Welcome back, Council Leader Song Feng."

The longma nodded at them and got off his cloud, flapping his own wings and soaring through the heavenly land. He was in the Third Circle of the Heavens, so he only saw the regular angels, archangels and principalities. These angels were either born in this class or could not advance to the higher Circles. They weren't entirely the lowest in terms of roles, but they did not have the luxury as the second or first circle of the angels; therefore, they were classified as the low class angels.

Song Feng did not have time to mingle any longer. Spreading out his wings and giving them one good pump, he breezed through the Circles. He had to head back to the Council. He had to warn them about what Waccruwk had told him, and prepare them for the worst case scenario.

They're not going to take it well, but they have to know. If there is a way we can save the universe, we'll find it.

✦✧✦ BONUS SCENE ✦✧✦

"What a menace!"

"He's going to destroy us all!"

"I told you all and I will say it again: we should have killed him!"

High in the Heavens in the First Circle, where the sky was much brighter than in the Second or Third Circle of the Heavens, resided a grand building sitting upon a large cloud. It was plated in shining gold that shone majestically. This was the Council building, home to the most powerful of angels: the seraphims, the cherubims, and the thrones. Song Feng had called for a council meeting to break the news of his encounter. In the Council, the members argued with one another. Song Feng watched over them.

The Council consisted of 7 angels (minus Song Feng): a Qilin named Liao Chen, a fenghuang named Sun Heng, a griffin named Skeiron, komainu twins Mamoru and Chinmoku, a wolpertinger named Nakia, and a peryton named Glacia. They were all seraphims, angels who hailed from the First Circle and were well respected amongst all angels. Song Feng glanced sadly; the longma, along with Waccruwk, was once one of those members, below where he stood. Before the passing of the old Council Leader, all voted in favor for Song Feng to take control. The Council was always kept at an odd total (including the Council Leader) in order for votes to be made easily without a tie. However, with the loss of Waccruwk and the ascension of Song Feng, the total members in the Councils was an even number for the first time in ages.

"Who said we should have killed him?" Mamoru asked.

The griffin tossed his head, drawing all attention to him. "I'm just saying," he said, "Waccruwk's death would have been much easier for all of us. It's the truth. Have Azrael take care of that good-for-nothing traitor."

The longma's body tensed up. The idea of his good friend dead and in Hell with sinful demons was an awful image his mind came up with. He would hate to see it happen. There still had to be some good in the cockatrice, even if his anger blinded him. *But if it's what the God of Hell decides on his soul, so be it.* Song Feng lowered his head. *The Gods know better than us.*

Mamoru appeared shocked, while their twin sibling, Chinmoku, shook their head in disapproval.

"Y-You can't possibly believe that, Councilman Skeiron!" Nakia whimpered.

"I do believe that!" Skeiron answered without hesitation.

"But...all living beings are born with goodness in them!"

Nakia understands it, Song Feng added.

"Not that treacherous chicken! He will be our demise! And if we don't do something about it, *it will* happen! So we should kill him! We should send a power angel to finish the job for us."

Everyone appeared horrified.

"We do not resort to that temptation to darkness," Song Feng interrupted, standing up from his place. "We are not to be lower than those corrupted with sin. You know that, Coun-

✦✦ BONUS SCENE ✦✦

cilman Skeiron." *And I'm not one that would plan out a murder of an ex.*

Skeiron bowed. "I do, Council Leader Song Feng. I apologize." He rolled his eyes. "Buuut...I'm just saaayinggg...I know a few powers who can help us. Just say the word, and I'll hit them up in a heartbeat."

"There is no 'just saying' in any of this, Councilman Skeiron!" Glacia whined, stomping her hoof. "Sinful temptation does not have a say in any second thoughts. We have to focus on what we can do now without giving in to the temptation! Something to alleviate the situation at hoof." She narrowed her eyes at him. "And we are *not* going to hire a power to *kill*."

Glacia was right. Even if Waccruwk was aiding in the eventual end of the universe, the Council knew that killing him would not be the answer to go with. Song Feng ran a hoof over his long whiskers, ignoring the painful beating of his heart. The situation was more delicate than ever before. It had to be resolved soon before anything bad happened.

Skeiron and Glacia continued their argument, practically butting heads as they went back and forth on Skeiron's proposal to send a power angel.

"But that's kinda their job. To fight the demonic forces. It's what powers do. Waccruwk is a demonic force!"

"We're not going to have all of the Heavens know of this! It would look bad on us!"

"How would it look bad on us!? We're getting rid of an evil that will destroy both the Heavens and the mortal realm! If anything, they will be thanking us for taking action."

"It just will!"

"I don't see how, but, okay. Fine then! I'm at a loss!"

"I am as well!"

"Fantastic!"

"Then what should we do?" Nakia intervened once the heat had died down.

The Council angels went silent after their argument, staring at one another in deep thought. A few of them mumbled but none spoke up. Song Feng lowered his eyes; he wondered what they were all thinking, wondering what was the best course to save the fate of the universe. Was there any salvation for the impending destruction of the universe? Was this truly the end? Was there anything they could do? Or was this the game Providence was playing, using everyone as his pawns? Song Feng had never felt so much pain in his chest.

"What should we do, Council Leader Song Feng?" Liao Chen asked him, looking to him hopefully.

The seraphims looked to Song Feng, who turned his head with widened eyes. Everyone followed suit, practically falling to their knees as if he was Ellowyn. They bowed and raised their arms.

"Yes, Council Leader Song Feng! You are wise! And kind! What should we do?" Sun Heng said, spreading her orange wings.

✦✧✦ BONUS SCENE ✦✧✦

"We can trust Council Leader Song Feng to guide us through this tough time," Nakia squeaked happily.

"Indeed we can!" spoke Liao Chen.

The longma looked to his council members. His whiskers twitched. It was inevitable they would call out to him for guidance, for his wisdom and answer. He had to do something if he was to save everyone and fast. The fate of the universe literally depended on his hooves at this point.

...He had one plan. The only thing that could possibly help them. But he rethought his plan. Was it even a good one? Should he tell the Council? What would they say on something so ridiculous and outrageous!?

"We do not resort to that temptation to darkness. We are not to be lower than those corrupted with sin."

His own words came back to haunt him.

"I have something, but...I am unsure how much you would all be in favor," he said to them, suddenly weak to his knees. "For...For it may possibly be...immoral.."

He winced, waiting for their shocked responses.

However, surprisingly, instead–

"I'm sure we can find a way to work with it," Mamoru said, with Chinmoku nodding.

The other Council members murmured in agreement.

"We can."

"Indeed."

"Yeah! Tell us what is on your mind?"

Song Feng stared at them, and took a deep breath. If they were all in agreement, then that was all he had to hear. Besides, like Mamoru said, they can work around it and shape it to be for the good of their cause.

"Alright. Here's the plan..."

...

✦✧✦ BONUS SCENE ✦✧✦

~ Waccruwk's POV... ~

What a shame.

The cockatrice took a deep breath and laid down in his nest after his friend left. He turned back to his crystals. They glowed brightly again, reflecting how calm he was becoming after the encounter. Though there were still some that remained dim. He was troubled.

He should be glad that Song Feng did not challenge him, but deep down, he badly wanted his former friend to end his life. Why had he not? It would be so easy for everyone both living and in the Heavens if Song Feng had fought him and defeated him, sending his soul to Hell where he belonged without being judged by Okalani and Azrael. The prophecy would have ceased to exist, the dark creature would not visit him (he knew the dark creature would still find another way, but he didn't want to think about that right about now), and the dark creature would not gain their powers. Everything would be saved. The universe would continue normally like nothing ever happened.

I wish he could have killed me when I gave him the chance, he lamented to himself.

But no. Song Feng's heart was too righteous. He was too pure to even think about killing someone, especially someone he knew and loved. Even if it meant saving the universe from a total apocalypse.

Sensitive, he is. Even for as long as I've known him. I both hate it and admire him.

The cockatrice walked further into his cave, his head in a bow as he kept moving forward with determination. The light began to dim as Waccruwk headed away from the light of the crystals. He wondered what the longma was telling the Council. He can already hear all the terrible things he was telling the Council. *"He was going to attack me! He wanted to fight me! Can you believe him? He's definitely evil, and you guys were right all along! So we're all going to die because of him!"* Probably something along those lines, Waccruwk liked to guess what his former friend would say. What would be everyone's reaction to Song Feng's statements? Probably the same. Shock, anger, demand. Anything but *"Oh okay, he doesn't wanna listen? Cool, we don't care! We'll let him destroy the universe and kill us all! WOO!"*

The cockatrice shook his head free from those ridiculous statements he was making up.

It didn't matter to him anyway.

They didn't matter. The Council, the rest of the angels, the Gods. They were nothing but puppets to a great being who couldn't control Her own sinful desires. Pure angels following their Gods like sheep.

The irony.

The cockatrice reached the end of the cave, where a larger crystal sat, shining brighter than the other ones. It was a large rock, with many sharp points protruding like needles on a cactus. He began to settle in his nest he had made next to this crystal when a

♦✧♦ BONUS SCENE ♦✧♦

ticking sound caught his attention. He got back up, stretching his legs and waddling over towards the sound. He smiled.

"Tick tock indeed, my friend," he said to himself. "Like the sound of a steady heart, you beat on. Don't you worry. I hear you."

Behind the larger crystal laid a chest. It was dark brown in color, as dark as the bark of an oak tree, laced with gold and having a gold lock that shone like a tiny bell coiled around a sheep's neck. Waccruwk couldn't figure out where this chest had come from, as any evidence of an owner had purposefully been scratched off from existence. The cockatrice used his talon to pick open the lock, careful not to damage it. Once he heard the click and snap, he laid the lock in his wing and set it to the side. When he opened the chest, he saw the single pocket watch that sat inside. "I have not forgotten about you." He picked it up, staring at it. "How glad I am that Song Feng has not found the chest." He opened it to check the time.

"9 o'clock? How strange." The cockatrice chuckled. "It feels much later than that. Ah. Such is the bliss of time. A conception. An illusion. No one ever uses it because of how absurd you are. Wretched, cursed thing." He looked back down at it, watching the small black hand ticking away on a white background without a care in the world. He didn't think a simple tinkery that made a repetitive sound would mesmerize him. Probably because it reminded him of how fast the day truly was.

"Hm?" The cockatrice tipped his head. "What was that?"

The pocket watch continued to tick.

It wasn't any normal ordinary ticking. The way this pocket watch ticked registered into vague words when you listen carefully and knew of the ticking pattern.

4 ticks. In a particular pattern.

"T i m e?"

"Oh. Your time will be soon. I promise you. Someone worthy of your power will arrive and be your master. You will arise once again to claim what you've lost when you were still alive. Revenge will be soon."

12 aggressive ticks. This time, a sentence.

"B e t t e r n o t l i e."

It was a broken sentence, but the implications were clear as day.

"When have I ever lied to you?" he asked the pocket watch curiously.

11 ticks.

"R i p p e d m e o u t."

12 different ticks.

"I m p r i s o n e d m e."

13 ticks.

"F o r y o u r d e s i r e."

The cockatrice rolled his eyes. "Someone woke up in a cranky and salty mood."

✦✧✦ BONUS SCENE ✦✧✦

The ticking of the pocket watch grew more aggressive and louder and louder at Waccruwk's remark.

6 ticks. Another broken sentence. *(Well, the following ticks would be broken sentences, but they were understandable enough to be passed this time.)*

"K n o w m e ?"

4 ticks.

"A G o d !"

7 ticks.

"F o o l i s h !"

8 ticks.

"B e t r a y m e."

7 ticks.

"W i l l d i e !"

12 ticks.

"H a t e t r a i t o r s."

The same 12 ticks repeated in an endless cycle.

"H a t e t r a i t o r s. H a t e t r a i t o r s. H a t e t r a i t o r s. H a t e t r a i t o r s. H a t e t r a i t o r s. H a t e –"

Behind him, Waccruwk's crystals brightened one by one in intensity. The cockatrice felt his breathing hitch. He was worried, agitated at the threatening words, but he forced himself to keep calm. He remembered these same kinds of threats when he ripped out the one who was in his body and kept it in the pocket watch. They were empty promises to him.

"Alright! Alright, hush!" Waccruwk shouted at the pocket watch, shaking it with fervor. "I hear you already; I will not betray you again!"

The endless 12 ticks finally stopped. Then–

4 ticks.

"L i a r."

The cockatrice shut his eyes and rubbed his beak. He doesn't like to listen, does he? "Whatever. As I said, revenge will be soon."

7 ticks.

"R e v e n g e?"

Waccruwk closed the pocket watch. "Yes. Your revenge. Of course. Now keep your rotting, non-existent pelt on."

Though it was closed, the cockatrice could still hear the ticking of the machine. He could make out certain words.

The same 7 ticks.

"R e v e n g e. R e v e n g e."

4 ticks.

"S o o n."

10 ticks. Another sentence.

✦✧✦ BONUS SCENE ✦✧✦

"I w i l l a r i s e."

5 ticks.

"A g a i n."

Normally, the sound would have driven him nuts and made him smash the stupid thing into many pieces. All while screaming "SHUT UP ALREADY!! MY HEAD IS READY TO EXPLODE FROM YOUR STUPID NOISE!!" But he was calm. He did not let the pocket watch irritate him any further and throw him off balance. The cockatrice turned back around to the chest. He laid the pocket watch inside delicately. He stared at it for one last time.

"Tick tock. Tick tock. We shall await, The One Lost to Time. For the dark creature. For The Timekeeper."

13 loud, muffled ticks. Repeated thrice.

"T h e T i m e k e e p e r. T h e T i m e k e e p e r. T h e T i m e k e e p e r."

Waccruwk grinned. Everything was going according to plan. The chest was closed, and the pocket watch faded into the obscurity of the darkness.

~ The story continues in Book 2: The Fallen Angel ~

A MINI GUIDE INTO THE WORLD OF BEGINNING OF TIME

Beginning of Time is a world not yet known to the current FASSAV characters but soon would be known as events go by. It is a world completely different yet related to the FASSAV universe. A universe once ruled by Gods, it would soon come to fall into despair following the discovery of a dark path long forgotten.

Here is a list of characters important to this universe, what their lifestyle was like and what major events had occurred. (As of Book 1)

A MINI GUIDE INTO THE WORLD OF BEGINNING OF TIME

MAIN CHARACTERS

Prince Wonwoo

-The Lion Prince/Lion Prince of the Promised Dynasty

New Name: Scolamander

Name Meaning: "to live by helping out with a rounded heart"

New Name Meaning: unknown

Title: Prince Wonwoo of the Promised Dynasty

Surname: Honeycutt

Birthday: August 1097 B.E.

Zodiac Sign: Leo

Age: 26 (by Terra Cycle 1123 B.E.)

Gender: Cis male

Species: Cave lion

Family Tree

Mother: Queen Cora

Father: King Jung-hwa

Siblings: unnamed cubs (deceased)

Paternal Uncle: Prince Hyun-sik (deceased)

Paternal Grandfather: King Boipelo (deceased)

Paternal Grandmother: Queen Hawa

Paternal Great-grandfather: King Saturhorimau (deceased)

Paternal Great-grandmother: Queen Haukea (deceased)

Former Fiancee: Princess Okome (deceased)

Girlfriend: Moth

-The lion prince of the Promised Dynasty, Prince Wonwoo is a childish and lively young lion who lives on pranks and fun activities. The only surviving child of the Lion King and Lion Queen of the Promised Dynasty, he has been spoiled rotten. He doesn't like acting like an adult and hates taking responsibility sometimes. He also has a lot of anxiety due to pressures from his father the King. Although a jokester at heart, he knows his limits and will stop if something goes too far.

Prince Scamander

-The Wolf Prince/Wolf Prince of the Demoniacal Kingdom

Name Meaning: "limping man, awkward man"

Title: Prince Scamander of the Demoniacal Kingdom

Surname: Snapdragon

Birthday: May 1094 B.E.

Zodiac Sign: Taurus

Age: 29 (by Terra Cycle 1123 B.E.)

Gender: Cis male

Species: Dire wolf-wyvern hybrid

Family Tree

Mother: Queen Zirconia

Father: King Titanosaurus

Sister: Princess Okome (deceased)

Paternal Grandfather: King Oromir (deceased)

Paternal Grandmother: Queen Bernadette

Paternal Great-Grandfather: King Wyvern (deceased)

Paternal Great-Grandmother: Queen Skydamire (deceased)

Paternal Uncle: Prince Livyatan

Cousins: Basilosaurus, Odobenocetops, Janjucetus, Dorudon, Incakujira

-The wolf prince of the Demoniacal Kingdom, Prince Scamander is brooding and constantly in a serious mood. He takes a lot after his father, and definitely takes after King Wyvern, his great-grandfather. He does not like the Promised Dynasty for various reasons. While he may appear cold and aloof, he is lenient and overprotective towards his sister Princess Okome. He does not like when his sister is being used as a tool for personal gains in the Kingdom. Though he has good intentions, he comes off as rude and intense.

King Jung-hwa

-The Lion King/Lion King of the Promised Dynasty

Name Meaning: "A righteous man"

Title: King Jung-hwa of the Promised Dynasty

Surname: Honeycutt

Birthday: March 1064 B.E.

Zodiac Sign: Pisces

Age: 59 (by Terra Cycle 1123 B.E.)

Gender: Cis male

Species: Cave lion

Family Tree

Mother: Queen Hawa

Father: King Boipelo (deceased)

Brother: Prince Hyun-sik (deceased)

Wife: Queen Cora

Son: Prince Wonwoo

Children: unnamed cubs (deceased)

Grandfather: King Saturhorimau (deceased)

Grandmother: Queen Haukea (deceased)

Kingship

~ Reign: December 1085 B.E.-present day

~ Coronation: December 1085 B.E.

~ Total Terra Cycles of Reign: 38 terra cycles

-The lion king of the Promised Dynasty, King Jung-hwa is a gentle and kind soul. He is a beloved king and well-liked. But beware: while he may seem like a gentle giant, King Jung-hwa won't hesitate to assert his aggression towards those who threaten his family and his Dynasty.

King Titanosaurus

-The Wolf King/Wolf King of the Demoniacal Kingdom

Name Meaning: Named after the dinosaur of the same name

Title: King Titanosaurus of the Demoniacal Kingdom

Surname: Snapdragon

Birthday: May 1067 B.E.

Zodiac Sign: Gemini

Age: 56 (by Terra Cycle 1123 B.E.)

Gender: Cis male

Species: Dire wolf-wyvern hybrid

<u>Family Tree</u>

Mother: Queen Bernadette

Father: King Oromir (deceased)

Brother: Prince Livyatan

Wife: Queen Zirconia

Son: Prince Scamander

Daughter: Princess Okome (deceased)

Nephews: Basilosaurus, Odobenocetops, Janjucetus, Dorudon

Niece: Incakujira

Paternal Grandfather: King Wyvern (deceased)

Paternal Grandmother: Queen Skydamire (deceased)

Mother-in-Law: ???

Father-in-Law: ???

Sister-in-Law: Sivatherium

Kingship

~ Reign: May 1085 B.E.-present day

~ Coronation: May 1085 B.E.

~ Total Terra Cycles of Reign: 38 terra cycles

-The wolf king of the Demoniacal Kingdom, King Titanosaurus is stoic and cold, never showing emotions or even a simple smile. He is only friendly towards his wife and children. He is a sturdy King who rules with stern. He has maintained a good relationship with his twin brother, Livyatan, as the two grew up with their abusive mother. He never knew about his father, King Oromir, as he had died moments after his birth. He never let his childhood trauma get to him unlike his brother.

Princess Okome

-The Wolf Princess/Wolf Princess of the Demoniacal Kingdom

Name Meaning: Unknown

Title: Princess Okome of the Demoniacal Kingdom

Surname: Snapdragon

Birthday: January 1096 B.E.

Zodiac Sign: Capricorn

Age: 21, almost 22 at death

Cause of Death: Accidentally killed by Prince Wonwoo

Gender: Cis female

Species: Dire wolf-wyvern hybrid

Family Tree

Mother: Queen Zirconia

Father: King Titanosaurus

Brother: Prince Scamander

Paternal Grandfather: King Oromir (deceased)

Paternal Grandmother: Queen Bernadette

Paternal Great-Grandfather: King Wyvern (deceased)

Paternal Great-Grandmother: Queen Skydamire (deceased)

Paternal Uncle: Prince Livyatan

Cousins: Basilosaurus, Odobenocetops, Janjucetus, Dorudon, Incakujira

Fiance: Prince Wonwoo

-The wolf princess of the Demoniacal Kingdom and the princess Prince Wonwoo was betrothed to, Princess Okome's personality is not like the Demoniacal Kingdom. She is a soft and kind-hearted wolf with a big heart. So kind in fact, you would think that she is a Promised Dynasty member. Her kindhearted personality leaves her feeling out of place in the Demoniacal Kingdom, since some Kingdom members cannot stand her cheery and bright persona. Though she has a good relationship with her family, she's most closest to her brother Prince Scamander. She strives for freedom and wants to live her life. After she met Prince Wonwoo, the prince she was to marry for an alliance of the Promised Dynasty and the Demoniacal Kingdom, she fell in love with him, growing close to him.

ROYAL FAMILY

Queen Zirconia

-The Wolf Queen/Wolf Queen of the Demoniacal Kingdom

Name Meaning: Named after the white crystalline

Title: Queen Zirconia of the Demoniacal Kingdom

Surname: Snapdragon

Maiden Name: ???

Birthday: ??? 1066 B.E.

Age: 56-57 (by Terra Cycle 1123 B.E.)

Gender: Cis female

Species: Dire wolf

<u>Family Tree</u>

Mother: ???

Father: ???

Husband: King Titanosaurus

Son: Prince Scamander

Daughter: Princess Okome (deceased)

Mother-in-Law: Queen Bernadette

Father-in-Law: King Oromir (deceased)

Brother-in-Law: Prince Livyatan

Grandfather-in-Law: King Wyvern (deceased)

Grandmother-in-Law: Queen Skydamire (deceased)

Queenship
--

~ Reign: January 1086 B.E.-present day

~ Coronation: January 1086 B.E.

~ Total Terra Cycles of Reign: 37 terra cycles

-The wolf queen of the Demoniacal Kingdom. Queen Zirconia is as gentle as Princess Okome. She grew up living a relatively normal life with her parents. She is very family oriented and loves being with her husband and children. She helps even out King Titanosaurus and Prince Scamander with her warm aura.

Queen Cora

-The Lion Queen/Lion Queen of the Promised Dynasty

Name Meaning: "Heart; Maiden"

Title: Queen Cora of the Promised Dynasty

Surname: Honeycutt

Maiden Name: ???

Birthday: March 1064 B.E.

Zodiac Sign: Pisces

Age: 59 (by Terra Cycle 1123 B.E.)

Gender: Cis female

Species: Cave lion

Family Tree

Mother: ???

Father: ???

Husband: King Jung-hwa

Son: Prince Wonwoo

Children: Unnamed cubs (deceased)

Mother-in-Law: Queen Hawa

Father-in-Law: King Boipelo (deceased)

Brother-in-Law: Prince Hyun-sik (deceased)

Grandfather-in-Law: King Saturhorimau (deceased)

Grandmother-in-Law: Queen Haukea (deceased)

Queenship

~ Reign: February 1086 B.E.-present day

~ Coronation: February 1086 B.E.

~ Total Terra Cycles of Reign: 37 terra cycles

-The lion queen of the Promised Dynasty. Queen Cora cares a lot for her family and loves her husband and son very much. She is fiercely protective of her son (having had failed pregnancies and previous miscarriages before Prince Wonwoo) and won't hesitate to lose her life when saving him from danger. She loves children with all her heart due to her strong sense of family and will worry over any child she encounters. Her desire to have a family was at first met with much hardship as she and King Jung-hwa failed to conceive many times. But the grief of her unborn cubs didn't stop her from loving her only surviving cub to death.

Prince Livyatan

-The Wolf Prince/Wolf Prince of the Demoniacal Kingdom

Name Meaning: Named after the extinct genus of sperm whale of the same name

Title: Prince Livyatan of the Demoniacal Kingdom

Surname: Snapdragon

Birthday: May 1067 B.E.

Zodiac Sign: Gemini

Age: 56 (by Terra Cycle 1123 B.E.)

Gender: Cis male

Species: Dire wolf-wyvern hybrid

Family Tree

Mother: Queen Bernadette

Father: King Oromir (deceased)

Brother: King Titanosaurus

Wife: Sivatherium

Sons: Basilosaurus, Odobenocetops, Janjucetus, Dorudon

Daughter: Incakujira

Nephew: Prince Scamander

Niece: Princess Okome (deceased)

Paternal Grandfather: King Wyvern (deceased)

Paternal Grandmother: Queen Skydamire (deceased)

Sister-in-Law: Queen Zirconia

-The wolf prince of the Demoniacal Kingdom second in line to the throne, Prince Livyatan is said to be a complete clone of his twin brother King Titanosaurus. He acts first before thinking, often letting his feelings take over his reason, and will not hesitate to speak his mind. The trauma of his father's untimely demise and abusive mother left him bitter and cruel and feeling distant from his loved ones (except for his brother).

MINOR CHARACTERS

Cayman

Name Meaning: "Crocodile"

Birthday: ???

Age: 26 (by Terra Cycle 1123 B.E.)

Gender: Cis male

Species: Cave lion

-Cayman is Prince Wonwoo's cubhood friend. He is extremely jittery and does not have a lot of confidence. Despite this, he is willing to do stupid shenanigans with his friend.

Atiena

Name Meaning: "Guardian of the night"

Birthday: ???

Age: late 30s-early 40s

Gender: Cis female

Species: Spotted Hyena

-A hyena originally from the Demoniacal Kingdom, she and her cackle–the Night Stalkers–immigrated to the Promised Dynasty in hopes for a better life. She was unsatisfied with the way King Titanosaurus ran the Dynasty and further dissatisfied when she learned King Jung-hwa was too soft of a King. She and her cackle became local bullies, terrorizing Promised Dynasty members, which included Prince Wonwoo.

Hakuba

Name Meaning: "white horse"

Rank: Commander of the Promised Dynasty Army

Birthday: ??? 1064 B.E.

Age: 59 (by Terra Cycle 1123 B.E.)

Gender: Cis female

Species: Horse

-One of King Jung-hwa's most trusted guards. Hakuba is a favorite in the Royal Family. She was entrusted to King Jung-hwa when she was a foal by King Boipelo, which allowed her to have a strong relationship with the Royal Family. She became Prince Wonwoo's babysitter and main bodyguard when he was born, and the two have a friendly relationship.

Korikuma

Name Meaning: "ice bear" in Japanese

Birthday: ???

Age: ??

Gender: Cis female

Species: Polar bear-grizzly bear hybrid

Family Tree

Mother: Unnamed mother

Father: ???

-Korikuma is a polar bear hybrid that Prince Wonwoo first meets when he leaves the Promised Dynasty. Korikuma is friendly and loves making new friends. She doesn't agree with her mother's views on inlanders and will openly speak against her.

Mabel

Name Meaning: "Loveable"

Birthday: ???

Age: ??

Gender: Cis female

Species: Cat

-A cat that leads a group of pirates called the Sharktooths of the Hidden Cove. Little is known about her, apart from the fact she is the great-granddaughter of the first leader of the Shell Clan, ran away from the inland clans and joined the pirates. She is on a mission to reform the Shell Clan back to their glory days.

Seabury

Name Meaning: "settlement near the sea"

Birthday: ???

Age: ??

Gender: Cis male

Species: Crocodile

-A crocodile who is a member of the Sharktooths of the Hidden Cove. He wears an eyepatch on his right eye. He is a suave and charming crocodile, putting up a great persona before he unveils who he truly is.

Aleena

Name Meaning: "Light, fair"

Title: Tropic Bloom Aleena

Birthday: ??? 1078 B.E.

Age: 45 (by Terra Cycle 1123 B.E.)

Gender: Cis female

Species: Peruvian Spider Monkey

Family Tree

Adopted Sister: Vermilion

-Aleena is the leader of the Tropic Clan. She is wise and compassionate, always having her clan members' well-being first in her agenda. She is reputed as a great leader and a fearsome protector. Her body bears scars from fights she's had, mainly with crocodiles.

Vermilion

Name Meaning: a brilliant red color

Birthday: ??? 1090 B.E.

Age: 33 (by Terra Cycle 1123 B.E.)

Gender: Cis female

Species: Howler monkey

Family Tree

Adopted Sister: Aleena

-Vermilion is a howler monkey from the Tropic Clan who saved Prince Wonwoo alongside Kitwana. She is a spunky and outgoing monkey. According to her adopted sister, she can have a bit of a crude humor, letting her sarcasm run her mouth at inappropriate times. She was best friends with Kitwana the jaguar before his demise and Prince Wonwoo before he left the Tropic Clan. It is implied that Vermilion developed a crush on Prince Wonwoo, hinted by the lion prince when he spent time with Moth, and he would notice her obvious jealousy.

A MINI GUIDE INTO THE WORLD OF BEGINNING OF TIME

Kitwana

Name Meaning: "pledged to survive"

Age: ?? at death

Cause of Death: Killed by crocodiles

Gender: Cis male

Species: Jaguar

-Kitwana was a jaguar from the Tropic Clan who saved Prince Wonwoo alongside Vermilion. He was described as gentle, heroic and brave. He bore many scars from his many fights with crocodiles, earning him his name. A terra cycle before Prince Wonwoo leaves the Tropic Clan, he is ambushed and killed by the same crocodile pod that attacked Prince Wonwoo, as an act of revenge by the crocodile leader for the death of the old leader at his paws. His death was heavily mourned by all in the Tropic Clan, though Vermilion was affected badly by it, since they were close friends.

Moth

Name Meaning: named after the insect

Title: Guard of the Tropic Clan

Birthday: ??? 1099 B.E.

Age: 24 (by Terra Cycle 1123 B.E.)

Gender: Cis female

Species: Margay

Family Tree

Boyfriend: Prince Wonwoo

-Moth is a member of the Tropic Clan. She is a spunky and sarcastic feline. She fell in love with Prince Wonwoo when he had resided in the Tropic Clan, becoming his girlfriend.

ANCIENT CHARACTERS

King Saturhorimau

-The Lion King/Lion King of the Promised Dynasty

-Founder of the Promised Dynasty

-The First Lion King

Name Meaning: a lion from The Story of Magellan: And the Discovery of the Philippines

Former Title: King Saturhorimau of the Promised Dynasty

Surname: Honeycutt

Birthday: January 1001 B.E.

Zodiac Sign: Aquarius

Age: 60 at death

Cause of Death: Natural Causes

Gender: Cis male

Species: Cave lion

Family Tree

Mother: ??? (deceased)

Father: ??? (deceased)

Wife: Queen Haukea (deceased)

Son: King Boipelo (deceased)

Grandsons: King Jung-hwa, Prince Hyun-sik (deceased)

Great-grandson: Prince Wonwoo

Great-grandchildren: Unnamed cubs (deceased)

Daughter-in-Law: Queen Hawa

Granddaughter-in-Law: Queen Cora

<u>Kingship</u>

~ Reign: July 1018 B.E.-February 1061 B.E.

~ Coronation: July 1018 B.E.

~ Total Terra Cycles of Reign: 43 terra cycles

-The first King and founder of the Promised Dynasty, Saturhorimau is a kind lion who cared about everyone. He always put others before himself. He was good friends with Wyvern, creating a bond that was near brotherly. However, since Saturhorimau was chosen as the new land's preacher, his relationship with Wyvern deteriorated, and the two ended up as sworn enemies.

King Wyvern

-The Dragon King/Dragon King of the Demoniacal Kingdom

-Founder of the Demoniacal Kingdom

-The First Dragon King

Name Meaning: named after his species

Former Title: King Wyvern of the Demoniacal Kingdom

Surname: Snapdragon

Birthday: May 1000 B.E.

Zodiac Sign: Taurus

Age: 57 at death

Cause of Death: ???

Gender: Cis male

Species: Wyvern

Family Tree

Mother: ??? (deceased)

Father: ??? (deceased)

Wife: Queen Skydamire (deceased)

Son: King Oromir (deceased)

Grandsons: King Titanosaurus, Prince Livyatan

Great-grandsons: Prince Scamander, Basilosaurus, Odobenocetops, Janjucetus, Dorudon

Great-granddaughters: Princess Okome (deceased), Incakujira

Daughter-in-Law: Queen Bernadette

Granddaughter-in-Laws: Queen Zirconia, Sivatherium

Kingship

~ Reign: July 1018 B.E.-December 1057 B.E.

~ Coronation: July 1018 B.E.

~ Total Terra Cycles of Reign: 39 terra cycles

-The first King and founder of the Demoniacal Kingdom, Wyvern is a ruthless and cunning dragon. (A wyvern specifically but you get the point...) Jealous of the attention his friend Saturhorimau was getting, Wyvern sought ways to get himself as the center of attention. Ways that would soon prove to be dark and sinister...

King Boipelo

-The Lion King/Lion King of the Promised Dynasty

-The Second Lion King

Name Meaning: "A very proud person"

Former Title: King Boipelo of the Promised Dynasty

Surname: Honeycutt

Birthday: February 1043 B.E.

Zodiac Sign: Pisces

Age: 56 at death

Cause of Death: Complications from an unknown illness

Gender: Cis male

Species: Cave lion

Family Tree

Mother: Queen Haukea (deceased)

Father: King Saturhorimau (deceased)

Wife: Queen Hawa

Sons: King Jung-hwa, Prince Hyun-sik (deceased)

Grandson: Prince Wonwoo

Grandchildren: Unnamed cubs (deceased)

Daughter-in-Law: Queen Cora

<u>Kingship</u>

~ Reign: February 1061 B.E.-December 1085 B.E.

~ Coronation: February 1061 B.E.

~ Total Terra Cycles of Reign: 24 terra cycles

-The King of the Promised Dynasty before King Jung-hwa, King Boipelo was described as proud and valiant. He continued to strengthen Halcyonwick and his Dynasty after his father passed. Despite his prideful nature, he had a good heart that many said he took after King Saturhorimau. He was also very family-oriented, spending as much time with them as he could. He was struck with a mysterious illness that slowly weakened him. This illness forced him to step down from the throne, crowning his son as the King. Despite his ailment, he still found time to be with his son and grandson.

A MINI GUIDE INTO THE WORLD OF BEGINNING OF TIME

King Oromir

-The Wolf King/Wolf King of the Demoniacal Kingdom

-The First Wolf King

-The Second Dragon King

Name Meaning: Unknown

Former Title: King Oromir of the Demoniacal Kingdom

Surname: Snapdragon

Birthday: April 1042 B.E.

Zodiac Sign: Aries

Age: 25 at death

Cause of Death: Unknown; Suspected Attempted Murder

Gender: Cis male

Species: Half wyvern, half dire wolf

Family Tree

Mother: Queen Skydamire (deceased)

Father: King Wyvern (deceased)

Wife: Queen Bernadette

Sons: King Titanosaurus, Prince Livyatan

Grandsons: Prince Scamander, Basilosaurus, Odobenocetops, Janjucetus, Dorudon

Granddaughters: Princess Okome (deceased), Incakujira

Daughter-in-Laws: Queen Zirconia, Sivatherium

Kingship

~ Reign: June 1057 B.E.-May 1067 B.E.

~ Coronation: June 1057 B.E.

~ Total Terra Cycles of Reign: 10 terra cycles

-The King of the Demoniacal Kingdom before King Titanosaurus, King Oromir is a figure of mystery. A half wyvern, half wolf creature, he had helped his father, King Wyvern, build Coldwyvern when he was just 12 terra cycles old. After the death of his father, 15 terra cycles old Oromir ascended to the throne and continued to grow the Demoniacal Kingdom. He is well known for his power to ensure Coldwyvern would be forever closed off to the Promised Dynasty and to the other clans for that matter. (He is lesser known for adding the medieval aspect to Coldwyvern.) He was also known to be a complete narcissist, completely full of himself and caring only about himself. His reign was short-lived, sitting at 10 terra cycles when the King unexpectedly collapsed during a celebration to honor the birth of his sons. He was the youngest reigning King and also the youngest King to die. His death was concluded to be an accident. A rumor began to spread that someone had assassinated the King out of either revenge or wanting power, although his killer has never been found to this day…

Queen Skydamire

-The Wolf Queen/Wolf Queen of the Demoniacal Kingdom

-The First Wolf Queen

Name Meaning: Unknown

Former Title: Queen Skydamire of the Demoniacal Kingdom

Surname: Snapdragon

Maiden Name: ???

Birthday: ??? ~1009-1010 B.E.

Zodiac Sign: ???

Age: ~31-32 at death

Cause of Death: Complications during childbirth

Gender: Cis female

Species: Dire wolf

Family Tree

Husband: King Wyvern (deceased)

Son: King Oromir (deceased)

Grandsons: King Titanosaurus, Prince Livyatan

Great-grandsons: Prince Scamander, Basilosaurus, Odobenocetops, Janjucetus, Dorudon

A MINI GUIDE INTO THE WORLD OF BEGINNING OF TIME

Great-granddaughters: Princess Okome (deceased), Incakujira

Mother-in-Law: ??? (deceased)

Father-in-Law: ??? (deceased)

Daughter-in-Law: Queen Bernadette

Granddaughter-in-Laws: Queen Zirconia, Sivatherium

Queenship

~ Reign: ???? B.E.-April 1042 B.E.

~ Coronation: ???? B.E.

~ Total Terra Cycles of Reign: ?? terra cycles

-The beloved wife of King Wyvern, Queen Skydamire was adored by all. Unlike her husband, she was a very calm and collected wolf, without ever a care to feel any type of anger. She never intended or thought she would be a Queen, but her love for King Wyvern was too great for her to reject the Royal life. Her death came as a shock to the Demoniacal Kingdom, having her life cut short during the birth of her and King Wyvern's son King Oromir. King Wyvern was completely devastated by the loss of his wife, refusing to take another as he only felt love for her and no other creature.

Queen Haukea

-The Lion Queen/Lion Queen of the Promised Dynasty

-The First Lion Queen

Name Meaning:

Former Title: Queen Haukea of the Promised Dynasty

Surname: Honeycutt

Maiden Name: ???

Birthday: ??? 1004 B.E.

Zodiac Sign: ???

Age: 60 at death

Cause of Death: Unknown

Gender: Cis female

Species: Cave lion

Family Tree

Husband: King Saturhorimau (deceased)

Son: King Boipelo (deceased)

Grandsons: King Jung-hwa, Prince Hyun-sik

Great-grandson: Prince Wonwoo

Great-grandchildren: Unnamed cubs (deceased)

Mother-in-Law: ??? (deceased)

Father-in-Law: ??? (deceased)

Daughter-in-Law: Queen Hawa

Granddaughter-in-Law: Queen Cora

Queenship

~ Reign: ???? B.E.-???? B.E.

~ Coronation: ???? B.E.

~ Total Terra Cycles of Reign: ?? terra cycles

-Not much information exists about the wife of King Saturhorimau. This was done by the first lion king in order to protect her from harm.

Queen Bernadette

-The Wolf Queen/Wolf Queen of the Demoniacal Kingdom

-The Second Wolf Queen

Name Meaning: Brave bear; strong

Former Title: Queen Bernadette of the Demoniacal Kingdom

Surname: Snapdragon

Maiden Name: ???

Birthday: ??? 1045 B.E.

Zodiac Sign: ???

Age: 77-78

Gender: Cis female

Species: Dire wolf

Family Tree

Husband: King Oromir (deceased)

Sons: King Titanosaurus, Prince Livyatan

Grandsons: Prince Scamander, Basilosaurus, Odobenocetops, Janjucetus, Dorudon

Granddaughters: Princess Okome (deceased), Incakujira

Mother-in-Law: Queen Skydamire (deceased)

A MINI GUIDE INTO THE WORLD OF BEGINNING OF TIME

Father-in-Law: King Wyvern (deceased)

Daughter-in-Laws: Queen Zirconia, Sivatherium

Queenship

~ Reign: ???? B.E.-May 1085 B.E.

~ Coronation: ???? B.E.

~ Total Terra Cycles of Reign: ?? terra cycles

-A rather mysterious gal, Queen Bernadette can only be described as extremely apathetic and cold. She wasn't like this before, however; before her marriage with King Oromir, she was known to be a lively and energetic wolf. Something within her changed after her marriage with the dire wolf-wyvern hybrid, and while she did love her husband, she felt her life had changed too much for her to process. She raised her sons with a firm and cold paw after the untimely demise of her husband and very rarely showed affection to them. As much as she loved her sons, she never hesitated to demonstrate her power over them, reminding them what she could do to them if they stepped out of line. This abusive lifestyle and mindset would lead to devastating effects on her sons, especially to Prince Livyatan.

It has been said that Prince Livyatan drove away their mother from the Demoniacal Kingdom as soon as King Titanosaurus ascended to the throne, where she now resides in territories unknown.

Queen Hawa

-The Lion Queen/Lion Queen of the Promised Dynasty

Name Meaning:

Former Title: Queen Hawa of the Promised Dynasty

Surname: Honeycutt

Maiden Name: ???

Birthday: ??? 1044 B.E.

Zodiac Sign: ???

Age: 79

Gender: Cis female

Species: Cave lion

Family Tree

Husband: King Boipelo (deceased)

Sons: King Jung-hwa, Prince Hyun-sik (deceased)

Grandson: Prince Wonwoo

Grandchildren: Unnamed cubs (deceased)

Mother-in-Law: Queen Haukea (deceased)

Father-in-Law: King Saturhorimau (deceased)

Daughter-in-Law: Queen Cora

A MINI GUIDE INTO THE WORLD OF BEGINNING OF TIME

Queenship

~ Reign: ???? B.E.-???? B.E.

~ Coronation: ???? B.E.

~ Total Terra Cycles of Reign: ?? terra cycles

-Queen Hawa is very loving and kind. She cared much for her subjects when she was still Queen.

Farlan

Name Meaning: "Son of the furrows"

Birthday: ???; sometime before 1000 B.E.

Age: ?? at death

Cause of Death: Brain Hemorrhage

Gender: Nonbinary

Pronouns: he/him

Species: Diprotodon

Family Tree

Mother: Unnamed mother (deceased)

-A strange creature from the Promised Dynasty who only wears a mask carved with a sad face on it and a poor farmer, Farlan is a Diprotodon who has the strange ability to see into the future. He gained this unusual ability after the death of his mother made him lost with grief. How he obtained it is up to speculation. Some say he used dark magic, which is the most popular theory. His newfound ability caused him to go officially mad and be locally known as the crazed old coot who rants and raves about future warnings. Though deemed a threat, Farlan is a fairly harmless fellow who just wants to have his voice heard.

MYTHICAL CHARACTERS

**These characters will appear more in Book 2.

Song Feng

Name Meaning: Song - "strong; powerful; soothing"; Feng - "sharp blade; wind; summit"

Rank: Council Leader of the Heavens

Age: Immortal

Gender: Cis male

Species: Longma

-A mythical creature from the Heavens. Song Feng leads the Council in the Heavens as Council Leader. He represents spirituality and goodwill. He was good friends with Waccruwk the cockatrice until the day the Council received a prophecy that involved Waccruwk in with the forces of darkness. Song Feng was torn at the news but, pressured by the Council (and even the Gods), he had no choice, and he swiftly exiled his best friend from the Council and the Heavens entirely. He managed to keep somewhat of a contact after his friend was exiled, but their relationship began to deteriorate quickly.

Waccruwk

Name Meaning: Unknown

Former Rank: Member of the Council of the Heavens

Age: ??

Gender: Cis male

Species: Cockatrice

-A mythical creature formerly from the Heavens. Waccruwk was once a Council member in the Council of the Heavens when a prophecy shockingly revealed that he was to turn evil, causing the destruction of the universe. Unable to take risks, Song Feng-his best friend (also crush) and new Leader of the Council-had him exiled to the Earth, stripping him of his status. This exile left Waccruwk bitter and feeling rejected, isolating himself in a cave of crystals. In there, he found the secrets to the truth and has been known to be feared by the Council in the Heavens...

Liao Chen

Name Meaning: Unknown

Rank: Member of the Council of the Heavens

Age: Immortal

Gender: ???

Species: Qilin

-Liao Chen is one of the members of the Council of the Heavens.

Sun Heng

Name Meaning: Unknown

Rank: Member of the Council of the Heavens

Age: Immortal

Gender: Cis female

Species: Fenghuang

-Sun Heng is one of the members of the Council of the Heavens.

Skeiron

Name Meaning: Unknown

Rank: Member of the Council of the Heavens

Age: Immortal

Gender: Cis male

Species: Griffin

-Skeiron is one of the members of the Council of the Heavens. He is hot-tempered and irrational, often speaking his mind instead of keeping them to himself.

Mamoru and Chinmoku

Name Meaning: "defend, protect" (Mamoru); "silence" (Chinmoku)

Rank: Member of the Council of the Heavens

Age: Immortal

Gender: ???

Species: Komainu

-Mamoru and Chinmoku are members of the Council of the Heavens. They are twins. Mamoru is the talkative one while Chinmoku hardly ever opens their mouth.

Nakia

Name Meaning: Unknown

Rank: Member of the Council of the Heavens

Age: Immortal

Gender: ???

Species: Wolpertinger

-Nakia is one of the members of the Council of the Heavens. They have a soft heart and can be easily timid.

Glacia

Name Meaning: "glacier"

Rank: Member of the Council of the Heavens

Age: Immortal

Gender: Trans Female (MtF)

Species: Peryton

-Glacia is one of the members of the Council of the Heavens.

PLANTS

**Yes. Plants.

Fern

Name Meaning: a type of plant

Age: ??

Gender: Male

Species: Venus Flytrap

-A Venus Flytrap Prince Scamander decided to own as a pet. Prince Scamander says it has a sassy personality, picky in what it eats.

Esme

Name Meaning: "to be loved"

Age: Ancient; old

Gender: Female(?)

Species: Acacia Tree

. . .

-A very, very old tree in the Tropic Clan territory. It is said to be as old as the universe. It is also the site of great tragedy, which spawned a legendary tale of a curse.

A MINI GUIDE INTO THE WORLD OF BEGINNING OF TIME

THE KINGDOMS

**There's currently 2 major Kingdoms: The Promised Dynasty and the Demoniacal Kingdom. There are also many small clans that exist throughout the land. How many there are is yet to be fully documented.

The Promised Dynasty

-The Promised Dynasty is a group of animals and one of the two prominent Kingdoms. They are wise, caring, and compassionate. They worship all the goodness and virtues in the world and also worship the Gods and Heavens that created their universe.

Known Living Members

*King Jung-hwa (cave lion) ♂

*Queen Cora (cave lion) ♀

*Prince Wonwoo (cave lion) ♂

*Ex-Queen Hawa (cave lion) ♀

*Hakuba (a horse) ♀

*Luta (a meerkat) ♂

*Cayman (a lion) ♂

*Atiena (a spotted hyena) ♀

*The Night Stalkers (a gang of spotted hyenas) (mostly females)

*Rashima (a maned wolf) ♀

BEGINNING OF TIME

*An unnamed dog soldier ♂

*Cornelius (a great horned owl) ♂

*An unnamed raccoon ♂

*Carmentis (a capybara doctor) ♀

*Jiro (an elephant doctor) ♂

*Arkaitz (a giant otter doctor) ♂

Known Deceased Members

*King Saturhorimau (cave lion) ♂

*Queen Haukea (cave lion) ♀

*King Boipelo (cave lion) ♂

*Prince Hyun-sik (cave lion) ♂

*King Jung-hwa's and Queen Cora's unnamed cubs (various genders)

*Farlan (Diprotodon)

*Zakath (Smilodon) ♀

*Alexandrei (Andrewsarchus) ♂

*Xiao (Diacodexis) ♀

*Tuur (Hemicyon) {?}

*Jinsalih (Daphoenus) ♀

*Cadwallader (cave bear) ♂

A MINI GUIDE INTO THE WORLD OF BEGINNING OF TIME

*Fingal (Xenocyon) {?}

*Clawtrax (Eremotherium) ♂

*A Thylacoleo {?}

*A Thylacosmilus {?}

*An Embolotherium {?}

*An Epicyon {?}

The Demoniacal Kingdom

-The Demoniacal Kingdom is a group of animals and one of the two prominent Kingdoms. They are aggressive, cold, and do not take kindly to the Promised Dynasty. They worship all things having to do with evil, the darkness and the sins.

Known Members

*King Titanosaurus (wolf-dragon hybrid) ♂

*Queen Zirconia (dire wolf) ♀

*Prince Scamander (wolf-dragon hybrid) ♂

*Princess Okome (wolf-dragon hybrid) ♀

*Prince Livyatan (wolf-dragon hybrid) ♂

*Basilosaurus (wolf-dragon hybrid) ♂

*Odobenocetops (wolf-dragon hybrid) ♂

*Janjucetus (wolf-dragon hybrid) ♂

*Dorudon (wolf-dragon hybrid) ♂

*Incakujira (wolf-dragon hybrid) ♀

*Tokira (a tiger) ♂

*Enky (a black leopardess) ♀

*Arvolf (a red fox) ♂

*Cyclone (a giant panda) ♂

*Atiena (a spotted hyena) ♀ - former member

A MINI GUIDE INTO THE WORLD OF BEGINNING OF TIME

*The Night Stalkers (a gang of spotted hyenas) - former members (mostly females)

Known Deceased Members

*King Wyvern (wyvern) ♂

*Queen Skydamire (dire wolf) ♀

*King Oromir (wolf-dragon hybrid) ♂

The Shell Clan

-The Shell Clan is a group of animals that live up north in the land by the sea. They are known as the friendliest of all minor clans. Although they are friendly, a few of its members are extremely hostile when it comes to those not of their clan. The history of this clan is rather secretive, and few know of its dark truth...

Known Members

*Shell Broken Savaria (species unknown) ♀

*Korikuma (a polar bear-grizzly bear hybrid) ♀

*Korikuma's mother (a polar bear) ♀

*An unnamed seal guard {?}

*An unnamed seal lion {?}

*Tihkoosue (a little penguin) ♂

*Mabel (a cat) ♀

*Seabury (a crocodile) ♂

*Sea otters (various genders)

*Canines (various genders)

*Felines (various genders)

The Tropic Clan

-The Tropic Clan is a group of animals that live up north in the land. They live in a rainforest and are well adapted to its surroundings.

Known Members

*Tropic Bloom Aleena (a Peruvian Spider Monkey) ♀

*Vermilion (a howler monkey) ♀

*Kitwana (a jaguar) ♂

*A bush dog doctor {?}

*A llama doctor ♂

*Moth (a margay) ♀

*Shikazu (a dhole pup) ♂

*A baby orangutan {?}

*Dusk (an okapi calf) ♀

*Graund (a gaur calf) ♂

*Ms. Flayke (a forest elephant) ♀

LOCATIONS

Halcyonwick

-The city where the Promised Dynasty lives. It sits in the middle of a deforested section of Divine Kingfisher Woods. It is a large city of lights and impressive infrastructure. The castle where the Royal Family resides is a tall golden building that shines in the lights.

Coldwyvern

-The city where the Demoniacal Kingdom lives. While defined as a city, its size is more akin to a small town. It is built on the base of a mountain. It has a dark medieval design to it, while also copying some of Halcyonwick's infrastructure. Coldwyvern has harsh winters and cold summers.

Divine Kingfisher Woods

-A forest just a few miles from Halcyonwick. It is known for its thick vegetation and the dangerous river Dragon's Wrath. It was named after a kingfisher swooped into the river and made it out alive, which Saturhorimau believed was a sign from the Heavens.

Dragon's Wrath

-A never-ending river that cuts through Divine Kingfisher Woods and leads to a waterfall. Dragon's Wrath got its name due to how dangerous the currents are, like how King Wyvern was dangerous with his dark magic. It is said that no one has ever survived Dragon's Wrath as the currents are too strong for anyone to fight back. It is unknown how many lives this river has claimed, since bodies are usually never recovered after they fall in.

Heaven's Eye

-A pool surrounded in a white mist that exists at the end of Dragon's Wrath in an abandoned cave. No one knows how this pool came to be, but it's believed to be created by the Heavens (possibly from an ancient being who resided there before they disappeared, never to be discovered). Only select creatures could see this pool. It was discovered and named by Farlan when he first got his powers.

Morning Dew Park

-A park within Halcyonwick. It is known for its large lake in the center. Various ducks and geese reside in this park. The park is a favorite amongst the Royal Family as a relaxation spot.

TERMINOLOGY

General Terms + Phrases

-Jinamizi: A term often uttered by Prince Wonwoo; the word is a real word of Swahili origin, and it means "nightmare"

-Inlander: A term used by the clans by the ocean to describe someone who resides more inland; used as a derogatory term

-Outland: A term that describes going beyond one's territory

-Curse the wyvern!: A phrase used by the Demoniacal Kingdom to describe their frustration. Similar phrases include "by the wyvern!"

-By the Gods!: A phrase used by the Promised Dynasty to describe their frustration

-By Ellowyn's galaxy: A phrase used by the Promised Dynasty when upholding a promise. First mentioned by Queen Cora.

-Great Ellowyn: A phrase used by the Promised Dynasty

-May Morana take you in her loving embrace and hopefully be blessed by Okalani: A phrase used by the Promised Dynasty when a predator kills their prey. First mentioned by Prince Wonwoo.

-Underneath Dagny's bright sun or Gau's dim moon, Ellowyn will bless us: A phrase used to describe when one is to meet someone again. First mentioned by Moth.

A Mini Guide into the World of Beginning of Time

Time Terms

-Terra Cycle: A term used to describe a year; it is also used to tell how old someone is, i.e. 20 terra cycles old = 20 years old

-New Terra Cycle Day: A term used to describe the new year; it's equivalent to New Year's Day

-Gau's First Rise: Moonrise

-Gau's Peak: Midnight

-Gau's Rest: Moonset

-Dagny's First Rise: Sunrise

-Dagny's Peak: Afternoon

-Dagny's Rest: Sunset

Phenomenon/Weather Terms

-Gau's Coup Day: A term that means a solar eclipse; legend goes of Gau–the God of Night and the Moon–wanting to keep the moon in place of the sun for a whole day

-Lavian's Rage: A term that means an earthquake; legend goes of Lavian–the God of the Land and Sea–throwing an unknown tantrum, destroying the land that he had created

Rank Terms

-Shell Broken: a rank that refers to the leader of the Shell Clan

-Tropic Bloom: a rank that refers to the leader of the Tropic Clan

MAJOR EVENTS THROUGHOUT HISTORY

The Creation of the Universe

* Date: Before 1000 B.E.

-The creation of the Universe was an event that occurred before 1000 B.E.

Premise: In an age not defined, nothingness exploded into the universe that stands today. From the great explosion, a shapeshifter God by the name of Ellowyn was created from a small clump of matter and was granted powers by the newfound energy of the universe.

Description: With her powers given to her by the newfound energy, she created the universe. She created the galaxy, the stars, the planets, the sun. She created it all.

The Birth of the Gods

* Date: Before 1000 B.E.

-The birth of the Gods was an event that occurred before 1000 B.E.

Premise: Sometime while governing the newly made universe, Ellowyn grew exhausted.

Description: She came up with an idea to split her roles. Using the cosmic matter she gathered, she bundled them up and gave them a form. In total, she created 12 forms for 12 roles who would be born for those roles. But these forms were only empty husks, a shell with nothing inside. There obviously had to be more than a shell. A life. So, Ellowyn gave them something important that every creature must have: a heart containing a soul of purity and goodness. She gave these empty forms those hearts, and soon rose the Gods that would come to be worshipped: Abella and Morana (the Goddesses of Life and Death respectively), Okalani and Azrael (the Goddess of the Heavens and the God of Hell respectively), Lavian and Wuxjun (the Gods of the Land and Sea and of the Skies respectively), Dagny and Gau (the Goddesses of Day and the Sun and Night and the Moon respectively), Ayumu and Kishi (the Goddess of Dreams and Visions and the God of Nightmares and Omens respectively) and Aklene and Ziton (the Goddess of Nature and the God of Destruction respectively).

Aftermath & Legacy: The creation of the Gods would give way into the first known life forms in the newly made Earth.

The First Release of Evil

* Date: Before 1000 B.E.

The First Rising of the Sea

* Date: Before 1000 B.E.

-The First Rising of the Sea was an event that was the first incidence of earthquakes and the rising of the ocean.

Premise: Lavian and Wuxjun helped give rise to the Earth the very Kingdoms and clans exist on today. With his massive strength, Lavian dug and rose the land, shaping them to his accord. With his slender body, Wuxjun soared through the skies, encasing the Earth in air to protect it from the cold empty void of space.

Description: Lavian had enough of Ziton's tricks and threw a massive tantrum. He shook the Earth, destroying the land he had created. Wuxjun attempted to calm him down, but he would not listen to reason. Days turned to weeks, and weeks to months, and Lavian's anger still have yet to subside. Wuxjun turned to Ellowyn for guidance, where he was given clouds to give to Lavian to cry and vent in. This eventually worked, and Lavian's anger subsided. Ellowyn made Lavian and Ziton meet each other in order to come to an agreement. Wuxjun soon used Lavian's tears to heal the Earth.

. . .

The First Gau's Coup Day

* Date: Before 1000 B.E.

-The First Gau's Coup Day was an event that was the first incidence of a solar eclipse.

Premise: Dagny and Gau were responsible for the rising of both the sun and the moon, the rising of day and night. Dagny was assigned to the day, and Gau was assigned to the night. The two worked in harmony as they helped bring both light and dark to the land. One day, Gau was a bit curious on what would happen if he kept the moon in place instead of the sun for a day. He did not have malicious intent, as devious and mysterious he was, but more it was curiosity that got the better of him. Though there may have been a bit of jealousy, but Gau refused to admit it. So he went through with his impulsive thought.

Description: One morning, as Dagny raised the sun, Gau arose and intervened, completely engulfing the sun with the moon and casting a huge shadow all over the land. Dagny was understandably angry and asked her brother what he was doing. Gau was vague but simply responded: "Today's my day." Dagny thought he meant this was his day to take over control, so, the two had a battle that led to the most confusing day in all of history. When Ellowyn was made aware of their scuffle, she swooped down and promptly ended the fight, moving the moon back in its place and letting the sun be free again. She scolded both of them, and ever since then, Dagny and Gau kept their peace in order to please Ellowyn.

Aftermath & Legacy: It is said every few years, Gau would try to have his day, to which Dagny agreed on the terms that Gau's day would not last for one whole day. Gau agreed with whatever his sister told him, and a term later emerged that would describe a time period when the moon would swallow the sun (a solar eclipse if you will): Gau's Coup Day.

The Great War Between Good and Evil

* Date:

-July 1017 B.E. - July 1018 B.E. (1 year)

-July 1017 B.E. - present (106 years) [de jure]

* Combatants:

-Wyvern's allies

-Saturhorimau's allies

* Leaders:

-Saturhorimau

-Wyvern

* Deaths and Losses

-Saturhorimau's group: Farlan's mother, many unnamed allies; few others injured

-Wyvern's group: many unnamed allies; few others injured

* Outcome:

-Stalemate; Wyvern separates from the group to create the Demoniacal Kingdom while Saturhorimau creates the Promised Dynasty; the two establish themselves as kings and begin the royal lineage

-The infamous war that gave birth to the two Kingdoms, the Great War Between Good and Evil (also known as the Great War)

was a major conflict enacted by Wyvern and his allies against Saturhorimau and his allies. It took place over 100 terra cycles ago in the Terra Cycle 1017 B.E.

Premise: Sometime before 1000 B.E., the land was created, and everyone lived in harmony. Saturhorimau and Wyvern were close friends and were somewhat leaders of the group of animals. One day, a heavenly being descended down to the Earth and spoke to Saturhorimau, proclaiming him as the land's preacher. Jealous that he wasn't chosen and slowly losing the respect he was getting after this proclamation, Wyvern sought ways to regain his lost attention. A month prior to the war, Wyvern had just discovered dark magic via a strange creature in a cave and perfected it, sharing his newfound abilities to all around the land. Saturhorimau is shocked at the evil forces and demands that Wyvern stop this. Wyvern refuses, saying he's been having animals admire him and following him. Wyvern gave Saturhorimau an ultimatum: either give up his powers and the land or die.

Description of The Battle: Saturhorimau and Wyvern meet, and Saturhorimau once again tries to convince Wyvern to stop. Wyvern–too consumed by his own dark desires and temptations–commands his allies to attack, which makes Saturhorimau send his allies into battle. The war goes on for 1 terra cycle, and it is bloody. Many lives were lost, leading to many unintended generational trauma that would come. During the final hours of the war in July 1018 B.E., the two meet for a final clash. Wyvern leaps at Saturhorimau and slices through Saturhorimau's throat, severing his jugular vein; the young lion begins to die under his talons. Wyvern, although suddenly feeling upset that his friend is dying, rants that this was his own fault, that all of what was happening was because of him. Suddenly, the clouds break free and Heavenly creatures descend, appearing in front of Wyvern. Wyvern is shaken by the angels and he calls off his allies. After Saturhorimau is revived by the Heavens, he declares the war over. The two separate, with Wyvern taking his allies with him and splitting the land between them.

Aftermath & Legacy: Apart from the fact the war helped give rise to the two Kingdoms, the Great War left a lasting effect on both the Promised Dynasty and the Demoniacal Kingdom. Despite the fact a treaty was agreed to and they officially stopped fighting in 1018 B.E., the war never technically ended and certain events would occur afterwards that they consider still to be part of the war. The Demoniacal Kingdom is still bitter over their "loss" and continue to desire ways to take control of the land as Wyvern would have wanted. The Promised Dynasty have very close-minded beliefs about the Demoniacal Kingdom, believing them all to be evil and power-hungry. It also led to a rise of many being fearful whenever King Wyvern was brought up. Though it's still a real strong belief, Prince Wonwoo lets loose of his beliefs to a certain degree and finds some good in the Demoniacal Kingdom, though it is quickly shattered following certain events that would soon befall.

A MINI GUIDE INTO THE WORLD OF BEGINNING OF TIME

The War For Prince Wonwoo

* Date:

-July 1118 B.E. - June 1122 B.E. (3 years)

* Combatants:

-The Promised Dynasty

-The Demoniacal Kingdom

* Leaders:

-King Jung-hwa

-King Titanosaurus

* Deaths and Losses:

-The Promised Dynasty: unnamed guards + soldiers

-The Demoniacal Kingdom: unnamed guards + soldiers

* Outcome:

-Prince Wonwoo on the run until his capture

-The war for Prince Wonwoo was a war that took place in July 1118 B.E. It was a building war that eventually exploded when the time was right.

Premise: 7 months before the war, in December 1117 B.E., King Titanosaurus and King Jung-hwa agree on an arranged marriage between the lion king's son Prince Wonwoo and the wolf king's daughter Princess Okome as a means to bring the two Kingdoms back together. Although met with heavy criticisms, they still went ahead with the plan, meeting up in Halcyonwick in January 1118 B.E., a day after the New Terra Cycle Day. Upon first seeing one another, Prince Wonwoo and Princess Okome fell in love and started to go out with each other. A week later and a day before Princess Okome's birthday, the two were on a date when Demoniacal Kingdom guards appeared to assess and check on Princess Okome. After being harassed by one of the guards, Prince Wonwoo attacks one of the guards, trying to teach them a lesson which ended in Princess Okome's death. Prince Scamander, having been made aware of his sister's death, yells to Prince Wonwoo that the Promised Dynasty will pay for what he did.

Description of The Battle: On July 1118 B.E., King Jung-hwa gathered his guards and soldiers for another meeting. The Demoniacal Kingdom attacked not long after. King Jung-hwa leads everyone to battle, having his wife and son hide in the basement. Demoniacal soldiers ambush the Promised Dynasty guards, killing them and attacking Queen Cora and Prince Wonwoo along with the soldiers that were charged with guarding them. Prince Wonwoo flees against his own will, falling into Dragon's Wrath.

Aftermath & Legacy: The Demoniacal Kingdom continue to search for the lion prince, but they begin to lose hope and give in to the thought he most likely perished. Prince Scamander, however, does not believe it, and, with much convincing to his father, has the Kingdom continuing to search for the lion prince but they do so on the down low. The capturing of Prince Wonwoo proved to be a delicate operation for the Demoniacal Kingdom, as it would lead to unintended consequences later on.

ABOUT THE AUTHOR

Adriana Rodriguez has gone by the alias SavageKiku and lives by it. Residing in California where she was born, she's loved making stories ever since she was a little child. She is a big fan of reading, writing, drawing, enjoying music of all kinds (ranging from rock to JPop), going on long rides, planes/plane rides, history and being with her two dogs Kifli and Ash. She also enjoys animation, especially indie animation, and loves watching cartoons, citing them as her huge inspiration for making stories. Currently working as a phone operator in a hospital, she has aspirations to go to school for arts and animation.

www.ingramcontent.com/pod-product-compliance
Lightning Source LLC
Chambersburg PA
CBHW031958080125
20085CB00004B/12